The daughter of a town marshal, **Linda Lael Miller** is a *New York Times* bestselling author of more than one hundred historical and contemporary novels. Linda's books have hit #1 on the *New York Times* bestseller list seven times. Raised in Northport, Washington, she now lives in Spokane, Washington. www.LindaLaelMiller.com

Delores Fossen, a *USA TODAY* bestselling author, has sold over seventy-five novels, with millions of copies of her books in print worldwide. She's received a Booksellers' Best Award and an RT Reviewers' Choice Best Book Award. She was also a finalist for a prestigious RITA® Award. You can contact the author through her website at www.deloresfossen.com.

#1 *New York Times* Bestselling Author

LINDA LAEL MILLER

THAT FOREVER FEELING

Previously published as *Daring Moves*

**HARLEQUIN
BESTSELLING
AUTHOR
COLLECTION**

**HARLEQUIN®
BESTSELLING
AUTHOR
COLLECTION**

Recycling programs
for this product may
not exist in your area.

ISBN-13: 978-1-335-74497-5

That Forever Feeling
First published as Daring Moves in 1990. This edition published in 2022.
Copyright © 1990 by Linda Lael Miller

Security Blanket
First published in 2008. This edition published in 2022.
Copyright © 2008 by Delores Fossen

For questions and comments about the quality of this book,
please contact us at CustomerService@Harlequin.com.

Harlequin Enterprises ULC
22 Adelaide St. West, 41st Floor
Toronto, Ontario M5H 4E3, Canada
www.Harlequin.com

Printed in U.S.A.

CONTENTS

Visit her Author Profile page at Harlequin.com,
or lindalaelmiller.com, for more titles!

THAT FOREVER FEELING

Linda Lael Miller

Chapter 1

The line of people waiting for an autograph reached from the bookstore down the length of the mall to the specialty luggage shop. With a sigh, Amanda Scott bought a cup of coffee from a nearby French bakery, bravely forgoing the delicate, flaky pastries inside the glass counter, and took her place behind a man in an expensive tweed overcoat.

Distractedly he turned and glanced at her, as though somehow finding her to blame for the delay. Then he pushed up his sleeve and consulted a slim gold watch. He was a couple of inches taller than Amanda, with brown hair that was only slightly too long and hazel eyes flecked with green, and he needed a shave.

Never one to pass the time in silence if an excuse to chat presented itself, Amanda took a steadying sip of her coffee and announced, "I'm buying Dr. Marshall's book for my sister, Eunice. She's going through a nasty divorce." The runaway bestseller was called *Gathering Up the Pieces*, and it was meant for people who had suffered some personal loss or setback.

The stranger turned to look back at her. The pleasantly mingled scents of new snow and English Leather seemed to surround him. "Are you talking to me?" he inquired, drawing his brows together in puzzlement.

Amanda fortified herself with another sip of coffee. She hadn't meant to flirt; it was just that waiting could be so tedious. "Actually, I was," she admitted.

He surprised her with a brief but brilliant smile that practically set her back on the heels of her snow boots. In the next second his expression turned grave, but he extended a gloved hand.

"Jordan Richards," he said formally.

Gulping down the mouthful of coffee she'd just taken, Amanda returned the gesture. "Amanda Scott," she managed. "I don't usually strike up conversations with strange men in shopping malls, you understand. It's just that I was bored."

Again that blinding grin, as bright as sunlight on water.

"I see," said Jordan Richards.

The line moved a little, and they both stepped forward. Amanda suddenly felt shy, and wished she hadn't gotten off the bus at the mall. Maybe she should have gone straight home to her cozy apartment and her cat.

She reminded herself that Eunice would benefit by reading the book and that, with this purchase, her Christmas shopping would be finished. After today she could hide in her work, like a soldier crouching in a foxhole, until the holidays and all their painful associations were past.

"Too bad about Eunice," Jordan Richards remarked.

"I'll give her your condolences," Amanda promised, a smile lighting her aquamarine eyes.

The line advanced, and so did Amanda and Jordan.

"Good," he said.

Amanda finished her coffee, crumpled the cup and tossed it into a nearby trash bin. Beside the bin there was a sign that read Is Therapy For You? Attend A Free Minisession With Dr. Marshall After The Book Signing. Beneath was a diagram of the mall, with the public auditorium colored in.

"So," she ventured, "are you buying *Gathering Up the Pieces* for yourself or somebody else?"

"I'm sending it to my grandmother," Jordan answered, consulting his watch again.

Amanda wondered if he had to be somewhere else later, or if he was just an impatient person.

"What happened to her?" she asked sympathetically.

Jordan looked reluctant, but after a few moments and another step forward as the line progressed, he said, "She had some pretty heavy-duty surgery a while back."

"Oh," Amanda said, and without thinking, she reached out and patted his arm so as not to let the mention of the unknown grandmother's misfortune pass without some response from her.

Something softened in Jordan Richards's manner at the small demonstration. "Are you attending the 'free minisession'?" he asked, gesturing toward the sign. The expression in his eyes said he fully expected her to answer no.

Amanda smiled and lifted one shoulder in a shrug. "Why not? I've got the rest of the afternoon to blow, and I could learn something."

Jordan looked thoughtful. "I suppose nobody has to talk if they don't want to."

"Of course not," Amanda replied confidently, even

though she had no idea what would be required. Some of the self-help groups could get pretty wild; she'd heard of people walking across burning coals in their bare feet, or letting themselves be dunked in hot tubs.

"I'll go if you'll sit beside me," Jordan said.

Amanda considered the suggestion only briefly. The mall was a well-lit place, crowded with Christmas shoppers. If Jordan Richards were some kind of weirdo—and that seemed unlikely, unless crackpots were dressing like models in *Gentlemen's Quarterly* these days—she would be perfectly safe. "Okay," she said with another shrug.

After the decision was made, they lapsed into a companionable silence. Nearly fifteen minutes had passed by the time Jordan reached the author's table.

Dr. Eugene Marshall, the famous psychology guru, signed his name in a confident scrawl and handed Jordan a book. Amanda had her volume-autographed and followed her new acquaintance to the cash register.

Once they'd both paid, they left the store together.

There was already a mob gathered at the double doors of the mall's community auditorium, and according to a sign on an easel, the minisession would start in another ten minutes.

Jordan glanced at the line of fast-food places across the concourse. "Would you like some coffee or something?"

Amanda shook her head, then reached up to pull her light, shoulder-length hair from under the collar of her coat. "No, thanks. What kind of work do you do, Mr. Richards?"

"Jordan," he corrected. He took off his overcoat and draped it over one arm, then loosened his tie and collar slightly. "What kind of work do you think I do?"

Amanda assessed him, narrowing her blue eyes. Jordan looked fit, and he even had a bit of a suntan, but she doubted he worked with his hands. His clothes marked him as an upper-management type, and so did that gold watch he kept checking. "You're a stockbroker," she guessed.

He chuckled. "Close. I'm a partner in an investment firm. What do you do?"

People were starting to move into the auditorium and take seats, and Amanda and Jordan moved along with them. With a half smile, she answered, "Guess."

He considered her thoughtfully. "You're a flight attendant for a major airline," he decided after several moments had passed.

Amanda took his conjecture as a compliment, even though it was wrong. "I'm the assistant manager of the Evergreen Hotel." They found seats near the middle of the auditorium, and Jordan took the one on the aisle. Amanda was just daring to hope she was making a favorable impression, when her stomach rumbled.

"And you haven't had lunch yet," Jordan stated with another of those lethal, quicksilver grins. "It just so happens that I'm a little hungry myself. How about something from that Chinese fast-food place I saw out there—after we're done with the minisession, I mean?"

Again Amanda smiled. She seemed to be smiling a lot, which was odd, because she hadn't felt truly happy since before James Brockman had swept into her life, turned it upside down and swept out again. "I'd like that," she heard herself say.

Just then Dr. Marshall walked out onto the auditorium stage. At his appearance, Jordan became noticeably uncomfortable, shifting in his seat and drawing one Italian-leather-shod foot up to rest on the opposite knee.

The famous author introduced himself, just in case someone who had never watched a TV talk show might have wandered in, and announced that he wanted the audience to break up into groups of twelve.

Jordan looked even more discomfited, and probably wouldn't have participated if a group hadn't formed around him and Amanda. To make things even more interesting, at least to Amanda's way of thinking, the handsome, silver-haired Dr. Marshall chose their group to work with, while his assistants took the others.

"All right, people," he began in a tone of pleasant authority, "let's get started." His knowing gray eyes swept the small gathering. "Why does everybody look so worried? This will be relatively painless—all we're going to do is talk about ourselves a little." He looked at Amanda. "What's your name?" he asked directly. "And what's the worst thing that's happened to you in the past year?"

She swallowed. "Amanda Scott. And—the worst thing?"

Dr. Marshall nodded with kindly amusement.

All of the sudden Amanda wished she'd gone to a matinee or stayed home to clean her apartment. She didn't want to talk about James, especially not in front of strangers, but she was basically an honest person and *James* was the worst thing that had happened to her in a very long time. Not looking at Jordan, she answered, "I fell in love with a man and he turned out to be married."

"What did you do when you found out?" the doctor asked reasonably.

"I cried a lot," Amanda answered, forgetting for the

moment that there were twelve other people listening in, including Jordan.

"Did you break off the relationship?" Dr. Marshall pressed.

Amanda still felt the pain and humiliation she'd known when James's wife had stormed into her office and made a scene. Before that, Amanda hadn't even suspected the terrible truth. "Yes," she replied softly with a miserable nod.

"Is this experience still affecting your life?"

Amanda wished she dared to glance at Jordan to see how he was reacting, but she didn't have the courage. She lowered her eyes. "I guess it is."

"Did you stop trusting men?"

Considering all the dates she'd refused in the months since she'd disentangled herself from James, Amanda supposed she had stopped trusting men. Even worse, she'd stopped trusting her own instincts. "Yes," she answered very softly.

Dr. Marshall reached out to touch her shoulder. "I'm not going to pretend you can solve your problems just by sitting in on a minisession, or even by reading my book, but I think it's time for you to stop hiding and take some risks. Agreed?"

Amanda was surprised at the man's insight. "Agreed," she said, and right then and there she made up her mind to read Eunice's copy of *Gathering Up the Pieces* before she wrapped it.

The doctor's attention shifted to the man sitting on Amanda's left. He said he'd lost his job, and the fact that Christmas was coming up made things harder. A woman in the row behind Amanda talked about her child's serious illness. Finally, after about twenty minutes had passed, everyone had spoken except Jordan.

He rubbed his chin, which was already showing a five o'clock shadow, and cleared his throat. Amanda, feeling his tension and reluctance as though they were her own, laid her hand gently on his arm.

"The worst thing that ever happened to me," he said in a low, almost inaudible voice, "was losing my wife."

"How did it happen?" the doctor asked.

Jordan looked as though he wanted to bolt out of his chair and stride up the aisle to the doors, but he answered the question. "A motorcycle accident."

"Were you driving?" Dr. Marshall's expression was sympathetic.

"Yes," Jordan replied after a long silence.

"And you're still not ready to talk about it," the doctor deduced.

"That's right," Jordan said. And he got up and walked slowly up the aisle and out of the auditorium.

Amanda followed, catching up just outside. She didn't quite dare to touch his arm again, yet he slowed down at the sound of her footsteps. "How about that Chinese food you promised me?" she asked gently.

Jordan met her eyes, and for just a moment, she saw straight through to his soul. What pain he'd suffered.

"Sure," he replied, and his voice was hoarse.

"I'm all through with my Christmas shopping," Amanda announced once they were seated at a table, Number Three Regulars in front of them from the Chinese fast-food place. "How about you?"

"My secretary does mine," Jordan responded. He looked relieved at her choice of topic.

"That's above and beyond the call of duty," Amanda

remarked lightly. "I hope you're giving her something terrific."

Jordan smiled at that. "She gets a sizable bonus."

"Good."

It was obvious Jordan was feeling better. His eyes twinkled, and some of the strain had left his face.

"I'm glad company policy meets with your approval."

It was surprising, considering her unfortunate and all-too-recent experiences with James, but it wasn't until that moment that Amanda realized that she hadn't checked Jordan's hand for a wedding band. She glanced at the appropriate finger, even though she knew it would be bare, and saw a white strip where the ring had been.

"Like I said, I'm a widower," he told her with a slight smile, obviously having read her glance accurately.

"I'm sorry," Amanda told him.

He speared a piece of sweet-and-sour chicken. "It's been three years."

It seemed to Amanda that the white space on his ring finger should have filled in after three years. "That's quite a while," she said, wondering if she should just get up from her chair, collect her book and her coat and leave. In the end she didn't, because a glance at her watch told her it was still forty minutes until the next bus left. Besides, she was hungry.

Jordan sighed. "Sometimes it seems like three centuries."

Amanda bit her lower lip, then burst out, "You aren't one of those creeps who goes around saying he doesn't have a wife when he really does, are you? I mean, you could have remarried."

He looked very tired all of a sudden, and pale beneath his tan. Amanda wondered why he hadn't gotten around to shaving.

"No," he said. "I'm not married."

Amanda dropped her eyes to her food, ashamed that she'd asked the question, even though she wouldn't have taken it back. The experience with James had taught her that a woman couldn't be too careful about such things.

"Amanda?"

She lifted her gaze to see him studying her. "What?"

"What was his name?"

"What was whose name?"

"The guy who told you he wasn't married."

Amanda cleared her throat and shifted nervously in her chair. The thought of James didn't cause her pain anymore, but she didn't know Jordan Richards well enough to tell him just how badly she'd been hoodwinked. A sudden, crazy panic seized her. "Gosh, look at the time," she said, pulling back her sleeve to check her watch a split second after she'd spoken. "I'd better get home." She bolted out of her chair and put her coat back on, then reached for her purse and the bag from the bookstore. She laid a five-dollar bill on the table to pay for her dinner. "It was nice meeting you."

Jordan frowned and slowly pushed back his chair, then stood. "Wait a minute, Amanda. You're not playing fair."

He was right. Jordan hadn't run away, however much he had probably wanted to, and she wouldn't, either.

She sank back into her seat, all too aware that people at surrounding tables were looking on with interest.

"You're not ready to talk about him," Jordan said, sitting down again, "and I'm not ready to talk about her. Deal?"

"Deal," Amanda said.

They discussed the Seattle Seahawks after that, and the Chinese artifacts on display at one of the museums. Then Jordan walked with her to the nearest corner and waited until the bus pulled up.

"Goodbye, Amanda," he said as she climbed the steps.

She dropped her change into the slot and smiled over one shoulder. "Thanks for the company."

He waved as the bus pulled away, and Amanda ached with a bittersweet loneliness she'd never known before, not even in the awful days after her breakup with James.

When Amanda arrived at her apartment building on Seattle's Queen Anne Hill, she was still thinking about Jordan. He'd wanted to offer to drive her home, she knew, but he'd had the good grace not to, and Amanda liked him for that.

In her mailbox she found a sheaf of bills waiting for her. "I'll never save enough to start a bed and breakfast at this rate," she complained to her black-and-white long-haired cat, Gershwin, when he met her at the door.

Gershwin was unsympathetic. As usual, he was interested only in his dinner.

After flipping on the lights, dropping her purse and the book onto the hall table and hanging her coat on the brass-plated tree that was really too large for that little space, Amanda went into the kitchenette.

Gershwin purred and wound himself around her ankles as she opened a can of cat food, but when she scraped it out onto his dish, he abandoned her without compunction.

While Gershwin gobbled, Amanda went back to the mail she'd picked up in the lobby and flipped through it again. Three bills, a you-may-have-already-won and a letter from Eunice.

Amanda set the other envelopes down and opened the crisp blue one with her sister's return address printed in italics in one corner. She was disappointed when she realized that the letter was just another litany of Eunice's soon-to-be-ex-husband's sins, and she set it aside to finish later.

In the bathroom she started water running into her huge claw-footed tub, then stripped off the skirt and sweater she'd worn to the mall. After disposing of her underthings and panty hose, Amanda climbed into the soothing water.

Gershwin pushed the door open in that officious way cats have and bounded up to stand on the tub's edge with perfect balance. Like a tightrope walker, he strolled back and forth along the chipped porcelain, telling Amanda about his day in a series of companionable meows.

Amanda listened politely as she bathed, but her mind was wandering. She was thinking about Jordan Richards and that recently removed wedding band of his.

She sighed. All her instincts told her he was telling the truth about his marital status, but those same instincts had once insisted that James was all right, too.

Amanda was waiting when the bus pulled up at her corner the next morning. The weather was a little warmer, and the snow, so unusual in Seattle, was already melting.

Fifteen minutes later Amanda walked through the huge revolving door of the Evergreen Hotel. Its lush Oriental carpets were soft beneath the soles of her shoes, and crystal chandeliers winked overhead, their multicolored reflections blazing in the floor-to-ceiling mirrors.

Amanda took the elevator to the third floor, where

the hotel's business offices were. As she was passing through the small reception area, Mindy Simmons hailed her from her desk.

"Mr. Mansfield is sick today," she said in an undertone. Mindy was small and pretty, with long brown hair and expressive green eyes. "Your desk is buried in messages."

Amanda went into her office and started dealing with problems. The plumbing in the presidential suite was on the fritz, so she called to make sure Maintenance was on top of the situation. A Mrs. Edman in 1203 suspected one of the maids of stealing her pearl earring, and someone had mixed up some dates at the reception desk—two couples were expecting to occupy the bridal suite on the same night.

It was noon when Amanda finished straightening everything out—Mrs. Edman's pearl earring had fallen behind the television set, the plumbing in the presidential suite was back in working order and each of the newlywed couples would have rooms to themselves. At Mindy's suggestion, she and Amanda went to the busy Westlake Mall for lunch, buying salads at one of the fast-food restaurants and taking a table near a window.

"Two more weeks and I start my vacation," Mindy stated enthusiastically, pouring dressing from a little carton over her salad. "Christmas at Big Mountain. I can hardly wait."

Amanda would just as soon have skipped Christmas altogether if she could have gotten the rest of the world to go along with the idea, but of course she didn't say that. "You and Pete will have a great time at the ski resort."

Mindy was chewing, and she swallowed before answering. "It's just great of his parents to take us along—we could never have afforded it on our own."

With a nod, Amanda poked her fork into a cherry tomato.

"What are you doing over the holidays?" Mindy asked.

Amanda forced a smile. "I'm going to be working," she reminded her friend.

"I know that, but what about a tree and presents and a turkey?"

"I'll have all those things at my mom and stepdad's place."

Mindy, who knew about James and all the dashed hopes he'd left in his wake, looked sympathetic. "You need to meet a new man."

Amanda bristled a little. "It just so happens that a woman can have a perfectly happy life without a man hanging around."

Mindy looked doubtful. "Sure," she said.

"Besides, I met someone just yesterday."

"Who?"

Amanda concentrated on her salad for several long moments. "His name is Jordan Richards, and—"

"Jordan Richards?" Mindy interrupted excitedly. "Wow! How did you ever manage to meet him?"

A little insulted that Mindy seemed to think Jordan was so far out of her orbit that even meeting him was a feat to get excited about, Amanda frowned. "We were in line together at a bookstore. Do you know him?"

"Not exactly," Mindy admitted, subsiding a little. "But my father-in-law does. Jordan Richards practically doubled his retirement fund for him, and they're always writing about him in the financial section of the Sunday paper."

"I didn't know you read that section," Amanda remarked.

"I don't," Mindy admitted readily, unwrapping a bread stick. "But we have dinner with my in-laws practically every Sunday, and that's all Pete and his dad ever talk about. Did he ask you out?"

"Who?"

"Jordan Richards, silly."

Amanda shook her head. "No, we just had Chinese food together and talked a little." She deliberately left out the part about how they'd gone to the minitherapy session and the way she'd reacted when Jordan had asked her about James.

Mindy looked disappointed. "Well, he did ask for your number, didn't he?"

"No. But he knows where I work. If he wants to call, I suppose he will."

A delighted smile lit Mindy's face. Positive thinking was an art form with her. "He'll call. I just know it."

Amanda grinned. "If he does, I won't be able to accept the glory—I owe it all to an article I read in *Cosmo*. I think it was called 'Big Girls Should Talk to Strangers,' or something like that."

Mindy lifted her diet cola in a rousing roast. "Here's to Jordan Richards and a red-hot romance!"

With a chuckle, Amanda touched her cup to Mindy's and drank a toast to something that would probably never happen.

Back at the hotel more crises were waiting to be solved, and there was a message on Amanda's desk, scrawled by the typist who'd filled in for Mindy during lunch. Jordan Richards had called.

A peculiar tightness constricted Amanda's throat, and

a flutter started in the pit of her stomach. Mindy's toast echoed in her ears: *"Here's to Jordan Richards and a red-hot romance."*

Amanda laid down the message, telling herself she didn't have time to return the call, then picked it up again. Before she knew it, her finger was punching out the numbers.

"Striner, Striner and Richards," sang a receptionist's voice at the other end of the line.

Amanda drew a deep breath, squared her shoulders and exhaled. "This is Amanda Scott," she said in her most professional voice. "I'm returning a call from Jordan Richards."

"One moment, please."

After a series of clicks and buzzes another female voice came on the line. "Jordan Richards's office. May I help you?"

Again Amanda gave her name. And again she was careful to say she was returning a call that had originated with Jordan.

There was another buzz, then Jordan's deep, crisp voice saying, "Richards."

Amanda hadn't expected a simple thing like the man saying his name to affect her the way it did. It was the strangest sensation to feel dizzy over something like that. She dropped into the swivel chair behind her desk. "Hi. It's Amanda."

"Amanda."

Coming from him, her own name had the same strange impact as his had had.

"How are you?" he asked.

Amanda swallowed. She was a professional with a very responsible job. It was ridiculous to be overwhelmed by something so simple and ordinary as the timbre of a man's voice. "I'm fine," she answered. Nothing more imaginative came to her, and she sat there behind her broad desk, blushing like an eighth-grade schoolgirl trying to work up the courage to ask a boy to a sock hop.

His low, masculine chuckle came over the wire to surround her like a mystical caress. "If I promise not to ask any more questions about you know who, will you go out with me? Some friends of mine are having an informal dinner tonight on their houseboat."

Amanda still felt foolish for talking about James in the therapy session, then practically bolting when Jordan brought him up again over Chinese food. Lately she just seemed to be a mass of contradictions, feeling one way one minute, another the next. What it all came down to was the fact that Dr. Marshall was right—she needed to start taking chances again. "Sounds like fun," she said after drawing a deep breath.

"Pick you up at seven?"

"Yes." And she gave him her address. A little thrill went through her as she laid the receiver back on its cradle, but there was no more time to think about Jordan. The telephone immediately rang again.

"Amanda Scott."

The chef's assistant was calling. A pipe had broken, and the kitchen was flooding fast.

"Just another manic day," Amanda muttered as she hurried off to investigate.

Chapter 2

It was ten minutes after six when Amanda got off the bus in front of her apartment building and dashed inside. After collecting her mail, she hurried up the stairs and jammed her key into the lock. Jordan was picking her up in less than an hour, and she had a hundred things to do to get ready.

Since he'd told her the evening would be a casual one, she selected gray woolen slacks and a cobalt-blue blouse. After a hasty shower, she put on fresh makeup and quickly wove her hair into a French braid.

Gershwin stood on the back of the toilet the whole time she was getting ready, lamenting the treatment of house cats in contemporary America. She had just given him his·dinner when a knock sounded at the door.

Amanda's heart lurched like a dizzy ballet dancer, and she wondered why she was being such a ninny. Jordan Richards was just a man, nothing more. And so what if he was successful? She met a lot of men like him in her line of work.

She opened the door and knew a moment of pure exaltation at the look of approval in Jordan's eyes.

"Hi," he said. He wore jeans and a sport shirt, and his hands rested comfortably in the pockets of his brown leather jacket. "You look fantastic."

Amanda thought he looked pretty fantastic himself, but she didn't say so because she'd used up that week's quota of bold moves by talking about James in front of people she didn't know. "Thanks," she said, stepping back to admit him.

Gershwin did a couple of turns around Jordan's ankles and meowed his approval. With a chuckle, Jordan bent to pick him up. "Look at the size of this guy. Is he on steroids or what?"

Amanda laughed. "No, but I suspect him of throwing wild parties and sending out for pizza when I'm not around."

After scratching the cat once behind the ears, Jordan set him down again with a chuckle, but his eyes were serious when he looked at Amanda.

Something in his expression made her breasts grow heavy and her nipples tighten beneath the smooth silk of her blouse. "I suppose we'd better go," she said, sounding somewhat lame even to her own ears.

"Right," Jordan agreed. His voice had the same effect on Amanda it had had earlier. She felt the starch go out of her knees and she was breathless, as though she'd accidentally stepped onto a runaway skateboard.

She took her blue cloth coat from the coat tree, and Jordan helped her into it. She felt his fingertips brush her nape as he lifted her braid from beneath the collar, and hoped he didn't notice that she trembled ever so slightly at his touch.

His car, a sleek black Porsche—Amanda decided then and there that he didn't have kids of his own—was parked at the curb. Jordan opened the passenger door and walked around to get behind the wheel after Amanda was settled.

Soon they were streaking toward Lake Union. It was only when he switched on the windshield wipers that Amanda realized it was raining.

"Have you lived in Seattle long?" she asked, uncomfortable with a silence Jordan hadn't seemed to mind.

"I live on Vashon Island now—I've been somewhere in the vicinity all my life," he answered. "What about you?"

"Seattle's home," Amanda replied.

"Have you ever wanted to live anywhere else?"

She smiled. "Sure. Paris, London, Rome. But after I graduated from college, I was hired to work at the Evergreen, so I settled down here."

"You know what they say—life is what happens while we're making other plans. I always intended to work on Wall Street myself."

"Do you regret staying here?"

Amanda had expected a quick, light denial. Instead she received a sober glance and a low, "Sometimes, yes. Things might have been very different if I'd gone to New York."

For some reason Amanda's gaze was drawn to the pale line across Jordan's left-hand ring finger. Although the windows were closed and the heater was going, Amanda suppressed a shiver. She didn't say anything until Lake Union, with its diamondlike trim of lit houseboats, came into sight. Since the holidays were approaching, the place was even more of a spectacle than usual.

"It looks like a tangle of Christmas tree lights."

Jordan surprised her with one of his fleeting, devastating grins.

"You have a colorful way of putting things, Amanda Scott."

She smiled. "Do your friends like living on a houseboat?"

"I think so," he answered, "but they're planning to move in the spring. They're expecting a baby."

Although lots of children were growing up on Lake Union, Amanda could understand why Jordan's friends would want to bring their little one up on dry land. Her thoughts turned bittersweet as she wondered whether she would ever have a child of her own. She was already twenty-eight—time was running out.

As he pulled the car into a parking lot near the wharves and shut the engine off, she sat up a little straighter, realizing that she'd left his remark dangling. "I'm sorry... I... How nice for them that they're having a baby."

Unexpectedly Jordan reached out and closed his hand over Amanda's. "Did I say something wrong?" he asked with a gentleness that almost brought tears to her eyes.

Amanda shook her head. "Of course not. Let's go in— I'm anxious to meet your friends."

David and Claudia Chamberlin were an attractive couple in their early thirties, he with dark hair and eyes, she with very fair coloring and green eyes. They were both architects, and framed drawings and photographs of their work graced the walls of the small but elegantly furnished houseboat.

Amanda thought of her own humble apartment with Gershwin as its outstanding feature, and wondered if Jordan thought she was dull.

Claudia seemed genuinely interested in her, though, and her greeting was warm. "It's good to see Jordan back in circulation—finally," she confided in a whisper when she and Amanda were alone beside the table where an array of wonderful food was being set out by the caterer's helpers.

Amanda didn't reply to the comment right away, but her gaze strayed to Jordan, who was standing only a few feet away, talking with David. "I guess it's been pretty hard for him," she ventured, pretending to know more than she did.

"The worst," Claudia agreed. She pulled Amanda a little distance farther from the men. "We thought he'd never get over losing Becky."

Uneasily Amanda recalled the pale stripe Jordan's wedding band had left on his finger. Perhaps, she reflected warily, there was a corresponding mark on his soul.

Later, when Amanda had met everyone in the room and mingled accordingly, Jordan laid her coat gently over her shoulders. "How about going out on deck with me for a few minutes?" he asked quietly. "I need some air."

Once again Amanda felt that peculiar lurching sensation deep inside. "Sure," she said with a wary glance at the rain-beaded windows.

"The rain stopped a little while ago," Jordan assured her with a slight grin.

The way he seemed to know what she was thinking was disconcerting.

They left the main cabin through a door on the side, and because the deck was slippery, Jordan put a strong arm around Amanda's waist. She was fully independent, but she still liked the feeling of being looked after.

The lights of the harbor twinkled on the dark waters of the lake, and Jordan studied them for a while before asking, "So, what do you think of Claudia and David?"

Amanda smiled. "They're pretty interesting," she replied. "I suppose you know they were married in India when they were there with the Peace Corps."

Jordan propped an elbow on the railing and nodded. "David and Claudia are nothing if not unconventional. That's one of the reasons I like them so much."

Amanda was slightly deflated, though she tried hard not to reveal the fact. With her ordinary job, cat and apartment, she knew she must seem prosaic compared to the Chamberlins. Perhaps it was the strange sense of hopelessness she felt that made her reckless enough to ask, "What about your wife? Was she unconventional?"

He turned away from her to stare out at the water, and for a long moment she was sure he didn't intend to answer. Finally, however, he said in a low voice, "She had a degree in marine biology, but she didn't work after the kids were born."

It was the first mention he'd made of any children— Amanda had been convinced, in fact, that he had none. "Kids?" she asked in a small and puzzled voice.

Jordan looked at her in a way that was almost, but not quite, defensive. "There are two—Jessica's five and Lisa's four."

Amanda knew a peculiar joy, as though she'd stumbled upon an unexpected treasure. She couldn't help the quick, eager smile that curved her lips. "I thought—well, when you were driving a Porsche—"

He smiled back at her in an oddly somber way. "Jessie and Lisa live with my sister over in Port Townsend."

Amanda's jubilation deflated. "They live with your sister? I don't understand."

Jordan sighed. "Becky died two weeks after the accident, and I was in the hospital for close to three months. Karen—my sister—and her husband, Paul, took the kids. By the time I got back on my feet, the four of them had become a family. I couldn't see breaking it up."

An overwhelming sadness caused Amanda to grip the railing for a moment to keep from being swept away by the sheer power of the emotion.

Reading her expression, Jordan gently touched the tip of her nose. "Ready to call it a night? You look tired."

Amanda nodded, too close to tears to speak. She had a tendency to empathize with other people's joys and sorrows, and she was momentarily crushed by the weight of what Jordan had been through.

"I see my daughters often," he assured her, tenderness glinting in his eyes. He kissed her lightly on the mouth, then took her elbow and escorted her back inside the cabin.

They said their goodbyes to David and Claudia Chamberlin, then walked up the wharf to Jordan's car. He was a perfect gentleman, opening the door for Amanda, and she settled wearily into the suede passenger seat.

Back at Amanda's building, Jordan again helped her out of the car, and he walked her to her door. Amanda waited until the last possible second to decide whether she was going to invite him in, breaking her own suspense by blurting out, "Would you like a cup of coffee or something?"

Jordan's hazel eyes twinkled as he placed one hand on either side of the doorjamb, effectively trapping Amanda between his arms. "Not tonight," he said softly.

Amanda's blue eyes widened in confusion. "Don't look now," she replied in a burst of daring cowardice, "but you're sending out conflicting messages."

He chuckled, and his lips touched hers, very tenderly.

Amanda felt a jolt of spiritual electricity spark through her system, burning away every memory of James's touch. Surprise made her draw back from Jordan so suddenly that her head bumped hard against the door.

Jordan lowered one hand to caress her crown, and she felt the French braid coming undone beneath his fingers.

"Careful," he murmured, and then he kissed her again.

This time there was hunger in his touch, and a sweet, frightening power that made Amanda's knees unsteady.

She laid her hands lightly on his chest, trying to ground this second mystical shock, but he interpreted the contact differently and drew back.

"Good night, Amanda," he said quietly. He waited until she'd unlocked her door with a trembling hand, and then he walked away.

Inside the apartment Amanda flipped on the living room light, crossed to the sofa and sagged onto it. She felt as though she were leaning over the edge of a great canyon and the rocks were slipping away beneath her feet.

Gershwin hurled himself into her lap with a loud meow, and she ran one hand distractedly along his silky back. Dr. Marshall had said it was time she started taking chances, and she had an awful feeling she was on the brink of the biggest risk of her life.

The massive redwood-and-glass house overlooking Puget Sound was dark and unwelcoming that night when Jordan pulled into the driveway and reached for the small remote control device lying on his dashboard. He'd barely made the last ferry to the island, and he was tired.

As the garage door rolled upward, he thought of Amanda, and shifted uncomfortably on the seat. He would have given half his stock portfolio to have her sitting beside him now, to talk with her over coffee in the kitchen or wine in front of the fireplace…

To take her to his bed.

Jordan got out of the car and slammed the door behind him. The garage was dark, but he didn't flip on a light until he reached the kitchen. Becky had always said he had the night vision of a vampire.

Becky. He clung to the memory of her smile, her laughter, her perfume. She'd been tiny and spirited, with dark hair and eyes, and it seemed to Jordan that she'd never been far from his side, even after her death. He'd loved her to an excruciating degree, but for the past few months she'd been steadily receding from his mind and heart. Now, with the coming of Amanda, her image seemed to be growing more indistinct with every passing moment.

Jordan glanced into the laundry room, needing something real and mundane to focus on. A pile of jeans, sweatshirts and towels lay on the floor, so he crammed as much as he could into the washing machine, then added soap and turned the dial. A comforting, ordinary sound resulted.

Returning to the kitchen, Jordan shrugged out of his leather jacket and laid it over one of the bar stools at the counter. He opened the refrigerator, studied its contents without actually focusing on a single item, then closed it again. He wasn't hungry for anything except Amanda, and it was too soon for that.

Too soon, he reflected with a rueful grin as he walked through the dining room to the front entryway and the stairs. He hadn't bothered with such niceties as timing with the women he'd dated over the past two years—in truth, their feelings just hadn't mattered much to him, though he'd never been deliberately unkind.

He trailed his hand over the top of the polished oak banister as he climbed the stairs. With Amanda, things were different. Timing was crucial, and so were her feelings.

The empty house yawned around Jordan as he opened his bedroom door and went inside. In the adjoining bathroom he took off his clothes and dropped them neatly into the hamper, then stepped into the shower.

Thinking of Amanda again, he turned on the cold water and endured its biting chill until some of the intolerable heat had abated. But while he was brushing his teeth, Amanda sneaked back into his mind.

He saw her standing on the deck of the Chamberlins' boat, looking up at him with that curious vulnerability showing in her blue-green eyes. It was as though she didn't know how beautiful she was, or how strong, and yet she had to, because she was out there making a life for herself.

Rubbing his now-stubbled chin, Jordan wandered into the bedroom, threw back the covers and slid between the sheets. He felt the first stirrings of rage as he thought about the mysterious James and the damage he'd done to Amanda's soul. Jordan had seen the bruises in her eyes every time she'd looked at him, and the memory made him want to find the bastard who'd hurt her and systematically tear him apart.

Jordan turned onto his stomach and tried to put the

scattered images of the past two days out of his thoughts. This time, just before he dropped off to sleep, was reserved for thoughts of Becky, as always.

He waited, but his late wife's face didn't form in his mind. He could only see Amanda, with her wide, trusting blue eyes, her soft, spun-honey hair, her shapely and inviting body. He wanted her with a desperation that made his loins ache.

Furious, Jordan slammed one fist into the mattress and flipped onto his back, training all his considerable energy on remembering Becky's face.

He couldn't.

After several minutes of concentrated effort, all of it fruitless, panic seized him, and he bolted upright, switched on the lamp and reached for the picture on his nightstand.

Becky smiled back at him from the photograph as if to say, *Don't worry, sweetheart. Everything will be okay.*

With a raspy sigh, Jordan set the picture back on the table and turned out the light. Becky's favorite reassurance didn't work that night. Maybe things would be okay in the long run, but there was a lot of emotional white water between him and any kind of happy ending.

It was Saturday morning, and Amanda luxuriated in the fact that she didn't have to put on makeup, style her hair, or even get dressed if she didn't want to. She really tried to be lazy, but she felt strangely ambitious, and there was no getting around it.

She climbed out of bed and padded barefoot into the kitchen, where she got the coffee maker going and fed Gershwin. Then she had a quick shower and dressed in battered jeans, a Seahawks T-shirt and sneakers.

She was industriously vacuuming the living room rug, when the telephone rang.

The sound was certainly nothing unusual, but it fairly stopped Amanda's heart. She kicked the switch on the vacuum cleaner with her toe and lunged for the telephone, hoping to hear Jordan's voice since she hadn't seen or heard from him in nearly a week.

Instead it was her mother. "Hello, darling," said Marion Whitfield. "You sound breathless. Were you just coming in from the store or something?"

Amanda sank onto the couch. "No, I was only doing housework," she replied, feeling deflated even though she loved and admired this woman who had made a life for herself and both her daughters after the man of the house had walked out on them all.

"That's nice," Marion commented, for she was a great believer in positive reinforcement. "Listen, I called to ask if you'd like to go Christmas shopping with me. We could have lunch, too, and maybe even take in a movie."

Amanda sighed. She still didn't feel great about Christmas, and the stores and restaurants would be jam-packed. The theaters, of course, would be full of screaming children left there by harried mothers trying to complete their shopping. "I think I'll just stay home, if you don't mind." She stated the refusal in a kindly tone, not wanting to hurt her mother's feelings.

"Is everything all right?"

Amanda caught one fingernail between her teeth for a moment before answering, "Mostly, yes."

"It's time you put that nasty experience with James Brockman behind you," Marion said forthrightly.

The two women were friends, as well as mother and daughter, and Amanda was not normally secretive with

Marion. However, the thing with Jordan was too new and too fragile to be discussed; after all, he might never call again. "I'm trying, Mom," she replied.

"Well, Bob and I want you to come over for dinner soon. Like tomorrow, for instance."

"I'll let you know," Amanda promised quickly as the doorbell made its irritating buzz. "And stop worrying about me, okay?"

"Okay," Marion answered without conviction just before Amanda hung up.

Amanda expected one of the neighbor children, or maybe the postman with a package, so when she opened the door and found Jordan standing in the hallway, she felt as though she'd just run into a wall at full tilt.

For his part, Jordan looked a little bewildered, as though he might be surprised to find himself at Amanda's door. "I should have called," he said.

Amanda recovered herself. "Come in," she replied with a smile.

He hesitated for a moment, then stepped into the apartment, his hands tucked into the pockets of his jacket. He was wearing jeans and a green turtleneck, and his brown hair was damp from the Seattle drizzle. "I was wondering if you'd like to go out to lunch or something."

Amanda glanced at the clock on the mantel and was amazed to see that it was nearly noon. The morning had flown by in a flurry of housecleaning. "Sure," she said. "I'll just clean up a little—"

He reached out and caught hold of her hand when she would have disappeared into her bedroom. "You look fine," he told her, and his voice was very low, like the rumble of an earthquake deep down in the ground.

By sheer force of will, Amanda shored up her knees,

only to have him pull her close and lock his hands lightly behind the small of her back. A hot flush made her cheeks ache, and she had to force herself to meet his eyes.

Jordan chuckled. "Do I really scare you so much?" he asked.

Amanda wet her lips with the tip of her tongue in an unconscious display of nervousness. "Yes."

"Why?"

The question was reasonable, but Amanda didn't know the answer. "I'm not sure."

He grinned. "Where would you like to go for lunch?"

She would have been content not to go out at all, preferring just to stand there in his arms all afternoon, breathing in his scent and enjoying the lean, hard feel of his body against hers. She gave herself an inward shake. "You know, I just refused a similar invitation from my mother, and she would have thrown in a movie."

Jordan laughed and smoothed Amanda's bangs back from her forehead. "All right, so will I."

But Amanda shook her head. "Too many munchkins screaming and throwing popcorn."

His expression changed almost imperceptibly. "Don't you like kids?"

"I love them," Amanda answered, "except when they're traveling in herds."

Jordan chuckled again and gave her another light kiss. "Okay, we'll go to something R-rated. Nobody under seventeen admitted without a parent."

"You've got a deal," Amanda replied.

Just as he was helping her get into her coat, the telephone rang. Praying there wasn't a disaster at the Evergreen to be taken care of, Amanda answered, "Hello?"

"Hello, Amanda." She hadn't heard that voice in six

long months, and the sound of it stunned her. It was James.

Grimacing at Jordan, she spoke into the receiver. "I don't want to talk to you, now or ever."

"Please don't hang up," James said quickly.

Amanda bit down on her lip and lowered her eyes. "What is it?"

"Madge is divorcing me."

She drew a deep breath and let it out again. "Congratulations, James," she said, not with cruelty but with resignation. After all, it was no great surprise, and she had no idea why he felt compelled to share the news with her.

"I'd like for you and me to get back together," he said in that familiar tone that had once rendered her pliant and gullible.

"There's absolutely no chance of that," Amanda replied, forcing herself to meet Jordan's gaze again. He was standing at the door, his hand on the knob, watching her with concern but not condemnation. "Goodbye, James." With that, she placed the receiver back in its cradle.

Jordan remained where he was for a long moment, then he crossed the room to where Amanda stood, bundled in her coat, and gently lifted her hair out from under her collar. "Still want to go out?" he asked quietly.

Amanda was oddly shaken, but she nodded, and they left the apartment together. The phone began ringing again when they reached the top of the stairs, but this time Amanda made no effort to answer it.

"I guess I can't blame him for being persistent," Jordan remarked when they were seated in the Porsche. "You're a beautiful woman, Amanda."

She sighed, ignoring the compliment because it didn't register. "I'll never forgive James for lying to me the way he did," she got out. Tears stung her eyes as she remembered the blinding pain of his deceit.

Jordan pulled out into the rainy-day traffic and kept his eyes on the road. "He wants you back," he guessed.

Amanda noticed that his hands tensed slightly around the steering wheel.

"That's what he said," she confessed, staring out at the decorated streets but not really seeing them.

"Do you believe him?"

Amanda shrugged. "It doesn't matter whether I do or not. I've made my decision and I'm not going to change my mind." She found some tissue in her purse and resolutely dried her eyes, trying in vain to convince herself that Jordan hadn't noticed she was crying.

He drove to a pizza joint across the street from a mall north of the city. "This okay?" he asked, bringing the sleek car to a stop in one of the few parking spaces available. "We could order takeout if you'd rather not go in."

Amanda drew a deep breath, composing herself. The time with James was behind her, and she wanted to keep it there, to enjoy the here and now with Jordan. Christmas crowds or none. "Let's eat here," she said.

He favored her with a half grin and came around to open her door for her. As she stood, she accidentally brushed against him, and felt that familiar twisting ache deep inside herself. She was going to end up making love with Jordan Richards, she just knew it. It was inevitable.

The realization that he was reading her thoughts once more made Amanda blush, and she drew back when he took her hand. His grip only became firmer, however, and she didn't try to pull away again. She was in the mood to follow where Jordan might lead—which, to

Amanda's way of thinking, made it a darned good thing they were approaching the door of a pizza parlor instead of a bedroom.

Chapter 3

The pizza was uncommonly good, it seemed to Amanda, but memories of the R-rated movie they saw afterward made her fidget in the passenger seat of Jordan's Porsche. "I've never heard of anybody doing that with an ice cube," she remarked with a slight frown.

Jordan laughed. "That was interesting, all right."

"Do you think it was symbolic?"

He was still grinning. "No. It was definitely hormones, pure and simple."

Amanda finally relaxed a little and managed to smile. "You're probably right."

Since there were a lot of cars parked in front of Amanda's building, a sleek silver Mercedes among them, Jordan parked almost a block away. It seemed natural to hold hands as they walked back to the entrance.

Amanda was stunned to see James sitting on the bottom step of the stairway leading up to the second floor. He was wearing his usual three-piece tailor-made suit, a necessity for a corporate chief executive officer like himself, and his silver gray hair looked as dashing as ever.

His tanned face showed signs of strain, however, and the once-over he gave Jordan was one of cordial contempt.

Amanda's first instinct was to let go of Jordan's hand, but he tightened his grip when she tried.

Meanwhile James had risen from his seat on the stairs. "We have to talk," he said to Amanda.

She shook her head, grateful now for Jordan's presence and his grasp on her hand. "There's nothing to say."

The man she had once loved arched an eyebrow. "Isn't there? You could start by introducing me to the new man in your life."

It was Jordan who spoke. "Jordan Richards," he said evenly, without offering his hand.

James studied him with new interest flickering in his shrewd eyes. "Brockman," he answered. "James Brockman."

A glance at Jordan revealed that he recognized the name—anyone active in the business world would have—but he clearly wasn't the least bit intimidated. He simply nodded an acknowledgment.

Amanda ran her tongue over her lips. "Let us pass, James," she said. She'd never spoken so authoritatively to him before, but she took no pleasure in the achievement because she knew she wouldn't have managed it if Jordan hadn't been there.

James did not look at Amanda, but at Jordan. Some challenge passed between them, and the air was charged with static electricity for several moments. Then James stepped aside to lean against the banister, leaving barely enough room for Jordan and Amanda to walk by.

"Richards."

Jordan stopped, still holding Amanda's hand, and looked back at James over one shoulder in inquiry.

"I'll call your office Monday morning. I'd be interested to know what we have in common—where investments are concerned, naturally."

Amanda felt her face heat. Again she tried to pull away from Jordan; again he restrained her. "Naturally," Jordan responded coldly, and then he continued up the stairway, bringing Amanda with him.

"I'm sorry," she said the moment they were alone in her apartment. She was leaning against the closed door.

"Why?" Jordan asked, reaching out to unbutton her coat. He helped her out of it, then hung it on the brass tree. Amanda watched him with injury in her eyes as he removed his jacket and put it with her coat.

She had been leaning against the door again, and she thrust herself away. "Because of James, of course."

"It wasn't your fault he came here."

She sighed and stopped in the tiny entryway, her back to Jordan, the fingers of one hand pressed to her right temple. She knew he was right, but she was slightly nauseous all the same. "That remark he made about what the two of you might have in common…"

Jordan reached out and took her shoulders in his hands, turning her gently to face him. "Your past is your own business, Amanda. I'm interested in the woman you are now, not the woman you were six months or six years ago."

Amanda blinked, then bit her upper lip for a moment. "But he meant—"

He touched her lip with an index finger. "I know what he meant," he said with hoarse gentleness. "When and if it happens for us, Amanda, you won't be the first woman I've been with. I'm not going to condemn you because I'm not the first man."

With that, the subject of that aspect of Amanda's relationship with James was closed forever. In fact, it was almost as though the subject hadn't been broached. "Would you like some coffee or something?" she asked, feeling better.

Jordan grinned. "Sure."

When Amanda came out of the kitchenette minutes later, carrying two mugs of instant coffee, Jordan was studying the blue-and-white patchwork quilt hanging on the wall behind her couch. Gershwin seemed to have become an appendage to his right ankle.

"Did you make this?"

Amanda nodded proudly. "I designed it, too."

Jordan looked impressed. "So there's more to you than the mild-mannered assistant hotel manager who gets her Christmas shopping done early," he teased.

She smiled. "A little, yes." She extended one mug of coffee and he took it, lifting it to his lips. "I had a good time today, Jordan."

When Amanda sat down on the couch, Jordan did, too. His nearness brought images from the movie they'd seen back to her mind. "So did I," he answered, putting his coffee down on the rickety cocktail table.

Damn that guy with the ice cube, Amanda fretted to herself as Jordan put his hands on her shoulders again and slowly drew her close. It seemed to her that a small eternity passed before their lips touched, igniting the soft suspense Amanda felt into a flame of awareness.

The tip of his tongue encircled her lips, and when they parted at his silent bidding, he took immediate advantage. Somehow Amanda found herself lying down on the sofa instead of sitting up, and when Jordan finally pulled away from her mouth, she arched her neck. He kissed the pulse point at the base of her throat, then progressed to the one beneath her right ear. In the meantime, Amanda could feel her T-shirt being worked slowly up her rib cage.

When he unsnapped her bra and laid it aside, revealing her ripe breasts, Amanda closed her eyes and lifted her back slightly in a silent offering.

He encircled one taut nipple with feather-light kisses, and Amanda moaned softly when he captured the morsel between his lips and began to suckle. She entangled her hands in his hair and spread her legs, one foot high on the sofa back, the other on the floor, to accommodate him.

The eloquent pressure of his desire made Amanda ache to be taken, but she was too breathless to speak, too swept up in the gentle incursion to ask for conquering. When she felt the snap on her jeans give way, followed soon after by the zipper, she only lifted her hips so the jeans could be peeled away. They vanished, along with her panties and her sneakers, and Jordan began to caress her intimately with one hand while he enjoyed her other breast.

The ordinary light in the living room turned colors and made strange patterns in front of Amanda's eyes as Jordan kissed his way down over her satiny, quivering belly to her thighs.

She whimpered when he burrowed into her deepest secret, gave a lusty cry when he plundered that secret with his mouth. Her hips shot upward, and Jordan cupped his hands beneath her bottom, holding her in his hands as he would sparkling water from a stream. "Jordan," she gasped, turning her head from side to side in a fever of passion when he showed her absolutely no mercy.

He flung her over the savage brink, leaving her to convulse repeatedly at the top of an invisible geyser. When the last trace of response had been wrung from her, he lowered her gently back to the sofa.

She lay there watching him, the back of one hand resting against her mouth, her body covered in a fine mist of perspiration. Jordan was sitting up, one of her bare legs draped across his lap, his eyes gentle as he laid a hand on Amanda's trembling belly as if to soothe it.

"I want you," she said brazenly when she could speak.

Jordan smiled and traced the outline of her jaw with one finger, then the circumferences of both her nipples. "Not this time, Mandy," he answered, his voice hardly more than a ragged whisper.

Amanda was both surprised and insulted. "What the hell do you mean, 'not this time'? Were you just trying to prove—"

Jordan interrupted her tirade by bending to kiss her lips. "I wasn't trying to prove anything. I just don't want you hating my guts when you wake up tomorrow."

Amanda's body, so long untouched by a man, was primed for a loving it wasn't going to receive. "You're too late," she spat, bolting to an upright position and righting her bra and T-shirt. "I *already* hate your guts!"

Jordan obligingly fetched her jeans and panties from the floor where he'd tossed them earlier. "Probably, but you'll forgive me when the time is right."

She squirmed back into the rest of her clothes, then stood looking down at Jordan, one finger waggling. "No, I won't!" she argued hotly.

He clasped her hips in his hands and brought her forward, then softly nipped the place he'd just pillaged so sweetly. Even through her jeans, Amanda felt a piercing response to the contact; a shock went through her, and she gave a soft cry of mingled protest and surrender.

Jordan drew back and gave her a swat on the bottom. "See? You'll forgive me."

Amanda would have whirled away then, but Jordan caught her by the hand and wrenched her onto his lap. When she would have risen, he restricted her by catching hold of her hands and imprisoning them behind her back.

With his free hand, he pushed her T-shirt up in front again, then boldly cupped a lace-covered breast that throbbed to be bared to him once more. "It's going to be very good when we make love," he said firmly, "but that isn't going to happen yet."

Amanda squirmed, infuriated and confused. "Then why don't you let me go?" she breathed.

He chuckled. "Because I want to make damn sure you don't forget that preview of how it's going to be."

"Of all the arrogance—"

Jordan pulled down one side of her bra, causing the breast to spring triumphantly to freedom. "I've got plenty of that," he breathed against a peak that strained toward him.

Amanda moaned despite herself when he took her into his mouth again.

"Umm," he murmured, blatant in his enjoyment.

Utter and complete surprise possessed Amanda when she realized she was being propelled to another release, with Jordan merely gripping her hands behind her and feasting on her breast. She didn't want him to know, and yet her body was already betraying her with feverish jerks and twists.

She bit down hard on her lower lip and tried to keep herself still, but she couldn't. She was moving at lightning speed toward a collision with a comet.

Jordan lifted his mouth from her breast just long

enough to mutter, "So it's like that, is it?" before driving her hard up against her own nature as a woman.

She surrendered in a burst of surprised gasps and sagged against Jordan, resting her head on his shoulder when it was finally over. "H-how did that happen?"

Still caressing her breast, Jordan spoke against her ear. "No idea," he answered, "but it damned near made me change my mind about waiting."

Amanda lay against his chest until she'd recovered the ability to stand and to breathe properly, then she rose from his lap, snapped her bra and pulled down her T-shirt. In a vain effort to regain her dignity, she squared her shoulders and plunged the splayed fingers of both hands through her hair. "You don't find me attractive—that's it, isn't it?"

"That's the most ridiculous question I've ever been asked," Jordan answered, rising a little awkwardly—and painfully, it seemed to Amanda—from the sofa. "I wouldn't have done the things I just did if I didn't."

"Then why don't you want me?"

"Believe me, I do want you. Too badly to risk lousing things up so soon."

Amanda wasn't satisfied with that answer, so she turned on one heel and fled into the bathroom, where she splashed cold water on her face and brushed her love-tousled hair. When she came out, half fearing that Jordan would be gone, she found him standing at the window, gazing out at the city.

Calmer, she stood behind him, slipped her arms around his lean waist and kissed his nape. "Stay for supper?"

He turned in her embrace to smile down into her eyes. "That depends on what's on the menu."

Amanda was mildly affronted, remembering his rejection. "It isn't me," she stated with a small pout, "so you can relax."

He laughed and gave her another playful swat on the bottom. "Take it from me, Mandy—I'm not relaxed."

She grinned, glad to know he was suffering justly, and kissed his chin, which was already darkening with the shadow of a beard. "Nobody has called me 'Mandy' since first grade," she said.

"Good."

"Why is that good?" Amanda inquired, snuggling close.

"Because it saves me the trouble of thinking up some cutesy nickname like 'babycakes' or 'buttercup.'"

She laughed. "I can't imagine you calling me 'buttercup' with a straight face."

"I don't think I could," he replied, bending his head to kiss her thoroughly. Amanda's knees were weak when he finally drew back.

"You delight in tormenting me," she protested.

His eyes twinkled. "What's for supper?"

"Grilled cheese sandwiches, unless we go to the market," Amanda answered.

"The market it is," Jordan replied. Once again, in the entryway he helped Amanda into her coat.

"You have good manners for a rascal," Amanda remarked quite seriously.

Jordan laughed. "Thank you—I think."

They walked to a small store on the corner, where food was overpriced but fresh and plentiful. Amanda selected two steaks, vegetables for a salad and potatoes for baking.

"Does your fireplace work?" Jordan asked, lingering in front of a display of synthetic logs.

Amanda nodded, wondering if she could stand the romance of a crackling fire when Jordan was so determined not to make love to her. "Are you trying to drive me crazy, or what?" she countered, her eyes snapping with irritation.

He gave her one of his nuclear grins, then picked up two of the logs and carried them to the checkout counter, where he threw down a twenty-dollar bill. He would have paid for the food, too, except that Amanda wouldn't let him.

She did permit him to carry everything back to the apartment, however, thinking it might drain off some of his excess energy.

When they were back in Amanda's apartment, he moved the screen from in front of the fireplace as Gershwin meowed curiously at his elbow. After opening the damper, he laid one of the logs he'd bought in the grate. Amanda glanced at the label on the other log and saw it was meant to last a full three hours.

She grinned as she got her favorite skillet out of the drawer underneath the stove. Two logs totaled six hours. Maybe Jordan would change his mind about waiting before that much time slipped past.

Dusting his hands together, he came into the kitchenette, and Amanda could see the flicker of the fire reflected on the shiny front of her refrigerator door. Without being asked, he took the vegetables out of the bag and began washing them at the sink.

Amanda went to his side, handing him both the potatoes. "You're pretty handy in a kitchen, fella," she remarked in a teasing, sultry voice.

Jordan's eyes danced when he looked at her, and his expression said he was pretty handy in a few other rooms, too. "Thanks." He scrubbed the potatoes and handed them back to Amanda, who put a little swing in her hips as she walked away because she knew he was watching.

He laughed. "You need a spanking."

Amanda poked the potatoes with a fork and set them in the tiny microwave oven her mother and stepfather had given her the Christmas before. "Very kinky, Mr. Richards."

Jordan chuckled as he went back to chopping vegetables, and Amanda found the wooden salad bowl she'd bought in Hawaii and set it on the counter beside him.

They ate at the glass table in Amanda's living room, the fire dancing on the hearth and casting its image on their wineglasses. Darkness had long since settled over the city, and Amanda wondered why she hadn't noticed when the daylight fled.

"Tell me about your daughters," she said when the meal was nearly over.

Jordan pushed his plate away and took a sip of his wine before replying. "They're normal kids, I guess. They like to watch *Sesame Street*, have me read the funny papers to them, things like that."

Amanda felt sad, but if someone had asked, she would have had to admit she wasn't thinking about Jordan's children at all. She was remembering how it felt when her dad had gone away that long-ago Christmas Day, swearing never to come back. And he hadn't. "Do you miss them?" she asked.

"Yes," he admitted frankly. "But I know they're better off with Karen and Paul."

"Why?" Amanda dared to ask.

Jordan lifted his shoulders in a slight shrug. "I told you—my sister and her husband took them in when I was in the hospital. I'm more like an uncle to them than a father. They wouldn't understand if I uprooted them now."

Amanda wasn't so sure, but she didn't say that because she knew she'd already overstepped her bounds in some ways. If Jordan didn't want to raise his own children, that was his business, but it made Amanda wonder what would happen if the two of them were ever married and had babies. If she died, would he just send the kids to live with someone else?

She refilled her wineglass and took a healthy sip.

There was a look of quiet understanding in Jordan's eyes as he watched her. "What have I done now?" he asked.

"Nothing," Amanda lied, setting her glass down and jumping up to begin clearing the table.

Jordan rose from his chair and elbowed her aside. "Go and sit by the fire. I'll take care of this."

Apparently giving orders had become a habit with Jordan over the course of his successful career. "I'll help," she insisted, following him into the kitchen with the salad bowl in her hands.

Jordan scraped and rinsed the plates, and Amanda put them, along with the silverware and glasses, into the dishwasher.

"Somebody trained you rather well," she commented grudgingly.

He gave her a meltdown grin. "Thanks for noticing," he said with a slight leer.

Amanda's face turned pink. "I was talking about cooking and doing dishes!"

Jordan smiled at her discomfiture. "Oh," he said, but he sounded patently unconvinced.

Amanda put what remained of the salad in a smaller

bowl, covered that tightly with plastic wrap, then stuck it into the refrigerator. She longed to ask him what kind of wife Becky had been, but she didn't dare. She knew he'd say she'd been wonderful, and Amanda wasn't feeling grown-up enough to deal with that.

He was leaning against the sink, watching her, his arms folded in front of his chest. "James is a lot older than you are," he said.

The remark was so out of left field that Amanda was momentarily stunned by it. "I know," she finally managed, standing in the doorway that led to the living room.

"Where did you meet him?"

Amanda couldn't think why she was answering, since they had agreed not to talk about James, but answer she did. "At the hotel," she replied with a sigh. "He taught a management seminar there a year and a half ago."

"And you went?"

She couldn't read Jordan's mood either in his eyes or his voice, and she was unsettled by the question. "Yes. He asked me out to dinner the first night, and after that I saw him whenever he was in Seattle on business."

Jordan crossed the room and enfolded Amanda in his arms, and the relief she felt was totally out of proportion to the circumstances.

"I have to know one thing, Mandy. Do you love him?"

She shook her head. "No." She tasted wine on Jordan's lips when he kissed her. And she tasted wanting. *Do you still love Becky?* she longed to ask, but she was too afraid of the answer to voice the question.

Slipping his arm around her waist, Jordan ushered Amanda into the living room, where they sat on a hooked rug in front of the fireplace. He gripped her hand and stared into the flames in the silence for a long time, then he turned, looked into her fire-lit eyes and said, "I'm sorry, Mandy. I didn't have any right to ask about James."

She let her head rest against the place where his arm and shoulder met. "It's okay. I made a fool of myself, and I can admit that now."

Jordan caught her chin in his hand and wouldn't let her look away. "Let's get one thing straight here," he said in gentle reproach. "The only mistake you made was trusting the bastard. He's the fool."

Amanda sighed. "That's a refreshing opinion. Most people either say or imply that I should have known better."

"Not this people," Jordan answered, tasting her lips.

Although it seemed impossible, Amanda wanted Jordan more now than she had on the couch earlier when he'd brought her face-to-face with her own womanhood. She longed to take him by the hand and lead him to her bed, but the thought of a second rebuff stopped her. In fact, she supposed it was about time she started taking the advice her mother had given her in ninth grade and play hard to get.

She moved a little apart from Jordan, stiffened her shoulders and raised her chin. "Maybe you should go," she said.

Jordan showed no signs of leaving. Instead he put his hands on Amanda's shoulders and lowered her to the hooked rug, stretching out beside her and laying one hand brazenly on her breast. The nipple tightened obediently beneath his palm.

Amanda moved to rise, but Jordan pressed her back down again, this time with a consuming kiss. "Don't you dare start anything you don't intend to finish," she ordered in a raspy whisper when at last he'd drawn away from her mouth. Having obtained the response he wanted from her right breast, he was now working on her left.

"I'll finish it," he vowed in a husky murmur, "when the time is right."

He lowered his hand to her belly, covering it with splayed fingers, and Amanda's heart pounded beneath her T-shirt. She pulled on his nape until his mouth again joined with hers, and the punishment for this audacious act was the unsnapping of her jeans.

"Damn it, Jordan, I don't like being teased."

He pulled at the zipper, and then his hand was in between her jeans and her panties, just resting there, soaking up her warmth, making her grow moist. That part of her body was like an exotic orchid flowering in a hothouse.

"Tough," he replied with a cocky grin just before he bent and scraped one hidden nipple lightly with his teeth, causing it to leap to attention.

Amanda's formidable pride was almost gone, and she had to grasp the rug and bite down on her lower lip to keep from begging him to make love to her.

"This night is just for you," he told her, his hand making a fiery circle at the junction of her thighs. "Why can't you accept that?"

"Because it isn't normal, that's why," Amanda gasped, trying to hold her hips still but finding it impossible. "You're a man. You're supposed to have just one thing on your mind. You're supposed to be trying to jump my bones."

He laughed at that. "What a chauvinistic thing to say."

Amanda groaned as he continued his sweet devilment. "I've never seen anything in *Cosmopolitan* that told what to d-do when this happens," she complained.

Again Jordan laughed. "I can tell you what to do," he said when he'd recovered himself a little. "Enjoy it."

Amanda was beginning to breathe hard. "Damn you, Jordan—I'll make you pay for this!"

"I'm counting on that," he said against her mouth.

Moments later Amanda was soaring again. She dug her fingers into Jordan's shoulders while she plunged her heels into the rug, and everyone in the apartment building would have known how well he'd loved her if he hadn't clamped his mouth over hers and swallowed her cries.

"If this is some kind of power game," Amanda sputtered five minutes later when she could manage to speak, fastening her jeans and sitting up again, "I don't want to play."

"You could have fooled me," Jordan responded.

Amanda gave a strangled cry of frustration and anger. "I can't imagine why I keep letting you get away with this."

"I can," he replied. "It feels good, and it's been a long time. Right?"

Amanda let her forehead rest against his shoulder, embarrassed. "Yes," she confessed.

He kissed the top of her head. "I should have dessert before dinner more often," he teased.

Amanda groaned, unable to look at him, and he chuckled and lifted her chin for a light kiss. "You're impossible," she murmured.

"And I'm leaving," he added with a glance at his watch. "It's time you were in bed."

Bleakness filled Amanda at the thought of climbing into bed alone, and she was just about to protest, when

Jordan laid a finger to her nose and asked, "Will you go Christmas shopping with me tomorrow?"

Amanda would have gone to Zanzibar. "Yes," she answered like a hypnotized person.

Jordan kissed her again, leaving her lips warm and slightly swollen. "Good night," he said. And then, after a backward look and a wave, he was gone.

Chapter 4

The telephone jangled just as Amanda finished with her makeup the next morning. She'd managed to camouflage the shadows under her eyes—the result of sleeping only a few hours—with a cover stick.

"Hello?" she blurted into the receiver of her bedside telephone, hoping Jordan wasn't calling to back out of their shopping trip.

"If I remember correctly," her mother began dryly without returning the customary greeting, "you were supposed to call last night and let us know whether you were coming over for supper."

Amanda stretched the phone cord as far as her closet, where she took out black wool slacks. "Sorry, Mom," she answered contritely. "I forgot, but you'll be glad to know it was because of a man." She went to the dresser for her pink cashmere sweater while waiting for her mother to digest her last remark.

"A man?" Marion echoed, unable to hide the pleasure in her voice.

"And James was here yesterday," Amanda went on after pulling the sweater on over her head.

Marion drew in her breath. "Don't tell me you're seeing him again—"

"Of course not, Mom," Amanda scolded, propping the receiver between her shoulder and her ear while she wriggled into the sleek black pants.

"You're deliberately confusing me," Marion accused.

Amanda sighed. "Listen, I'll tell you everything tomorrow, okay? I'll stop by after work and catch you up on all the latest developments."

"So there is somebody besides James?" Marion pressed, sounding pleased.

"Yep," Amanda answered just as the door buzzer sounded. "Gotta go—he's here."

"Bye," Marion said cooperatively, and promptly hung up.

Amanda was brushing her hair as she hurried through the apartment to open the door. She was smiling, since she expected Jordan, but she found a delivery man from one of the more posh department stores in the hallway, instead. He was holding two silver gift boxes, one large and one fairly small. "Ms. A. Scott?" he asked.

Amanda nodded, mystified.

"These are for you—special express delivery," the man said, holding on to the packages while he shoved a clipboard at Amanda. "Sign on line twenty-seven."

She found the appropriate line and scrawled her name there, and the man gave her the packages in return for the clipboard.

After depositing the boxes on the couch and rummaging through her purse for a tip, she closed the door and lifted the lid off the smaller box. A skimpy aqua bikini lay inside, but there was no card or note to explain.

She opened the large box and gasped, faced with the rich, unmistakable splendor of sable. A small envelope lay on top, but Amanda didn't need to read it to know the gifts were from James.

As a matter of curiosity, she looked at the card: "Honeymoon in Hawaii, then on to Copenhagen? Call me. James."

With a sigh, Amanda tossed down the card. She was just about to call the store and ask to return the two boxes, when there was a knock at the door.

She rushed to open it and found Jordan standing in the hallway, looking spectacular in blue jeans, a lightweight yellow sweater and a tweed sport jacket.

"Hi," he said, his bright hazel eyes registering approval as he looked at her.

"Come in," Amanda replied, stepping back and holding the door open wide. "I'm just about finished with my hair. Pour yourself a cup of coffee and I'll be right out."

He stopped her when she would have turned away from him, and lightly entangled the fingers of one hand in her hair. "Don't change it," he said hoarsely. "It looks great."

Amanda's heart was beating a little faster just because he was close and because he was touching her. Since she didn't know what to say, she didn't speak.

Jordan kissed her lightly on the lips. "Good morning, Mandy," he said, and his voice was still husky. Amanda had a vision of him carrying her off to bed, and heat flooded her entire body, a blush rising in her cheeks.

"Good morning," she replied, her voice barely more than a squeak. "How about that coffee?"

His gaze had shifted to the boxes on the couch. "What's this?" There was a teasing reproach in his eyes when they returned to her face. "Opening your presents before Christmas, Mandy? For shame."

Amanda had completely forgotten the unwanted gifts, and the reminder deflated her spirits a little. "I'm sending them back," she said, hoping Jordan wouldn't pursue the subject.

His expression sobered. "James?"

Amanda licked her lips, then nodded nervously. She wasn't entirely displeased to see a muscle in Jordan's cheek grow taut, then relax again.

"Persistent, isn't he?"

"Yes," Amanda admitted. "He is." And after that there seemed to be nothing more to say—about James, anyway.

"Let's go," Jordan told her, kissing her forehead. "We'll get some breakfast on the way."

Amanda disappeared into the bedroom to put on her shoes, and when she came out, Jordan was studying the quilt over her couch again, his hands in his hip pockets.

"You know, you have a real talent for this," he said.

Amanda smiled. James had always been impatient with her quilting, saying she ought to save the needlework for when she was old and had nothing better to do. "Thanks."

Jordan followed her out of the apartment and waited patiently while she locked the door. He held her elbow lightly as they went down the stairs, once again giving her the wonderful sensation of being protected.

The sun was shining, which was cause for rejoicing in Seattle at that time of year, and Amanda felt happy as Jordan closed the car door after her.

When he slid behind the wheel, he just sat there for a

few minutes and looked at her. Then he put a hand in her hair again. "Excuse me, lady," he said, his voice low, "but has anybody told you this morning that you're beautiful?"

Amanda flushed, but her eyes were sparkling. "No, sir," she answered, playing the game. "They haven't."

He leaned toward her and gave her a lingering kiss that made a sweet languor blossom inside her.

"There's an oversight that needs correcting," he murmured afterward. "You're beautiful."

Amanda was trembling when he finally turned to start the ignition, fasten his seat belt and steer the car out into the light Sunday morning traffic. Something was terribly wrong in this relationship, she reflected. It was supposed to be the man who wanted to head straight for the bedroom, while the woman held out for knowing each other better.

And yet it was all Amanda could do not to drag Jordan out of the car and back up the stairs to her apartment.

"What's the matter?" Jordan asked, tossing a mischievous glance her way that said he well knew the answer to that question.

Amanda folded her arms and looked straight ahead as they sped up a freeway ramp. The familiar green-and-white signs slipped by overhead. "Nothing," she said.

He sighed. "I hate it when women do that. You ask them what's wrong and they say 'nothing,' and all the while you know they're ready to burst into tears or clout you with the nearest blunt object."

Amanda turned in her seat and studied his profile for a few moments, one fingernail caught between her teeth. "I wasn't about to do either of those things," she finally said. She didn't quite have the fortitude to go the rest of the way and admit she was wondering why he didn't seem to want her.

Jordan reached out and laid a hand gently on her knee, once again sending all her vital organs into a state of alarm.

"What's the problem, then?"

She drew in a deep breath for courage and let it out slowly. "If we sleep together, you'll be the second man I've ever been with in my life, so it's not like I'm hot to trot or anything. But I usually have to fight guys off, not wait for them to decide the time is right."

He was clearly suppressing a smile, which didn't help.

"'Hot to trot'? I didn't think anybody said that anymore."

"Jordan."

He favored her with a high-potency grin. "Believe me, Mandy, I'm a normal man and I want you. But you're going to have to wait, because I've got no intention of—forgive me—screwing this up."

Amanda sighed and folded her arms. "Exactly what is it you're waiting for?"

His wonderful eyes were crinkled with laughter, even though his mouth was unsmiling.

"Exactly what is it you want me to do?" he countered. "Pull the car over to the side of the freeway and, as you put it last night, 'jump your bones'?"

Amanda blushed. "You make me sound like some kind of loose woman," she accused.

He took her hand and squeezed it reassuringly. "I can't even imagine that," he said in a soothing voice. "Now what do you say we change the subject for a while?"

That seemed like the only solution. "Okay," Amanda agreed. "Remember how you admired the quilt I made?"

Jordan nodded, switching lanes to be in position for an upcoming exit. "It's great."

"Well, I've been designing and making quilts for years. Someday I hope to open a bed and breakfast somewhere, with a little craft shop on the premises."

He grinned as he took the exit. "I'm surprised. Given your job and the fact that you live in the city, I thought you were inclined toward more sophisticated dreams."

"I was," Amanda said, recalling some of the glamorous, exciting adventures she had had with James. "But life changes a person. And I've always liked making quilts. I've been selling them at craft shows for a long time, and saving as much money as I could for the bed and breakfast."

Jordan was undoubtedly thinking of her humble apartment when he said, "You must have a pretty solid nest egg."

Amanda sighed, feeling discouraged all over again. "Not really. The real estate market is hot around here, what with so many people moving up from California, and the prices are high."

They had left the freeway, and Jordan pulled the car into the parking lot of a family-style restaurant near the mall. "Working capital is one of my specialties, Mandy. Maybe I can help you."

Amanda surprised even herself when she shook her head so fast. She guessed it was partly pride that made her do that, and partly disappointment that he wasn't trying to talk her out of establishing a business in favor of something else. Like getting married and starting a family.

"Did we just hit another tricky subject?" Jordan asked

good-naturedly, when he and Amanda were walking toward the restaurant.

She shrugged. "I want the bed and breakfast to be
all my own."

Jordan opened the door for her. "What if you decide
to get married or something?"

Amanda felt a little thrill, even though she knew Jordan wasn't on the verge of proposing. She would have
refused even if he had. "I guess I'll cross that bridge
when I come to it."

A few minutes later they were seated at a small table
and given menus. They made their selections and sipped
the coffee the waitress had brought while they waited
for the food.

"Who are we shopping for today?" Amanda asked,
to get the conversation going again. Jordan was sitting
across from her, systematically making love to her with
his eyes, and she was desperate to distract him.

"Jessie and Lisa mostly, though I still need to get
something for Karen and Paul."

Something made Amanda ask, "What about your parents?"

Sadness flickered in the depths of Jordan's eyes, but
only for a moment. "They were killed in a car accident
when I was in college," he replied.

Amanda reached out on impulse and took his hand. It
seemed to her that Jordan had had more than his share of
tragedy in his life, and she suddenly wanted to share her
mother and stepfather with him. "I'm sorry."

He changed the subject so abruptly his remark was
almost a rebuff. "What do you think Karen would like?"

Amanda was annoyed and a little hurt. "How would
I know? I've never even met the woman."

The waitress returned with their breakfast, setting bacon and eggs in front of Jordan and giving Amanda wheat toast and a fruit compote. When they were alone again, Jordan replied, "Karen's thirty-five, a little on the chubby side—and totally devoted to Paul and the girls."

Amanda tried to picture the woman and failed. "Do she and Paul have children of their own?"

Jordan was mashing his eggs into his hash browns. "No."

She speared a melon ball and chewed it distractedly. "That's sad," she said after swallowing.

"These things happen," Jordan replied.

Amanda looked straight into his eyes. "I guess Karen would be pretty upset if she ever had to give Jessica and Lisa back to you," she ventured to say.

He returned her bold, assessing stare. "I wouldn't do that to her or to the girls," he said, and there was no hint of mischief about him this time. He was completely serious.

Things were a little strained between them throughout the rest of the meal, but as soon as they reached the toy store at the mall, they were both caught up in the spirit of the season. They bought games for the girls, and dolls, and little china tea sets.

Amanda couldn't remember the last time she'd had so much fun, and her eyes were sparkling as they stuffed everything into the back of the Porsche.

From the toy store they headed to a big-name department store where, after great deliberation, they chose expensive perfume and bath powder for Karen and a sweater for her husband.

They had lunch in a fast-food hamburger place

jammed to the rafters with excited kids, and by the time they returned to Amanda's apartment, she was exhausted.

"Coming in?" she asked at the door because, in spite of everything he'd said about waiting, she'd been entertaining a discreet fantasy all morning.

Jordan shook his head. "Not today," he said. "I've got to drive up to Port Townsend and look in on the kids."

Amanda was hurt that he didn't want to take her along, but she hid it well. After all, she didn't have the right to any injured feelings. "Say hello for me," she said softly.

He kissed her, lightly at first, then with an authority that brought the fantasy to the forefront of her mind. Amanda surreptitiously gripped the doorknob to keep from sliding to the floor.

"I'll be out of town most of next week," he said when the kiss was over. "Is it okay if I call?"

Is it okay? She would be shattered if he didn't. "Sure," she answered in a tone that said it wouldn't matter one way or the other because she'd be busy with her glamorous, sophisticated life.

Jordan waited until she'd unlocked the door and stepped safely inside, then she heard him walking away.

She tossed aside her purse, kicked off her shoes and hung up her coat. The coming week yawned before her like an abyss.

Ignoring the boxes still sitting on her couch, she bent distractedly to pet a meowing Gershwin, then stumbled into her bedroom, stripped off her clothes and crawled back into the unmade bed. All those hours she hadn't slept the night before were catching up with her.

Later she awoke to full darkness, the weight of Gershwin curled up on her stomach and the ringing of the phone.

Groping with one hand, she found the receiver, brought it to her ear and yawned, "Hello?"

"It's Mom," Marion announced. "How are you, dear?"

Amanda yawned again. "Tired. And hungry."

"Perfect," Marion responded with her customary good cheer and indefatigable energy. "Drag yourself over here, and I'll serve you a home-cooked meal that will put hair on your chest."

Amanda giggled, rubbing her eyes and stretching. The movement made Gershwin jump down from her stomach and land with a solid *thump* on the floor. "There's one flaw in your proposal, Mom. Who needs hair on their chest?"

Marion laughed. "Just get in your car and drive over here. Or should I send Bob, so you don't have to go wandering around in that dark parking lot behind your building?"

"There's an attendant," Amanda said, sitting up. "I'll drive over as soon as I've had a quick shower to revive myself."

Marion agreed, and the conversation came to an amicable end.

With her hair pulled back into a ponytail, Amanda was wearing jeans, a football jersey and sneakers when she arrived at her parents' house in another part of the city. And she was making a determined effort not to think about Jordan and the fact that he hadn't asked her to go to Port Townsend with him.

Her mother, a slender, attractive woman with shoulder-length hennaed hair and skillfully applied makeup, met her at the front door. Marion looked wonderful in her trim green jumpsuit, and her smile and hug were both warm.

"Bob's in the living room, cussing that string of Christmas tree lights that always goes on the blink," the older woman confided in a merry whisper.

Amanda laughed and wandered into the front room. There were cards everywhere—they lined the top of the piano, the mantel and were arranged into the shape of a Christmas tree on one wall. Amanda had been putting hers in a desk drawer that year.

"Hi, Bob," she said, giving her stepfather a hug. He was a tall man, with thinning blond hair and kindly blue eyes, and he'd been very good to Marion. Amanda loved him for that reason, if for no other.

He was standing beside a fresh-smelling, undecorated pine tree, which was, as usual, set up in front of the bay window facing the street. The infamous string of lights was in his hands. "I don't know why she won't let me throw these darned things out and buy new ones," he fussed in a conspiratorial whisper. "It's not as if we couldn't afford to."

Amanda chuckled. "Mom's sentimental about those lights," she reminded him. "They've been on the tree since Eunice and I were babies."

"Speaking of your sister," Marion remarked from the kitchen doorway, wiping her hands on her white apron, "we had a call from her today. She's coming home for Christmas."

Amanda was pleased. This was a hard time in Eunice's life; she needed to get away from the wreckage of her marriage, if only for a week or two. "What about her job at the university?"

Marion shrugged. "I guess she's taking time off. Bob and I are picking her up at the airport late next Friday night."

Amanda left Bob to his Christmas tree light quandary and followed her mother into the bright, fragrant kitchen, where they had had so many talks before. "Seattle will be a shock to Eunice after Southern California," she remarked.

Marion gave her a playful flick with a dish towel. "Forget the harmless chitchat," she said with a grin. "What's going on in your life these days? Who's the new man, and what the devil was James doing, dropping by?"

Drawing up a battered metal stool, Amanda sat down at the breakfast counter Bob had built when he remodeled the kitchen, and started cutting up the salad vegetables her mother indicated. "James is getting divorced," she said, avoiding Marion's gaze. "Evidently he has some idea that we can get back together."

"I presume you set him straight on that."

"I did." Amanda sighed. "But I'm not sure he's getting the message. He sent me a sable jacket and a silk bikini today, along with an invitation to Hawaii and Copenhagen."

The oven door slammed a touch too hard after Marion pulled a pan of fragrant lasagna from it. "You'd never guess he was such a scumbag, would you?"

Amanda grinned and tossed a handful of chopped celery into the salad bowl. "You've got to stop watching all those cop shows, Mom. It's affecting your vocabulary."

"No way," replied Marion, who had a minor crush on Don Johnson. "So, who's the other guy?"

"Did I say there was another guy?"

"I think so," Marion replied airily, "but you wouldn't have had to. There's a sparkle in your eyes and your cheeks are pink."

"His name is Jordan Richards," Amanda said. Personally she attributed any sparkle in her eyes or color in her cheeks to the nap she'd taken.

Marion stopped slicing the lasagna to look directly at her daughter. "And?"

"And he makes me crazy, that's what."

Marion beamed. "That's a good sign."

Amanda wondered if her mother would still be of the same opinion if she knew just how hard her daughter had fallen. And how bold she'd been. "I guess so."

"What does he do for a living?" Bob asked from the kitchen doorway. Since it was a classic parental question, Amanda didn't take offense.

"He's a partner in an investment firm—Striner, Striner and Richards."

Bob whistled and tucked his hands in his pockets. "That's the big time, all right."

"Amanda doesn't care how much money he makes," Marion said with mock haughtiness. "She just wants his body."

At this, both Amanda and Bob laughed.

"Mom!" Amanda protested.

"It's true," Marion insisted. "I'd know that look anywhere. Now let's all sit down and eat."

They trooped into the dining room, where Marion had set a festive table using the special Christmas dishes that always came out of storage, along with the nativity set, on the first of December. Despite the good food and the conversation, Amanda's mind was on Jordan.

"About those presents James sent you," Marion began when she and Amanda were alone in the kitchen again, washing dishes while Bob fought it out with the Christmas tree lights. "You are sending them back, aren't you?"

Amanda favored her mother with a rueful smile. "Of course I am. First thing tomorrow."

"Some women would have their heads turned, you know, by such expensive things."

"Expensive is right. All James wants in return for his presents is my soul. What a bargain."

Marion finished washing the last pot, drained the sink and washed her hands. "I'm glad you're wise enough to see that."

Amanda shrugged. "I don't know how smart I am," she replied. "The only reason I'm so sure about everything where James is concerned is that I don't love him anymore. I'm not sure what I'd do if I still cared."

"I am," Marion said confidently. "You've always had a good head on your shoulders. That's why I think this new man must really be something."

Amanda indulged in a smile as she shook out the dish towel and hung it on the rack to dry. "He is." But her smile faded as she thought of those two little girls living far away from their father with an aunt and uncle, and of Becky, cut down before she'd even had a chance to live.

"What is it?" Marion wanted to know. She had already poured two cups full of coffee, and she carried them to the kitchen table while waiting for Amanda to answer.

Amanda sank dejectedly into one of the chairs and cupped her hands around a steaming mug. "He's a widower, and I think—well, I think he might have some problems with commitment."

"Don't they all?" Marion asked, stirring artificial sweetener into her coffee.

"Bob didn't," Amanda pointed out, her voice solemn. "He loved you enough to marry you, even though he knew you had two teenage daughters and a pile of debts."

Marion looked thoughtful. "How long have you known this man?"

"Not very long," Amanda confessed. "About ten days, I guess."

Marion chuckled and shook her head. "And you're already bandying words like 'commitment' about?"

"No. I'm only *thinking* words like 'commitment.'"

"I see. Well, this is serious. Why do you think he wouldn't want to settle down?"

Amanda ran the tip of her index finger around the rim of her coffee mug. "He has two little girls, and they don't live with him—his sister and brother-in-law are raising them. He sort of bristled when I asked him about it."

Marion laid a hand on her daughter's arm. "You're a little gun-shy, dear, and that's natural after what happened with James. Just give yourself some time."

Time. Jordan was asking the same thing of her. Didn't anyone act on impulse anymore?

Marion smiled at her daughter's frustrated expression. "Just take life one day at a time, Amanda, and everything will work out."

Amanda nodded, and after chatting briefly with her mother about Eunice's upcoming visit, she put on her coat, kissed both her parents goodbye and went out to her nondescript car.

"You be careful to park where the attendant can see you," Bob instructed her just before she pulled away from the curb.

The attendant was on duty, and Amanda parked where there was plenty of light.

It turned out, however, that it was the inside of her building that she should have looked out for, not the parking lot.

James was sitting on the stairs again, and this time she didn't have Jordan along to act as a buffer.

"I'm glad you're here," Amanda said in a cold voice. "You can take back the fur and the bikini."

James's handsome, distinguished face fell. "You still haven't forgiven me, have you?" he asked in a pained voice, spreading his hands wide for emphasis. "Baby, how many times do I have to tell you? Madge and I haven't been in love for years."

Amanda ached as she remembered Madge Brockman's raging agony during the confrontation. "Maybe *you* haven't been," she muttered sadly.

James either didn't hear the remark or chose to ignore it. "Just let me talk to you. Please."

Having summoned up the courage she needed, Amanda passed him on the narrow stairway. "Nothing you can say will change my mind, James." She reached her door and unlocked it as he made to follow her. "So just take your presents and give them to some other fool."

Suddenly James caught her elbow in a hard grasp and wrenched her around to face him. "You're in love with Richards, aren't you? The boy wonder! You think he's pretty hot stuff, I'll bet! Well, let me tell you something— I could buy and sell him ten times over!"

Amanda pulled free of James, stormed over to the couch, picked up the boxes and shoved them at him. "Take these and get out!"

He stared at her as though she'd lost her mind.

"And while you're at it, you can just take everything *else* you've ever given me, too!"

With that, she strode into the bedroom and yanked open her jewelry box, intending to return the gold brace- let and pearl earrings she'd forgotten about. She only became aware that James had followed her when he cried out.

Turning, Amanda saw him clasp his chest with one hand and topple to the floor.

Chapter 5

James's face was contorted with pain, and he was only partially conscious. "Help—me—" he groaned.

Amanda lunged for the phone on her bedside table, punched 911 and barked out her address when someone came on the line. She followed that with a brief description of the problem.

"Someone will be there in a few minutes," the woman on the telephone assured her. "Is the patient conscious?"

James was clearly in agony, but he was awake. "Yes."

"Then just cover him up and make him as comfortable as you can—and try to reassure him. The paramedics will take care of everything else when they get there."

Amanda hung up and draped James with a quilt dragged from her bed. When it was in place, she knelt beside him and grasped his hand.

"It's going to be okay, James," she said, her eyes stinging with tears. "Everything is going to be okay."

His free hand was clenched against his chest. "Hurts—so much...crushing..."

"I know," Amanda whispered, holding his knuckles

to her lips. She could hear sirens in the distance. "Help will be here soon."

A loud knock sounded at the door just a few minutes later.

"In here!" Amanda called, and soon two paramedics burst into the bedroom, bringing a stretcher and some other equipment. She scrambled out of the way and perched on the end of her bed, still unmade from her nap earlier, watching as James was examined, loaded onto the stretcher and given oxygen and an IV.

"Any history of heart disease?" one of the men asked Amanda as he and his partner lifted the stretcher.

"I—I don't know," Amanda whispered.

"We'll be taking him to Harborview Hospital, if you'd like to come along," the other volunteered.

Amanda only sat there, gripping the edge of the mattress and shaking her head, unable to tell them she wasn't James's wife.

When the telephone rang a full hour later, she was still sitting in the exact same place.

"H-hello?"

Jordan's voice was warm and low. "Hello, Mandy. Is something wrong?"

Amanda dragged her forearm across her face, wiping away tears that had long since dried. *James had a heart attack in my bedroom*, she imagined herself answering.

She couldn't explain the situation to Jordan over the phone, she decided, sinking her teeth into her lower lip.

"Mandy?" Jordan prompted when the silence had stretched on too long.

"I thought you were in Port Townsend," she managed in a small voice that was hoarse from crying.

"I just got back," he answered. "As a matter of fact,

I'm spending the night in a hotel out by the airport, since my plane leaves so early tomorrow."

Amanda swallowed hard and did her best to sound ordinary. There would be time enough to tell Jordan what had happened when he got back from his business trip. "Wh-where are you going?"

"Chicago. Mandy, what's the matter?"

She closed her eyes. "We can talk about it when you get home."

There was a long pause while he digested that. "Is this something I should know about?"

Amanda nodded, even though he wasn't there to see her. "Yes," she admitted, "but I can't talk about it like this. I have to be with you."

"I could get in the car and be there in half an hour."

Amanda would have given anything short of her very soul to have Jordan there in the room with her, to be held and comforted by him. But she'd only known him a little while, and she had no right to make demands. "I'll be okay," she said softly.

After that, there didn't seem to be much to say. Jordan promised to phone her from Chicago the first chance he got and Amanda wished him well, then the call was over.

Amanda had barely replaced the receiver, when the bell jangled again, startling her. If it had been Jordan she would have relented and asked him to come over, but the voice on the other end of the line was a woman's.

"Well, I must say, I half expected you to be at the hospital, clutching James's hand and swearing your undying love."

Amanda closed her eyes again, feeling as though she'd been struck. The caller was Madge Brockman, James's estranged wife. "Mrs. Brockman, I—"

"Don't lie to me, please. I just spoke to someone on the hospital staff, and they told me James had suffered a heart attack 'at the home of a friend.' It didn't take a genius to figure out just who that 'friend' might be."

Deciding to let the innuendos pass unchallenged, Amanda asked, "Is James going to be all right?"

"He's in critical condition. I'm flying in tonight to sit with him."

It was a relief to know James wouldn't be going through this difficult time alone. "Mrs. Brockman, I'm very sorry—for everything."

The woman hung up with a slam, leaving Amanda holding the receiver in one trembling hand and listening to a dial tone. Slowly she put down the phone, then crouched to unplug it from the outlet. After disconnecting the living room phone, as well, she took a long, hot shower and crawled into bed.

The sound of her alarm and faceful of bright sunshine woke her early the next morning. The memory of James lying on her bedroom floor in terrible pain was still all too fresh in her mind.

But Amanda had a job, so, even though she would have preferred to stay in bed with her face turned to the wall, she fed the cat, showered, dressed and put on makeup. Once she'd pinned her hair up in a business-like chignon, she reconnected the telephones and called the hospital.

James was in stable condition.

Longing for Jordan, who might have been able to put the situation into some kind of perspective, Amanda pulled on her coat and gloves and left her apartment.

Late that afternoon, just as she was preparing to go home for the day, Jordan called. He was getting ready to have dinner with some clients, and there was something clipped about his voice. Something distant.

"Feeling better?" he asked.

Amanda heard a whole glacier of emotion shifting beneath the tip of the iceberg. "Not a whole lot," she admitted, "but it's nothing for you to worry about."

She could almost see him hooking his cuff links. "I read about James in the afternoon edition of the paper, Amanda."

So he knew about the heart attack, and she was no longer 'Mandy.' "Word gets around," she managed, propping one elbow on her desk and sinking her forehead into her palm.

"Is that what you didn't want to talk about last night?"

There was no point in trying to evade the question further. "Yes. It happened in my bedroom, Jordan."

He was quiet for a long time. Much too long.

"Jordan?"

"I'm here. What was he doing in your bedroom, or don't I have the right to ask?"

Tears were brimming in Amanda's eyes, and she prayed no one would step into her office and catch her displaying such unprofessional emotions. "Of course you have the right. He came over because he wanted to persuade me to start seeing him again. I told him to take back the things he gave me, and then I remembered some jewelry he'd given me a long time ago. I went to get them, and he followed me." She drew in a shaky breath, then let it out again. "He got very angry, and he was yelling at me. He just—just fell to the floor."

"My God," Jordan rasped. "What kind of shape is he in now?"

"When I called the hospital this morning, he was stable."

Jordan's voice was husky. "Mandy, I'm sorry."

Amanda didn't know whether he meant he was sorry for doubting her, or he was sorry about James's misfortune. "I wish you were here," she said, testing the water. Everything would ride on his reply.

"So do I," he answered.

Relief flooded over Amanda. "You're not angry?"

He sighed. "No. I guess I just lost my head for a little while there. Do you want me to come back tonight, Mandy? There's a flight at midnight."

"No." She shook her head. "Stay there and set the financial world on its ear. I'll be okay."

"Promise?"

For the first time since before James's collapse, Amanda smiled. "I promise."

"In that case, I'll be back sometime on Friday night. How about penciling me into your busy schedule, Ms. Scott?"

Amanda chuckled. "Consider yourself penciled."

"In fact," he went on, "have a bag packed. I'll stop and pick you up on my way home from the airport."

"Have a bag packed?" Amanda echoed. "Wait a minute, Jordan. What are you proposing here?"

He hesitated only a moment before answering, "I want you to spend the weekend at my place."

Amanda's throat tightened. "Is this the Jordan I know—the one who insists on taking things slow and easy?"

"The same," Jordan replied, his words husky. "I need to have you under the same roof with me, Mandy. Whether we sleep together is entirely up to you."

She plucked some tissue from the box on her desk and began wiping away the mascara stains on her cheeks. "That's mighty mannerly of you, Mr. Richards," she drawled.

"See you Friday," he replied.

And after just a few more words, Amanda hung up.

It was some time before she got out of her chair, though. She'd had some violent ups and downs in the past twenty-four hours, and her emotional equilibrium was not what it might have been.

After taking a few minutes to sit with her head resting on her folded arms, Amanda finished up a report she'd been working on, then slipped into the ladies' room to repair her makeup. Leaving the elevator on the first floor of the hotel, she encountered Madge Brockman.

Mrs. Brockman was a slender, attractive brunette, expensively dressed and clearly well educated. There were huge shadows under her eyes.

"Hello, Amanda," she said.

At first Amanda thought it was just extraordinarily bad luck that she'd run into Mrs. Brockman, but moments later she realized the woman had been waiting in the lobby for her. "Hello, Mrs. Brockman. How is James?"

James's wife reached for Amanda's arm, then let her hand fall back to her side. "I was wondering if you wouldn't have a drink with me or something," she said awkwardly. "So we could talk."

Amanda took a deep breath. "If there's going to be a scene—"

Madge shook her head quickly. "There won't be, I promise."

Hoping Mrs. Brockman meant what she'd said, Amanda followed her into the cocktail lounge, where they took a quiet table in a corner. When the waiter came, Amanda asked for a diet cola and Mrs. Brockman ordered a gin and tonic.

"The doctor tells me James is going to live," Mrs. Brockman said when the drinks had arrived and the waiter was gone again.

Amanda dared a slight smile. "That's wonderful."

Madge looked at her with tormented eyes. "James admitted he went to your apartment on his own last night, and not because you'd invited him. He—he's a proud man, my James, so it wasn't easy for him to say that you'd rejected him."

Not knowing what to say, Amanda simply waited, her hands folded in her lap, her diet cola untouched.

"He's agreed to come back home to California with me when he gets out of the hospital," Mrs. Brockman went on. "I don't know if that's a new start or what, but I do know this much—I love James. If there's any way we can begin again, well, I want a fighting chance."

"It's over between James and me," Amanda said gently. "It has been for months and months."

Mrs. Brockman's eyes held a flicker of hope. "You were telling the truth six months ago when I confronted you in your office, weren't you? You honestly didn't know James was married."

Amanda sighed. "That's right. As soon as I found out, I broke it off."

"But you loved him, didn't you?"

Amanda felt a twinge of the pain that time and hard work and Jordan had finally healed. "Yes."

"Then why didn't you hold on? Why didn't you fight for him?"

"If he'd been my husband instead of yours, I would

have," Amanda answered, reaching for her purse. She wasn't going to be able to choke down so much as a sip of that cola. "I'm not cut out to be the Other Woman, Mrs. Brockman. I want a man I don't have to share."

Madge Brockman smiled sadly as Amanda stood up. "Have you found one?"

"I hope so," Amanda answered. Then she laid a hand lightly on Mrs. Brockman's shoulder, just for a moment, before walking away.

Jordan arrived at seven o'clock on Friday night, looking slightly wan, his expensive suit wrinkled from the trip. "Hi, Mandy," he said, reaching out to gather her close.

Dressed for the island in blue jeans, walking boots and a heavy beige cable-knit sweater, Amanda went into his arms without hesitation. "Hi," she answered, tilting her head back for his kiss.

He tasted her mouth before moving on to possess it entirely. "I don't suppose you're going to be merciful enough to tell me what you've decided," he said, sounding a little breathless, when the long kiss was over.

"About what?" Amanda asked with feigned innocence, and kissed the beard-stubbled underside of his chin. Of course she knew he wanted to know what the sleeping arrangements would be on the island that night.

Jordan laughed hoarsely and gave her a swat. "You know damn well 'about what'!" he lectured.

Despite the weariness she felt, Amanda grinned at him. "If you guess right, I'll tell you," she teased.

He studied her with tired, laughing, hungry eyes. "Okay, here's my guess. You're going to say you want to sleep in the guest room." •

Amanda rocked back on her heels, resting against his hands, which were interwoven behind her, and said nothing.

"Well?" Jordan prodded.

"You guessed wrong," Amanda told him.

"Thank God," he groaned.

Amanda laughed. "Let's go—we'll miss the ferry."

Jordan's lips, warm and moist, touched hers. "We could just stay here—"

"No way, Mr. Richards," Amanda protested, pulling back. "You invited me to go away for the weekend and I want to *go away.*"

"What about the cat?" Jordan reasoned as Gershwin jumped onto the back of an easy chair and meowed plaintively.

"My landlady is going to take care of him," Amanda said, pulling out of Jordan's embrace and picking up her suitcase and overnight case. "Here," she said, shoving the suitcase at him.

"I like a subtle woman," Jordan muttered, accepting it.

Soon they were leaving the heart of the city behind for West Seattle, where they caught the Southworth ferry. Once they were on board the enormous white boat, however, they remained in the car instead of going upstairs to the snack bar with most of the other passengers.

"I've missed you," Jordan said, leaning back in the seat, resting his hand on Amanda's upper thigh and gripping her fingers.

"And I've missed you," Amanda answered. They'd already run through all the small talk; Jordan had told her about his business trip and she'd detailed her hectic week. By tacit agreement, they hadn't discussed James's heart attack.

Jordan splayed the fingers of his left hand and ran them through his rumpled hair, then gave a heavy sigh. He moved his thumb soothingly over Amanda's knuckles. "Do you have any idea how much I want you?"

She lifted his hand to her mouth and kissed it. "How much?"

He chuckled. "Enough to wish this were a van instead of a sports car." Jordan turned in the seat and cupped Amanda's chin in his hand. "You're sure you're ready for this?" he asked gently.

Amanda nodded. "I'm sure. How about you?"

Jordan grinned. "I've been ready since I turned around and saw you standing in line behind me."

"You have not."

"Okay," he admitted, "it started after that, when you threw five bucks on the table to pay for your Chinese food. For just a moment, when you thought I was going to refuse it, you had blue fire in your eyes."

"And?"

"And I had this fantasy about the whole mall being deserted—except for us, of course. I made love to you right there on the table."

Amanda felt a hot shiver go through her. "Jordan?"

His lips were moving against hers. "Yes?"

"We're fogging up the windows. People will notice that."

He chuckled and drew back. "Maybe we should go upstairs and have some coffee or something, then."

She felt the rough texture of his cheek against her palm. "Then what kind of fantasies would you be having?"

"I'd probably start imagining that we were right here, alone in a dark car, with nobody around." Slowly he unbuttoned the front of her coat. "I suppose I'd picture myself touching you like this." He curved his fingers around her breast.

Even through the weight of her sweater and the lacy barrier of her bra, Amanda could feel his caress in every nerve. "Jordan."

He moved his hand beneath the sweater and then, to the accompaniment of a little gasp of surprised pleasure from Amanda, beneath the bra. Cupping her warm breast, he rolled the nipple gently between his fingers. "I'd be thinking about doing this, no doubt."

Amanda was squirming a little, and her breath was quickening. "Damn it, Jordan—this isn't funny. Someone could walk by!"

"Not likely," he murmured, touching his mouth to hers as he continued to fondle her.

Although she knew she should, Amanda couldn't bring herself to push his hand away. What he was doing felt too good. "S-someone might see—they'd think…"

Jordan bent his head to kiss the pulse point at the base of her throat. "They'd think we were necking. And they'd be right." Satisfied that he'd set one nipple to throbbing, he proceeded to attend the other. "Ummm. Where were you on prom night, lady?"

"Out with somebody like you," Amanda gasped breathlessly.

Jordan chuckled and continued nibbling at her throat. She felt the snap on her jeans pop, heard the faint whisper of the zipper. "Did he do this?"

The windows were definitely fogging up. "No…" Amanda moaned as he slid his fingers down her warm abdomen to find what they sought.

"Lift up your sweater," Jordan said. "I want to taste you."

Amanda whimpered a halfhearted protest even as she obeyed, but when she felt his mouth close over a distended nipple, she groaned out loud and entangled her fingers in his hair. In the meantime he continued the other delicious mischief, causing Amanda to fidget on the seat.

She ran her hands down his back, then up to his hair again in a frantic search for a place to touch him and make him feel what she was feeling. His name fell repeatedly from her lips in a breathless, senseless litany of passion.

Just as the ferry horn sounded, Amanda arched her back and cried out in release. Her body buckled over and over again against Jordan's hand before she sagged into the seat, temporarily soothed. Gradually her breathing steadied.

"Rat," she said when her good sense returned. She righted her bra and pulled her sweater down while Jordan zipped and snapped her jeans. Not two seconds after that, the first of the passengers returning from the upper deck walked past the car and waved.

Amanda's cheeks glowed as Jordan drove off the ferry minutes later.

"Relax, Mandy," he said, shoving a tape into the slot on the dashboard. The car filled with soft music. "I'm on your side, remember?"

She ran her tongue over her lips and turned in the seat to look at him. Her body was still quivering like a resonating string on some exotic instrument. "I'm not angry—just surprised. Nobody's ever been able to make me forget where I was."

"Good," Jordan replied, turning the Porsche onto a paved road lined with towering pine trees. "I'd be something less than thrilled if that was a regular thing with you."

Amanda gazed out the window for a moment, then looked back at Jordan. "Is it a regular thing with you?" she asked, almost in a whisper.

He looked at her, but she couldn't read his expression in the darkness. "There have been women since Becky, if that's what you mean. But if it'll make you feel better, none of them has ever had quite the same effect on me that you do. And I've never taken any of them to the island."

Amanda didn't know whether she felt better or not. She peered at his towering house as they pulled into the driveway, but all she could see was a shadowy shape and a lot of dark windows.

The garage door opened at the push of a button, and Jordan pulled in and got out, then turned on the lights before coming around to open Amanda's door for her. Gripping the handle of her suitcase in one hand, the other hand pressed to the small of her back, he escorted her through a side door and into a spacious, well-designed kitchen.

Amanda stopped when he set the suitcase down on the floor. "Did you live here with Becky?" she blurted. She'd known she wouldn't have the courage to ask if she waited too long.

"No," Jordan answered, taking the overnight case from her hand and setting it on the counter.

She shrugged out of her coat, avoiding his eyes. "Oh."

"Are you hungry or anything?" Jordan asked, glancing around the kitchen as though he expected it to be changed somehow from the last time he'd seen it.

"I could use a cup of coffee," Amanda admitted. "Maybe with a little brandy in it."

Jordan chuckled and disappeared with her coat. When he came back, he was minus his suit jacket and one hand was at his throat, loosening his tie. "The coffee maker's there on the counter," he said, pointing. "The other stuff is in the cupboard above it. Why don't you start the coffee brewing while I bring my stuff in from the car?"

It sounded like a reasonable idea to Amanda, and she was thankful for something to occupy her. What she and Jordan were about to do was as old as time, but she felt like the first virgin ever to be deflowered. She nodded and busily set about making coffee.

Jordan made one trip to the garage and then went upstairs. When he returned, he stood behind Amanda and put his arms around her. "Are you sure you want coffee? It's late, and that's the regular stuff."

His lips moved against her nape, and she couldn't help the tremor that went through her. "I guess not," she managed to say.

Without another word, Jordan lifted her into his arms and carried her through the dark house and up a set of stairs. The light was on in his spacious bedroom, and Amanda murmured an exclamation at the low-key luxury of the place.

The bed was enormous, and it faced a big-screen TV equipped with a VCR and heaven-only-knows-what other kinds of high-tech electronic equipment. One wall was made entirely of windows, while another was lined with mirrors, and the gray carpet was deep and plush.

Amanda glanced nervously at the mirrors and saw her own wide eyes looking back at her.

Jordan kicked off his shoes, flung his tie aside and vanished into the bathroom, whistling and unbuttoning his shirt as he went. A few moments later Amanda heard the sound of a shower running.

Quickly she scrambled off the bed and found her suitcase, still feeling like a shy virgin. Suddenly the skimpy black nightgown she'd brought along didn't look sturdy enough, so she helped herself to a heavy terry-cloth robe from Jordan's closet. After hastily stripping, she wrapped herself in the robe and tied the belt with a double knot.

When Jordan came out sometime later, he was wearing nothing but a towel around his waist. His hair was blow-dried and combed back from his face, and his eyes twinkled at Amanda when he saw her sitting fitfully on the edge of the chair farthest from the bed.

"Scared?" he asked, approaching her and pulling her gently to her feet.

"Of course not," Amanda lied. The truth was, she was terrified.

Jordan undid the double knot at her waist as though it were nothing. "I guess I should have invited you to share my shower," he said, his voice a leisurely rumble.

"I had one at home," Amanda was quick to point out.

He opened the robe, laid it aside and looked at her, slowly and thoroughly, before meeting her eyes again. His lips quirked. "You're awfully nervous, considering how mad you were when I wouldn't make love to you last week."

Amanda moved to close the robe, but Jordan grasped her wrists and stopped her. He subjected her to another lingering assessment before pushing the garment off her shoulders with warm, gentle hands. It fell silently to the floor.

"We—we could turn the light out," she dared to suggest as Jordan lifted her again and carried her back to the bed.

"We could," he agreed, stretching out beside her, "but we're not going to."

He'd shaved, and his face was smooth and fragrant. He took her mouth and mastered it skillfully, leaving Amanda dizzy and disoriented when he drew away.

Tenderly he turned Amanda's head so that she was facing the mirrors, and a moan lodged in her throat when she saw him move his hand toward her breast.

"Jordan," she whispered.

"Shhh," he murmured against the tingling flesh of her neck, and Amanda was quiet, her eyes widening as she watched her conquering begin.

Chapter 6

The dark blue velour bedspread felt incredibly soft against Amanda's bare skin, and she forgot the mirrored wall and even the lights as Jordan kissed and caressed her. Although she tried, she couldn't hold back the soft moans that escaped her, or the whispered pleas for release.

But Jordan would not be hurried. "All in good time, Mandy," he assured her, his mouth at her throat. "All in good time. Just relax."

"Relax?" Amanda gave a rueful semihysterical chuckle at the word. "Now? Are you crazy?"

He trailed his lips down over her collarbone, over the plump rounding of one breast. "Ummm-hmm," he said just before he took her nipple into his mouth. In the meantime he was stroking the tender skin on the insides of Amanda's thighs.

"Stop teasing me," she whimpered, moving her hands through his hair and over the muscular sleekness of his back.

"Never," he paused long enough to say. He left off tormenting Amanda to reach for a pillow, which he deftly tucked underneath her bottom. And then he caressed her in earnest.

Amanda was frantic. Jordan had been subjecting her to various kinds of foreplay for a week, and she simply couldn't wait any longer for gratification. Her body demanded it.

"Jordan," she pleaded, half-blind with the need of him, "*now*. Oh, please—"

She felt him part her legs, then come to rest between them. "Mandy," he rasped like a man being consumed by invisible fire. In one fierce, beautiful thrust, he was a part of her, but then he lay very still. "Mandy, open your eyes and look at me."

She obeyed, but she could barely focus on his features because she was caught up in a whirlwind of sensation. The pillow raised her to him like a pagan offering, and her body was still reacting to the single stroke he'd allowed her. "Jordan," she pleaded, and all her desperation, all her need, echoed in the name.

He kissed her thoroughly, his tongue staking the same claim that the other part of his body was making on her. Finally he began to move upon her, slowly at first, making her ask for every motion of his powerful hips, but as Amanda's passion heated, so did his own. Soon they were parting and coming together again in a wild, primitive rhythm.

Amanda was the first to scale the peak, and the splintering explosion in her senses was everything she'd hoped it would be. Her body arched like a bow with the string drawn tight, and her cries of surrender echoed off the walls.

Jordan was more restrained, but Amanda saw a panorama of emotions cross his face as he gave himself up to her in a series of short, frenzied thrusts.

They lay on their sides, facing each other, legs still entwined, for long minutes after their lovemaking had ended.

Jordan gave a raspy chuckle.

"What's funny?" Amanda asked softly, winding a tendril of his rich brown hair around one finger.

"I was just thinking of the first time I saw you. You were bored with waiting in line, so you struck up a conversation. I wondered if you were a member of some weird religious sect."

Amanda gave him a playful punch in the chest.

He laughed and leaned over to kiss her. "Let's go down to the kitchen," he said when it was over. "I'm starving."

Jordan rose off the bed and retrieved the yellow bathrobe from the floor, tossing it to Amanda. He took a hooded one of striped silk from the closet and put that on. Together, they went downstairs.

Jordan plundered the cupboards, while Amanda perched on a stool, watching him and sipping a cup of the coffee she'd made earlier. He finally decided on popcorn and thrust a bag into the microwave.

"This is a great house," Amanda said as the oven's motor began to whir. "What I've seen of it, anyway."

Jordan was busy digging through another cupboard for a serving bowl that suited him. "Thanks."

"And it's pretty big." Saying those words gave Amanda the same sense of breathless anticipation she would have felt if she'd walked outside with the intention of plunging a toe into the frigid sound.

He set a red bowl on the counter with a thump, and

the grin he gave her was tinged with exasperation. "Big enough for a couple of kids, I suppose," he said.

Amanda shrugged and lifted her eyebrows. "Seems like you could fit Jessica and Lisa in here somewhere."

The popcorn was snapping like muted gunfire inside its colorful paper bag. For just a moment, Jordan's eyes snapped, too. "We've been over that, Amanda," he said.

She took another sip of her coffee. "Okay. I was just wondering why you'd want a house like this when you live all alone."

The bell on the microwave chimed, and Jordan took the popcorn out, carefully opened the bag and dumped the contents into the bowl. The fragrance filled the kitchen, causing Amanda to decide she was hungry, after all.

"Jordan?" she prompted when he didn't reply.

He picked up a kernel and tossed it at her. "How about cooling it with the questions I can't answer?"

Amanda sighed and wriggled off the stool. "I'm sorry," she said. "Your living arrangements are none of my business, anyway."

Jordan didn't counter that statement. He simply took up the bowl and started back through the house and up the stairs. Amanda had no choice but to follow.

Returning to the bed, they settled themselves under the covers, with pillows at their backs, the popcorn between them, and Jordan switched on the gigantic TV screen.

The news was on. "I'm not in the mood to be depressed," Jordan said, working the remote control device with his thumb until a cable channel came on.

Amanda settled against his shoulder and crunched

thoughtfully on a mouthful of popcorn. "I've seen this movie before," she said. "It's good."

Jordan slipped an arm around her and plunged the opposite hand into the bowl. "I'll take your word for it."

Images flickered across the screen, the popcorn diminished until there were only yellow kernels in the bottom of the bowl and the moon rose high and beautiful beyond the wall of windows. Amanda sighed and closed her eyes, feeling warm and contented.

The next thing she knew, it was morning, and Jordan was lying beside her, propped up on one elbow, smiling. "Hi," he said. He'd showered, and his breath smelled of mint toothpaste.

Amanda was well aware she hadn't and hers didn't. "Hi," she responded, speaking into the covers.

Jordan laughed and kissed her forehead. "Breakfast in twenty minutes," he said, and then he rose off the bed and walked away, wearing only a pair of jeans.

The moment he was gone, Amanda dashed to the bathroom. When he returned in the prescribed twenty minutes, he was carrying a tray and Amanda was sitting cross-legged in the middle of the bed. She'd exchanged Jordan's robe for a short nightgown of turquoise silk, and she grinned when she saw the tray in his hands.

"Room service! I'm impressed, Mr. Richards."

He set the food tray carefully in her lap, and Amanda's stomach rumbled in anticipation as she looked under various lids, finding sliced banana, toast, orange juice and two slices of crisp bacon. "Our services are *très* expensive, *madame*," he teased in a very good French accent.

"Put it on my credit card," Amanda bantered back, and picked up a slice of bacon and bit into it.

Jordan chuckled, still playing the Frenchman. "Oh, but *madame*, this we cannot do." He reached out to touch the tip of her right breast with his index finger, making the nipple turn button-hard beneath its covering of silk. "Zee policy is strictly cash and carry."

Amanda's eyes were sparkling as she widened them in mock horror. "We have a terrible problem then, *monsieur*, for I haven't a franc to my name. Not a single, solitary one!"

"This is a true pity," Jordan continued, laying a light, exploratory finger to Amanda's knee and drawing it slowly down to her ankle. "I am afraid you cannot leave this room until you have made proper restitution."

Amanda ate in silence for a time, while Jordan lingered, watching her with mischievous expectancy in his eyes. "Aren't you going to eat?" she asked, forgetting the game for a moment, and she went red the instant the words were out of her mouth.

Jordan chuckled, took the tray from her lap and set it aside. "About the price of your room, *madame*. Some agreement must be reached."

Recovered from her earlier embarrassment, Amanda slipped her arms around Jordan's neck and kissed him softly on the lips. "I'm sure we can work out something to our mutual satisfaction, *monsieur*."

He drew the silk nightgown gently over her head and tossed it away. *"Oui,"* he answered, laying a hand to her bare thigh even as he pressed her back onto the pillows.

Amanda groaned as he moved his hand from her thigh to her stomach, and when instinct caused her to draw up her knees, he claimed her with a finger in a sudden motion of his hand.

The sensation was exquisite, and Amanda arched her

neck, her eyes drifting closed as Jordan choreographed a dance for her eager body. She groaned as Jordan's tongue tamed a pulsing nipple.

"Of course," he told her in that same accented English, "the customer, she must always have satisfaction first."

Only moments later, Amanda was caught in the throes of a climax that caused her to thrash on the bed and call Jordan's name even as she clutched blindly at his shoulders.

"Easy," he told her, moving his warm lips against her neck. "Nice and easy."

Amanda sagged back to the mattress, her breath coming in fevered gasps, her eyes smoldering as she watched Jordan slip out of his jeans and poise himself above her. "No more waiting," she said. "I want you, Jordan."

He gave her only a portion of his magnificence at first, but then, when she traced the circumference of each of his nipples with a fingertip, he gave a low growl and plunged into her in earnest. And the whole splendid rite began all over again.

"A Christmas tree?" Amanda echoed, standing in the middle of Jordan's living room with its high, beamed ceilings and breathtaking view of the mountains and Puget Sound. She was wearing jeans, sneakers and a sweatshirt, like Jordan, and there was a cozy fire snapping on the raised hearth.

"Is that so strange?" Jordan asked. "After all, it is December."

Amanda assessed the towering tinted glass window that let in the view. "It would be a shame to cover that up," she said.

Jordan pinched her cheek. "Thank you, Ebenezer

Scrooge," he teased. Then he widened his eyes at her. "What is it with you and Christmas, anyway?"

With a sigh, Amanda collapsed into a cushy chair upholstered in dark blue brushed cotton, her arms folded. "I guess I'd like to let it just sort of slip past unnoticed."

"Fat chance," Jordan replied, perching on the arm of her chair. "It's everywhere."

"Yeah," Amanda said, lowering her eyes.

He put a finger under her chin and lifted. "What is it, Mandy?"

She tried to smile. "My dad left at Christmas," she admitted, her voice small as she momentarily became a little girl again.

"Ouch," Jordan whispered, pulling her to her feet. Then he sank into the chair and drew Amanda onto his lap. "That was a dirty trick."

"You don't know the half of it," Amanda reflected, staring out at mountains she didn't really see. "We never heard another word from him, ever. He didn't even take his presents."

Jordan pressed Amanda's head against his shoulder. "Know what?" he asked softly. "Hating Christmas isn't going to change what happened."

She lifted her head so that she could look into Jordan's eyes. "It's the hardest time of the year when you've lost somebody you loved."

He kissed her forehead. "Believe me, Mandy, I know that. The first year after Becky died, Jessie asked me to write a letter to Santa Claus for her. She wanted him to bring her mother back."

Amanda smoothed the hair at Jordan's temple, even though it wasn't rumpled. "What did you do?"

"My first impulse was to get falling-down drunk

and stay that way until spring." He sighed. "I didn't, of course. With some help from my sister, I explained to Jessie that even Santa couldn't pull off anything that big. It was tough, but we all got through it."

"Don't you miss them?" Amanda dared to ask, her voice barely more than a breath. "Jessica and Lisa, I mean?"

"Every day of my life," Jordan replied, "but I've got to think about what's best for them." His tone said the conversation was over, and so did his action. He got out of the chair, propelling Amanda to her feet in the process. "Let's go cut a Christmas tree."

Amanda smiled. "I haven't done that since I was still at home. My stepdad used to take my sister and me along every year—we drove all the way to Issaquah."

"So," Jordan teased with a light in his eyes, "your memories of Christmas aren't all bad."

Recalling how hard Bob had tried to make up not only for Marion's loss, but the girls', as well, Amanda had a warm feeling. "You're right," she admitted.

Jordan squinted at her and twisted the end of an imaginary mustache. This time his accent was Viennese, and he was, according to Amanda's best guess, Sigmund Freud. "Absolutely of course I am right," he said.

And then he pulled Amanda close and kissed her soundly, and she found herself wanting to go back upstairs.

That wasn't in the cards, however. Jordan had decided to cut down a Christmas tree, and his purpose was evidently unshakable. They put on coats, climbed into the small, late-model pickup truck parked beside the Porsche and sped off toward the tree farm.

Slogging up and down the rows of Christmas trees

while the attendant walked behind them with a chain saw at the ready, Amanda actually felt festive. The piney smell was pungent, the air crisp, the sky painfully blue.

"How about this one?" Jordan said, pausing to inspect a twelve-footer.

Amanda looked at him in bewilderment. "What about it?"

Jordan gave her a wry glance. "Do you like it?" he asked patiently.

Amanda couldn't think why it mattered whether she liked the tree or not, but she nodded. "It's beautiful."

"We'll take this one," Jordan told the attendant.

They stood back while the man in the plaid woolen coat and blue overalls felled the tree, and followed when he dragged it off toward the truck.

By the time the tree had been paid for and tied down in the back of Jordan's truck, it was noon and Amanda was famished.

Jordan favored her with a sidelong grin when they were seated in the cab. "Hungry?"

"How do you always know?" Amanda demanded, half surprised and half exasperated. A person couldn't have a private thought around this man.

"I'm psychic," Jordan teased, starting the engine. "Of course, the fact that you haven't eaten in four hours and your stomach is rumbling helped me come to the conclusion. How does seafood sound?"

"Wonderful," Amanda replied. The scent of the tree was on her clothes and Jordan's, and she loved its pungency.

They drove to a café overlooking the water and took a table next to a window, where they could see a ferry passing, along with the occasional intrepid sailboat and a number of other small vessels. Jordan flirted with the middle-aged waitress, who obviously knew him and gave Amanda a kindly assessment with heavily made-up eyes.

"So, Jordan Richards," the older woman teased, "you've been stepping out on me."

Jordan grinned. "Sorry, Wanda."

Wanda swatted him on the shoulder with a plastic-covered menu. "I'm always the last to know," she said. Her eyes came back to Amanda again. "Since Jordan doesn't have enough manners to introduce us, we'll just have to handle the job ourselves. My name's Wanda Carson."

Amanda smiled and held out her hand. "Amanda Scott," she replied.

After shaking Amanda's hand, Wanda laid the menus down and said, "We got a real good special today. It's baked chicken with rice."

Jordan ordered the special, perhaps to atone for "stepping out on" Wanda, but Amanda had her heart set on seafood, so she ordered deep-fried prawns and French fries.

Amanda couldn't remember ever enjoying a meal more than she did that one, but honesty would have forced her to admit it was not the food but the company that made it special.

On the way back to Jordan's house, they stopped at a variety store, which was crowded with shopping carts and people, and bought an enormous tree stand, strings of lights, colorful glass ornaments and tinsel. "I gave away the stuff Becky and I had," he admitted offhandedly while they waited in line to pay.

A bittersweet pang squeezed Amanda's heart at the thought, but she only smiled.

They spent a good hour just dragging the massive tree inside the house and setting it up. It fell over repeatedly, and Jordan finally had to put hooks in the wall and tie it in place. It towered to the ceiling, every needle of its fresh, green branches filling the room with perfume.

"It's beautiful," Amanda vowed, resting her hands on her hips.

Jordan was bringing a high stepladder in from the garage. "So are you," he told her, setting the ladder up beside the tree. "In fact, why don't you come over here?"

Amanda laughed and shook her head. "No thanks. This fly knows a spider when she sees one."

Assuming a pretend glower, Jordan stomped over to Amanda, put his fingers against her ribs and tickled her until she toppled onto the couch, shrieking with laughter.

Then he pinned her down with his body and stretched her arms far above her head. "Hello, fly," he said, his eyes twinkling as he placed his mouth on hers.

"Hello, spider," Amanda responded, her lips touching his. Just as the piney scent of the tree pervaded the house, Jordan's closeness permeated her senses.

Things might have progressed from there if the telephone hadn't rung, but it did, and Jordan reached over Amanda's head to grasp the receiver. There was a note of impatience in his voice when he answered, but his expression changed completely when the caller spoke.

He sat up on the edge of the couch, Amanda apparently forgotten. "Hi, Jessie. I'm fine, honey. How are you?"

Amanda suddenly felt like an eavesdropper. She got up from the couch and tiptoed out of the living room and up the stairs. She was pacing back and forth across the bedroom, when she noticed an overturned photograph on the bedside table.

An ache twisted in the pit of her stomach as she walked over, grasped the photograph and set it upright. A beautiful dark-haired woman smiled at her from the picture, her eyes full of love and laughter.

"Hello, Becky," Amanda whispered sadly, recalling the white stripe on Jordan's finger where his wedding band had been.

Becky seemed to regard her with kind understanding.

Amanda set the photo carefully back on the bedside table and stood up. A fathomless sorrow filled her; she felt as though she'd made love to another woman's husband. But this time she'd known what she was doing.

Turning her back on the picture, Amanda found her suitcase and her overnighter and packed them both. She was just snapping the catches on the suitcase, when the door opened and Jordan came in.

His gaze shifted from Amanda to the photograph and back again. "Is this about the picture?" he asked quietly.

Amanda lowered her head. "I'm not sure."

"Not good enough, Mandy." Jordan's voice was husky. "Until ten minutes ago when my daughters called, everything was okay. Then you came up here and saw the picture, and you packed your clothes."

She made herself look at him, and it hurt that he lingered in the doorway instead of crossing the room to take her into his arms. "I guess I feel like this is her house and you're her husband. It's kind of like being the other woman all over again."

"That's crazy."

Amanda shook her head. "No, it isn't. Look at your left hand, Jordan. You can still see where the wedding band was. When did you take it off? Two weeks ago? Last month?"

Jordan folded his arms. "What does it matter when I took it off? The point is, I'm not wearing it anymore. And as for the picture, I just forgot to put it away, that's all."

"The night we had dinner at my place, you told me I wasn't ready for a relationship. I think maybe *you're* the one who isn't ready, Jordan."

He sprang away from the door frame, strode across the room and took the suitcase and overnighter from Amanda's hands, tossing them aside with a clatter. "Remember me? I'm the guy whose mind you blew in that bed over there," he bit out. "Damn it, have you forgotten the way it was with us?"

"That isn't the issue!" Amanda cried, frustrated and confused.

"Isn't it?" Jordan asked, clasping her wrists in his hands and wrenching her close to him. "You're scared, Amanda, so you're looking for an excuse to make a quick exit. That way you won't have to face what's really happening here."

Amanda swallowed hard. "What *is* happening here?" she asked miserably.

Jordan withdrew from her, albeit reluctantly, except for the grip he'd taken on her hand. "I don't know exactly," he confessed, calmer now. "But I think we'd damn well better find out, don't you?"

At Amanda's nod, he led her out of the bedroom and down the stairs again. She sank despondently into an easy chair while he built up the fire on the hearth.

"I don't want to be the other woman, Jordan," she said when he turned to face her.

He crossed the room, knelt in front of her and placed

one of her blue-jeaned legs over each arm of the chair, setting her afire all over again as he stroked the insides of her thighs. "You're the *only* woman," he answered, and he nipped at one of her nipples through the bra and sweatshirt that covered it. "Show me your breasts, Mandy."

It was a measure of her obsession with him that she pulled up her sweatshirt and unfastened the front catch on her bra so that she spilled out into full view. He grasped her knees, holding them up on the arms of the chair as he leaned forward to tease one nipple with his tongue.

Amanda remembered that there was somebody else in Jordan's life, but she couldn't remember a face or a name. Perspiration glowed on her upper lip as Jordan took his pleasure at her breasts, moving his right hand from one knee to the other, slowly following an erotic path.

Finally, when Amanda was half-delirious with wanting, he kissed his way down over her belly and lightly bit her through the denim at the crossroads of her thighs.

Amanda moaned helplessly and moved to close her legs, and Jordan allowed that, but only long enough to unsnap her jeans and dispose of them, along with her panties and shoes. Then he put her knees back into their original position, opened his own jeans and took her in a powerful, possessive thrust so pleasurable that she nearly fainted.

She longed to embrace Jordan with her legs, as well as her arms, but he didn't permit it. It was a battle of sorts, but Amanda couldn't be sure who was the loser, since every lunge Jordan made wrung a cry of delight from her throat.

Her climax made her give a long, low scream as she pressed her head into the chair's back. Jordan, both hands still holding her knees, uttered a desolate groan as his body convulsed and he spilled himself into Amanda.

Once the gasping aftermath was over and Amanda's breathing and heart rate had gone back to normal, she was angry. Jordan hadn't forced her, but he had turned her own body against her, and that was a power no one had ever had over Amanda before.

She moved to fasten her bra, but Jordan, still breathing hard, his eyes flashing with challenge, interrupted the action and took her tingling breasts gently but firmly into his hands. "We're not through, Amanda," he ground out.

"The hell we aren't!" she sputtered.

Keeping his hands where they were, he turned his head and lightly kissed the back of her knee.

Amanda trembled. "Damn it, Jordan…"

He moved his lips along her inner thigh, leaving a trail of fire behind them, and slid one of his hands down to rest on her lower abdomen, finding the hidden plum and making a small circle around it with the pad of his thumb. "Yes?" he answered at his leisure.

A whimper escaped Amanda, and Jordan chuckled at the sound, still working his lethal magic. "You were saying?" he prompted huskily.

Amanda reached backward to grasp the top of the chair, fearing she would fly away like a rocket if she didn't. "We're n-not through," she concluded.

Her reward was another baptism in sweet fire, and it made a believer out of her through and through.

The next day was cold and pristinely beautiful, and Jordan and Amanda decided to leave the tree undecorated and take a drive around the island. That was when Amanda saw the house.

It stood between Jordan's place and the ferry terminal, and she couldn't imagine why she hadn't noticed it before. It was white with green shutters, and very Victorian, and there was even a lighthouse within walking distance. Best of all a For Sale sign stood in the yard, swinging slowly in the salty breeze.

"Jordan, stop!" Amanda cried, barely able to restrain herself from reaching out and grasping the steering wheel.

After giving her one half-amused, half-bewildered look, Jordan steered the truck onto the rocky, rutted driveway leading past a tumbledown mailbox and a few discarded tires and empty rabbit pens.

Amanda was out of the truck a moment after they came to a jolting halt.

Chapter 7

The grass in the yard was overgrown, and the outside of the building needed paint, but neither of these facts dampened Amanda's enthusiasm. She hurried around the back of the house and found a screened porch that ran the full length of the place. On the upper floor there were lots of windows, providing an unobstructed view of the water and the mountains.

It was the perfect place for a bed and breakfast, and Amanda felt a thrill of excitement race through her blood.

A moment later, though, as Jordan caught up to her, her spirits plummeted. The place had obviously been neglected for a long time and would cost far more than she had to spend. People were willing to pay a premium price for waterfront property.

"I could help you," Jordan suggested, reading her mind.

Amanda quickly shook her head. A personal loan could poison their relationship if things went wrong later on, and besides, she wanted the accomplishment to be her own.

After they'd walked around the house and looked into

the windows, Amanda wrote down the name of the real estate company and the phone number, tucking the information into her purse.

She could hardly wait to get to a telephone, and Jordan, discerning this, headed straight for the café where Wanda worked. While he chatted with the waitress and ordered clubhouse sandwiches, Amanda dialed the real estate agency's number and got an answering machine. She left her name and her numbers for home and work in Seattle and returned to the table.

"No luck?" Jordan asked as she sat down across from him in the booth and reached for the cup of coffee he'd ordered for her.

"They'll get in touch," Amanda answered with a little shrug. "I don't know why I'm so excited. I probably won't be able to afford the place, anyway."

Jordan's eyes twinkled as he looked at her. "That was a negative thing to say," he scolded. "You're not going to get anywhere in life if you don't believe in yourself."

"Thank you, Norman Vincent Peale," Amanda said somewhat irritably as she wriggled out of her coat and set it aside. "Just because you could probably write a check for the place on the spot doesn't mean I'd be able to."

The clubhouse sandwiches arrived, and Jordan picked up a potato chip and crunched it between his teeth. "Okay, so I have a knack with money. I should have— it's my business. And I don't understand why you won't let me help."

"I have my reasons, Jordan."

"Like what?"

Amanda shrugged. "Suppose in two days or two weeks we decide we don't want to see each other anymore. If I owed you a big chunk of money, things could get pretty sticky."

Jordan shook his head. "That's just an excuse, Mandy. People borrow money to start businesses every day of the week."

In the short time they'd known each other, Amanda had to admit that Jordan had learned to read her well. "I want it to be mine," she confessed. "Is that too much to ask?"

"Nope," Jordan replied good-naturedly, and after that they dropped the subject and talked of other things.

They spent the rest of the afternoon exploring the beach fronting the property Amanda wanted to buy, and the time sped by. Too soon the weekend was over and Jordan was putting her suitcase and overnighter in the back of the Porsche.

Even the prospect of separation was difficult for Amanda. "How about having dinner at my place before you come back?" she asked somewhat shyly as Jordan pushed the button to turn on the answering machine in his study.

He smiled at her. "Smooth talker," he teased.

Amanda barely stopped herself from suggesting that he bring fresh clothes and a toothbrush, as well. All her life she'd been a patient, methodical person, but where this man was concerned, she had a dangerous tendency to be impulsive. She trembled a little when Jordan kissed her, and devoutly hoped he hadn't noticed.

During the ferry ride back to Seattle, they drank coffee in the snack bar, and when they reached the city, Amanda asked Jordan to stop at a supermarket. She bought chicken, fresh corn and potatoes.

Gershwin greeted them with a mournful meow when

they entered Amanda's apartment. Appeasing his pique was easy, though; Jordan simply opened a can of cat food and set it on the floor for him.

Amanda was busy cutting up the chicken and washing the corn, so Jordan wandered back into the living room and used the log left from his last visit to start a fire on the hearth.

"We forgot to decorate your tree," Amanda said when he returned to the kitchenette to lean against the counter, watching her put floured chicken pieces into a hot skillet.

"It'll keep," Jordan answered. When she'd finished putting the chicken on to brown, he took her into his arms. "Mandy, Karen's bringing the girls to Seattle Friday night. They're going to spend two weeks with me."

Amanda was pleased, but a little puzzled that he'd waited until now to mention it. "That's great. I guess you found that out when the kids called."

He nodded.

"Why didn't you tell me?"

Jordan shrugged. "If you recall, we were a little busy after that phone call," he pointed out. "And then I was trying to work out how to ask you to spend next weekend on the island with us."

Amanda broke away long enough to turn the chicken pieces and put the corn on to boil. "I don't think that would be a very good idea, Jordan," she finally said, looking back at him over her shoulder. "After all, we aren't married, and we don't want to confuse the kids."

"How could we confuse them? They're not teenagers, Amanda. They're too small to understand about sex."

Amanda shook her head. "Kids know something is going on, whether they understand what it is or not. They sense emotional undercurrents, Jordan, and I don't want to get off on the wrong foot with them." She turned down the heat under the chicken and covered it with a lid. "Now how about a glass of wine?"

Jordan nodded his assent, but he looked distracted. After uncorking the bottle and pouring a glass for himself and for Amanda, he wandered into the living room.

Amanda followed, perching on the arm of the sofa while he stood at the window, watching the city lights.

"Come on, Jordan," she urged gently. "'Fess up. You're scared, aren't you? When was the last time you were responsible for your kids for two weeks straight?"

There was a hint of anger in his eyes when he turned to look at her. "I've been 'responsible' for them since they were born, Amanda."

"Maybe so," she retorted quietly, "but somebody else did the nitty-gritty stuff—first Becky, then your sister. You don't have any idea how to really take care of your daughters, do you?"

Jordan was offended initially, but then his ire gave way to a sort of indignant resignation. "Okay," he admitted, "you've got me. I wanted you to spend next weekend with us because I need moral support."

Amanda went back to the kitchen for plates and silverware, then began to set the small, round table in the living room. "You know my phone number," she said. "If you want moral support, you can call me. But you don't need somebody else in the way when you're bonding with your kids, Jordan."

"Bonding? Hell, you've been reading too many pop psychology books."

"You have a right to your opinion," Amanda responded, "but I'm not going to be there to act as a buffer. You're on your own with this one, buddy."

Jordan gave her an irate look, but then his expression softened and he took her in his arms. "Maybe I can't change your mind," he told her huskily, "but I can sure as hell let you know what you'll be missing."

Amanda pushed him away. "The chicken will burn."

Jordan chuckled. "Okay, Mandy, you win. For now."

Twenty minutes later they sat down to a dinner of fried chicken, corn on the cob, mashed potatoes and gravy. Amanda's portable TV set was turned to the evening news, and the ambience of the evening was quietly domestic.

When they were through eating, Amanda began clearing the table, only to have Jordan stop her by slipping his arms around her waist from behind. "Aren't you forgetting something?" he asked, his voice a low rumble as he bent his head to kiss her nape and sent a jagged thrill swirling through her system.

"W-what?" Amanda asked, already a little breathless.

Jordan slid his hands up beneath her shirt to cup the undersides of her breasts. "Dessert," he answered.

Amanda was trembling. "Jordan, the food—"

"The food will still be here when we're through."

"No, it won't," Amanda argued, following her protest with a little moan as Jordan unfastened her bra and rubbed her nipples to attention with the sides of his thumbs. "G-Gershwin will eat it."

His lips were on her nape again. "Who cares?"

Amanda realized that she didn't. She turned in Jordan's embrace and tilted her head back for his kiss.

While taming her mouth, he grasped her hips in his hands and pressed her close, making her feel his size and power.

She was dazed when he drew back, pliant when he steered her toward the bedroom and closed the door behind them.

The small room was shadowy, the bed neatly made. Jordan set Amanda on the edge of the mattress and knelt to slowly untie her shoes and roll down her socks. For a time he caressed her feet, one by one, and Amanda was surprised at the sensual pleasure such a simple act could evoke.

When she was tingling from head to foot, he rose and pulled her shirt off over her head, then smoothed away the bra he'd already opened. He pressed Amanda onto her back to unsnap her jeans and remove them and her panties, and she didn't make a move to stop him. All she could do was sigh.

After the last of her garments was tossed away, Jordan began removing his own clothes. They joined Amanda's in a pile on the floor.

"Jordan," Amanda whispered, entwining her fingers in his hair as he stretched out beside her, "don't make me wait. Please."

He gave her a nibbling kiss. "So impatient," he scolded sleepily, trailing his lips down over her chin to her neck. "Lovemaking takes time, Mandy. Especially if it's good."

Amanda remembered their session in Jordan's living room the day before. It had been fast and ferocious, and if it had been any better, it would have killed her. She moaned as Jordan made a slow, silken circle on her belly with his hand. "I can only stand so much pleasure!" she whimpered in a lame protest.

Jordan chuckled. "We're going to have to raise your tolerance," he said.

* * *

Two hours later, when both Jordan and Amanda were showered and dressed and the table had been cleared, he reached for his jacket and shrugged into it. Amanda had to fight back tears when he kissed her, as well as pleas for him to spend the night. On a practical, rational level, she knew they both needed to let things cool down a little so they could get some perspective.

But when she'd closed the door behind Jordan, Amanda rested her forehead against it for a long moment and bit down hard on her lower lip. It was all she could do not to run out into the hallway and call him back.

Slowly she turned from the door and went about her usual Sunday night routine, choosing the outfits she would wear to work during the coming week, manicuring her nails and watching a mystery program on TV.

The bed was rumpled, and it still smelled of Jordan's cologne and their fevered lovemaking. Forlornly Amanda remade it and crawled under the covers, the small TV she kept in her room turned to her favorite show.

Two minutes after that week's victim had been done in, the telephone rang. Hoping for a call from the real estate agent or from Jordan, Amanda reached for the receiver on her bedside table and answered on the second ring.

"Amanda?"

The voice was Eunice's, and she sounded as though she'd been crying for a week.

Amanda spoke gently to her sister, because they'd always been close. "Hi, kid," she said, for she was the older of the two and Eunice had been "kid" since she was born. "What's the problem?"

"It's Jim," Eunice sobbed.

Now there's a real surprise, Amanda thought ruefully while she waited for her sister to recover herself.

"There's been someone else the whole time," Eunice wept, making a valiant, sniffling attempt to get a hold on herself.

Amanda was painfully reminded of what Madge Brockman had gone through because of her. "Are you sure?" she asked gently.

"She called this afternoon," Eunice said. "She said if Jim wouldn't tell me, she would. He's moved in with her!"

For a moment Amanda knew a pure, white-hot rage entirely directed at her soon-to-be ex-brother-in-law. Since her anger wouldn't help Eunice in any way, she counted to herself until the worst of it had passed. "Honey, this doesn't look like something you can change. And that means you have to accept it."

Eunice was quiet for almost a minute. "I guess you're right," she admitted softly. "I'll try, Amanda."

"I know you will," Amanda replied, wishing she could be nearer to her sister to lend moral support.

"Mom tells me you've met a guy." Eunice snuffled. "That's really great, Mand. What's he like?"

Amanda remembered making love with Jordan on the very bed she was lying in, and a wave of heat rolled over her. She also remembered the photograph of Becky and the white strip of skin on Jordan's left hand ring finger. "He's moderately terrific," she answered demurely.

Eunice laughed, and it was a good sound to hear. "Maybe I can meet him when I come home next week."

"I'd like that," Amanda replied. "And I'm glad you're coming home. How long can you stay?"

"Perhaps forever," Eunice replied, sounding blue

again. "Everywhere I turn here, there's another reminder of Jim staring me in the face."

Amanda spoke gently. "Don't misunderstand me, sis, because I'd love for you to live in Seattle again, but I hope you realize you can't run away from your problems. You'll still have to find a way to work them out."

"That might be easier with you and Mom and Bob nearby," Eunice said quietly.

"You know we'll help in any way we can," Amanda assured her.

"Yeah, I know. It means the world to know you're there for me, Mand—you and Mom and Daddy Bob. But listen, I'll get off the line now because I know you're probably trying to watch that murder show you like so much. See you next week."

Amanda smiled. "You just try and avoid it, kid."

After that, the two sisters said their goodbyes and hung up. Amanda, having lost track of her TV show, switched off the set and the lamp on her bedside table and wriggled down between the covers.

How empty the bed seemed without Jordan sprawled out beside her, taking more than his share of the space.

Two days passed before Amanda saw Jordan again; they met for lunch in a hotel restaurant.

"Did you ever hear from the real estate agent?" Jordan asked, drawing back Amanda's chair for her.

She sank into it, inordinately relieved just to be with him again. She wondered, with a chill, if she wasn't letting herself in for a major bruise to the soul somewhere down the line. "She called me at work yesterday. The down payment is five times what I have in the bank."

Jordan sat down across from her and reached out for

her hand, which she willingly gave. "Mandy, I can lend you the money with no problem."

"You must be loaded," Amanda teased, having no intention of accepting, "if you can make an offer like that without even knowing how much is involved."

He grinned one of his melting grins. "I confess—I called the agency and asked."

Amanda shook out her napkin and placed it neatly on her lap. It was time to change the subject. "Who's going to take care of the kids while you're working?" she asked.

"Much to the consternation of Striner and Striner," said Jordan, "I'm taking two weeks off. I figure I'm going to need all my wits about me."

Amanda laughed. "No doubt about that."

Jordan leaned forward in his chair with a look of mock reprimand on his face. "I'll thank you to extend a little sympathy, here, Ms. Scott. You're looking at a man who has no idea how to take care of two little girls."

"They need to eat three times a day, Jordan," Amanda pointed out with teasing patience, "and it's a good idea if they have a bath at night, followed by about eight hours of sleep. Beyond that, they mainly just need to know they're loved."

Jordan was turning his table knife from end to end. "You're sure you won't come out for the weekend?"

"My sister is arriving on Friday night—in pieces, from the sounds of things."

"Ah," Jordan answered as a waiter brought menus and filled their water glasses. "The recipient of *Gathering Up the Pieces*, the pop psychology book of the decade. I'm sorry to hear things haven't improved for her."

Amanda sighed. "They've gone from bad to worse,

actually," she replied. "But there's hope. Eunice is intelligent, and she's attractive, too. She'll work through this."

"Maybe she could work through the first part of it—say next Saturday and Sunday—without you?"

Amanda shook her head as she opened her menu. "Don't you ever give up?"

"Never," Jordan replied. "It's my credo—keep bugging them until they give in to shut you up."

Amanda laughed. "Such sage advice."

They made their selections and placed their orders before the conversation continued. Jordan reached out and took Amanda's hand again when the waiter was gone.

"I've missed you a whole lot."

"Then how come you didn't call?"

"I've been in meetings day and night, Amanda. Besides, I figured if I heard your voice, I wouldn't be able to stop myself from walking into your office and taking you on your desk."

Amanda's cheeks burned, but she knew her eyes were sparkling. "Jordan," she protested in a whisper, "this is a public place."

"That's why you're not lying on the table with your skirt up around your waist," Jordan answered with a perfectly straight face.

"You have to be the most arrogant man I've ever met," Amanda told him, but a smile hovered around her mouth. She couldn't very well deny that Jordan could make her do extraordinary things.

The waiter returned with their seafood salads, sparing Jordan from having to answer. His reply probably would have been cocky, anyway, Amanda figured.

The conversation had turned to more conventional subjects, when Madge Brockman suddenly appeared beside the table. There was a look of infinite strain in her face as she assessed Amanda, then Jordan.

Amanda braced herself, having no idea whether to expect a civil greeting or violent recriminations. "Hello, Mrs. Brockman," she said as Jordan pushed back his chair to stand. "I'd like you to meet Jordan Richards."

"Do sit down," Madge Brockman said when she and Jordan had shaken hands.

Jordan remained standing. "How is your husband?" he asked, knowing Amanda wouldn't dare ask.

"He's recovering," Madge replied with a sigh. "And he's adamant about wanting a divorce."

"I'm sorry," Amanda said softly.

The older woman managed a faulty smile. "I'll get over it, I guess. Well, if you'll excuse me, I'm supposed to meet my attorney, and I see him sitting right over there."

Jordan dropped back into his chair when Mrs. Brockman had walked away. "Are you okay?" he asked.

Amanda pushed her salad away. Even though she'd done it inadvertently, she was partly responsible for destroying Mrs. Brockman's marriage, and the knowledge was shattering. "No," she answered. "I'm not okay."

"It wasn't your fault, Amanda."

There it was again, that strange clairvoyance of his.

"Yes, it was—part of it, at least. I didn't even bother to ask if James was married. And now look what's happening."

Jordan gave a ragged sigh. Apparently his appetite had fled, too, for he set down his fork and sank back in his chair, one hand to his chin.

"The man's marital status wouldn't have made a difference to a lot of women, you know," he remarked. "For instance, you're the first one I've dated who's asked me whether I was married."

"Okay, so infidelity is widespread. So is cocaine addiction. That doesn't make either of them right."

Jordan raised his eyebrows. "I wasn't saying it did, Mandy. My point is, you're being too damn hard on yourself. So you made a mistake. Welcome to the human race."

Amanda met Jordan's gaze. "Were you faithful to Becky?" she asked, having no idea why it was suddenly so important to know. But it was.

"That's none of your damn business," Jordan retorted politely, making a steeple under his chin with his hands, "but I'll answer, anyway. I was true to my wife, and she was true to me."

Amanda had known, in some corner of her heart, that Jordan was a man of his word, and she believed him. "Were you ever tempted?"

"About a thousand times," he replied. "But there's a difference between thinking about something and doing it, Mandy. Now, do you want to ask me about my bank balance or my tax return? Or maybe how I voted in the last election?"

Amanda smiled. "You've made your point, Mr. Richards. I'm being nosy. But I'm glad you were faithful to Becky."

"So am I," Jordan said, as by tacit agreement they rose to go. "When am I going to see you again, Mandy?"

Amanda held off answering until the bill was paid and they were walking down the sidewalk, wending their way through hordes of Christmas shoppers. "When do you want to see me?"

"As soon as possible."

"You could come to dinner tonight."

"Amanda Scott, you have a silver tongue. I'll bring the wine and the food, so don't cook."

Amanda's smile was born deep inside her, and it took its time reaching her mouth. "Seven?"

"Eight," Jordan said as they stopped in front of the Evergreen Hotel. "I have a meeting, and it might run late."

She stood on tiptoe to kiss him briefly. "I'll be waiting, Mr. Richards."

He grinned as he rubbed a tendril of her hair between his fingers. "Good," he answered.

His voice made Amanda's knees quiver beneath her green suede skirt.

When Amanda reached her desk, there was a message waiting for her. In a flash, work—and Jordan—fled her uppermost thoughts. The hospital had called about James, and the matter was urgent.

Amanda's fingers trembled as she reached for the panel of buttons on her telephone. She punched out the numbers written on the message slip and, when an operator answered, asked for the designated extension.

"Intensive Care," a sunny voice said when the call was put through. "This is Betsy Andrews."

Amanda sank into her desk chair, a terrible headache throbbing beneath her temples. "My name is Amanda Scott," she said in a voice that sounded surprisingly crisp and professional. "I received a message asking me to call about Mr. Brockman."

There was a short silence while the nurse checked her records. "Yes. Mr. Brockman isn't doing very well, Ms. Scott. And he's constantly asking for you."

Amanda closed her eyes and rubbed one temple with

her fingertips. She'd broken up with James long ago, and had refused his gifts and his requests for a reconciliation. When was it going to be over? "I see."

"His wife has explained the—er—situation to us," the nurse went on, "but Mr. Brockman still insists on seeing you."

"What is his doctor's recommendation?"

"It was his idea that we call you. We all feel that, well, maybe Mr. Brockman would calm down if he could just have a short visit from you."

Amanda glanced at her watch. Her headache was so intense that the numbers blurred. "I could stop by briefly after work." James had won this round. Under the circumstances, there was no way she could refuse to visit him. "That would be about six o'clock."

Betsy Andrews sounded relieved. "I'll be off duty then, but I'll make a note in the record and tell Mr. Brockman you'll be coming in."

"Thank you," Amanda said with a defeated sigh. Once she'd hung up, she reached for the phone again, planning to call Jordan, but her hand fell back to the desk. She was a grown woman, and this was her problem, not Jordan's. She couldn't go running to him every time some difficulty came up.

Pulling open her desk drawer, Amanda took out a bottle of aspirin, shook two tablets into her palm and swallowed them with water from the tap in her bathroom. Then she rolled up her sleeves and did her best to concentrate on her work.

At six-fifteen she approached James's door in the Intensive Care Unit, having gotten directions from a nurse.

He was lying in a room banked with flowers. Tubes led into his nose and the veins in both his hands. He seemed to sense Amanda's arrival and turned to look at her.

She approached the bed. "Hello, James," she said.

"You came," he managed, his voice hoarse and broken.

She nodded, unable for the moment to speak. And not knowing what to say.

"I'm going to die," he told her.

Amanda shook her head, her eyes filling with tears. She didn't love James anymore, but she had once, and it was hard to see him suffer. "No."

His eyes half-closed, he pleaded with her, "Just tell me there's a chance for us, and I'll have a reason not to give up."

Amanda started to tell him there was someone else, that there could never be anything between the two of them again, but something stopped her in the last instant. Some instinct that he really meant to die if she didn't give him hope, and she couldn't just abandon him to death. She bit down on her lower lip, then whispered, "All right, James. Maybe we could—start again."

Chapter 8

Jordan was due to arrive a little more than twenty minutes after Amanda reached her apartment. Gershwin was hungry and petulant, and the boxes containing the fur jacket and the skimpy bikini James had sent were still sitting on the hallway table. Amanda had intended to return them to the department store and ask the clerk to credit James's account, but she hadn't gotten around to it.

Now, without stopping to analyze her motives—certainly she meant to tell Jordan about her promise to James—she stuffed the boxes into the back of her bedroom closet and hastily changed into a silky beige jumpsuit. She had just misted herself with cologne, when the door buzzer sounded.

After drawing a deep breath to steady herself, Amanda dashed through the apartment and opened the door. Jordan was standing in the hallway, a tired grin on his face, a bottle of wine and several bags from a Chinese take-out place in his arms.

Looking at him, Amanda thought of how it would be to have him walk out of her life forever, and promptly lost her courage. She told herself it wasn't the right time to tell him about James.

Smiling shakily, she took the wine and fragrant bags from him and stood on tiptoe to kiss his cheek.

He shrugged out of his overcoat and hung it on the coat tree while Amanda carried the food to the table. She hadn't put out place settings yet, so she hurried back to the kitchenette for plates, silverware, wineglasses and a cork screw.

Jordan looked at her strangely when she returned. "Is something wrong, Mandy?"

Amanda swallowed. *Tell him*, ordered the voice of reason. *Just come right out and tell him you're planning to visit James in the hospital until he's out of danger.* "Wr-wrong?" she echoed.

"You seem nervous."

Amanda imagined the scenario: herself telling Jordan that she meant to pretend she was still in love with James just until he was stronger, Jordan saying the idea was stupid, getting angry, walking out. Maybe forever. "I'm okay," she lied.

Jordan popped the cork on the wine bottle. "If you say so," he said with a sigh, and they both sat down at the table to consume prawns, fried noodles and chow mein. Their conversation, usually so free and easy, was guarded.

When they were through with dinner, Jordan made Amanda stay at the table, nursing a second glass of wine, while he cleared away the debris of their meal. Returning, he put gentle hands on Amanda's shoulders and began massaging her tense muscles.

"Will you stay tonight?" she asked, holding her breath after the words were out. She needed Jordan desperately, but at the same time she knew guilt would prevent her from enjoying their lovemaking.

Jordan sighed. "You've been through a lot lately, Mandy. I think it would be better if we let things cool off a little."

She turned to look up at him with worried eyes. "Is this the brush-off, Mr. Richards?"

He smiled and bent to kiss her forehead. "No. I just think you need some extra rest." With that, he turned and crossed the room to the entryway. He reached for his overcoat and put it on.

Amanda stood up quickly and went to him. Even though Jordan didn't know what was going on, he sensed something, and he was already distancing himself from her. She had to tell him. "Jordan—"

He interrupted her with a kiss. "Good night, Mandy. I'll talk to you tomorrow."

Amanda tried to call out to him, but the words stopped in her throat. In the end she simply closed the door, locked it and stood there leaning against the panel, wondering how she'd gotten herself into such a mess.

True to his word, Jordan called her the next morning at work, but their conversation was brief because he was busy and so was Amanda. She threw her mind into her job in order to distract herself from the fact that she had, in effect, lied to him. And a chilling instinct told her that deceit was one thing Jordan wouldn't tolerate.

At six-thirty that evening, Amanda walked into James's room in Intensive Care, after first making sure Madge wasn't there. She was wearing jeans and a sweater, and was carrying a bouquet of flowers from the gift shop downstairs.

He smiled thinly when he saw her and extended one hand. "Hello, Amanda."

She took his hand and bent to kiss his forehead. "Hi. How are you feeling today?"

"They're moving me out of the ICU tomorrow," he answered.

But he looked very sick to Amanda. He was gaunt, and his skin still had a ghastly pallor to it.

"That's good."

"You look wonderful."

Amanda averted her eyes for a moment, feeling like a highly paid call girl. What she was doing was all wrong, but how could she turn her back on another human being, allowing him to give up and die? That would be heartless. "Thanks."

James's grip on her hand was remarkably firm. "You're better off without that Richards character," he confided. "He might have made his mark in the business world, but he's really nothing more than an overgrown kid. Killed his own wife with his recklessness, you know."

Amanda was willing to go only so far with this charade, and listening to James bad-mouth Jordan was beyond the boundary. Somewhat abruptly she changed the subject. "Is there anything you'd like me to bring you? Magazines or books?"

He shook his head. "All I want is to know I'm going to get well and see you wear—and not wear—that blue bikini."

Feeling slightly ill, Amanda nonetheless managed a smile. "You shouldn't be thinking thoughts like that," she scolded. She had to get out of that room or soon she'd be smothered. "Listen, the nurses made me promise not to stay too long, so I'm going now. But I'll be back after work tomorrow."

When she would have walked away, James held her fast by the hand. "I want a kiss first," he said, a shrewd expression in his eyes.

Amanda shook her head, unable to grant his request. She smiled brittlely and said in a too-bright voice, "You're too ill for that." Ignoring his obvious disappointment, she squeezed his hand once and then dashed out of the room, calling a hasty farewell over her shoulder.

Only when Amanda was outside in the crisp December air was she able to breathe properly again. She went home, flung her coat onto the couch and took a long, scalding hot shower. No matter how she tried, though, she couldn't wash away the awful feeling that she was selling herself.

In an effort to escape, Amanda telephoned the real estate agency on Vashon Island the next morning to see if the Victorian house had been sold. It hadn't, and even though she had no means of buying it herself, the news lifted her flagging spirits.

She visited James that night, and the next, and he seemed to be improving steadily. He told her repeatedly that she was his only reason for holding on.

By Friday, when Eunice was due to arrive, Amanda was practically a wreck. She had been avoiding Jordan's calls for several days, and she could barely concentrate on her job.

Marion noticed her elder daughter's general dishevelment when they met at the airport in front of the gate assigned to Eunice's flight. "What on earth is the matter with you?" she demanded. "You have bags under your eyes and you must have lost five pounds since I saw you last week!"

Amanda would have given anything to be able to confide in her mother, but she didn't want to spoil Eunice's homecoming—her sister would need all of Marion's and Bob's support. She shrugged and managed a halfhearted smile. "You know how it is. Falling in love takes a lot out of a person."

Marion's gaze was slightly narrowed and alarmingly shrewd. "You're not fooling me, you know," she said. "But just because I don't have time to drag it out of you now doesn't mean I won't."

Bob was just returning from parking the car, and he smiled and gave Amanda a hug. "You're looking a little peaky," he pointed out good-naturedly.

"She's up to something," Marion informed him just before the passengers from Eunice's flight began pouring out of the gate.

Amanda was the first to reach her brown-eyed, dark-haired sister, and they embraced. Tears stung both their eyes.

After the usual hassles of getting the luggage from the baggage carousel and fighting the traffic out of the airport, they drove back to the family home. Eunice chattered the whole time about how glad she was to be in Seattle again, how miserable she'd been in California, how she wished she'd never met Jim, let alone married him. By the time they reached the quiet residential area where Bob and Marion lived, Eunice had exhausted herself.

She stumbled into the room she and Amanda had once shared and collapsed on one of the twin beds.

Amanda took a seat on the other one. "I'm glad you're back," she said.

Her sister sat up on the bed and began unbuttoning her coat. "I didn't exactly return in triumph, like I thought I would," Eunice observed sadly. "Oh, Amanda, my life is a disaster area."

"I know what you mean," Amanda answered sadly, thinking of the deception she hadn't had the courage to straighten out.

Eunice yawned. "Maybe tomorrow we can put our heads together and figure out how to get ourselves back on track."

With a smile, Amanda opened her sister's suitcase and found a nightgown for her. "Here," she said, tossing the billow of pink chiffon into Eunice's lap. "Get some sleep."

When Eunice had disappeared into the adjoining bathroom, Amanda returned to the kitchen. Her mother was sitting at the table, sipping decaffeinated coffee, and Bob was in the living room, listening to the news.

"How's Eunice?" Marion asked.

Amanda wedged her hands into the front pockets of her worn brown corduroy pants. "She'll be okay once she gets a perspective on things."

"And what about you?"

"I'm in a fix, Mom," Amanda admitted, staring at the darkened window over the kitchen sink. "And I don't know how to get out of it."

Marion went to the counter, poured a cup of coffee from the percolator and brought it back to the table for Amanda. "Sit down and tell me about it."

Amanda sank into the chair. "Some very good things have been happening between Jordan and me," she said, closing her fingers around the cup to warm them. "I never thought I'd meet anybody like him."

Marion smiled. "I feel the same way about Bob."

Amanda touched her mother's hand fondly. "I know."

"So what's the problem?"

"About a week ago," Amanda began reluctantly, "someone from the hospital called and said James was asking for me. He was in the ICU at the time, so I didn't feel I could ignore the whole thing. I went to see him, and while I was there, he told me he'd given up, that he was going to die."

Marion's lips thinned in irritation, but she seemed to know how hard it was for Amanda to keep up her momentum, so she didn't interrupt.

"Essentially, he said I was the only reason he had to go on living, and if I didn't want him, he was just going to give up. So I've been visiting him and pretending we'll be getting back together again once he's well."

Marion sighed heavily. "Amanda."

"I know it sounds crazy, but I feel guilty enough without being the reason somebody died!"

Marion reached out and covered Amanda's hand with her own. "I suppose you haven't told Jordan any of this."

"I'm afraid to. Maybe it would have been all right if I'd mentioned it that very first night after I spoke to James, when Jordan and I were together for dinner, but I couldn't bring myself to do it. I was too afraid he'd make me choose between him and James."

"I didn't think there was any question of a choice," Marion said. "You're in love with Jordan Richards, whether you know it or not."

Amanda bit her lower lip for a moment. "I guess I am."

"Tell him the truth, Amanda," Marion urged. "Don't

put it off for another second. March right over to that phone and call him."

"I can't," Amanda said with a shake of her head. "It's not something I can say over the telephone, and besides, his little girls will be there. This is their first night together, and I don't want to spoil it."

"You're going to regret it if you don't straighten this out," Marion warned.

"I think it might already be too late," Amanda said brokenly, and then she rose from her chair, emptied her coffee into the sink and set the cup down. "You just concentrate on Eunice, Mom, and don't worry about me."

Marion shook her head as she got up to see her daughter to the door. "Talk to Jordan," she insisted as Amanda put on her coat and wrapped a colorful knitted scarf around her neck.

Amanda nodded and hurried through the cold night to her car.

The light on her answering machine was blinking when she arrived home, and after brewing herself a cup of tea, she pushed the Play button and sat down at the little table in her living room to listen.

The first call was from James. He'd missed her that night and hoped she'd come to visit in the morning.

Amanda closed her eyes against the prospect, though she knew she would have to do as he asked. Maybe if she used Eunice's visit as an excuse, she could get away after only a half hour or so.

The next message nearly made her spill her tea. "This is Madge Brockman," an angry female voice said, "and I just wanted to tell you that you're not going to get away with this. You took my husband, and I'm going to take something from you." After those bitter words, the woman had hung up with a crash.

Amanda was struggling to compose herself, when yet another voice came on. "Mandy, this is Jordan. I've survived supper, and the kids' baths and story time. I have a new respect for mothers. Call me, will you?" There was a click, and then the machine rewound itself.

Despite the fact that Madge Brockman's call had shaken her to her soul, Amanda reached for the phone and dialed Jordan's number at the island house.

He answered on the second ring.

"Hi, Jordan. It's Amanda."

"Thank God," he replied with a lilt to his voice.

"How are the girls?" She dabbed at her eyes with her sleeve and resisted an impulse to sniffle.

"They're fine. Mandy, are you all right?"

"I—I need to see you. Could I c-come out there?"

Jordan hesitated, then said, "Sure. If you hurry, you can still make the last ferry. Mandy—"

"I'll be there as soon as I can," Amanda broke in, and then she hung up the phone and dashed into her bedroom. She pulled her suitcase out from under the bed and tossed in two pairs of jeans, two sets of clean underwear and two sweaters. Then, after snatching up her toothbrush and makeup bag, she made sure Gershwin had plenty of food and water and hurried out of the apartment.

Several times on the way to West Seattle Amanda's eyes were so full of tears that she nearly had to pull over to the side of the road. But finally she drove on board the ferry and parked.

Safe in the bottom of the enormous boat, she let her forehead rest against the steering wheel and sobbed.

By the time she'd reached Vashon Island and driven to Jordan's house, however, she was beginning to feel a little foolish. She wasn't a child, she told herself sternly, and she couldn't expect Jordan to solve her problems. She might have backed out of the driveway and raced back to the ferry dock if Jordan hadn't come outside to greet her.

He was wearing sneakers, jeans and a Seahawks sweatshirt, and he looked so good to Amanda that she nearly burst into tears again.

Without a word, he opened the door and helped her out, then fetched her suitcase and overnighter from the backseat. Amanda preceded him into the house, wondering what she was going to say.

There was a fire snapping on the hearth, and after setting her luggage down in the entryway, Jordan helped Amanda out of her coat. "Sit down and I'll get you some brandy," he said hoarsely after kissing her on the cheek.

Amanda took a seat on the raised stone hearth of the fireplace, hoping the warmth would take the numb chill out of her soul.

When Jordan sat down next to her and handed her a crystal snifter with brandy glowing golden in the bottom, her heart turned over. She knew she'd waited too long to explain things; she was going to lose him.

"Talk to me, Mandy," he said when she was silent, studying him with miserable eyes.

"I can't," she replied, setting the brandy aside untouched. "Will you just hold me, Jordan? Just for a few minutes?"

Gently he pulled her into his arms and pressed her head to his shoulder. He moved his hand soothingly up and down her back, but he didn't ask any questions or make any demands, and Amanda loved him more than ever for that.

Amanda had just about worked up her courage to tell him about her promise to James, when a small, curious voice asked, "Who's that, Daddy?"

Amanda started in Jordan's arms, but he held her fast. She turned her head and saw a little dark-haired girl standing a few feet away. She was wearing a pink quilted robe and tiny fluffy slippers to match.

"This is Amanda, Jess. Amanda, my daughter, Jessica."

"Hi," Amanda managed.

"How come you're hugging her?" Jessica wanted to know. "Did she fall down and hurt herself?"

"Sort of," Jordan answered. "Why don't you go back to bed now, honey? You can get to know Amanda better in the morning."

Jessica's smile was so like Becky's that Amanda was shaken by it. "Okay. Good night, Daddy. Good night, Amanda."

When the little girl was gone, Amanda sat there in Jordan's arms, sorely wishing she hadn't intruded. She didn't belong here.

"I shouldn't have come," she said, bolting to her feet.

Jordan pulled her back so that she landed on his lap. "You've missed the last ferry, Mandy," he pointed out. "Besides, I'm not letting you go anywhere in the shape you're in."

Amanda swallowed hard. "I can't sleep with you— not with your daughters in the house."

"I understand that," Jordan replied. "I have a guest room."

Why did he have to be so damned reasonable?

Amanda fretted. She didn't deserve his patience or his kindness. "Okay," she said lamely, reaching for her brandy and downing the whole thing practically in one gulp. Maybe that would give her the courage to say what she needed to say.

But it only made her woozy and very nauseous. Jordan lifted her into his arms and carried her to the guest room, where he undressed her like a weary child, put her into one of his pajama tops because she'd forgotten to bring a nightgown and tucked her in.

"Jordan, I made a terrible mistake."

He kissed her forehead. "We'll talk tomorrow," he said. "Go to sleep."

Exhaustion immediately conquered Amanda, and when she awakened, it was morning. Jordan had brought her things to her room. There was a small bathroom adjoining, so she showered, brushed her teeth and put on make-up. When she arrived in the kitchen, wearing jeans and a blue sweater, she felt a hundred percent better than she had the night before.

Jordan was making pancakes on an electric griddle and cooking bacon in the microwave, while his daughters sat at the table, drinking their orange juice and watching him with amusing consternation. While Jessica resembled Becky, the smaller child, Lisa, looked like Jordan. She had his maple-brown hair and hazel eyes, and she smiled broadly when she saw Amanda.

Again, despite her improved mood, Amanda felt like an imposter shoving herself in where she didn't belong. She would have fled to her car if she hadn't known it would only compound her problems.

"Hungry?" Jordan asked, his eyes gentle as he studied Amanda's face.

She nodded, and, seeing that there were four places set at the table, took a chair beside Lisa.

"That's Daddy's chair," Jessica pointed out.

Amanda started to move, but Jordan slapped his hand down on her shoulder and pushed her back.

"It doesn't matter where Amanda sits," he said.

Jessica didn't take offense at the correction, and Amanda reached for the orange juice carton with a trembling hand. She was more than ready to tell Jordan the truth now, but it didn't look as though she was going to get the opportunity. After all, she couldn't just drop an emotional bombshell in front of his daughters.

Jordan's cooking was good, and Amanda managed to put away three pancakes and a couple of strips of bacon even though she couldn't remember the last time she'd been so nervous.

"I think it's about time we decorated that Christmas tree, don't you?" Jordan asked when the meal was over.

The girls gave a rousing cheer and bounded out of their chairs and into the living room.

"You'll have to get dressed first," Jordan called after them. Despite his lack of experience, he seemed to be picking up the fundamentals of active fatherhood rather easily.

"Lisa can't tie her shoes," Jessica confided from the kitchen doorway.

"Then you can do it for her," Jordan replied, beginning to clear the table.

Amanda insisted on helping, and the moment Jordan heard the kids' feet pounding up the stairway, he took her into his arms and gave her a thorough kiss. She melted against him, overpowered, as always, by his strange magic.

"It's very good to have you here, lady," he said in a rumbling whisper. "I just wish I could take you upstairs and spend about two hours making love to you."

Amanda shivered at the prospect. She wished that, too, with all her heart, but once she told Jordan about her visits to James's hospital room and her pretense of rekindling their affair, he probably wouldn't ever want to touch her again.

The idea of never lying in Jordan's arms another night, never feeling the weight of his body or going crazy under the touch of his hands or his mouth, made a hard lump form in her throat.

"Still not ready to talk?" he asked, touching the tip of her nose with a gentle finger.

Amanda shook her head.

"There's time," Jordan said, and he kissed her again, making her throw her arms around his neck in an instinctive plea for more.

"Daddy!" a little voice shouted from upstairs. "I can't find my red shoes!"

Amanda pushed away from Jordan as though he'd struck her, and lifted the back of one hand to her mouth when he turned away to go and help his daughter.

While he was gone, Amanda's bravery completely deserted her. She found her purse and dashed for her car, leaving her luggage behind in Jordan's guest room. He ran outside just as she pulled out of the driveway, but Amanda didn't stop. She put her foot down hard on the accelerator and drove away.

A glance at her watch told her the ferry wouldn't leave for another twenty minutes, and Amanda was half-afraid Jordan would toss the kids in the car and come chasing after her. Since she couldn't face him, she drove to the café where they'd eaten on a couple of occasions.

After parking her car behind a delivery truck, Amanda went into the restaurant, took a chair as far from the front door as she could and hid behind her menu until Wanda arrived.

"Well, hello there," the pleasant woman boomed. "Where's Jordan?"

"He's—busy. Could I get a cup of coffee?"

Wanda arched one artfully plucked eyebrow, but she didn't ask any more questions. She just brought a cup to Amanda's table and filled it from the pot in her other hand.

"Thanks," Amanda said, wishing she didn't have to give up the menu.

Jordan didn't show up, and Amanda was half disappointed and half relieved. She finished her coffee and went back to the ferry terminal just in time to board the boat.

Because she hoped there would be a message on the answering machine from Jordan and feared there would not, she went to the hospital first, instead of her apartment.

"You're late," James fussed when she walked into his room.

"I'm sorry—" Amanda began.

She'd forgotten what a master James was of the quick-silver change, and the brightness of his smile stunned her. "That's okay," he said generously. "I'm just glad you're here."

Amanda lowered her eyes. She would have given anything to be with Jordan and his children at that moment, helping to decorate the Christmas tree or even listening to a lecture. She regretted giving in to her impulse and running away. "Me, too," she lied.

"Tell me you love me," James said.

Amanda's heart stopped beating. She would have choked on the words if she'd tried to utter them.

For better or worse, Madge Brockman spared her the trouble. "Isn't this sweet?" she asked, sweeping like a storm into the room in a black full-length mink with a matching hat. Her eyes, full of poison, swung to Amanda. "To think I believed you when you said you and James were through."

"Amanda and I are going to be married," James protested, and he raised one hand to his chest.

Amanda was terrified.

"You idiot," Madge growled at him, gesturing wildly with one mink-swathed arm. "She's two-timing you with Jordan Richards!"

"That's a lie!" James shouted.

A nurse burst into the room. "Mr. Brockman, you must be calm!"

Terrified, Amanda backed blindly out into the hallway and ran to the elevator. It seemed to be her day for running away, she thought to herself as she got into her car and sped out of the parking lot.

For a time she just drove around Seattle, following an aimless path, trying to gather her composure. She considered visiting her mother, or one of her friends, but she couldn't, because she knew she'd break down and cry if she tried to explain things to anyone.

Finally Amanda drove back to her apartment building and went in through the rear entrance.

In the bathroom she splashed cold water on her face, washing away the tearstains, but her eyes were still puffy afterward, and her nose was an unglamorous red. It was no real surprise when the door buzzer sounded.

"Jordan or the tiger?" she asked herself with a sort of wounded fancy as she made her way determinedly across the living room and reached for the doorknob.

Chapter 9

Jordan stood in the hallway, holding Amanda's suitcase. He was alone, and his expression was quietly contemptuous.

For the moment Amanda couldn't speak, so she stepped back to let him pass. He set the luggage down with a clatter just inside the entryway and jammed his hands into the pockets of his leather jacket.

"Why the hell did you run off like that?" he demanded.

For a second or so, Amanda swung wildly between relief and dread. She turned away from Jordan, walked to the sofa and sank onto it. "You haven't had a call from Mrs. Brockman?" she asked in a small voice.

Without bothering to take off his jacket—he obviously didn't intend to stay long—Jordan perched on the arm of an easy chair. "James's wife? Why would she call me?"

Amanda swallowed. "I've been visiting James in the hospital," she blurted out. "I told him we could t-take up where we left off."

The color drained from Jordan's face. "What?"

"He said he was going to give up and die—that I was

all he had to live for. So I decided to pretend I still loved him, just until he was strong enough to go on his own."

"And you believed that?" His voice was low, lethal.

"Of course I believed it!" Amanda flared.

"Well, you've been had," Jordan replied coldly.

Amanda stared at him, wounded, her worst suspicions confirmed. "I knew you wouldn't understand, Jordan," she said. "That's why I was afraid to tell you."

"Damn it," he rasped, "don't make excuses. A lie is a lie, Amanda, and there's no room in my life for games like this!"

"It wasn't a game! You didn't see him, hear him…"

Jordan was on his feet again, his hands back in his pockets. "I didn't have to." He walked to the door and stood there for a moment with his back to Amanda. "I could understand your wanting to help," he said in parting. "But I'll never understand why you didn't tell me about it." With that, he opened the door and walked out.

Amanda jumped off the couch and raced to the entryway—she couldn't lose him, she *couldn't*—but at the door she stopped. Jordan had judged her and found her guilty, and he wasn't going to change his mind.

It was over.

Slowly Amanda closed the door. With a concerned meow, Gershwin circled her ankles. "He's gone," she said to the cat, and then she went into the bedroom, found the fur jacket and the skimpy bikini, and returned to her car.

With every mile she drove, Amanda became more certain that Jordan had been right: James had used emotional blackmail to get her to come back to him. She could see now that he'd given a performance every time she'd visited his room; she recalled the shrewd expression in his eyes, the things he'd said about Jordan.

"Fool!" Amanda muttered to herself, flipping on her windshield wipers as a light rain began to fall.

When she reached the hospital, Amanda marched inside, carrying the fur coat over her arm and the bikini in her purse. Some of her resolution faded as she got into the elevator, though. James had a serious heart condition, and for a time he'd been in real danger. Suppose what she meant to say caused him to suffer another attack? Suppose he died and it was her fault?

Amanda approached James's room reluctantly, then stopped when she heard him laughing. "Face it, Richards," he said. "You lose. In another week or two I'll be out of this place. And believe me, Amanda will be more than happy to fly off to Hawaii with me and make sure I recuperate properly."

Her first instinct was to flee, but Amanda couldn't move. She stood frozen in the hallway, resting one hand against the wall.

Jordan said something in response, but Amanda didn't hear what it was—maybe because the thundering of her heart drowned it out.

The scraping of a chair broke Amanda's spell, and she didn't know whether to stay and face Jordan or dodge into the little nook across the hall where a coffee machine stood. In the end she decided she'd done enough running away for a lifetime, and stayed where she was.

When Jordan walked out of James's room, he stopped cold for a moment, but then a weary expression of resignation came over his face.

"I'm going to tell him the truth," she said, her voice hardly more than a whisper.

Jordan shrugged. "It's a little late for that, isn't it?"

His eyes dropped to the rich sable jacket draped over her arm. "Merry Christmas, Amanda."

Amanda saw all her hopes going down the drain, and something inside drove her to fight to save them. "Jordan, be reasonable. You know I never meant for things to turn out this way!"

He looked at her for a moment, then walked around her, as he would something objectionable lying on the sidewalk, and strode off down the hall.

Amanda watched him go into the elevator. He looked straight through her as the doors closed.

It was a few moments before she could bring herself to walk into James's room and face him. She no longer feared that her news would cause him another heart attack; now it was her anger she struggled to control.

Finally she was able to force herself through the doorway. She laid the coat at the foot of James's bed without meeting his eyes, then took the bikini from her purse and put it with the coat. When she thought she could manage it without hysterics, she turned to him and said, "You had no right to manipulate me that way."

"Amanda." His voice was a scolding drawl, and he stretched out his hand to her.

She evaded his grasp. "It's over, James. I can't see you anymore."

Surprisingly James smiled at her and let his hand fall to his side. "You might as well come back to me, baby. It's plain enough that Richards is through with you."

Hot rage made Amanda's backbone ramrod straight, but she didn't allow her anger to erupt in a flow of nasty retorts. Clinging to the last of her dignity, she whispered, "Maybe the time I had with Jordan will have to last me a lifetime. But he's the only man I'll ever love." With that, she turned and walked out.

"You'll be back!" James shouted after her. "You'll come begging for my forgiveness! Damn it, Amanda, nobody walks out on me…"

While a nurse rushed into James's room, Amanda went straight on until she got to the elevator. She pushed the button and waited circumspectly for a ride to the main floor, even though her emotions were howling in her spirit like a storm. She wanted to be anywhere but there, anybody besides herself.

She'd hoped Jordan might be lingering somewhere downstairs, or maybe in her section of the parking lot, but there was no sign of him.

Beyond tears, she climbed behind the wheel of her car and started toward the house where she and Eunice had grown up.

She knocked at the door and called out "It's me!" and her mother instantly replied with a cheerful "Come in!"

Bob, it turned out, was putting in some overtime at the aircraft plant where he worked, but Marion and Eunice were wrapping festive presents on the dining room table. Eunice looked a little tired, but other than that she seemed to be in good spirits. Marion was taking her usual delight in the yuletide season, but her face fell when she got a look at her elder daughter.

"Merciful heavens," she sputtered, rushing over and forcing Amanda into a chair. "You're as pale as Marley's ghost! What on earth is the matter?"

Just minutes before, Amanda had been convinced she had no tears left to cry, but now a despondent wail escaped her and tears streamed down her face.

Eunice immediately rushed to her side. "Sis, what is

it?" she whispered, near tears herself. She had always cried whenever Amanda did, even if she didn't know what was bothering her sister.

"It's Jordan!" Amanda sobbed. "He's gone—he never wants to see me again..."

"Get her a glass of water," Marion said to Eunice. She rested her hands on Amanda's shoulders, much as Jordan once had, trying to soothe away the terrible tension.

Eunice reappeared moments later, looking stricken, a glass of water in one hand.

"You told him," Marion said as Amanda sipped the cold water.

Eunice dragged up a chair beside her. "Told him what?"

Setting the water down with a thump, Amanda blurted out the whole story—how she'd fallen hopelessly in love with Jordan, how James had hoodwinked her into ruining everything. She ended with an account of the scene in James's hospital room when she'd given back his gifts once and for all.

"What kind of lunkhead is this Jordan," Eunice demanded, "that he doesn't understand something so simple?"

Amanda dragged her sleeve across her eyes, feeling like a five-year-old with both knees skinned raw. Only it was her heart that was hurting. "He's angry because I didn't tell him about it from the first." She paused to sniffle, and her mother produced a handful of tissues in that magical way mothers have. "I tried, I honestly did, but I was so scared of losing him."

"Men," muttered Eunice. "Who needs them?"

"I do," chorused Amanda and Marion. And at that, all three women laughed.

Eunice patted Amanda's shoulder. "Don't worry. After he thinks about it for a while, he'll forgive you."

Amanda shook her head, dabbing at her puffy eyes with a wad of damp tissue. "You don't know Jordan. He's probably never told a lie in his life. He just flat out doesn't understand deception."

"Maybe he's never lied," Marion said briskly, "but he's made mistakes, just like the rest of us. When he calms down, Amanda, he'll call."

Amanda prayed her mother was right, but the hollow feeling in the center of her heart made that seem unlikely.

An hour later, when Amanda announced that she was going home, Eunice grabbed her coat and insisted on riding along. She'd make supper, she said, and the two of them could just hang around the way they had in high school.

"I wasn't planning to stick my head in the oven or anything, if that's what you're worried about," Amanda said with a sad smile as she backed her car out of her parents' driveway.

Eunice grinned. "And singe those gorgeous, golden tresses? I should hope not."

Amanda laughed at the image. "You know what, kid? It's good to have you back."

Her younger sister patted her arm. "I'll be around awhile, I think," she replied. "There's an opening for a computer programmer at the university. I have an interview the day after Christmas."

"There's really no hope of getting back together with Jim, then?" Amanda asked as they wended their way through rainy streets, the windshield wipers beating out a rhythmic accompaniment to their conversation.

Eunice shook her head. "Not when there's somebody else involved," she said.

Amanda nodded. Just the idea of Jordan seeing another woman was more than she could tolerate, even with the relationship in ruins.

After parking the car, Amanda and Eunice dashed through the rain to the store on the corner and bought popcorn, a log for the fireplace, a pound of fresh shrimp and the makings for a salad.

Back at Amanda's apartment, Eunice prepared and cooked the succulent shrimp while Amanda washed and cut up the vegetables.

"You don't even have a Christmas tree," Eunice complained later when she was kneeling on the hearth, lighting the paper-wrapped log.

Amanda shrugged. "I was just planning to skip the whole holiday," she said.

"Knowing Jordan didn't change that?"

"When I was with him, he was all I thought about," Amanda explained. "Same thing when I wasn't with him."

Eunice grinned and got to her feet, dusting her hands off on the legs of her jeans as if she'd just carried wood in from the wilderness like a pioneer. "You could always throw yourself at his feet and beg for forgiveness."

Amanda lifted her chin stubbornly and went to the living room window. "I explained everything to him, and he wouldn't listen."

Rain pattered at the glass and made the people on the sidewalks below hurry along under their colorful umbrellas. Amanda wondered how many of them were happy and how many had broken hearts.

"You shouldn't give up if you really care about the guy," Eunice said softly.

Amanda sighed. "I didn't give up, Eunice," she said. "He did."

At that, the two sisters dropped the subject of Jordan and talked about other Christmases.

Jordan had his own reasons for welcoming the rain, and after he drove on board the ferry to Vashon Island, he stayed in the car, staring bleakly at the empty van ahead of him. He felt hollow and numb, as though all his vitals had shriveled up and disappeared, but he knew the pain would come eventually, and he dreaded it.

After losing Becky, Jordan had made up his mind never to really care about another woman again. That way, he'd reasoned in his naïveté, he'd never have to suffer the way he had after his wife's death.

The trouble was, he'd reckoned without Amanda Scott.

He'd fallen hard for her without ever really being aware of what was happening. Had he told her that he loved her? He couldn't remember.

Maybe things would have been different if he had.

Jordan shook his head. He was being stupid. Telling her he cared wouldn't have prevented her from deceiving him. He drifted into a restless sleep, haunted by dreams of things that might have been, and when the ferry's horn blasted, he was startled. He hadn't been aware of the passing time.

Once the boat docked and his turn came, Jordan drove down the ramp, just as he had a million times before. Rain danced on the pavement, and wet gulls hid out be-

neath the picnic tables in the park he passed. The world
was the same, and yet it was different.

He was alone again.

When he entered the kitchen through the garage door
minutes later, he heard the stereo blasting. Taking off his
jacket and running a hand through his rumpled hair, he
went into the living room.

Jessie and Lisa had dragged their presents out from
under the mammoth Christmas tree he and Amanda
had chosen together, and piled them up in two teeter-
ing stacks. The babysitter, a teenage girl from down the
road, was curled up on the couch, chattering into the
telephone receiver.

Sighting Jordan, his daughters flung themselves at
him with shrieks of glee, and he lifted one in each arm,
making the growling sound they loved and pretending
to be bent on chewing off their ears.

The babysitter, a plain little thing with thick glasses,
hung up the telephone and tiptoed over to the stereo to
turn it off.

Jordan let the girls down to the floor, took out his
wallet and paid the sitter. The moment she was gone,
Jessie folded her arms and announced, "Lisa has more
presents than I do."

Jordan pretended to be horrified. "No!"

"Count them for yourself," Jessie challenged.

He knelt and began to count. The red-and-silver
striped package on the top of Lisa's stack turned out to
be the culprit. "This one is for both of you," Jordan said,
tapping at the gift tag with his finger. "See? It says 'Lisa
and Jessie.'"

Jessie examined the tag studiously and was then satisfied that it was still a just world. "Where did Amanda

go?" she asked, looking at him with Becky's eyes. "Why did she run away?"

Jordan had no idea how to explain Amanda's abrupt disappearance. He still didn't understand it completely himself. "She's at her apartment, I guess," he finally answered.

"But why did she runned away?" Lisa asked, rubbing her eye with the back of one dimpled hand.

"She probably went to heaven, like Mommy," Jessie said importantly.

Her innocent words went through Jordan like a lance. Young as they were, these kids were developing a strategy for being left—Mommy went to heaven; Daddy doesn't have time for us; Amanda was just passing through.

Jordan kissed both his girls resoundingly on the forehead. "Amanda's not in heaven," he said, sounding hoarse even to himself. "She's in Seattle. Now put these presents back under the tree before Santa finds out you've been messing around with them and fills your stockings with clam shells."

The telephone rang just as Jordan was rising to his feet, but he didn't lunge for it, even though that was his first instinct. He answered in a leisurely, offhand way, but his heart was pounding.

"Hi, little brother. It's Karen," his sister said warmly. "How are the monkeys getting along?"

Jordan forced himself to chuckle; he felt like weeping with disappointment. So it wasn't Amanda. What would he have said to her if it had been? "Do they always pile their presents in the middle of the living room?" he countered, trying to sound lighthearted.

Karen laughed. "No, that's a new one," she said. "How are you doing, Jord?"

He ran a hand through his hair. "Me? I'm doing great." *For somebody who's just had his insides torn out, that is.*

"No problems with memories?"

Jordan sighed and watched his children as they put their colorful gifts back underneath the tree. It seemed hard to believe there had ever been a time when he found it difficult even to look at them because they reminded him so much of Becky. "I guess I'm over that," he said huskily.

"Sounds to me like things are a little rocky."

Karen had always been perceptive. "It's something else," he said. The pain he'd been expecting was just starting to set in. "Listen, Karen, you and Paul and I have to have a talk about the girls. I want to spend more time with them."

"Took you long enough," Karen responded, her voice gentle.

Jordan remembered how she'd helped him through those dark days after Becky had died; she'd been there for him while he was in the hospital, and later, too. If she'd been in his living room instead of miles away on the peninsula, he'd have told her about Amanda.

"Better late than never," he finally replied.

"Paul and I will be down on Christmas Eve, as planned," Karen went on, probably sensing that Jordan wasn't going to confide anything important over the phone. "Save some room under that tree, because we're bringing a carload of loot, and Becky's parents will send boxes of stuff."

Jordan chuckled and shook his head. "Just what they need," he said, watching the greedy munchkins playing tug-of-war with a box wrapped in shiny blue paper. "See you Christmas Eve, sis."

Karen said a few more words, then hung up.

"I'm hungry," said Lisa as a stain spread slowly through the fabric of her plaid jeans.

"She peed her pants," Jessie pointed out quite unnecessarily.

With a grin, Jordan swept his younger daughter up in his arms and carried her off to the bathroom.

'Twas the night before Christmas, and Amanda Scott was feeling sorry for herself. She sat with her feet up in front of the fire while her mother, stepfather and sister bundled up to go to the midnight service at church.

"No fair peeking in the stockings while we're gone," said Bob with a smile and a shake of his finger.

Marion and Eunice were less understanding. They both looked as though they wanted to shake her.

"Moping around this house won't change anything," Marion scolded.

"Yeah," Eunice agreed, gesturing. "Put on your coat and come with us."

"I'm wearing jeans and a sweatshirt, in case you haven't noticed," Amanda pointed out archly. Bob had on his best suit, and Marion and Eunice were both in new dresses.

"Nobody's going to notice," Marion fussed, and she looked so hopeful that Amanda would change her mind that Amanda relented and pushed herself out of the chair.

Soon, she was settled beside Eunice in the backseat of her parents' car. It was so much like the old days that for a while Amanda was able to pretend her life wasn't in ruins.

"Maybe a little angel will whisper in Jordan's ear and he'll call you," Eunice said in a low voice as Marion and Bob sang carols exuberantly in the front seat.

Amanda gave her sister a look. "And maybe Saint Nicholas will land on our roof tonight in a sleigh drawn by eight tiny reindeer."

"Okay, then," Eunice responded, bristling, "why don't you call him?"

The truth was that Amanda had dialed Jordan's number a hundred times since they'd parted. Once she'd even waited to hear him say hello before hanging up. "Gee, why don't I?" she retorted. "Or better yet, I could plunge headfirst off an overpass. I just *love* pain."

Eunice folded her arms. "Don't be such a poop, Amanda. I'm only trying to help."

"It isn't working," Amanda responded, turning her head to look out at the festive lights trimming roofs and windows and shrubbery.

The church service was soothing, as family traditions often are, and Amanda was feeling a little better when they drove back home. They all sat around the tree, sipping eggnog and listening to carols, and when Bob and Marion finally retired for the night, Eunice dug a package out from under a mountain of gifts and extended it.

Amanda accepted the present, but refused to open it until she had found her gift to Eunice. It was another tradition; as girls, the sisters had always made their exchange just before going to bed.

When Amanda opened her gift, she laughed. It was a copy of *Gathering Up the Pieces*, the same book she'd bought for Eunice.

Eunice was amazed when she opened her package. "I don't believe this," she whispered, a wide smile on

her face. She turned back the flyleaf. "And it's auto-
graphed. Wow."

"I waited in line for hours to get it signed," Amanda
exaggerated. She was remembering meeting Jordan that
day, and feeling all the resultant pain.

"Let's go to bed and read ourselves to sleep," Eunice
suggested, standing up and switching off the Christmas
tree. Its veil of tinsel seemed to whisper a silvery song
in the darkness.

"Good idea," Amanda answered.

She was all the way up to chapter three before she finally closed her eyes.

The kids were asleep and so, as far as Jordan knew,
were Paul and Karen. He sat up in bed, switched on the
lamp and reached for the telephone on the nightstand.
The picture of Becky had been moved to a shelf in his
study, but he looked at the place where it had stood and
said, "Know what, Becky? I've got it bad."

A glance at his watch told him it was after two in the
morning. If he called Amanda now, he would be sure to
wake her up, but he didn't care. Whatever happened, he
had to hear her voice and wish her a merry Christmas.

He punched out the number and waited, nervous as
a high school kid. While the call went through, a number of scenarios came to mind—such as James answering with a sleepy "Hello." Or Amanda telling him to go
straight to hell.

Instead he got a recorded voice. "Hi. This is Amanda
Scott, and I can't come to the phone right now…"

Jordan hung up without leaving a message, switched
off the light and lay back on his pillows. She was probably at her parents' place, he told himself.

Or maybe she was in Hawaii, helping James recuperate.

Jordan turned onto his stomach and slammed one fist into the pillow. He knew the lush plains and contours of Amanda's body, and he begrudged them to every other man on earth. They were his to touch, and no one else's.

His groin knotted as he recalled how it was to bury himself in Amanda's depths, to feel her hands moving on his back and the insides of her thighs against his hips. She'd lain beneath him like a temptress, her eyes smoldering, her body rising to meet his, stroke for stroke, her hands curled on the sides of the pillow.

But then, as release approached, she would bite down hard on her lower lip and roll her eyes back, focusing dreamily on nothing at all. A low, keening whimper would escape her as she surrendered completely, breaking past her clamped teeth to become a shameless groan...

Jordan sat bolt upright in bed and switched on the lamp again. He couldn't quite face the prospect of a cold shower, but he was too uncomfortable to stay where he was. He tossed back the covers, reached for his robe and tied it tightly around his waist. The cloth stood out like canvas stretched over a tent pole.

Feeling reasonably certain he wouldn't meet anybody, Jordan slipped out of his room and down the darkened stairs. In the kitchen he poured himself a glass of chocolate milk and carried it back to the living room. There he sat, staring at the silent glimmer of the dark Christmas tree, the bulging shapes of the stockings. The thin light of a winter moon poured in through the smoked-glass windows, making everything look unfamiliar.

"Jordan?" It was Karen's voice, and seconds before she switched on the lights, he grabbed a sofa pillow and laid it on his lap. His plump, pretty sister, bundled in her practical blue chenille robe, looked at him with concern. "Are you all right?"

"No," Jordan answered, tossing back the last of his chocolate milk as though it could give him the same solace as brandy or good whiskey. Since it was safe to set aside the pillow, he did. "Don't ever let anybody tell you it's 'better to have loved and lost, than never to have loved at all,'" he advised, sounding for all the world like a melancholy drunk. "I've done it twice, and I wish to God I'd joined the foreign legion, instead."

Karen sat down next to him. "So you're just going to give up, huh?"

"Yeah," Jordan answered obstinately. He had to change the subject, or risk being smothered in images of Amanda lying in somebody else's bed. "About the kids—"

"You want them back," Karen guessed with a gentle smile.

Jordan nodded.

Chapter 10

Amanda sat staring at the bank draft in amazement that dreary Saturday morning in February while a gray rain drizzled at the kitchen windows. "I don't understand," she muttered, glancing from Marion's smiling face to Bob's to Eunice's. "What's this for?"

Bob reached across the table to cover her hand with his. "I guess you could say it's an investment. You've been walking around here for two months looking as though you've lost your last friend, so your mother and I decided you needed a lift. It's enough for the down payment on that old house you wanted, isn't it?"

Amanda swallowed, reading the numbers on the check in disbelief. It was five times the down payment the owner demanded—Amanda still called once a week to see if the house had sold, and had gone to see it twice—and must have represented a major chunk of her parents' savings account. "I can't take this," she said. "You've worked so hard and budgeted so carefully..."

But Bob and Marion presented a united front, and they were backed up by a beaming Eunice, who was now working full-time at the university and living in her own apartment.

"You have to accept it," Marion said firmly. "We won't take no for an answer."

"But suppose I fail?" Since the breakup with Jordan, Amanda's confidence had taken a decided dip, and everything was more difficult than it should have been.

"You won't," Bob said with certainty. "Now call that real estate woman and make an offer before the place is snapped up by some doctor or lawyer looking for a summer house."

Amanda hesitated only a moment. Hope was fluttering in her heart like a bird rising skyward; for the first time in two months she could see herself as a happy woman. With a shriek of delight, she bolted out of her chair and dashed for the telephone, and Bob and Marion laughed until they had tears in their eyes.

The real estate agent was delighted at Amanda's offer, and offered to bring the papers over to Seattle for her to sign. They agreed to meet Monday morning at Amanda's office in the Evergreen Hotel.

When Amanda was off the phone, she turned to her parents. "I can't believe you're doing this for me—taking such a chance—"

"A person can't expect to win in life if they're afraid to take a risk," Bob said quietly.

Amanda went back to the table and bent to hug each of her parents. "You'll be proud of me," she promised.

"We already are," Marion assured her.

On Monday morning Amanda arrived at work with a carefully typed letter of resignation tucked into her briefcase. In another two weeks she would be rolling up her sleeves and making a start on her dream—or, at least, part of it.

She flipped through the messages on her desk, sorting them in order of importance, and at the same time looked into the future. The house she was buying was hardly more than a mile from Jordan's place. She was bound to meet him on the highway or run into him in the supermarket, and she wondered if she could deal with that.

Even after two months Amanda ached every time she thought of Jordan. Actually encountering him face-to-face might really set her back.

There was a rap at the door, and Mindy stepped in, smiling. "You look pretty cheerful today. What's going on? Did you and Jordan get back together or something?"

Amanda opened her briefcase and took out the letter of resignation, keeping her eyes down to hide the sudden pain the mention of Jordan had caused her. "No," she answered, "but I'll be leaving the Evergreen in a couple of weeks—I'm buying that house I wanted on Vashon Island."

"Wow," Mindy responded. "That's great!"

Amanda lifted her eyes to meet her friend's gaze. "Thanks, Mindy."

Mindy's brow puckered in a frown. "I'll miss you a lot, though."

"And I'll miss you." At that moment the intercom on Amanda's telephone buzzed, and she picked up the receiver as Mindy left the office. "Amanda Scott."

"Ms. Scott, this is Betty Prestwood, Prestwood Real Estate. I'm afraid I've been delayed, so I won't be arriving in the city until around noon. Could we possibly meet at Ivar's for lunch at twelve-fifteen? I'll have the proper papers with me, of course."

Amanda automatically glanced at her calendar, even though she already knew she was free for lunch that day. She probably would have eaten yogurt in her office or gone to the mall with Mindy for fast food. "That will be fine."

After ending that phone call, Amanda went to the executive manager's office suite and handed in her resignation. Mr. Mansfield, a middle-aged man with a bald head and an ulcer, was not pleased that his trusty assistant manager was leaving.

He instructed her to start preliminary interviews for a replacement as soon as possible.

Amanda spent the rest of the morning on the telephone with various employment agencies in the city, and when it came time to meet Mrs. Prestwood for lunch, she was relieved. It wasn't the food that attracted her, but the prospect of a break.

After exchanging her high heels for sneakers, Amanda walked the six blocks from the hotel to the seafood restaurant on the waterfront. The sun was shining, and the harbor was its usual noisy, busy self.

Mrs. Prestwood, a small, trim woman with carefully coiffed blond hair and tasteful makeup, was waiting by the reservations desk.

She and Amanda shook hands, then followed the hostess to a table by a window.

Just as Amanda was sitting down, she spotted Jordan—it was as though her eyes were magnetized to him. He looked very Wall Street in his three-piece suit as he lunched with two other men and a woman.

Evidently he'd sensed Amanda's stare, for his eyes shifted to her almost instantly.

For a moment the whole restaurant seemed to fall into

eerie silence for Amanda; she had the odd sensation of standing on the bottom of the ocean. It was only with enormous effort that she surfaced and forced her gaze to the menu the waitress had handed her. *Don't let him come over here*, she prayed silently. *If he does, I'll fall apart right in front of everybody.*

"Is something wrong?" Betty Prestwood asked pleasantly.

Amanda swallowed and shook her head, but out of the corner of her eye she was watching Jordan.

He had turned his attention back to his companions, especially the woman, who was attractive, in a tweedy sort of way, with her trim suit and her dark hair pulled back into a French twist. She was laughing at something Jordan had said.

Amanda made herself study the menu, even though she couldn't have eaten if her life depended on it. She finally decided on the spinach salad and iced tea, just for show.

Mrs. Prestwood brought out the contracts as soon as the waitress had taken their orders, and Amanda read them through carefully. Lunch had arrived by the time she was done, and in a glance she saw that Jordan and his party were leaving. He was resting his hand lightly on the small of the woman's back, and Amanda felt for all the world like a betrayed wife.

Forcing her eyes back to the contracts, she signed them and handed Mrs. Prestwood a check. Since the owner was financing the sale himself, it was now just a matter of waiting for closing. Amanda could rent the house in the interim if she wished.

She wrote another check, then stabbed a leaf of spinach with her fork. Try as she might, she couldn't lift it to her mouth. Her stomach was roiling angrily, unwilling to accept anything.

She laid the fork down.

"Is everything all right?" Mrs. Prestwood asked, seeming genuinely concerned.

Amanda lied by nodding her head.

"You don't seem very hungry."

Amanda managed a smile. Was Jordan sleeping with that woman? Did she visit him on the island on weekends? "I'm just getting over the flu," she said, which was at least a partial truth. She was probably coming down with it, not getting over it.

Mrs. Prestwood accepted that excuse and finished her lunch in good time. The two women parted outside the restaurant with another handshake, then Amanda started back up the hill to the hotel. By the time she arrived, her head was pounding and there were two people waiting to be interviewed for her job.

She talked to both of them and didn't pass either application on to Mr. Mansfield for his consideration. One had obviously considered herself too good for such a menial position, and the other had an offensive personal manner.

Amanda's headache got progressively worse as the afternoon passed, but she was too busy interviewing to go home to bed, and besides, she couldn't be sure the malady wasn't psychosomatic. She hadn't started feeling really sick until after she'd seen Jordan with that woman in the dress-for-success clothes.

At the end of the day Amanda dragged herself home, fed Gershwin, made herself a bowl of chicken noodle soup and watched the evening news in her favorite bathrobe. By the time she'd been apprised of all the shootings, rapes, drug deals and political scandals of the day, she was thoroughly depressed. She put her empty soup bowl in the sink, took two aspirin and fell into bed.

The next morning she felt really terrible. Her head seemed thick and heavy as a medicine ball, and her chest ached.

Reluctantly she called in sick, took more aspirin and went back to sleep.

A loud knocking at the door awakened her around eleven-thirty, and Amanda rolled out of bed, stumbled into the living room with one hand pressed to her aching head and called, "Who is it?"

"It's me," a feminine voice replied. "Mindy. Let me in—I come bearing gifts."

With a sigh, Amanda undid the chains, twisted the lock and opened the door. "You're taking your life in your hands, coming in here," she warned in a thick voice. "This place is infested with germs."

Mindy's pretty hair was sprinkled with raindrops, and her smile was warm. "I'll risk it," she said, stepping past Amanda with a stack of magazines and a box of something that smelled good. She grimaced as she assessed Amanda's rumpled nightgown and unbrushed hair. "You look like the victim in a horror movie," she observed cheerfully. "Sit down before you fall down."

Amanda dropped into a chair. "What's going on at the office?"

"It's bedlam," Mindy answered, setting the magazines and food down on the table to shrug out of her coat. "Mr. Mansfield is finding out just how valuable you really are." Her voice trailed back from the kitchenette, where she was opening cupboards and drawers. "He's been interviewing all morning, and he's such a bear today, he'll be lucky if anybody wants to work for him."

Amanda sighed. "I should be there."

Mindy returned from the kitchenette and handed Amanda a plate of the fried Chinese noodles she knew she loved. "And spread bubonic plague among your friends and coworkers? Bad idea. Eat this, Amanda."

Amanda took the plate of noodles and dug in with a fork. Although she still had no appetite, she knew her body needed food to recover, and she hadn't had anything to eat since last night's chicken soup. "Thanks."

Mindy glanced at the blank TV screen in amazement. "Do you mean to tell me you have a chance to catch up on all the soaps and you aren't even watching?"

"I'm sick, not on vacation," Amanda pointed out.

Mindy rushed to turn on the set and tune in her favorite. "Lord, will you look at him?" she asked, pointing to a shirtless hero soulfully telling a woman she was the only one for him.

"Don't listen to him," Amanda muttered. "As soon as you make one wrong move, he'll dump you."

"You *have* been watching this show!" Mindy accused.

Amanda shook her head glumly. "I was speaking from the perspective of real life," she said, chewing.

Mindy sighed. "I knew that rascal would be fooling around with Lorinda the minute Jennifer turned her back," she fretted, shaking her finger at the screen.

Amanda chuckled, even though she would have had to feel better just to die, and took another bite of the noodles Mindy had brought. "How do you know so much about the story line when you work every day?"

"I tape it," Mindy answered. Then, somewhat reluctantly, she snapped off the set and turned back to her mission of mercy. "Is there anything you want me to do at the office, Amanda? Or I could shop for you—"

Amanda interrupted with a shake of her head. "It's enough that you came over. That was really nice of you."

Mindy rose from the couch and put her hands on her slim hips. "I know. I'll make a bed for you on the couch so you can watch TV. Mom always did that for me when I was sick, and it never failed to cheer me up."

With that, Mindy disappeared into the bedroom, returning soon afterward with sheets, blankets and pillows. True to her word, she made a place for Amanda on the couch and all but tucked her in when she was settled with her magazines and the controls for the TV.

Before going back to work, she made Amanda a cup of hot tea, put the phone within reach and forced her to take more aspirin.

When Mindy was gone, Amanda got up to lock the door behind her, then padded back to the bed. She was comfortably settled when the telephone rang. A queer feeling quivered in the pit of her stomach as she remembered seeing Jordan in the restaurant the day before, felt again the electricity that passed between them when their eyes met. "Hello?" she said hopefully.

"Hello, Amanda."

The voice didn't belong to Jordan, but to Mrs. Prestwood. Amanda could pick up the keys to her house at the real estate office whenever she was ready.

Amanda promised to be there within the week, and asked Mrs. Prestwood to have telephone service hooked up at the house, along with electricity. Then she hung up and flipped slowly through the magazines, seeing none of the glossy photographs and enticing article titles. She was going to be living on the same island with Jordan, and that was all she could think about.

* * *

By the time Amanda recovered enough to return to work, half her notice was up and Mr. Mansfield had selected a replacement. Handing her her final paycheck, which was sizable because there was vacation pay added in, he wished her well. On her last day, he and Mindy and the others held a going away party for her in the hotel's elegant lounge, and Bob, Marion and Eunice attended, too.

That Friday evening, Amanda filled her car with boxes, one of which contained Gershwin, leaving the rest of her things behind for the movers to bring, and boarded the ferry for Vashon Island.

Since it was cold and dark in the bottom of the ship, she decided to venture upstairs to the snack bar for a cup of hot coffee. Just as she arrived, however, she spotted Jordan again. This time he was with his daughters, and the three of them were eating French fries while both girls talked at once.

Amanda's first instinct was to approach them and say hello, but in the end she lost her courage and slipped back out of the snack bar and down the stairs to her car. She sat hunched behind the wheel, waiting for the whistle announcing their arrival at Vashon Island to blast, and feeling miserable. What kind of life was she going to have in her new community if she had to worry about avoiding Jordan?

In those moments Amanda felt terribly alone, and the enormity of the things she'd done—giving up her job and apartment and borrowing such a staggering sum of money from her parents—oppressed her.

Finally the ferry came into port, and Amanda drove her car down the ramp, wondering if Jordan and the girls were in one of the cars ahead, or one behind. She didn't get a glimpse of them, which wasn't surprising, considering how dark it was.

When Amanda arrived at her new old house, the lights were on and Mrs. Prestwood was waiting in the kitchen to present the key, since Amanda had not had a chance to pick it up at the office. The old oil furnace was rumbling beneath the floor, filling the spacious rooms with warmth.

Amanda wandered through the rooms, sipping coffee from the percolator Betty Prestwood had thoughtfully loaned her and dreaming of the things she meant to do. There would be winter parties around the huge fireplace in the front parlor—she would serve mulled wine and spice cake with whipped cream. And in summer, guests could sleep on the screened sun porch if they wanted to, and be lulled into slumber by the quiet rhythm of the tide and the salty whisper of the breezes.

There were seven bedrooms upstairs, but only one bathroom. Amanda made a mental note to call in a plumbing contractor for estimates the next morning. She would have to add at least one more.

Amanda's private room, a small one off the kitchen, looked especially inviting after the long day she'd had. While Gershwin continued to explore the farthest reaches of his new home, she went out to the car to get the cot and sleeping bag she'd borrowed from her stepdad. After a bath upstairs, she crawled onto the cot with a book.

She hadn't read more than a page, when Gershwin suddenly landed in the middle of her stomach with a plop and meow.

Amanda let her book rest against her chin and stroked his silky fur. "Don't worry, Big Guy. We're both going to like it here." The instant the words were out of her mouth, though, she thought of the jolt that seeing Jordan and the girls had caused her, and her throat tightened painfully. "You'd think I'd be over him by now, wouldn't you?" she said when she could speak, her vision so blurred that there seemed to be two Gershwins lying on her stomach instead of one.

"Reoww," Gershwin agreed, before bending his head to lick one of his paws.

"Love is hell," Amanda went on with a sniffle. "Be glad you're neutered."

Gershwin made no comment on that, so Amanda dried her eyes and focused determinedly on her book again.

The next morning brought a storm in off Puget Sound. It slashed at the windows and howled around the corners of the house, and Gershwin kept himself within six inches of Amanda's feet. She left him only to carry in the boxes from the car and drive to the supermarket for food.

Since she'd prepared herself to encounter Jordan, Amanda was both relieved and disappointed when there was no sign of him. She filled her cart with groceries, taking care to buy a can of Gershwin's favorite food to make up for leaving him, and drove back over rain-slickened roads to the house.

The tempest raged all day, but Amanda was fascinated by it, rather than frightened. While Gershwin was sleeping off the feast Amanda had brought him, she put on her slicker and a pair of rubber boots she'd found in the basement and walked down to the beach.

Lightning cracked the sky like a mirror dropped on a hard floor, and the water lashed furiously at the rocky shoreline. Amanda stood with her hands in the pockets of her slicker, watching the spectacle in awe.

When she returned to the house half an hour later, her jeans were wet to her knees despite the rain garb she wore, and her hair was dripping. She felt strangely comforted, though, and when she saw Betty Prestwood's car splashing up the puddle-riddled driveway, she smiled and waved.

The two women dashed onto the enclosed porch together, laughing. Betty was only a few years older than Amanda, and they were getting to be good friends.

"There's an estate sale scheduled for today," Betty said breathlessly when they were in the kitchen and Amanda had handed her a cup of steaming coffee. "I thought you might like to go, since you need so much furniture. It's just on the other side of the island, and we could have lunch out."

Amanda was pleased that Betty had thought of her. Even though she had a surplus of funds, thanks to her own savings and the loan from Bob and Marion, it was going to cost a lot of money to get the bed and breakfast into operation. She needed to furnish the place attractively for a reasonable price. "Sounds great," Amanda said, ruefully comparing her soggy jeans and crumpled flannel shirt to Betty's stylish pink suit. "Just give me a few minutes, and I'll change."

Betty smiled. "Fine. Do you mind if I use the phone? I like to check in with the office periodically."

Amanda gestured toward the wall phone between the sink and stove. "Help yourself. And have some more coffee if you want it. I won't be long."

After finding a pair of black woolen slacks and a burgundy sweater, along with clean underthings and a towel and washcloth, Amanda dashed upstairs and took a quick, hot shower. When she was dressed, with her hair blow-dried and a light application of makeup highlighting her features, she hurried downstairs.

Betty was leaning against one of the kitchen counters, sipping coffee. "When are the movers coming?"

"Monday," Amanda answered, pulling on a pair of shoes that would probably be ruined the instant she wore them outside. "But even when all my stuff is here, the place is still going to echo like a cavern."

Betty laughed. "Maybe we can fix that this afternoon."

After saying goodbye to Gershwin, who still hadn't recovered from his stupor, Amanda pulled the ugly rubber boots she'd worn earlier on over her shoes, put on her slicker and followed Betty to her car.

Since the auction was scheduled for one o'clock, they had time for a leisurely lunch. Mercifully Betty suggested a small soup-and-sandwich place in town, rather than the roadside café Amanda knew Jordan frequented.

She ordered a turkey sandwich with bean sprouts, along with a bowl of minestrone, and ate with enthusiasm. She wasn't over Jordan, and she was still weak with lingering traces of the flu, but her appetite was back.

After lunch, she and Betty drove to a secluded house on the opposite side of the island, where folding chairs had been set up under huge pink-and-white striped canopies. Amanda's heart sank when she saw how many people had braved the nasty weather in search of a bargain, but Betty seemed to be taking a positive attitude, so she tried to follow suit.

The articles available for sale were scattered throughout the house—there were pianos and bedroom sets, tea services and bureaus, sets of china boasting imprints like Limoges and Haviland. Embroidered linens were offered, too, along with exquisite lace curtains and grandfather clocks, and wonderful old books that smelled of age and refinement.

Amanda's excitement built, and she crossed her fingers as she and Betty took their places in the horde of metal chairs.

A beautiful old sleigh bed with a matching bureau and armoire came up for sale first, and Amanda, thinking of her seven empty bedrooms, held up her bid card when the auctioneer asked for a modest amount to start the sale rolling.

A man in the back row bid against her, and it was nip and tuck, but Amanda finally won the skirmish with fairly minimal damage to her bank balance.

After that she bought linens, one of the grandfather clocks and a set of English bone china, while Betty purchased a full-length mirror in a cherrywood stand and an old jewelry box. At the end of the sale, Amanda made arrangements for the auction company to deliver her purchases, then wrote out a check.

It was midafternoon by then, and her soup and sandwich were beginning to wear off. Having lost sight of Betty in the crowd, she bought a hot dog with mustard and relish and a diet cola, then sat quietly in one of the folding chairs to eat.

She nearly choked when Jordan walked up, turned the chair in front of hers around and straddled it, his arms draped across the back. His expression was every bit as remote as it had been the last time she'd seen him, and Amanda prayed he couldn't hear her heart thudding against her rib cage.

"What are you doing here?" he asked, his voice insinuating that she was probably up to no good.

Amanda was instantly offended. She swallowed a chunk of her hot dog in a painful lump and replied, "I thought I'd try to steal some of the silverware, or maybe palm an antique broach or two."

He grinned, though the expression didn't quite reach his eyes. "You bought a bedroom set, a grandfather clock and some dishes. Getting married, Ms. Scott, now that Mrs. Brockman is out of the picture?"

It was all Amanda could do not to poke him in the eye with the rest of her hot dog. Obviously he didn't know she'd bought the Victorian house, and she wasn't about to tell him. "It'll be a June wedding," she said evenly. "Would you like to come?"

"I'm busy for the rest of the decade," Jordan answered in a taut voice, his hazel eyes snapping as he rose from the chair and put it back into line with the others. "See you around."

As abruptly as that, he was gone, and Amanda was left to sit there wondering why she'd let him walk away. When Betty returned, bringing along two of her friends to be introduced, Amanda was staring glumly at her unfinished hot dog.

Because Jessie and Lisa were staying with Becky's parents in Bellevue that weekend, Jordan was driving the Porsche. He strode back to it, oblivious to the rain saturating his hair and his shirt, and threw himself behind the wheel, slamming the door behind him.

Damn it all to hell, if Amanda was going to go on as if nothing had happened between them, couldn't she at least stay on her own turf? It drove him crazy, catching glimpses of her in restaurants, and in the midst of crowds waiting to cross streets, and in the next aisle at bookstores.

After slamming his palms against the steering wheel once, he turned the key in the ignition, and the powerful engine surged to life. The decision had been made by the time the conglomeration of striped canopies had disappeared from the rearview mirror; he would go home, change his clothes and spend the rest of the day in Seattle, working.

The plan seemed to be falling into place until an hour later, when he was passing by that Victorian place Amanda had liked so much. The lights were on, and there was a familiar car parked in the driveway.

He met Betty Prestwood's pink Cadillac midway between the highway and the house. She smiled and waved, and Jordan waved back distractedly, noticing for the first time that the For Sale sign was gone from the yard.

He braked the car to a stop and sprinted through the rain to the door, feeling a peculiar mixture of elation and outrage as he hammered at it with one fist.

Chapter 11

Amanda had just changed back into her jeans and a T-shirt when the thunderous knock sounded at the door. Expecting an enthusiastic salesperson, she was taken aback to find Jordan standing on her porch, dripping rainwater and indignation.

"Aren't you going to ask me in?" he demanded.

Amanda stepped back without a word, watching with round eyes as Jordan stomped into the warm kitchen, scowling at her.

"Well?" he prompted, putting his hands on his hips.

He seemed to have a particular scenario in mind, but Amanda couldn't think for the life of her what it would be.

She left him standing there while she went into her bathroom for a dry towel. Handing it to him upon her return, she asked, "Well, what?"

"What are you doing in this house? For that matter, what are you doing on this *island*?" He was drying his hair all the while he spoke, a grudging expression on his face.

Amanda hooked her thumbs in the waistband of her jeans and tilted her head to one side. "I own this house," she replied. "As for why I'm on the island, well—" she paused to shrug and spread her hands "—I guess I just didn't know I was supposed to get your approval before I stepped off the ferry."

Jordan flung the towel across the room, and it caught on the handle of the old-fashioned refrigerator. "Are you married to James?"

She went to the percolator and filled two cups with coffee, one for her and one for Jordan. "No," she answered, turning her head to look back at him over her shoulder. "I explained the situation to you. I was only trying to help James in my own misguided way. Where did you get the idea I meant to marry him?"

Jordan sighed and shoved his hand through damp, tangled hair. "Okay, so my imagination ran away with me. I tried to call you on Christmas Eve, and you weren't home. I had all these pictures in my mind of you lying on some secluded beach in Hawaii, helping James recuperate."

Although she was delighted, even jubilant, to know Jordan had tried to call her, she wasn't about to let on. She brought the coffee cup to him and held it out until he took it. "How would my lying on a secluded beach help James recuperate?"

"With you for a visual aid, a corpse would recuperate," he replied with a sheepish grin. His eyes remained serious. "I've missed you, Mandy."

She felt tears rising in her eyes and lowered her head while she struggled to hold them back. She didn't trust herself to speak.

Jordan took her coffee and set it, with his own, on the counter. "Don't you have any chairs in this place?"

Amanda made herself meet his eyes as she shook her head. "Not yet. The movers will be here on Monday."

He approached her, hooked his index fingers through the belt loops on her jeans and pulled her close. So close that every intimacy they'd ever shared came surging back to her memory at the contact, making her feel light-headed.

"I may have neglected to mention this before," he said in a voice like summer thunder rumbling far in the distance, "but I'm in love with you, and I have a feeling it's a lifetime thing."

Amanda linked her hands behind his neck, reveling in her closeness to Jordan and the priceless words he'd just said. "Actually, you did neglect to mention that, Mr. Richards."

He tasted her lips, sending a thrill careening through her system. "I apologize abjectly, even though you're guilty of the same oversight."

"Only too true," Amanda whispered, her mouth against his. "I love you, Jordan."

He ran his hands up and down her back, strong and sure and full of the power to set her senses aflame. He pressed his lips to her neck and answered with a teasing growl.

Amanda called upon all her self-control to lean back in his arms. "Jordan, we have things to talk about— things to work out. We can't just take up where we left off."

His fingers were hooked in her belt loops again. "I'll grant you that we have a lot to work through, and it's going to take some time. Why don't we go over to my place and talk?"

With considerable effort, Amanda willed her heart to slow down to a normal beat. She knew what was going to happen—it was inevitable—but she wanted to be sure they were on solid ground first. "We can talk here," she said, and she led him into the giant, empty parlor with its view of the sound. They sat together on a window seat with no cushion, their hands clasped. "I was wrong not to tell you I was seeing James again, Jordan, and I'm sorry."

He touched her lips with an index finger. Outside, beyond the rain-dappled glass, the storm raged on. "Looking back, I guess I wouldn't have been very receptive, anyway. I was feeling pretty possessive."

Amanda rested her head against his damp shoulder, unable to resist his warmth any longer, trembling as he traced a tingling pattern on her nape. "I thought I was going to die when I saw you at Ivar's with that corporation chick."

Jordan laughed and curved his fingers under her chin. "'Corporation chick'? That was Clarissa Robbins. She works in the legal department and is married to one of my best friends."

Amanda felt foolish, but she was also relieved, and she guessed that showed in her face, because Jordan was grinning at her. "You have your girls back," she said. "I saw you on the ferry last night."

Jordan nodded. "They didn't actually move in until a month ago. After all, they were used to living with Paul and Karen, so we just did weekends at first. And they're staying with Becky's parents until tomorrow night."

She tried to lower her head again, but Jordan wouldn't allow it.

"Think you could fall for a guy with two kids, Mandy?" he asked.

"I already have," she answered softly.

Jordan's mouth descended to hers, gentle at first, and then possessive and commanding. By the time he withdrew, Amanda was dazed.

"Show me the bridal suite," he said, rising to his feet and pulling Amanda after him.

She swallowed. "There's no bed in there, Jordan," she explained timidly.

"Where do you sleep?"

His voice was downright hypnotic. In fact, if he'd started undressing her right there in the middle of the parlor, she wouldn't have been able to raise an objection. "In a little room off the kitchen, but—"

"Show me," Jordan interrupted, and she led him back to where she slept.

"That'll never hold up," he said, eyeing the cot Amanda had spent the night on. With an inspired grin, he grabbed up the sleeping bag and pillow. "Now," he went on, grasping her hand again, "let's break in the bridal suite."

Amanda felt color rise in her cheeks, and she averted her eyes before leading the way around to the front of the house and up the stairs.

The best room faced the water and boasted its own fireplace, but it was unfurnished except for a large hooked rug centered in the middle of the floor.

Jordan spread the sleeping bag out on the rug and tossed the pillow carelessly on top of it, then stood watching Amanda with a mingling of humor and hunger in his eyes. "Come here, Mandy," he said with gentle authority.

She approached him shyly, because in some ways everything was new between them.

He slipped his hands beneath her T-shirt, resting them lightly on the sides of her waist; his hands were surprisingly warm.

"I love you, Amanda Scott," he told her firmly. "And in a month or a year or whenever you're ready, I'm going to make you my wife. Any objections?"

Amanda's lips were dry, and she wet them with her tongue. "None at all," she answered, and she drew in a sharp breath and closed her eyes as Jordan slid his hands up her sides to her breasts. With his thumbs he stroked her long-neglected nipples through the lacy fabric of her bra. When they stood erect, he pulled Amanda's T-shirt off over her head and tossed it aside.

"Let me look at you," he said, standing back a little.

Slowly, a little awkwardly, Amanda unhooked her bra and let it drop, revealing her full breasts. She let her hand fall back in ecstatic surrender as Jordan boldly closed his hands over her. When he bent his head and began to suckle at one pulsing nipple, she gave a little cry and entangled her hands in his hair.

He drew on both her breasts, one after the other, until she was half-delirious, and then he dropped to his knees on the sleeping bag and gently took Amanda's shoes from her feet. She started to sink down, needing union with him, but he grasped her hips and held her upright.

She bit down on her lower lip as she felt his finger beneath the waistband of her jeans. The snap gave way, and then the zipper, and then Amanda was bared to him, except for her panties and socks.

Her knees bent of their own accord, and her pelvis shifted forward as Jordan nipped at the hidden mound, all the time rolling one of her socks down. When her feet were bare, he pulled her panties down very slowly, and she kicked them aside impatiently, sure that Jordan would appease her now.

But he wasn't through tormenting her. He massaged the insides of her thighs, carefully avoiding the place that most needed his attention, and then lifted one of her knees and placed it over his shoulder.

Amanda was forced to link her hands behind his neck to keep from falling. "Oh," she whimpered as she realized what a vulnerable position she was in. "Jordan—"

He parted her with his fingers. "What?"

Her answer was cut off, and forced forever into the recesses of her mind when Jordan suddenly took her fully, greedily, into his mouth. She thrust her head back with the proud abandon of a tigress and gave a primitive groan that echoed in the empty room.

Jordan raised one hand to fondle her breast as he consumed her, and the two sensations combined to drive her to the very edge of sanity. She began to plead with him, and tug at the back of his shirt in a fruitless effort to strip him and feel his nakedness under her hands.

He lay back on the floor, bringing Amanda with him, and she rocked wildly in a shameless search for release while he moved his hands in gentle circles on her quivering belly. When he caught both her nipples between his fingers, Amanda's quest ended in a spectacular explosion that wrung a series of hoarse cries from her throat.

She sagged to the floor when it was over, only half-conscious, and Jordan arranged her on the sleeping bag before slowly removing his clothes. When he was naked, he tucked the pillow under her bottom and parted her knees, kneeling between them to tease her.

The back of one hand resting against her mouth, Amanda gave a soft moan. "Jordan—"

"Umm?" He gave her barely an inch of himself, but that was enough to arouse her all over again, to stir the fires he'd just banked. At the same time, he bent to sip at one of her nipples in a leisurely fashion.

Amanda groaned.

"What was that?" Jordan teased, barely pausing in his enjoyment of her breast.

"I want—oh, God, Jordan, please—I need you so much…"

He drew in a ragged breath, and she felt him tremble against the insides of her thighs as he gave her another inch.

She clutched at his arms, trying to pull him to her. "Jordan!" she wailed suddenly in utter desperation, and he gave her just a little more of himself.

Amanda couldn't wait any longer. She'd had release once, it was true, but her every instinct drove her toward complete fulfillment. She needed Jordan's weight, his substance, his force, and she needed it immediately.

With a fierce cry, she thrust her hips upward, taking him all the way inside her, and at that point Jordan's awesome control snapped.

Amanda watched through a haze of passion as he surrendered. Bracing his hands on the rug and arching his back, he withdrew and lunged into her again in a long, violent stroke, leaving no doubt as to the extent of his claim on her.

Triumph came at the peak of a sweet frenzy that tore a rasping shout from Jordan's throat and set Amanda's spirit to spiraling within her. For a few dizzying moments she was sure it would escape and soar off into the cosmos, leaving her body behind forever. The feeling passed, like a fever, and when Jordan fell to her, she was there to receive him.

He kissed her bare shoulder between gasps for air, and finally whispered, "Don't mind me. I'll be fine in a year or two."

Amanda's breath had just returned, and she laughed, moving her hands over his back in a gesture meant both to soothe and to claim. But her eyes were solemn when Jordan lifted his head to study her face a few moments later.

"Do you think it will take a long time for us to get things ironed out, Jordan?"

He kissed her forehead. "Judging by what just happened here, I'd say no."

"Good," she answered.

He traced the outline of her mouth with the tip of one finger. "Will you give me a baby, Mandy?" he asked huskily.

Her heart warmed within her, and seemed to grow larger. "Probably sooner than you think," she replied.

Jordan chuckled and drew her close to him, and they lay together for a long time, recovering. Remembering. Finally, he bent to kiss her once more before rising from her to reach for his clothes. He gave her a long look as she sat up and wrapped her arms around her knees, then sighed. "We've got a lot of talking to do," he said. "Now that there's some chance of concentrating, let's go over to my place and get started."

Amanda nodded and grabbed her jeans and panties. Because her things were scattered all over the rug, she wasn't able to dress as fast as Jordan, and he was brazen enough to watch her put on every garment.

Fifteen minutes later they pulled into his garage. When a blaze was snapping in the living room fireplace, they sat side by side on the floor in front of it, cross-legged and sipping wine.

Amanda started the conversation with a blunt but necessary question. "Are you still in love with Becky?"

Jordan considered her words solemnly and for a long time. "Not in the way you mean," he finally said, his eyes caressing Amanda he watched her reactions. "But I'll always care about her. It's just that I feel a different kind of love for her now. Sort of mellow and quiet and nostalgic."

Amanda nodded, then let her head rest against his shoulder. "In a way, she lives on in Jessie and Lisa."

Jordan sighed, watching the fire. He told her about the accident then, about feeling Becky's arms tighten around his waist in fear just before impact, about the pain, about being in the hospital when her funeral was held. "I felt responsible for her death for a long time," he said, "but I finally realized I was just using that as an excuse to go on mourning forever. Deep down inside, I knew it was really an accident."

Amanda gave him a hug.

"Thanks, Mandy," he said hoarsely.

She sat up straight to look at him. "For what?"

"For coming along when you did, and for being who you are. Until I met you, I didn't think love was an option for me."

The rain began to slacken in its seemingly incessant chatter on the roof and against the windows, and Amanda thought she saw a hint of sunshine glimmering at the edge of a distant cloud. She linked her arm through Jordan's and laid her temple to his shoulder, content just to be close to him.

Jordan intertwined his fingers with Amanda's, and his grip was strong and tight. With his other hand he tapped his wineglass against hers. "Here's to taking chances," he said softly.

The movers arrived on Monday, and so did the furniture Amanda had bought at the estate sale. She called in several plumbers for estimates on extra bathrooms, and that night she and Jordan and the girls sat around her kitchen table, eating chicken from a red-and-white striped bucket.

"I'm glad you didn't go to heaven," Jessie told Amanda, her dark eyes round and earnest.

"Me, too," Lisa put in, nibbling on a drumstick.

Amanda's gaze linked with Jordan's. "I could have sworn I visited there once," she said mysteriously.

Jordan gave her a look. "Dirty pool, lady," he accused.

"Uh-uh, Daddy," Jessie argued. "Amanda doesn't even *have* a pool."

"I stand corrected," Jordan told his daughter, but his eyes were on Amanda.

Tossing a denuded chicken bone onto her plate, Amanda stood up and bent to give greasy, top-of-the-head kisses to both Jessie and Lisa. "Thanks for being glad I'm around, gang," she told the girls in a conspiratorial whisper.

"You're welcome," Jessie replied.

Lisa was busy tilting the bucket to see if there was another drumstick inside.

Jordan watched Amanda with mischievous eyes as she dropped her plate into the trash and then leaned back against the sink with her arms folded.

"I suppose you people think I can't cook," she said.

No one offered a comment except for Gershwin, who came strolling into the kitchen with a cordial meow. The girls were delighted, and instantly abandoned what remained of their dinners to pet him.

When he realized he wasn't going to get any chicken, the cat wandered out of the room again. Jessie and Lisa were right behind him.

"Come here," Jordan said with just the hint of a grin.

"I've got no willpower at all where you're concerned," Amanda answered, allowing herself to be pulled onto his lap.

"Good. Will you marry me, Mandy?"

She tilted her head to one side. "Yes. But we agreed to wait, give things time—"

"We've had enough time. I love you, and that's never going to change."

Amanda kissed him. "If it's never going to change, then it won't matter if we wait."

He let his forehead fall against her breasts, pretending to be forlorn. "Do you know what it's going to do to me to go home tonight and leave you here?" he muttered.

She rested her chin on the top of his head. "You'll survive," she assured him. "I need a few months to get the business going, Jordan."

He sighed heavily. "Okay," he said with such a tone of martyrdom that Amanda laughed out loud.

Jordan repaid her by sliding a hand up under her shirt and cupping her breast.

Amanda squirmed and uttered a protest, but the steady strokes of his thumb across her nipple raised a fever in her. "We'll just have to be—flexible," she acquiesced with a sigh of supreme longing.

"We're not going to have much time alone together,"

Jordan warned, continuing his quiet campaign to drive her crazy. "Of course, if we were married, it would be perfectly natural for us to sleep together every night." He'd lifted one side of Amanda's bra so that her bare breast nestled in his hand.

"Jordan," Amanda whispered. "Stop it."

In the parlor, Amanda's television set came on, and the theme song of the girls' favorite sitcom filled the air. "A nuclear war wouldn't distract them from that show," Jordan said sleepily, lifting Amanda's T-shirt and closing his lips brazenly around her nipple.

She knew she should twist away, but the truth was, the most she could manage was to turn on Jordan's lap so that she could see the parlor doorway clearly. The position provided Jordan with better access to her breast, which he enjoyed without a hint of self-consciousness.

When he'd had enough, he righted her bra, pulled her shirt down and swatted her lightly on the bottom. "Well," he said with an exaggerated yawn, "it's a school night. I'd better take the girls home."

Amanda was indignant. "Jordan Richards, you deliberately got me worked up…"

He grinned and lifted her off his lap. "Yep," he confessed, rising from his chair and wandering idly in the direction of the parlor.

Flushed, Amanda flounced back and forth between the table and the trash can, disposing of the remains of dinner. After that, she wiped the table off in furious motions, and when she carried the dishcloth back to the sink, she realized Jordan was watching her with a twinkle in his eyes.

"In three days we could have a license," he said.

In the parlor, Jessie and Lisa laughed at some event

in their favorite program, and the sound lifted Amanda's heart. The children would always be Becky and Jordan's, but she loved them already, and she wanted to be a part of their lives almost as much as she wanted to be a part of their father's.

She walked slowly over to the man she loved and put her arms around his waist. "Okay, Jordan, you win. I want to be with you and the kids too much to wait any longer. But you'll have to be patient with me, because getting a new business off the ground takes a lot of time and energy."

His eyes danced with delight as he lifted one hand for a solemn oath. "I'll be patient if you will," he said.

Amanda bit down on her lower lip, worried. "I don't want to fail at this, Jordan."

He kissed her forehead. "We'll have to work at marriage, Mandy—just like everybody else does. But it'll last, I promise you."

"How can you be so sure?" she asked, watching his face for some sign of reservation or caution.

She saw only confidence and love. "The odds are in our favor," he answered, "and I'm taking the rest on faith."

It was September, and the maples and elms scattered between the evergreens across the road were turning to bright gold. They matched the lumbering yellow school bus that ground to a halt beside the sign that read Amanda's Place.

The bus door opened and Jessie bounded down the steps and leaped to the ground, then turned to catch hold of Lisa's hand and patiently help her down.

Amanda smiled and placed one hand on her distended

stomach, watching as her stepdaughters raced toward the house, their school papers fluttering in the autumn breeze.

"I made a house!" Lisa shouted, breathless with excitement as she raced ahead of her sister to meet Amanda on the step.

Amanda bent to properly examine the drawing Lisa had done in the afternoon kindergarten session. A crude square with windows represented the house, and there were four stick figures in front. "Here's me," Lisa said with a sniffle, pointing a pudgy little finger at the smallest form in the picture, "and here's Jessie and Daddy and you. I didn't draw the baby 'cause I don't know what he looks like."

Amanda kissed the child soundly on the forehead. "That's such a good picture that I'm going to put it up in the shop so everybody who comes in can admire it."

Lisa beamed at the prospect, sniffled again and toddled past Amanda and into the warm kitchen.

"How about you?" she asked Jessie, who had waited patiently on the bottom step for her turn. "Did you draw a picture, too?"

"I'm too big for that," Jessie said importantly. "I wrote the whole alphabet."

Putting an arm on the little girl's back, Amanda gently steered her into the kitchen. "Let's see," she said.

Jessie proudly extended the paper. "I already know enough to be in second grade," she said.

Amanda assessed the neatly printed letters marching smartly across Jessie's paper. "This is certainly one of the nicest papers I've ever seen," she said.

Jessie eyed her shrewdly. "Good enough to be in the shop like Lisa's picture?"

"Absolutely," Amanda replied. To prove her assertion, she strode through the big dining room, now completely furnished, and the large parlor, where Lisa was plunking on the piano, into the shop. Several of her quilts were displayed there, along with the work of many local craftspeople.

Her live-in manager, Millie Delano, was behind the cash register. It had been a slow day, but there were guests scheduled for the weekend, and the quilts and other items had sold extremely well over the summer. Amanda was making a go of her bed and breakfast, although it would be a long time before she got rich.

She held up both Lisa's picture and Jessie's printing for Millie's inspection. The pleasant middle-aged woman smiled broadly as Amanda made places for the papers on the bulletin board behind the counter and pinned them into place.

Jessie, who sometimes worried that her fondness for Amanda made her disloyal to her mother, beamed with pride.

The girls were settled in the kitchen, drinking milk and eating bananas, when Jordan arrived from the city. "Is my family ready to go home?" he asked, poking his head around the door.

Jessie and Lisa, who were always delighted to see him, whether he'd been away five minutes, five hours or five days, flung themselves at him with shrieks of welcome. Amanda, her hands resting on her protruding stomach, stood back, watching. Her eyes brimmed with tears as she thought how lucky she was to have the three of them filling her life with love and confusion and laughter.

After gently freeing himself from his daughters, Jordan walked over to Amanda and laid his hands on either side of her face. With his thumbs he brushed away her tears. "Hi, pregnant lady," he said. A quiet pride made Amanda's heart swell.

"Hi," she replied with a soft smile.

He gave her a leisurely kiss, then steered her toward the door. Her coat was hanging on a wooden peg nearby, and he helped her into it before handing Jessie and Lisa their jackets.

Amanda was struck again by the depth of her love for him when, in his tailored suit, he dropped to one knee to help Lisa with a jammed zipper. She couldn't have asked for a better father for her child than Jordan Richards.

When the hectic family project of preparing dinner was behind them, and Lisa and Jessie had had their baths, their stories and their good-night kisses, Jordan led Amanda into the living room. They sat on the sofa in front of a snapping fire, with their heads touching.

Jordan brought his hand to rest on Amanda's stomach, and when the baby kicked, his eyes were as bright as the flames on the hearth. Amanda couldn't help smiling.

He smoothed back a lock of her hair. "Tired?" he asked.

"Yes." Amanda sighed. "How about you?"

"Beat," Jordan replied. "Personally, I don't see that we have any choice but to go straight to bed."

Amanda laughed and thrust herself off the couch. "Last one there is a rotten egg!" she cried, waddling toward the stairs.

* * * * *

SECURITY BLANKET

Delores Fossen

To the Magnolia State Romance Writers.
Thanks for everything.

Chapter 1

The man was watching her.

Marin Sheppard was sure of it.

He wasn't staring, exactly. In fact, he hadn't even looked at her, though he'd been seated directly across from her in the lounge car of the train for the past fifteen minutes. He seemed to focus his attention on the wintry Texas landscape that zipped past the window. But several times Marin had met his gaze in the reflection of the glass.

Yes, he was watching her.

That kicked up her heart rate a couple of notches. A too-familiar nauseating tightness started to knot Marin's stomach.

Was it starting all over again?

Was he watching her, hoping that she'd lead him to her brother, Dexter? Or was this yet another attempt by her parents to insinuate themselves into her life?

It'd been over eight months since the last time this happened. A former "business associate" of her brother who was riled that he'd paid for a "product" that Dexter hadn't delivered. The man had followed her around Fort Worth for days. He hadn't been subtle about it, either, and that had made him seem all the more menacing. And she hadn't given birth to Noah yet then.

The stakes were so much higher now.

Marin hugged her sleeping son closer to her chest. He smelled like baby shampoo and the rice cereal he'd had for lunch. She brushed a kiss on his forehead and rocked gently. Not so much for him—Noah was sound asleep and might stay that way for the remaining hour of the trip to San Antonio. No, the rocking, the kiss and the snug embrace were more for her benefit, to help steady her nerves.

And it worked.

"Cute kid," she heard someone say. The man across from her. Who else? There were no other travelers in this particular section of the lounge car.

Marin lifted her gaze. Met his again. But this time it wasn't through the buffer of the glass, and she clearly saw his eyes, a blend of silver and smoke, framed with indecently long, dark eyelashes.

She studied him a moment, trying to decide if she knew him. He was on the lanky side. Midnight-colored hair. High cheekbones. A classically chiseled male jaw.

The only thing that saved him from being a total pretty boy was the one-inch scar angled across his right eyebrow, thin but noticeable. Not a precise surgeon's cut, a jagged, angry mark left from an old injury. It conjured images of barroom brawls, tattooed bikers and bashed beer bottles. Not that Marin had firsthand knowledge of such things.

But she would bet that he did.

He wore jeans that fit as if they'd been tailor-made for

him, a dark blue pullover shirt that hugged his chest and a black leather bomber jacket. And snakeskin boots—specifically diamondback rattlesnake. Pricey and conspicuous footwear.

No, she didn't know him. Marin was certain she would have remembered him—a realization that bothered her because he was hot, and she was sorry she'd noticed.

He tipped his head toward Noah. "I meant your baby," he clarified. "Cute kid."

"Thank you." She looked away from the man, hoping it was the end of their brief conversation.

It wasn't.

"He's what…seven, eight months old?"

"Eight," she provided.

"He reminds me a little of my nephew," the man continued. "It must be hard, traveling alone with a baby."

That brought Marin's attention racing across the car. What had provoked that remark? She searched his face and his eyes almost frantically, trying to figure out if it was some sort of veiled threat.

He held up his hands, and a nervous laugh sounded from deep within his chest. "Sorry. Didn't mean to alarm you. It's just I noticed you're wearing a medical alert bracelet."

Marin glanced down at her left wrist. The almond-shaped metal disc was peeking out from the cuff of her sleeve. With its classic caduceus symbol engraved in crimson, it was like his boots—impossible to miss.

"I'm epileptic," she said.

"Oh." Concern dripped from the word.

"Don't worry," she countered. "I keep my seizures

under control with meds. I haven't had one in over five years."

She immediately wondered why in the name of heaven she'd volunteered that personal information. Her medical history wasn't any of his business; it was a sore spot she didn't want to discuss.

"Is your epilepsy the reason you took the train?" he asked. "I mean, instead of driving?"

Marin frowned at him. "I thought the train would make the trip easier for my son."

He nodded, apparently satisfied with her answer to his intrusive question. When his attention strayed back in the general direction of her bracelet, Marin followed his gaze. Down to her hand. All the way to her bare ring finger.

Even though her former fiancé, Randall Davidson, had asked her to marry him, he'd never given her an engagement ring. It'd been an empty, bare gesture. A thought that riled her even now. Randall's betrayal had cut her to the bone.

Shifting Noah into the crook of her arm, she reached down to collect her diaper bag. "I think I'll go for a little walk and stretch my legs."

And change seats, she silently added.

Judging from the passengers she'd seen get on and off, the train wasn't crowded, so moving into coach seating shouldn't be a problem. In fact, she should have done it sooner.

"I'm sorry," he said. "I made you uncomfortable with my questions."

His words stopped her because they were sincere. Or at least he sounded that way. Of course, she'd been wrong before. It would take another lifetime or two for her to trust her instincts.

And that was the reason she reached for the bag again.

"Stay, *please*," he insisted. "It'll be easier for me to move." He got up, headed for the exit and then stopped, turning back around to face her. "I was hitting on you."

Marin blinked. "You…what?"

"Hitting on you," he clarified.

Oh.

That took her a few moments to process.

"Really?" Marin asked, sounding far more surprised than she wanted.

He chuckled, something low, husky and male. Something that trickled through her like expensive warm whiskey. "Really." But then, the lightheartedness faded from his eyes, and his jaw muscles started to stir. "I shouldn't have done it. Sorry."

Again, he seemed sincere. So maybe he wasn't watching her after all. Well, not for surveillance any way. Maybe he was watching her because she was a woman. Odd, that she'd forgotten all about basic human attraction and lust.

"You don't have to leave," Marin let him know. Because she suddenly didn't know what to do with her fidgety hands, she ran her fingers through Noah's dark blond curls. "Besides, it won't be long before we're in San Antonio."

He nodded, and it had an air of thankfulness to it. "I'm Quinn Bacelli. Most people though just call me Lucky."

She almost gave him a fake name. Old habits. But it was the truth that came out of her mouth. "Marin Sheppard."

He smiled. It was no doubt a lethal weapon in his arsenal of ways to get women to fall at his feet. Or into his bed. It bothered Marin to realize that she wasn't immune to it.

Good grief. Hadn't her time with Randall taught her anything?

"Well, Marin Sheppard," he said, taking his seat again. "No more hitting on you. Promise."

Good. She mentally repeated that several times, and then wondered why she felt mildly disappointed.

Noah stirred, sucked at a nonexistent bottle and then gave a pouty whimper when he realized it wasn't there. His eyelids fluttered open, and he blinked, focused and looked up at Marin with accusing blue-green eyes that were identical to her own. He made another whimper, probably to let her know that he wasn't pleased about having his nap interrupted.

Her son shifted and wriggled until he was in a sitting position in her lap, and the new surroundings immediately caught his attention. What was left of his whimpering expression evaporated. He examined his puppy socks, the window, the floor, the ceiling and the ruby-red exit sign. Even her garnet heart necklace. Then, his attention landed on the man seated across from him.

Noah grinned at him.

The man grinned back. "Did you have a good nap, buddy?"

Noah babbled a cordial response, something the two males must have understood, because they shared another smile.

Marin looked at Quinn "Lucky" Bacelli. Then, at her son. Their smiles seemed to freeze in place.

There was no warning.

A deafening blast ripped through the car.

One moment Marin was sitting on the seat with her son cradled in her arms, and the next she was flying across the narrow space right at Lucky.

Everything moved fast. So fast. And yet it happened in slow motion, too. It seemed part of some nightmarish dream where everything was tearing apart at the seams.

Debris spewed through the air. The diaper bag, the magazine she'd been reading, the very walls themselves. All of it, along with Noah and her.

Something slammed into her back and the left side of her head. It knocked the breath from her. The pain was instant—searing—and it sliced right through her, blurring her vision.

She and Noah landed in Lucky's arms, propelled against him. But he softened the fall. He turned, immediately, pushing them down against the seat and crawling over them so he could shelter them with his body. Still, the debris pelted her legs and her head. She felt the sting of the cuts on her skin and reached out for something, anything, to use as protection. Her fingers found the diaper bag, and she used it to block the shards so they wouldn't hit Noah.

The train's brakes screamed. Metal scraped against metal. The crackle and scorched smell of sparks flying, shouts of terror, smoke and dust filled the air.

Amid all the chaos, she heard her baby cry.

Noah was terrified, and his shrill piercing wail was a plea for help.

Marin tried to move him so she could see his face, so she could make sure he was all right, but her peripheral vision blurred. It closed in, like thick fog, nearly blinding her.

"Help my son," she begged. She couldn't bear his cries. They echoed in her head. Like razor-sharp daggers. Cutting right through her.

Sweet heaven, was he hurt?

There was some movement, and she felt Lucky maneuver his hand between them. "He's okay, I think."

His qualifier nearly caused Marin to scream right along with her son. "Please, help him."

Because she had no choice, because the pain was unbearable, Marin dropped her head against the seat. The grayness got darker. Thicker. The pain just kept building. Throbbing. Consuming her.

And her son continued to cry.

That was the worst pain of all—her son crying.

Somehow she had to help him.

She tried to move again, to see his face, but her body no longer responded to what she was begging it to do. It was as if she were spiraling downward into a bottomless dark pit. Her breath was thin, her heartbeat barely a whisper in her ears. And her mouth was filled with the metallic taste of her own blood.

God, was she dying?

The thought broke her heart. She wasn't scared to die. But her death would leave her son vulnerable. Unprotected.

That couldn't happen.

"You can't let them take Noah," she heard herself whisper. She was desperate now, past desperate, and if necessary she would resort to begging.

"Who can't take him?" Lucky asked. He sounded so far away, but the warmth of his weight was still on her. She could feel his frantic breath gusting against her face.

"My parents." Marin wanted to explain that they were

toxic people, that she didn't want them anywhere near her precious son. But there seemed so little breath left in her body, and she needed to tell him something far more important. "If I don't make it..."

"You will," he insisted.

Marin wasn't sure she believed that. "If I don't make it, get Noah out of here." She had to take a breath before she could continue. "Protect him." She coughed as she pulled the smoke and ash into her lungs. "Call Lizette Raines in Fort Worth. She'll know what to do."

Marin listened for a promise that he would do just that. And maybe Lucky Bacelli made that promise. Maybe he spoke to her, or maybe it was just her imagination when the softly murmured words filtered through the unbearable pain rifling in her head.

I swear, I'll protect him.

She wanted to see her son's face. She wanted to give him one last kiss.

But that didn't happen.

The grayness overtook her, and Marin felt her world fade to nothing.

Chapter 2

Working frantically, Lucky slung off the debris that was covering Marin Sheppard and her son.

No easy feat.

There was a lot of it, including some shards of glass and splintered metal, and he had to dig them out while trying to keep a firm grip on Noah. Not only was the baby screaming his head off, he wriggled and squirmed, obviously trying to get away from the nightmare.

Unfortunately, they were trapped right in the middle of it.

"You're okay, buddy," Lucky said to the baby. He hoped that was true.

Lucky quickly checked, but didn't see any obvious injuries. Heck, not even a scratch, which almost certainly qualified as a miracle.

As he'd seen Marin do, Lucky brushed a kiss on the boy's cheek to reassure him. Though it wasn't much help. Noah might have only been eight months old, but he no doubt knew something was horribly wrong.

This was no simple train derailment. An explosion.

An accident, maybe. Perhaps some faulty electrical component caused it. Or an act of terrorism.

The thought sickened him.

Whatever the cause, the explosion had caused a lot of damage. And a fire. Lucky could feel the flames and the heat eating their way toward them. There wasn't much time. A couple of minutes, maybe less.

And even then, getting out wasn't guaranteed.

They couldn't go through the window. There were jagged, thick chunks of glass still locked in place in the metal frame. It wouldn't be easy to kick out the remaining glass, and it'd cut them to shreds if he tried to go through it with Noah and Marin, especially since she was unconscious. Still, he might have to risk it. Lucky had no idea what he was going to face once he left the car and went into the hall toward the exit.

Maybe there was no exit left.

Maybe there was no other way out.

"Open your eyes, Marin," he said when he finally made it through the debris to her.

Oh, man.

There wasn't a drop of color in her face. And the blood. There was way too much of it, and it all seemed to be coming from a wound on the left side of her head. The blood had already seeped into her dark blond hair, staining one side of it crimson red.

"Look at me, Marin!" Lucky demanded.

She didn't respond.

Lucky shoved his fingers to her neck. It took him several snail-crawling moments to find her pulse. Weak but steady.

Thank God, she was alive.

For now.

But he didn't like the look of that gash on her head. Since she was breathing, there was no reason for him to do CPR, but he tried to revive her by gently tapping her face. It didn't work, and he knew he couldn't waste any more time.

Soon, very soon, the train would be engulfed in flames, and their chances of escape would be slim to none. They could be burned alive. He wasn't about to let that happen to her or the precious cargo in his arms. He'd made a promise to protect Noah, and that was a promise he intended to keep.

Moving Marin could make her injuries worse, but it was a risk he had to take. Placing Noah on her chest and stomach, he scooped them both up in his arms and hugged them tightly against him so that Noah wouldn't fall. Noah obviously wasn't pleased about that arrangement because he screamed even louder.

Lucky kicked aside a chunk of the displaced wall, and hurrying, he went through what was left of the doorway that divided the lounge car from the rest of the train. A blast of thick smoke shot right at him. He ducked his head down, held his breath and started running.

The hall through coach seating was an obstacle course. There was wreckage, smoke and at least a dozen other passengers also trying to escape. It was a stampede, and he was caught in the middle with Noah and Marin.

The crowd fought and shoved, all battering against each other. All fighting to get toward the end of the car. And they finally made it. Lucky broke through the emergency exit and launched himself into the fresh air.

Landing hard and probably twisting his ankle in the process, he didn't stop. He knew all too well that there could be a secondary explosion, one even worse than the first, so he carried Noah and Marin to a clear patch about thirty yards from the train.

The November wind was bitter cold, but his lungs were burning from the exertion. So were the muscles in his arms and legs. He had to fight to hold on to his breath. The air held the sickening smell of things that were never meant to be burned.

He lay Marin and Noah down on the dried winter grass beside him, but Noah obviously intended to be with Lucky. He clamped his chubby little arms around Lucky's neck and held on, gripping him in a vise.

"You're okay," Lucky murmured. And because he didn't know what else to say, he repeated it.

To protect Noah from the wind and cold, Lucky tucked him inside his leather jacket and zipped it up as far as he could. Noah didn't protest. But he did look up at him, questioning him with tear-filled eyes. That look, those tears broke Lucky's heart. It was a look that would haunt him for the rest of his life.

"Your mom's going to be all right," Lucky whispered.

He prayed that was true.

Lucky pulled Marin closer so his body heat would keep her warm, and used his hand and shirt sleeve as a compress. He applied some gentle pressure against her injured head, hoping it would slow the bleeding. She didn't move when he touched her, not even a twitch.

He heard the first wail of ambulance sirens. Already close. Thankfully, they were just on the outskirts of Austin so the response time would be quick. The firefighters wouldn't be far behind. Lucky knew the drill. They'd set up a triage system, and the passengers with the most severe, but treatable injuries would be seen first. That meant Marin. She'd get the medical attention she needed.

"You're going to stay alive, Marin," Lucky ordered. "You hear me? Stay alive. The medics are on the way. Listen to the sirens. Listen! They're getting closer. They'll be here in just a few minutes."

Noah volleyed uncertain glances between Lucky and his mother. He stuck out his quivering bottom lip. For a moment Lucky thought the little boy might burst into tears again, but he didn't. Maybe the shock and adrenaline caught up with him, because even though his eyes watered, he stuck his thumb in his mouth and snuggled against Lucky.

It wasn't a sensation Lucky had counted on.

But it was a damn powerful one.

What was left of his breath vanished, and feelings went through him that he'd never experienced. Feelings he couldn't even identify except for the fact that they brought out every protective instinct in his body.

"What are your injuries?" Lucky heard someone shout. He looked up and saw a pair of medics racing toward him. They weren't alone. More were running toward some of the other passengers.

"We're not hurt. But she is," Lucky said pulling back his hand from Marin's injured head.

The younger of the two, a dark-haired woman, didn't take Lucky's word about not being injured. She began to examine Noah and him. Noah whined and tried to bat her hands away when she checked his pupils. The other medic, a fortysomething Hispanic man, went to work on Marin.

"She's Code Yellow," the medic barked to his partner. "Head trauma."

That started a flurry of activity, and the woman yelled for a stretcher.

Code Yellow. Marin's condition was urgent, but she was likely to survive.

"I need your name," the female medic insisted, forcing his attention back to her. "And the child's."

Lucky's stomach clenched.

It was a simple request. And it was standard operating procedure for triage processing. But Lucky knew it was only the beginning of lots of questions. If he answered some of those questions, especially the part about Noah being a near stranger, they'd take the little boy right out of his arms, and the authorities would hold on to him until they could contact the next of kin.

The very thing that Marin didn't want to happen.

Because her parents and her brother, Dexter, were Noah's next of kin.

Some choice.

As if he understood what was going on, Noah looked up at him with those big blue-green eyes. There were no questions. No doubts. Not even a whimper.

But there was trust. Complete, unconditional trust.

Noah's eyelids fluttered down, his thumb went back in his mouth, and he rested his cheek against Lucky's heart.

Oh, man.

It seemed like some symbolic gesture, but it probably had more to do with the kid's sheer exhaustion than anything else. Still, Lucky couldn't push it aside. Nor could he push aside what Marin had asked of him when they'd been trying to stay alive.

If I don't make it, get Noah out of here. Protect him.

And in that crazy life-or-death moment, Lucky had promised her that he would do just that.

It was a promise he'd keep.

"Sir," the medic prompted. "I need you to tell me the child's name."

It took Lucky a moment to say anything. "I'm Randall Davidson. This is my son, Noah," he lied. He tipped his head toward Marin. "And she's my fiancé, Marin Sheppard."

In order to protect the frightened little boy in his arms, Lucky figured he'd have to continue that particular lie for an hour or two until Marin regained consciousness or until he could call her friend in Fort Worth. Not long at all, considering his promise.

He owed Noah and Marin that much.

And he might owe them a hell of a lot more.

Chapter 3

Marin heard someone say her name.

It was a stranger's voice.

She wondered if it was real or all part of the relentless nightmare she'd been having. A nightmare of explosions and trains. At least, she thought it might be a train. The only clear image that kept going through her mind was of a pair of snakeskin boots. Everything else was a chaotic blur of sounds and smells and pain. Mostly pain. There were times when it was unbearable.

"Marin?" she heard the strange voice say again.

It was a woman. She sounded real, and Marin thought she might have felt someone gently touch her cheek.

She tried to open her eyes and failed the first time, but then tried again. She was instantly sorry that she'd succeeded. The bright overhead lights stabbed right into her eyes and made her wince.

Marin groaned.

Just like that, with a soft click, the lights went away. "Better?" the woman asked.

Marin managed a nod that hurt, as well.

The dimmed lighting helped, but her head was still throbbing, and it seemed as if she had way too many nerves in that particular part of her body. The pain was also affecting her vision. Everything was out of focus.

"Where am I?" Marin asked.

Since her words had no sound, she repeated them. It took her four tries to come up with a simple audible three-word question. Quite an accomplishment though, considering her throat was as dry as west Texas dust.

"St. Mary's," the woman provided.

Marin stared at her, her gaze moving from the woman's pinned-up auburn hair to her perky cotton-candy-pink uniform. Her name tag said she was Betty Garcia, RN. That realization caused Marin to glance around the room.

"I'm in a hospital?" Marin licked her lips. They were dry and chapped.

"Yes. You don't remember being brought here?"

Marin opened her mouth to answer, only to realize that she didn't have an answer. Until a few seconds ago, she'd thought she was having a nightmare. She definitely didn't remember being admitted to a hospital.

"Are you real?" Marin asked, just to make sure she wasn't trapped in the dream.

The woman smiled. "I'm going to assume that's not some sort of philosophical question. Yes, I'm real. And so are you." She checked the machine next to the bed. "How do you feel?"

Marin made a quick assessment. "I feel like someone bashed me in the head."

The woman made a sound of agreement. "Not someone. *Something.* But you're better now. You don't remember the train accident?"

"The accident," Marin repeated, trying to sort through the images in her head.

"It's still under investigation," the nurse continued. She touched Marin's arm. "But the authorities think there was some kind of electrical malfunction that caused the explosion."

An explosion. She remembered that.

Didn't she?

"Thankfully, no one was killed," the woman went on. She picked up Marin's wrist and took her pulse. "But over a dozen people were hurt, including you."

It was the word *hurt* that made the memories all come flooding back. The call from her grandmother, telling Marin that she was sick and begging her to come home. The train trip from Fort Worth to San Antonio.

The explosion.

God, the explosion.

"Noah!" Marin shouted. "Where's my son?"

Marin jackknifed to a sitting position, and she would have launched herself out of the bed if Nurse Garcia and the blinding pain hadn't stopped her.

"Easy now," the nurse murmured. She released her grip on Marin's wrist and caught on to her shoulders instead, easing her down onto the mattress.

Marin cooperated, but only because she had no choice. "My son—"

"Is fine. He wasn't hurt. He didn't even get a scratch."

The relief was as overwhelming as the pain. Noah was all right. The explosion that had catapulted them through the air had obviously hurt her enough that she needed to be hospitalized, but her son had escaped unharmed.

Marin considered that a moment.

How had he escaped?

A clear image of Lucky Bacelli came into her head.

The man she'd been certain was following her. He'd promised to get Noah out, and apparently he had.

"I want to see Noah," Marin insisted. "Could you bring him to me now?"

Nurse Garcia stared at her, and the calm serenity that had been in her coffee-colored eyes quickly faded to concern. "Your son's not here."

Marin was sure there was some concern in her own eyes, as well. "But—"

"Do you have any idea how long you've been in the hospital?" the nurse interrupted.

Marin opened her mouth, closed it and considered the question. She finally shook her head. "How long?"

"Nearly two days."

"Days?" Not hours. Marin was sure it'd only been a few hours. Or maybe she was simply hoping it had been. "So where is he? Who's had my baby all this time?" But the moment she asked, the fear shot through her. "Not my parents. Please don't tell me he's with them."

A very unnerving silence followed, and Nurse Garcia's forehead bunched up.

That did it.

Marin pushed aside the nurse's attempts to restrain her and tried to get out of the bed. It wasn't easy, nowhere close, but she fought through the pain and wooziness and forced herself to stand up.

She didn't stay vertical long.

Marin's legs turned boneless, and she had no choice but to slouch back down on the bed.

"There isn't any reason for you to worry," the nurse assured her. "Your son is okay."

Marin gasped for breath so she could speak. "Yes, so you've said. But who has him?"

"Your fiancé, of course. His father."

What breath she'd managed to regain, Marin instantly lost. "His…father?"

Nurse Garcia nodded, smiling. The bunched up forehead was history.

Marin experienced no such calmness. Adrenaline and fear hit her like a heavyweight's punch.

Noah's father was dead. He was killed in a boating accident nearly eight months before Noah was even born. There was no way he could be here.

"Your fiancé should be arriving any minute," the nurse cheerfully added.

Nothing could have kept Marin in the bed. Ignoring the nurse's protest and the weak muscles in her legs, Marin got up and went in search of her clothes. But even if she had to leave the hospital in her gown, she intended to get out of there and see what was going on.

Nurse Garcia caught on to her arm. Her expression changed, softened. "Everything's okay. There's no need for you to panic."

Oh, yes, there was. Either Randall had returned from the grave or something was terribly wrong. Noah had no father, and she had no fiancé.

There was a knock at the door. One soft rap before it opened. The jeans, the black leather jacket. The boots.

Lucky Bacelli.

Not Randall.

"Where's Noah?" she demanded.

Lucky ignored her question and strolled closer. "You gave me quite a scare, you know that? I'm glad you're finally awake." And with that totally irrelevant observation, he smiled. A secretive little smile that only he and Mona Lisa could have pulled off.

"I want to see Noah," Marin snapped. "And I want to see him now."

Another smile caused a dimple to wink in his left cheek. He reached out, touched her right arm and rubbed softly. A gesture no doubt meant to soothe her. It didn't work. For one thing, it was too intimate. Boy, was it. For another, nothing would soothe her except for holding her son and making sure he was okay.

"The doctor wants to examine you before he allows any other visitors so Noah's waiting at the nurses' station," Lucky explained, his voice a slow, easy drawl. The sound and ease of Texas practically danced off the words. "And I'm sure they're spoiling him rotten."

Marin disregarded the last half of his comment. Her son was at the nurses' station. That's all she needed to know. She ducked around Lucky and headed toward the door. Marin had no idea where the nurses' station was, but she'd find it.

Lucky stepped in front of her, blocking her path. "Where are you going, darling?"

That stopped her in her tracks.

Darling?

He said it as if he had a right to.

That was well past being intimate. Then he slid his arm around her waist and leaned in close. Too close. It violated her personal space and then some. Marin slapped her palm on his chest to stop him from violating it further.

"Is there a problem?" Nurse Garcia asked.

"You bet there is," Marin informed her.

And she would have voiced exactly what that problem was if she'd had the chance.

She hadn't.

Because in that same moment, Lucky Bacelli curved his hand around her waist and gently pulled her closer to him. He put his mouth right against her ear. "This was the only way," he whispered.

Marin tried to move away, but he held on. "The only way for what?" she demanded.

"To keep you and Noah safe." He kept his voice low, practically a murmur.

Even with the pain and fog in her head and his barely audible voice, she understood what he meant. Lucky had needed to protect Noah from her parents, just as she'd asked him to do. He'd pretended to be Randall Davidson, a dead man. Marin couldn't remember how Lucky had known Randall's name. Had she mentioned it? She must have. Thankfully, her parents had never met Randall and knew almost nothing about him. They certainly didn't know he was dead. She'd kept that from them because if she'd explained his death, she would have also had to endure countless questions about their life together.

Marin stopped struggling to get away from him and wearily dropped her head on his shoulder. He'd lied, but he'd done it all for Noah's sake. "My parents tried to take him?"

Lucky nodded. "They tried and failed. But I'm pretty sure they'll be back soon for round two."

That wasn't a surprise. With her in a hospital bed, her parents had probably thought they could take over her life before she even regained consciousness. It'd been a miracle that Lucky had been able to stop them, and if he'd had to do that with lies, then it was a small price to pay for her to be able to keep her son from them.

"Thank you," Marin mouthed.

"Don't thank me." Lucky moved back enough to allow their gazes to connect. The gray in his eyes turned stormy. "I don't think that train accident was really an accident," he whispered.

Stunned, Marin shook her head. "What do you mean?"

It seemed as if he changed his mind a dozen times about what to say. "Marin, Noah and you were nearly killed because of me."

Chapter 4

Lucky braced himself for the worst. A slap to the face. A shouted accusation. But Marin just stepped back and stared at him.

"What did you say?" she asked. Lucky wasn't sure how she managed to speak. The air swooshed out of her body, and the muscles in her jaw turned to steel.

Lucky didn't repeat his bombshell. Nor did he explain. He glanced over at the nurse. "Could you please give me a few minutes alone with my fiancée?"

Nurse Garcia nodded. "But only if Ms. Sheppard gets back in bed."

"Of course." Lucky caught on to Marin to lead her in that direction, but he encountered some resistance. Their eyes met, and in the depth of all that blue and green, he saw the debate going on. He also saw the moment she surrendered.

He knew she expected her cooperation to get her some fast answers. Unfortunately, Lucky didn't have any answers that she was going to like.

"You have five minutes. I don't want Ms. Sheppard

getting too tired," the nurse informed them. "I'll see if I can figure out a way to get Noah in here so you can have a quick kiss and cuddle."

"Thank you," Marin told the woman without taking her gaze from Lucky. She didn't say another word until the nurse was out of the room.

"Start talking," Marin insisted, her voice low and laced with a warning. "What do you mean you're responsible for nearly getting us killed? The nurse said it was an accident. Caused by an electrical malfunction."

That warning was the only thing lethal looking about her. She was pale and trembling. Lucky got her moving toward the bed. He also gave her gown an adjustment so that it actually covered her bare backside. Then, he got on with his explanation.

"The police first believed the explosion was caused by something electrical," Lucky explained. "But there are significant rumblings that when the Texas Rangers came in, they found an incendiary device."

But that was more than just rumblings. The sheriff had confirmed it.

Which brought him back to Marin's question.

"I'm a PI. And a former cop," he told her. With just those few crumbs of info, he had to pause and figure out how to say the rest. Best not to give Marin too much too soon. She was still weak. But he owed her at least part of the truth. "I've been working on a case that involves some criminals in hiding."

Well, one criminal in particular. That was a detail he'd keep to himself for now.

"I think someone associated with the case I'm investigating might have set that explosive," Lucky explained.

"I believe there are people who don't want me to learn the truth about a woman who was murdered."

He waited for her reaction.

Marin paused, taking a deep breath. "I see."

Those two little words said a lot. They weren't an accusation. More like reluctant acceptance. He supposed that was good. It meant she might not slap him for endangering her son. Too bad. Lucky might have felt better if she *had* slapped him.

"The authorities know the explosion might be connected to you?" she asked.

"They know. The train was going through LaMesa Springs when the explosives went off. The sheriff there, Beck Tanner, is spearheading the initial investigation. He's already questioned me, and I told him about the case I was working on."

Sheriff Tanner would likely question Marin, too. Before that, Lucky would have to tell her the whole truth about why he was really on that train.

And the whole truth was guaranteed to make her slap him.

Or worse.

Marin looked down at her hands and brushed her fingers over her scraped knuckles. "The explosion wasn't your fault," she concluded. "You were just doing your job. And I put you in awkward position by asking you to protect Noah." She lifted her head. "I don't regret that. I can't."

Lucky pulled the chair next to her bed closer and sat down so they were at eye level. But they were still a safe distance from each other. Touching her was out. Her weakness and vulnerability clouded his mind.

And touching her would cloud his body.

He didn't need either.

"Yeah. After I met your parents, I totally understood why you asked me to take care of your little guy," Lucky continued. "Though at the time I thought I'd only have to keep that promise for an hour or two."

She nodded. "And then I didn't regain consciousness right away."

That was just the first of several complications.

"Like you asked, I tried getting in touch with your friend, Lizette Raines, in Fort Worth. She didn't answer her home phone, so I finally called someone I knew in the area and asked him to check on her. According to the neighbors, she's on a short trip to Mexico with her boyfriend."

Marin groaned softly. "Yes. She met him about two months ago, and I knew things were getting more serious, but she didn't mention anything about a trip."

She ran her fingers through the side of her shoulder-length hair and winced when she encountered the injury that had caused her concussion and the coma. In addition to the bandage that covered several stitches, her left temple was bruised—and the purplish stain bled all the way down to her cheekbone. It sickened him to see that on her face, to know what she'd been through.

And to know that it wasn't over.

This—whatever this was—was just beginning, and Lucky didn't care much for the bad turn it'd taken on that train.

"I wonder why Lizette didn't call me," Marin said. "She has my cell number."

"Your phone was lost in the explosion so even if she'd tried that number, she wouldn't have gotten you. Don't worry. Your friend's trip sounded legit, and none of your neighbors are concerned."

Before Lucky could continue, the door flew open, and a couple walked in. Not the nurse with Noah, but two people that Lucky had already met. And they were two people he had quickly learned to detest.

Marin's parents, Lois and Howard Sheppard.

The unexpected visit brought both him and Marin to their feet. It wasn't a fluid movement for Marin. She wobbled a bit when she got out of bed, and he slid his arm around her waist so she could keep her balance.

Lucky so wished he'd had time to prepare Marin for this. Of course, there was no preparation for the kind of backstabbing she was about to encounter.

"Mother," Marin said. Because she was pressed right against him, Lucky felt her muscles tense. She pulled in a long, tight breath.

No frills. That was the short physical description for the petite woman who strolled toward them. A simple maroon dress. Matching heels. Matching purse. Heck, even her lipstick matched. There wasn't a strand of her graying blond hair out of place. Lois Sheppard looked like the perfect TV mom.

She hurried toward Marin and practically elbowed Lucky out of the way so she could hug her daughter. When Lois pulled back, her eyes were shiny with tears.

"It's so good to see you, sweetheart," Lois said, her voice weepy and soft.

Marin stepped back out of her mother's embrace.

The simple gesture improved Lois's posture. "Marin, that's no way to act. Honestly, you'd think you have no manners. Aren't you even going to say hello to your father?"

"Hello," Marin echoed.

And judging from Marin's near growling tone, she didn't like her dad any better than Lucky did. Unlike Lois, Howard had a slick oily veneer that reminded Lucky of con artists and dishonest used car salesmen. Of course, his opinion probably had something to do with this whole backstabbing mission.

"Mother, why are you and Dad here?"

Lois shrugged as if the answer were obvious. "Because we love you. Because we're concerned about you. You're coming back to the ranch with us so you can have time to recuperate from your injuries. You know you're not well enough or strong enough to be on your own. You never have been. Clearly, leaving home was a mistake."

Lucky pulled Marin tighter into the crook of his arm.

"I'm not going with you," she informed her mother.

Lucky wanted to cheer her backbone, but he already knew the outcome of this little encounter.

There'd be no cheering today.

"Yes, you are," Lois disagreed. "I'm sorry, but I can't give you a choice about that. You and Noah are too important to us. And because we love you both so much, we've filed papers."

Lucky felt Marin's muscles stiffen even more. "What kind of papers?" Marin enunciated each syllable.

Lucky didn't wait for Lois Sheppard to provide the explanation. "Your folks are trying to use your hospital stay and your epilepsy to get custody of Noah." He turned his attention to Lois and made sure he smirked. "Guess what—not gonna happen."

The woman's maroon-red mouth tightened into a temporary bud. "I don't think you'll have much of a say in that, Randall."

"Lucky," he corrected. Because by damn he might have to play the part of Marin's slimeball ex, but Lucky refused to use the man's name. It'd been a godsend that neither of Marin's parents had ever met said slimeball. If they had, the charade of Lucky pretending to be him would have been over before it even started.

"I don't care what you call yourself," Howard interceded. "You're an unfit father. You weren't even there for the birth of your own son. You left Marin alone to fend for herself."

Lucky shoved his thumb to his chest. "Well, I'm here now."

"Are you?" Howard challenged.

"What the hell does that mean?" Lucky challenged right back.

Howard didn't answer right away, and the silence intensified with his glare. "It means I don't think you love my daughter. I think this so-called relationship between you two is a sham to convince Lois and me that we don't need to intervene in Marin's life."

Since that was the truth, Lucky knew it was time for some damage control. Later, he'd figure out if Howard really knew something or if this was a bluff.

Lucky pulled Marin closer to him. Body against body. Marin must have felt the same need for damage control because she came up on her toes and kissed him, a familiar peck of reassurance. Something a real couple would have shared.

That brief lip-lock speared through him, causing Lucky to remind himself that this really was a sham.

"What papers have they filed?" Marin asked him.

Lucky didn't take his gaze from Howard. "Your parents convinced a judge to review your competency as a parent. A crooked judge is my guess, because we have to go to your parents' ranch for an interview with a psychologist."

Lucky expected Marin to lose it then and there. Maybe a tirade or some profanity. He wouldn't have blamed her if she had. But her reaction was almost completely void of emotion.

"Mother, Dad, you're leaving now," Marin said. And she stepped out of Lucky's arms and sat back down on the bed. A moment passed before she looked at her mother again. "I'm tired. I need my rest. Nurse's orders."

Lois took a step closer, and even though she wasn't smiling, there was a certain victory shout in her stance. "If you don't return to the ranch and do this interview with the psychologist, the judge will intervene. Noah will be taken from you and placed in our custody."

And with that threat, Lois and Howard finally did what Marin had asked. They turned and walked out the door.

All that cool and calmness that Marin had displayed went south in a hurry. She began to shake, and for a moment Lucky thought she might be going into shock or on the verge of having a seizure.

Instead, she wrapped her arms around herself. "What do I have to do to make this go away?"

Since there was no easy way to put it, Lucky just laid it out there for her. "We'll have to go to the ranch because as your legal next of kin, your parents managed to get an emergency hearing in front of a judge who's also their friend. They persuaded this judge that you need to be medically monitored—by them, under their roof. And the judge signed a temporary order. Once we're at the ranch, we'll have the interview where we'll need to convince a psychologist that we're a happy couple fit to raise Noah. If we do that, the psychologist will pass that on to the judge, and there won't be another hearing. The temporary order will expire, and you'll keep sole custody of Noah."

Marin slowly lifted her eyes and looked at him. She didn't exactly voice a question, but there were plenty of nonverbal ones.

"The interview could be as early as tomorrow afternoon," Lucky added. "If the doctor releases you from the hospital today. That means we wouldn't have to keep up the charade for long. Then, after visiting with your grandmother, you can go home."

Well, maybe.

That was one of those gray areas that Lucky hadn't quite figured out. Marin might never be able go home. It might not be safe.

"And what happens if we come clean and tell everyone that you're not Noah's father?" she asked. But Marin immediately waved that off. "Then my parents will use that against me. They might even want a paternity test. They'll brand us as liars. And if the judge knows we lied about that, he'll assume we're lying about my ability to be a good parent."

The Sheppards might even try to file criminal charges against him for preventing them from taking Noah. The couple certainly had a lot of misplaced love, and they were aiming all of it at Marin and Noah.

"I'll fight it," Marin said, sounding not nearly as strong as her words. "I'll hire a lawyer and fight it."

"I've already talked to one," he assured her. "I called a friend of a friend, and she says to cooperate for now. Your mother and Howard might have this judge firmly in their pockets, and he's the one who arranged for the interview with the psychologist. I've requested a change of venue, and he denied it. The only way we could have gotten a delay is if you hadn't come out of the coma."

"Great. Just great." She paused a moment. "So you're saying we should go to the ranch and do as my parents say?"

"I don't think we have a choice."

Her chin came up. "Yes, I do. There's no reason to drag you into this. And you shouldn't have to be subjected to staying with my parents. You have no idea the emotional hell they'll put you through, especially since they believe we're a couple. A couple they want to see driven apart."

Lucky didn't doubt that. But there was another problem. "Marin, your parents aren't going to just give up. It took some fast talking for me to stop an immediate transfer of custody. Your mother was here early yesterday morning. She came prepared to take Noah then and there."

Marin groaned and buried her face in her hands. "Oh, God."

Lucky groaned right along with her. There were a lot of things wrong with their plan. For one thing, it wasn't legal. But what Marin's parents were trying to do wasn't right, either. So maybe two wrongs did make a right.

That still didn't mean this would be easy.

For two days, he'd have to pretend to be Noah's father and Marin's loving fiancé. The first was a piece of cake. It was that second one that was giving him the most trouble.

Lucky blamed it on the blazing attraction between them. Before he'd held Marin in his arms, before that brief kiss, he'd only lusted after her in his heart. Now, he was lusting after her in all kinds of ways. And he couldn't do anything about it.

Because Marin might become a critical witness when he busted his investigation wide open. She might be the key to finally getting justice. He couldn't compromise that—it was the most important thing in his life.

He couldn't get involved with Marin. He could only live a temporary lie.

"Okay," Marin mumbled. She cleared her throat. "So, you have to do the interview, whenever that'll be, but you don't have to stay at the ranch in Willow Ridge. You can drop Noah and me off and then say you have an urgent business appointment or something, that you'll return in time for the interview."

Lucky just stared at her, wondering how she was going to handle what he had to say.

"You're already having second thoughts?" Marin concluded.

"No. That interview has to happen. You have to keep custody of Noah."

Now it was Marin's turn to stay silent for several moments. "And you'd do this for me?" Marin asked. Her gaze met his again, and there was no cowering look in her eyes. Just some steel and attitude. "Why?"

She wasn't requesting information. She was demanding it.

This would have been a good time to tell another half truth. Especially since—much to his disgust—he was getting good at them.

But another lie would stick in his throat.

"I'm looking for your brother, Dexter," he confessed.

Her eyes immediately darkened, and he saw the pulse pound on her throat. "You followed me on the train?"

Lucky nodded. "I followed you."

"Why?" she repeated, though this one had even more steel than the original one.

"Because I thought you might lead me to him."

She tipped her eyes to the ceiling and groaned. "I was right about you. You're one of those men. The ones who've followed me and tried to scare me."

He reached out to her, but Marin batted his hands away. "Scaring you was never my intention. I just need to find your brother."

"What do you want from Dexter?" she snapped.

Lucky was betting this answer wasn't so obvious. "The truth?"

She sliced at him with a scalpel-sharp glare. "That would be nice for a change."

He debated if Marin was strong enough to hear this. Probably not. But there was no turning back now. He toyed with how he should say it. But there was only one way to deliver news like this. Quick and dirty.

He'd tell her the truth even if it made Marin hate him.

Chapter 5

Marin stared at Lucky, holding her breath.

Even though she'd only known him for a short period of time, she was already familiar with his body language.

Whatever he had to say wouldn't be good.

"What do you want from my brother?" she repeated.

Lucky stood and looked down at her. He met her gaze head-on. "I want him dead."

Everything inside her stilled. It wasn't difficult to process that frightening remark since she'd been through this before. For the past year, she'd had to deal with other men who had wanted to find Dexter, too. And like Lucky they probably had wanted him dead, as well. But this cut even deeper to the bone because Lucky had saved her son. He'd saved her.

And she trusted him.

Correction, she *had* trusted him. Right now, she just felt betrayed.

Marin tried to keep her voice and body calm, which was hard to do with her emotions in shreds. She silently cursed the pain that pounded through her head and made it hard to think. "Then, you already have what you want. Dexter *is* dead."

Lucky lifted his left shoulder. "I'm not so sure about that."

The other men hadn't been sure, either. But then neither had her own family. "If Dexter were alive, he would have contacted me by now. He wouldn't have let me believe he was dead."

At least she hoped that was true. But Marin couldn't be certain, especially considering the dangerous circumstances surrounding his disappearance.

"Let's just say that I know a different side of your brother," Lucky insisted. "The man I know would do anything—and I mean anything—to save himself. And in this case, making everyone think he's dead is about the only thing that could save him from the investors who poured millions of dollars into research that didn't pay off for them because Dexter didn't deliver what he promised he would."

She couldn't disagree with that. Marin had examined and reexamined every detail she could find about the night Dexter had disappeared.

Lucky had no doubt done the same.

"What do you know about the night my brother died?" she asked.

His eyes said "too much." "Your brother was a chemical engineer working on a privately funded project. He was supposed to be testing antidotes for chemical agents, specifically a hybrid nerve agent that might be used in a combat situation against ground troops. The investors believed they could sell this antidote to the Department of Defense for a large sum of money. But something went wrong. The Justice Department got some info that Dexter was selling secrets, and they were about to launch a full-scale investigation."

Yes, she knew all of that—after the fact. Before that night, however, Marin hadn't known exactly what Dexter's research project entailed. Even now, she doubted that she knew the entire truth. Maybe no one did. But something had indeed gone wrong with the project, and the Justice Department investigation hadn't happened as planned because there had been an explosion in the research facility.

There was also evidence of some kind of attack that night, and a security guard who was actually an undercover Justice Department agent had been killed. The body had been found in the rubble of the facility.

Unlike Dexter's.

No one had been able to locate his body or those of the two women who'd been in the facility that night. But Marin believed Dexter had indeed been killed in the attack, which might have been orchestrated by someone who wanted to get their hands on her brother's research project.

Since the project was missing, as well, Marin was convinced that the culprit had succeeded.

"Your brother is a criminal," Lucky informed her.

Even though she was in pain and exhausted, Lucky's words gave her a boost of anger and adrenaline that she needed. But then, defending her brother had always been a strong knee-jerk reaction.

"There were never any charges brought against Dexter," Marin reminded him.

"Because the authorities think he's dead."

"No. Because there's no evidence to indicate he's done anything wrong."

"There's evidence," Lucky insisted. "I just haven't found it. Yet. But before his disappearance, Dexter was working on more than a chemical antidote. A chemical weapon. He was playing both sides of the fence, and three days ago a key component of that weapon surfaced for sale on the black market."

Now, that she didn't know. But perhaps her parents did. According to the phone conversations she'd had with her grandmother, the federal authorities had kept her parents informed about the investigation, and they'd visited the ranch often.

"That's still not proof Dexter's alive," Marin insisted, certain that her voice no longer sounded so convinced of Dexter's innocence.

Lucky lifted his hands, palms up. "Who else would be trying to sell that component?"

"The person who stole it."

He didn't toss his hands in the air again, but he looked as if he wanted to do just that. "Other than some blood found at the scene, there's no proof that Dexter is dead. *None.* He would have hung on to that weapon and waited until the right time to sell it. Three days ago was apparently the right time for him because it appeared."

Marin took a moment to rein in her emotions. Despite his sometimes selfish behavior, she loved her brother and didn't want to believe he was capable of doing something like this. She'd grieved for him, and she missed him. Would Dexter have put the family and her through all that pain just to cover himself?

Maybe.

And if so, then maybe Lucky was telling the truth. "Assuming you're right, then what does this case have to do with you?"

"Dexter pissed off the wrong people, Marin," Lucky explained. "And I'm one of those people."

That didn't sound like something a PI would say about one of his cases. It sounded personal. "What do you mean?"

His jaw muscles stirred. He eased back down into the chair and scrubbed his hands over his face. "My sister was fresh out of her doctoral program at the University of Texas, and her first and only real job was working for Dexter."

Marin sucked in her breath. This was starting to move in a direction that she didn't want to go. "Not Brenna Martel?" Brenna had been a colleague, one of the women who went missing and was presumed dead. But Brenna hadn't just been Dexter's business associate. She'd been his lover.

"No. Not Brenna. His lab assistant, Kinley Ford." He waited a moment. "My dad died right after Kinley was born, my mom remarried shortly thereafter, and Kinley took our stepdad's surname."

That's why Marin hadn't immediately made the connection between Lucky and the woman. She hadn't met Kinley Ford, but since her brother's disappearance, she had seen a photo of the young chemical engineer who'd assisted Dexter on his last project.

Kinley Ford had her brother's eyes.

And those storm-gray eyes were drilling into her, waiting for her to answer.

"The police believe your sister was killed that night," Marin whispered. "And unlike Dexter, there's evidence to point to that."

He nodded. And swallowed hard. "The cops think Brenna was killed, too. They found blood from all three of them. Just a trace from Dexter. More than a pint from Brenna. Triple that from my sister. There's no way she could have lived with that much blood loss."

"But the police didn't find the bodies of either woman," she pointed out.

Lucky shrugged. "Dexter probably hid them somewhere before he gave up and set the explosives to blow up the research lab. There was evidence that someone had tried to clean up the crime scene."

Yes, she'd read that, as well, and along with the fact that there'd been no lethal quantities of her brother's blood found, she could understand why some people believed he was still alive.

And guilty.

Though Lucky hadn't convinced her that Dexter was alive, he had convinced her of something—the pain he was feeling over the loss of his sister. She understood that loss because she'd grieved for Dexter. "I'm sorry Kinley was killed."

"Yeah. So am I." She heard the pain. It was raw and still so close to the surface that she could practically feel it. "Your brother murdered her."

Marin didn't want to believe that, either. But she couldn't totally dismiss it. However, if Dexter was responsible, then it must have been an accident.

"You followed me because you thought I'd lead you to Dexter," she concluded.

He nodded. "I've been monitoring you for months. When I learned you were going to the ranch to see your grandmother, I figured Dexter would do the same."

A chill went through her. "You've been *monitoring* me? What the heck does that mean?"

He didn't get a chance to answer.

There was a tap at the door a split second before it opened. Marin didn't want the interruption. She wanted to finish this conversation with Lucky. But then, she saw that it wasn't her parents returning for round two. It was Nurse Garcia, and she had Noah in her arms.

The anger and frustration didn't exactly evaporate, but Marin did push aside those particular emotions along with her questions so that she could stand and go to her son. Just seeing him flooded her heart with love.

"Stay put. I'll bring this little guy to you," Nurse Garcia insisted. "I told the doctor you were awake and anxious for this visit. He was going to be tied up with another patient for an hour or so, but he agreed to let you see your son before the examination."

Noah smiled when he spotted Marin, and he began to pump his arms and legs. He babbled some excited indistinguishable sounds. Marin reached for him, and he went right into her arms. Nurse Garcia excused herself and left.

Marin didn't even try to blink her tears away. It was a miracle that she was holding her son, and an even greater miracle that he hadn't been hurt.

Noah tolerated the embrace for several seconds before he got bored. He leaned back and reached for the bandage on her head. Marin shifted him in her arms, and her son's attention landed on Lucky.

Noah immediately reached for him.

Her son had given her a warm reception, but it was mild compared to the one he gave Lucky. Noah squealed with delight and laughed when Lucky stood to give him a kiss on the cheek.

"I told you that your mom was okay, buddy," Lucky said to Noah.

When Noah's reach got more insistent and he began to fuss, Marin handed her son over to a man who was feeling more and more like her enemy.

"Sorry about that," Lucky mumbled, gathering Noah in his arms. "I've hardly let him out of my sight since the explosion. I guess he's gotten used to me."

"I guess." And she didn't bother to sound pleased about it.

"I wasn't sure what to feed him so I called a doctor friend and got some suggestions for formula and food. He said to go with rice cereal. I hope that was okay."

"Fine," she managed to say. "I guess you didn't have any trouble getting him to sleep?"

"Not really. But he's got a good set of lungs on him when he wants a bottle. Don't you, buddy?" Lucky grinned at Noah, the expression making him a little more endearing than she wanted at the moment.

Marin watched as Noah playfully batted at Lucky. Her son was at ease in this man's arms. More than at ease. The two looked like father and son. And they weren't. Lucky was simply a temporary stand-in.

Now, it was time to deal with reality.

The replacement father act had to be over soon, because she and Lucky obviously weren't on the same path. He not only hated her brother, he wanted revenge for his sister's death, and he'd been willing to use her to get to Dexter.

"Earlier you said you'd monitored me," she reminded him. "How?"

His grin evaporated, and even though he kept his attention on Noah, his expression became somber. "I rented the condo connected to yours."

The chill inside her got significantly colder. "You watched me? You listened in on my conversations?"

He nodded. "The walls between the condos are thin. It's not hard to overhear, if you're listening. And I was. I wanted to know if you were in contact with Dexter."

She silently cursed. "So you know I didn't. Still, you invaded my privacy."

"I did," Lucky readily admitted. "Because I had to do it. Whether you want to believe it or not, your brother's a dangerous man."

Marin groaned softly, looked at her son and blinked back more tears. "First, you save my son. You save me. And then you tell me that you've not only been spying on me, you want to kill my brother if by some miracle he's still alive."

"I don't want to kill him. I want him arrested so he can stand trial, be convicted and then get the death penalty."

"Oh, is that all?" The sarcasm dripped from her voice.

With Noah still gripped lovingly in his arms, Lucky stood back up. There was emotion in his eyes. But even though she owed this man a lot, she had just as much reason to despise him.

Marin hoped like the devil that she was keeping her temper in check because of her headache and Noah. Not because she was feeling anything like attraction for Lucky Bacelli.

But just looking at him gave her a little tug deep within her belly. She didn't want that tug to mean anything. She wanted it to go away. It was a primal reminder that no matter what he wanted from her brother, she was still hotly attracted to him.

"I'm not the only person after Dexter," Lucky continued. "Have you met Grady Duran?"

Oh, yes. And unlike what she was feeling for Lucky, there was no ambivalence when it came to Duran. She loathed Duran as much as she was afraid of him. Judging from their brief, heated encounters he thought she was a liar.

"Duran and my brother were in business together on the chemical antidote project. He believes Dexter is alive," she supplied. "For the past year he's been harassing me because he thinks I know more than I'm saying. The man's a bully, and he's dangerous."

"Did Duran hurt you?" Lucky immediately asked.

Marin's gaze rifled to his. Lucky's tone set off all sorts of alarms. That sounded like the tone of a man who was concerned.

About *her*.

Marin rethought that when she studied the ease he seemed to have when interacting with Noah. Maybe the alarm wasn't for her but for her son. That led her to another question.

Was there reason for concern?

"Duran didn't physically hurt me," Marin explained. "But he's one of the reasons I've tried to keep where I live secret. I was in Dallas for a while, but when he showed up, I moved to Fort Worth. The man frightens me because his desperation seems almost as intense as his determination to find Dexter."

Lucky's mouth tightened. "Duran probably knows about the chemical weapon's components surfacing on the black market. He might try to contact you again."

He paused, took a step toward her, halving the distance between them. "Marin, you have a lot to deal with, and you're not a hundred percent. Right now, just concentrate on recovering and getting through the interview that your parents set up."

Marin wanted to argue, but he was right. She also wanted to turn down Lucky's offer to pose as Noah's father. But she couldn't do that, either. She couldn't let her anger and pride cause her to lose custody. However, there was something she could do.

Something to put some distance between her and Lucky.

"All right," Marin agreed. "I'll check with the doctor and see how soon I can be discharged. Then, once he gives me the okay, I'll call a cab to take Noah and me to the ranch. When I know the exact time and place of the interview, I'll phone you and you can meet me at the psychologist's office. If all goes well, maybe it won't take more than an hour or two."

Lucky pulled in a deep breath and eased down on the bed beside her. The mattress creaked softly. "I should be at the ranch with you."

"No." Marin didn't even have to think about that— the tug in her belly had convinced her of that. "My parents will be expecting us to be a loving couple. In fact, they won't just be expecting it, they'll be looking for anything they can use against me to force me to return home for good."

"You need me there with you," he insisted.

She met his stare. The tug got worse. So, Marin dodged those lethal gray eyes. "I don't want to be coddled."

"Good." He leaned in, so close that it forced her to make eye contact again. "Because I'm not the coddling type."

No. He wasn't. There was a dangerous edge about him, and despite the gentleness he was showing her son, Marin didn't think this was his normal way of dealing with things. Lucky Bacelli was a lifetime bad boy.

The tug became a full-fledged pull.

Marin drew back. She had to. Because there was no room in her life for a man, especially this man who could make her feel things she didn't want to feel.

He inched even closer. "Marin, I'm not giving you a choice about this. I'm coming to the ranch with Noah and you."

His adamancy didn't sit well with her. Especially after all the things he'd just admitted.

Then, it hit her.

She finally got why Lucky was so adamant. "You think Dexter had something to do with that explosion on the train?"

He gave a crisp nod. "Who else?"

"Not Dexter. My brother wouldn't hurt me," she informed him.

"If not him, then someone who was trying to stop me from getting to him. And that person didn't care if you or Noah got hurt in the process."

Lucky snared her gaze. "Marin, what I'm saying is that Noah and you could still be in serious danger."

Chapter 6

Lucky caught on to Marin's arm to help steady her as she walked through the door of her old room at her parents' ranch. But Marin would have no part of accepting his help. With Noah clutched in her arms, she moved out of Lucky's grip and tossed him a warning glance.

He tossed her one of his own.

"We aren't going to pull this off if you're shooting daggers at me," he mumbled.

She'd been giving him the silent treatment since they left the hospital an hour earlier. And because Noah had hardly made a peep the entire trip to the ranch, it'd been a very quiet drive in the rental car she'd arranged so that they wouldn't be in the same vehicle with her parents.

Lucky wasn't sure what to say to her anyway. Truth was, he had let her down. He'd gone onto that train to follow her, and even though he'd gotten Noah and her out of the burning debris, that wasn't going to negate one simple fact.

Marin didn't trust him.

Heck, she didn't even like him.

And that would make these next forty-eight hours damn uncomfortable.

His opinion about that didn't change when he glanced around the room. There were plenty of signs of Marin's life here. Her earlier life, that is, when she was still her parents' daughter. Several framed pictures of her sat on the dresser. In one she wore a pale pink promlike dress; in another, a dark blue graduation gown. But the photo in the middle, the one most prominently displayed was a shot of her standing between her parents. It was the most recent of the photographs, probably taken just shortly before her move to Dallas–Fort Worth.

She looked miserable.

"I figured all of this stuff would have been put in storage," Marin grumbled. "Instead, they've made it a sort of shrine."

They had indeed.

From the background investigation Lucky had run on her, Marin had left Willow Ridge in a hurry after a bitter argument with her parents over her relationship with Randall, the jerk her parents had thankfully never met. Before that, she'd lived and worked just a few miles away, running her CPA business from an office on Main Street in Willow Ridge. Her apartment had been over her office, and according to a former town resident that Lucky had interviewed, Marin's parents had visited her every day.

Marin had then met Randall while on a short business trip to New Orleans. The problems with her parents had started when Marin began dating him and had refused to bring him home so they could meet him. Maybe she'd done that because subconsciously she hadn't trusted Randall, but it probably had more to do with the fact that her parents had disapproved of all of her previous relationships.

This fake one would be no different.

"Obviously, we can't ask for separate rooms," Marin grumbled.

She was right about that. But at least the suite was big, thank goodness. Probably at least four hundred square feet, with a bathroom on one side. On the other there was a sitting room that had been converted to a nursery— complete with a crib and changing table.

There was only one bed though, covered with a garnet-red comforter.

Lucky followed the direction of Marin's gaze—the bed had obviously caught her attention, as well.

"Only two days," he reminded her.

Her heavy sigh reminded him that those two days would seem like an eternity. It was also a reminder that he should at least try to do some damage control because Lucky was positive that things could get a lot worse than they already were.

Lucky took off his leather jacket and placed it over the back of a chair that was perched in front of an antique desk. He adjusted the compact-size handgun that he had tucked in a slide holster at the back of his jeans.

Marin's gaze went racing to his holster. "Is that a gun?" she asked.

"Yes. I always carry it. I'm a PI, remember?"

She opened her mouth, closed it and turned away.

Great. Now, they had another issue. "We have to talk," Lucky insisted.

Another sigh. Marin sank down onto the edge of the bed and lay Noah next to her. The little boy didn't stay put, however. He rolled onto his stomach and tried to crawl away, but Marin caught on to him. Soon the tiny floral pattern in the comforter caught his eye, and Noah stopped crawling and began to pick at the embroidery.

"There really isn't anything to talk about," Marin countered. "I think you've made everything perfectly clear."

But then, her gaze came to his again. Lucky didn't exactly see a carte blanche acceptance there, but he did see and feel a slight change in her. She probably knew her animosity, though warranted, wasn't going to do them any good.

"You really think Noah and I are still in danger?" she asked.

He considered his answer. "Yes. And if I could do anything to change that, I would."

She wearily pushed her hair away from her bandaged forehead. "So would I. I even thought if I distanced myself from you that the danger would go away." Marin waved him off when Lucky started to respond to that. "But if the danger is connected to Dexter and the people who might want him and that chemical weapon, then no matter where I am, the danger will find me."

Marin stared at him. "How do I stop the danger from finding Noah?"

Since this wasn't going to be an easy answer, Lucky sat down beside her. "I won't let anything happen to Noah, understand?"

She shook her head. Then, swallowed hard. "I can't lose him."

"I know." And because he truly understood her concern and fear, Lucky reached out and slid his arm around her.

Marin stiffened, and for a moment he thought she

might push him away. She didn't. But she didn't exactly melt into his arms, either. Still, this contact was better than the silent treatment.

Wasn't it?

Lucky rethought that when she looked at him. Just like that, he felt the hard punch of attraction. A punch he'd been trying to ward off since the first time he'd watched Marin with his surveillance equipment. Of course, he hadn't spoken to her then. At that time, he'd merely thought of her as Dexter Sheppard's sister who might have been hiding her brother's whereabouts. But she was more than that now.

And that wasn't good.

Lucky couldn't lose focus. He owed it to Kinley to find her killer, and he owed it to Noah to keep him safe. He couldn't do either if he was daydreaming about having sex with Marin.

But that little reminder didn't really help.

Next to him, Marin was warm, soft, and her scent was stirring things in him that were best left alone.

"On the train, you said you were hitting on me," she commented, her voice practically a whisper as if discussing a secret. "Why did you lie about that?"

Now, that riled him. "Who said I lied?"

"You were following me to find Dexter."

"And I was hitting on you. Despite what you think of me, I can do two things at once."

She frowned and glanced down at the close contact. "Is that what you're doing now—hitting on me?" And it wasn't exactly an invitation to continue.

The knock at the door stopped anything stupid he was about to say. Or do. Like kiss her blind just to prove the attraction that was already way too obvious.

"It's me," the visitor called out.

"My grandmother," Marin provided, and she got up to open the door.

The petite woman who gave Marin a long hug was an older version of Lois, Marin's mother. Except unlike Lois, this woman had some warmth about her. Of course, Marin had come all this way to see her, so obviously there wasn't the tension she had with her parents.

Lucky got to his feet, as well, though he didn't move far from the bed in case Noah crawled closer to the edge.

"I'm Helen," the woman said, introducing herself to Lucky. Her dusty-blue eyes were as easy as her smile. "Welcome to Willow Ridge."

Her eye contact was hospitable, unlike the frostiness he'd gotten from Marin's parents when they'd arrived minutes earlier. Helen's scrutiny lasted only a few seconds though before the woman's attention landed on Noah. She smiled again. No. She *beamed* and went to the bed to sit next to her great-grandson.

"My, my, now aren't you a handsome-looking young man," Helen concluded. Noah stared at her a moment before he returned the smile. That caused Helen to giggle with delight, and she scooped up the little boy in her arms. "Why don't we go out on the patio and have a little visit."

Lucky was about to question whether Marin was up to going outside, but she followed her grandmother to a pair of French doors that thankfully led to a glass enclosed patio. No sting of the winter wind here. It was warm, cozy and had an incredible view of the west pasture that was green with winter rye grass. With the sun just starting to set, the room was filled with golden light.

"How are you feeling?" Helen asked, her attention

going back to Marin. The older woman dropped down into one of the white wicker chairs.

"I'm fine," Marin assured her, taking the love seat next to her grandmother and son.

Everyone in that sunroom knew that was a lie. The dark smudgy circles beneath Marin's eyes revealed her draining fatigue. And then there was that bandage on her forehead, a stark reminder of how close she'd come to being killed. It would take Lucky a lifetime or two to forgive himself for not being able to stop what had happened.

"How are you feeling?" Marin countered.

Helen gave her a short-lived smile and showered Noah's cheeks with kisses. "I figured the only way to get you here was to tell you I was under the weather."

Marin mumbled something under her breath. Then, huffed. "When you called Lizette earlier this week and asked her to give me a message, you said you were sick, not under the weather. *Sick*. I was worried about you."

"I know, and considering what happened on the train, I'm sorry. But I'm not sorry you're here." Helen paused a moment. "All of these problems with your folks need to be worked out, and this was the only way I could think to do it."

"Grandma, it didn't resolve anything. Mom and Dad are trying to take Noah from me."

"I know, and I'm sorry about that, too. I did try to stop them, but you know how your mother is when she gets an idea in her head." The smile returned. "But they'll forget all about custody and such when Dexter comes home."

That grabbed Lucky's complete attention. "You think Dexter's alive?"

"Of course. And he won't miss the chance to see his

sister and nephew. I figure Dexter's been waiting for the best time to make his homecoming, and that time is now."

Lucky was about to agree, but Helen continued before he could speak. "I don't guess you'll be joining the family for dinner tonight?"

"No," Marin immediately answered. "Mom and Dad might have blackmailed me into staying here, but there's nothing in that judge's order that says I have to socialize with the people trying to take my son."

"I thought you'd feel that way. I'll make sure the cook brings in some trays for you two and some baby goodies for our little man here." Helen tipped her head toward the bedroom. "It's my guess that your folks have your suite bugged."

Lucky and Marin just stared at her.

Helen continued, "I heard them talking when they got back from the hospital after they saw you. Don't know where the bug is, but I'll bet my favorite broach that they put one somewhere in the bedroom."

"Why would they do that?" Lucky asked.

"Because they're suspicious. I don't know where Howard got the notion, but he thinks Lucky here is only out to break your heart. My advice, be careful what you say. And be just as careful what you do. Don't give Howard and Lois any ammunition to take this little boy. Because with a judge who's your dad's fishing buddy, they already have enough."

Marin groaned softly and started to get up. "I'll look for the bug."

Lucky put his hand on her shoulder and eased her back down. "I'll do it."

"You might not want to do that," Helen volunteered.

"I mean, you could think of a bug as a golden opportunity to give Howard and my often misguided daughter a dose of their own medicine. After all, they're using deceit to try to force Marin back here. Why don't you prove to them that you have nothing to hide, that you are what you say you are?"

Lucky could think of a reason—because it would be damn impossible to stay "in character" 24/7. He would have to disarm that eavesdropping device.

His cell phone rang. He considered letting it go to voice mail. Until he spotted the name on the caller ID.

"I have to take this," he told Marin, and since he couldn't go into the bugged bedroom, he stepped outside so he could have some privacy.

Winter came right at him. The wind felt like razor blades whipping at his shirt and jeans. But that didn't stop him. This call was exactly what he'd been waiting for.

"Cal," Lucky answered. As in Special Agent Cal Rico from the Justice Department. Just as important, Cal was his best friend and had been since they'd grown up together in San Antonio. "Please tell me you have good news about that train explosion."

"Some." But Cal immediately paused. "It looks as though someone left a homemade explosive device in a suitcase in one of the storage lockers near the lounge car."

The car where they'd been sitting.

"I don't suppose you saw anyone suspicious carrying a black leather suitcase?" Cal asked.

"No." But then, Lucky had been preoccupied with Marin. He'd allowed the attraction he felt for her to stop him from doing his job. And his job had been to make sure that no one had followed him while he'd been following Marin.

Obviously, he'd failed big-time.

"Did any of the other passengers notice the suitcase-carrying bomber?" Lucky leaned his shoulder against the sunroom glass, hoping he'd absorb some of the heat. Inside, Marin and her grandmother were still talking.

"No, but I'm about to start reviewing the surveillance disks."

That caught Lucky's attention. "What exactly was recorded?"

"All the main areas on the train itself, and the two depots where the train stopped in Fort Worth and then in Dallas."

Good. It was what he wanted to hear. "So anyone who boarded should be on that surveillance?"

"Should be. Of course, that doesn't rule out a person who was already on the train. The person could have been hiding there for a while just so they wouldn't be so obvious on surveillance."

Hell. But Lucky would take what he could get. These disks were a start.

"We'll scan the disks using the face recognition program," Cal continued. "And also check for anyone carrying a suitcase that matches the leather fragments we were able to find at the point of origin of the explosion. We might get something useful."

Lucky didn't like the possibility that they might not succeed. He had to find that bomber. Better yet, he had to prove the bomber was either Dexter or someone connected to him. And then, he had to stop this SOB before Marin and Noah were put in harm's way again.

From the other side of the glass, Noah grinned at him, a reminder of just what was at stake here.

"I want a copy of those surveillance disks," Lucky requested.

"I figured you would. And I thought about how many different ways to tell you no. You're no longer a cop, Lucky. I can't give you official authorization to see them."

Lucky cursed. "Then I hope you've worked out a way to do it unofficially because I need those disks. Someone tried to kill me, and I want to know who."

Cal groaned heavily enough for Lucky to hear it. "And that's how I'm going to get around the official part. A set of the disks are already on the way to the local sheriff there in Willow Ridge. He'll bring them out to you so you can view them as a witness looking for anything that you would consider suspicious."

Lucky released the breath that he didn't even know he'd been holding. "Thanks, Cal. I owe you."

"Yeah. You do. You can repay me by finding our unknown suspect on those disks." And with that assignment, Cal hung up.

Lucky didn't waste any time. He went back into the sunroom so he could question Helen about Dexter. So far, she was the only person who seemed to want to talk about Marin's brother. But when Lucky saw Marin's face, he immediately knew his questions about Dexter would have to wait.

"What's wrong?" he asked. He hadn't thought it possible, but she was even paler than she had been when they first arrived.

Marin exchanged an uneasy glance with her grandmother, who still had Noah in her arms. "There was a message left for me." She pointed to the phone on a wicker coffee table.

"It's a private line," Helen supplied, taking up the explanation. "Lois didn't have the line taken out when Marin moved. And since no one other than the cleaning lady ever goes out here, we didn't notice the message until just now."

Since this "message" had obviously upset both women, Lucky went to the phone and pressed the play button. It took a couple of seconds to work through Marin's old recorded greeting and the date and time of the call. Two days earlier at nine fifty-three in the morning. About the same time Marin had been on the train en route to Willow Ridge.

The answering machine continued, and a man's rusty voice poured through the sunroom. "Marin Sheppard, this is Grady Duran."

The very person who'd hounded Marin when she first moved to Dallas–Fort Worth.

"I'm tired of waiting for you to get chatty about Dexter," Duran continued. "And I'm tired of warning you of what could happen if you don't tell me where your brother is. My number will be on your caller ID. Get in touch with me. That's not a suggestion. Keep ignoring me, and you'll regret it."

Lucky felt the inevitable slam of anger. How dare this SOB threaten Marin, especially after everything she'd been through. But then, something else occurred to him.

Had Grady Duran been the one to set that explosive?

Lucky couldn't immediately see a motive for that, since Duran would want Marin alive. Well, alive until he got the info about Dexter's whereabouts. But maybe the explosion had been meant to scare her.

If so, it'd worked.

"Has Grady Duran ever been here at the ranch?" he asked Helen and Marin.

Marin shook her head. "I don't think so." Helen echoed the same.

Lucky took out his wallet, fished out the dog-eared photo and handed it to Helen. "Does he look familiar?"

Helen brought it closer to her face and studied the picture. Marin leaned in and looked at it, as well. Lucky had already studied it so long that he'd memorized every little detail. Kinley had sent it to him just a month before she was murdered.

The last picture taken of her.

Kinley was smiling, as usual. It was a victory photo of sorts, she'd said in her brief e-mail to Lucky. An office party to celebrate her boss getting a new research contract, which meant she'd be employed at least another year.

In the posed shot, her boss, Dexter, was on her right. Tall, blond and toned, he looked as if he'd be more at home on a California beach than a research lab. He was sporting a thousand-watt smile—smiles like that had probably gone a long way to helping him with the ladies.

Lucky also knew something else about that photo: Dexter had his arm slung a little too intimately over Kinley's shoulder.

On Kinley's left was a woman with light brown hair. Brenna Martel, Dexter's former lover and other lab assistant. And then there was Grady Duran, standing just off from the others. Wide shoulders, imposing dark stare, he wasn't looking like a man in a festive mood.

Odd, since of the four he was the only one who wasn't missing or dead.

"I remember her," Helen tapped Brenna's image. "Dexter brought her here a time or two. She's dead."

"Looks that way. Either that or she disappeared from the face of the earth. No one's touched her bank accounts or her other personal assets since the night of the explosion at the research facility. What about the other guy, Grady Duran? Ever seen him?"

"He wasn't at the ranch," Helen concluded. "But I'm pretty sure I saw him in town. He was in the parking lot of Doc Sullivan's office when I came out from having my blood pressure checked. That was Monday. I noticed because we don't get many strangers in Willow Ridge, especially this time of year."

Helen turned back to Lucky. "Is it a bad thing that this man's in town?"

"A suspicious thing," Lucky supplied. He didn't like the timing of Duran's reappearance. Monday was the day before the train explosion. "Did he say anything to you?"

"Not a word. In fact, he looked away and turned his head when I spotted him."

Lucky didn't care for that, either. Except that it could mean that Duran was here because he knew Dexter was nearby. That was both good and bad.

He looked at Noah, who had hardly been out of his arms for two days. Two days wasn't that long. But it was more than long enough. Lucky loved Noah. He couldn't have loved him more if he were his own son. With Dexter's possible return, that meant Lucky would have the additional challenge of protecting Noah in case something went wrong.

"You need to tell the sheriff that you saw this man," Lucky instructed Helen. "And while you're doing that, I'll ask him to keep a watch out for Duran in case he makes a return visit. I don't want him anywhere near here."

Helen's forehead bunched up. "You think there could be trouble?"

"Maybe."

But the truth was trouble was already on the way.

Chapter 7

Frustrated, Marin shut the dresser drawer with far more force than necessary. "Where is it?" she mumbled.

She'd looked at every inch of the furniture and still hadn't found an eavesdropping device. She glanced at Lucky, who was still examining her closet, but he didn't seem to be having any better luck than she was.

With Noah now asleep in his crib in the sitting room, Marin walked toward the closet. "Maybe Grandma was wrong about the bug," she whispered.

Lucky, too, was obviously frustrated, and he stopped his search to stare at her. "We could be going about this the wrong way," he said under his breath. "Maybe we should just blow off this bug and concentrate on making sure this place is as secure as it can be."

"You've already done that," she pointed out.

The sheriff, Jack Whitley, had already been alerted about Grady Duran possibly being in town, and he'd agreed to send out a deputy to patrol the ranch. The ranch hands had been instructed to keep an eye out for Grady, as well. And her parents had agreed to turn on the security system that they'd had installed but almost never used.

"I could arrange to have surveillance cameras brought in," Lucky explained, his voice not so soft now. "Then, I could monitor the perimeter of the ranch."

"The ranch is huge. Well over a thousand acres and with more than a dozen outbuildings." She glanced back at Noah to make sure he was okay. He was. Her son was on his side and still asleep. "Besides, we only have two days here. After that, I can make other arrangements for security."

Marin was still undecided about her future living arrangements. But returning to Fort Worth probably wasn't a wise move. She'd need a new place, a new home, far away from danger and from her parents. First though, she had to fight this custody challenge.

And she had to keep Noah safe.

Of course, Lucky had taken over that task as if he'd been ordained to protect her son. She couldn't exactly fault him for that. Yes, he'd lied to her about Dexter. Probably lied about hitting on her, as well. But she couldn't doubt that he had her son's best interest at heart.

"So, what do we do about this bug?" Marin mouthed.

Lucky glanced around. Scowled. "Howard and Lois?" he called out. "If you're listening, and you probably are, maybe the judge and the shrink would like to know how perverted you are. Eavesdropping on your daughter having sex with her fiancé. How sick is that, huh?"

Lucky stepped closer to her, placed his palm on the wall just behind her head, and made a throaty grunting sound. It was the exaggerated sound of a man in the throes of sex. He grunted some more, and Marin couldn't help it, she smiled.

Since she figured this was an impromptu outlet for all that pent-up frustration about her parents' antics, she added some moans of her own.

Lucky laughed. It was husky, low and totally male. And she didn't know why—maybe it was the sheer absurdity of their situation—but their charade did indeed help ease some of the frustration.

Well, for a moment or two.

Then, the frustration returned and went in a totally different direction. Or rather, a too familiar, dangerous direction.

Their eyes met and their gazes held. There it was again, that jolt of attraction that'd hit her when she first met him. Lucky was hot. But Marin remembered he was hands-off. He wanted her brother, and he'd been willing to use her to find him.

That reminder was still flashing through her head when Lucky lowered his head. She saw it coming. He was making a move on her. Slick. Effortless. Still, even though she saw it coming, she didn't do anything to stop it. She leaned closer into him, and his mouth found hers, letting the dreamy feel of his kiss wash over her.

He was gentle. A surprise. She'd thought he would be rough and demanding. A bad boy's kiss. But his mouth was as easy as his smooth Texas drawl.

Marin slipped her arms around his neck. First one, then the other. Everything inside her slowed to practically a crawl. Except her heart. It was racing, and she could feel it in her throat.

The slow crawling feeling didn't last long. It couldn't. Not with his clever kiss. When she'd first seen Lucky's face, she'd thought of him being in a bar brawl, of his rough exterior. Of those snug jeans that hugged all the interesting parts of his body. Now, all of that came into play. All of those had drawn her in.

Her body went from mindless resistance to being flooded with raging heat. His chest brushed her breasts. It was enough to urge her closer, to feel more of him. He was solid, all sinew and muscle, and she felt so soft in his arms.

He hooked his arm around her waist and snapped her to him. The gentleness vanished. Thank goodness! Because what good was it to lust after a rough and tumble bad boy if he held back one of the very things that made him bad?

Their bodies met head-on, a collision of sensations. The thoroughness of his touch. The firmness of his grip. His taste. The undeniable need of his mouth as he took the kiss and made it French.

Yes! she thought. Yes. This was her fantasy. Him, taking her like this. Not treating her with kid gloves.

And Lucky didn't disappoint.

His left hand went into her hair. Avoiding her injured forehead, he caught the strands of hair between his fingers and pulled back her head gently, but firmly so that he controlled the angle of the kiss. So that he controlled her.

Marin moved into the kiss, against him. Lucky moved, too, sliding his hand down her back, over her butt. He caught on to the back of her thigh, lifting it, just a little, to create the right angle so that his sex would touch hers.

Her breath vanished, and her vision blurred. She mumbled a word of profanity that she'd never used.

Every part of her responded. A slow, melting heat that urged her to take this further. She wanted Lucky. Not just his French kiss. Not just the clever pressure created by his erection now nestled against her. She wanted it all.

Right here. Right now.

Senseless and thinking with her body, Marin fought to regain control. It wasn't easy. She had to fight her way through the mindlessness of pure, raw desire and a fantasy she'd been weaving for hours. She remembered that having sex just wasn't a good idea. Thankfully, she got a jolt of help when she heard the bedroom door open.

"Noah," she said on a rise of breath.

Just like that, the heat was gone, and even though she turned to race back into the bedroom, Lucky launched himself ahead of her and beat her to it. However, the threat Marin had been prepared to face wasn't there.

Well, not exactly.

With a large thick envelope tucked beneath her arm, her mother, Lois, waltzed inside. Marin made a mental note to keep the door locked from now on—and to keep some distance between Lucky and her.

Lois glanced over at her grandson in the sitting room and gave the sleeping baby a thin smile. Her scrutiny of Lucky and her though lasted a bit longer, and Marin didn't think it was her imagination that her mother was displeased about something. Probably because both Lucky and she looked as if, well, they'd gotten lucky. For the sake of the facade, Marin tried to hang on to the well-satisfied look. It wasn't hard to do. That kiss had been darn memorable.

Which was exactly why she had to forget it.

Her mother snapped her fingers and in stepped a young dark-haired woman carrying a large tray of plates covered with domed silver lids. She set the tray on the desk in the corner and made a hasty exit.

"Your dinner," Lois announced. "Since you made it clear that you wouldn't be dining with us. There's some rice cereal and formula there for Noah, as well."

"Thank you," Lucky responded. "But Noah's already had his dinner—Grandmother brought it in. Oh, and next time, knock first."

Her mother looked as if she wanted to argue with that, but she didn't. Instead, she extracted the envelope and thrust it at Lucky. "Sheriff Whitley had his deputy bring this over for you. I suppose it's connected to the explosion?"

Neither Lucky nor Marin confirmed that. Nor would they. But it was no doubt the surveillance disks from the train that Lucky had told her about. Lucky examined the red tape that sealed the envelope, and Marin could see that someone had written their initials in permanent marker on that tape.

The sound her mother made was of obvious disapproval. "The sheriff apparently packaged it like that. He said if the seal was tampered with that he'd arrest my husband and me for obstruction of justice."

"Good for Sheriff Whitley," Lucky mumbled.

"The man isn't fit to wear that badge," Lois declared. But her expression softened when she looked at Marin. "You should at least eat dinner with your family."

"I would if my family were really a family." Marin paused a moment to put a chokehold on her temper. She didn't want to shout with Noah in the room. "Drop this interview. Apologize. Back off. And then I might have dinner with you."

"The interview has to happen, for your son's sake," her mother said without hesitation. "And it's for his sake that I can't back off."

"Neither can I," someone echoed. It was her father who stepped inside to join forces with her mother.

"Oh, goody," Marin mumbled.

Lucky placed the envelope on the foot of the bed and positioned himself closer to her, so that they were literally facing down her parents.

"By the way, did either of you know about the threatening phone message that Grady Duran left Marin on her private line?" Lucky asked.

It was a good question. One that Marin should have already thought to ask.

"That message," her father grumbled. "Marin's grandmother told us about it after her visit with you. No. We didn't know. But the sheriff does now. For all the good that'll do."

Apparently, her father wasn't any happier with the sealed envelope than her mother. Marin didn't care. She wanted the authorities to know about Grady Duran because it was her guess that he was the one responsible for that explosion, and she wanted him off the streets and behind bars.

Her father propped his hands on his hips. "I thought you should know, I just heard from your brother."

Marin could have sworn her heart stopped.

Lucky must have had a similar reaction because he didn't utter a word. Neither did her mother. And the three all stood there, staring at the man who'd just made the announcement she'd never thought she would hear.

"Dexter's not dead?" Marin finally managed to say.

"Obviously not. He just e-mailed me," Howard explained.

Lois pressed her hand to her chest and pulled in several quick breaths. "What did he say?"

"That he's alive and he wants to come home to see his family."

"Where is he?" Lucky demanded.

"Even if he had said, I wouldn't tell you. Dexter's worried about his safety, as he should be. He knows someone killed two of his employees and an agent who was posing as a security guard at the research facility. Whoever did that is trying to set him up to take the blame."

Marin figured Lucky wasn't buying that or this entire conversation.

Her father's eyes narrowed when he looked at Lucky. "But Dexter says he won't come while you're here, Randall. And he wants you to leave immediately."

It was another shock. Not that Dexter wanted to come home. But that he'd even mentioned Randall, Marin's dead ex-boyfriend.

"I want to see that e-mail," Lucky insisted.

"I'm sure you do," her father snarled. "But first I want you to answer one question. Since you've supposedly never met anyone in Marin's family, mind explaining how the hell my son knows you?"

Chapter 8

How the hell does my son know you?

Lucky hadn't been able to provide an answer to Howard Sheppard, nor had he speculated to the man. He'd ended the inquisition by walking away. Now, two hours later, he still didn't know the answer to Howard's question.

Was the e-mail bogus? And if it was real, did that mean Dexter knew who Lucky really was and why he was at the ranch?

Of course, another possibility was that Howard had asked Dexter to make that demand. After all, what better and faster way to get Lucky off the ranch than to tie Dexter's homecoming to his departure? It would give Howard and Lois everything they wanted.

Their son's return.

And their daughter and grandson at the ranch with no ally, other than Marin's grandmother, who was too old to put up much of a fight. After all, Helen hadn't been able to stop the Sheppards so far. That's why Lucky had refused to leave and then ordered Marin's parents out of the room.

Well, it was one of the reasons anyway.

That kissing session with Marin was another.

Pushing that uncomfortable thought aside, Lucky concentrated on the images from the surveillance disks on his laptop. So far, he hadn't seen anything or anyone suspicious, and he'd been looking for well over an hour. He'd hoped to have spotted Dexter doing something incriminating by now.

He heard Noah stir, and Lucky got up from the desk to check on him. But Noah was still sleeping peacefully in the crib in the sitting room.

Lucky leaned down, gave Noah a light kiss on the cheek and turned to go back to the bedroom, but another sound stopped him. Marin came out of the bathroom. Toweling her damp hair, she was dressed in a turquoise-blue robe that was nearly the same color as her eyes.

She didn't look so pale now, probably because the hot steamy shower had given her skin a pinkish flush. She'd changed the bandage on her forehead, replacing it was a Band-Aid that covered the stitches. It was less noticeable, even though it still exposed the bruise left from the impact.

"Everything okay?" she asked in a whisper.

He nodded. "Just making sure he's all right."

Marin walked closer, close enough for him to catch her scent. Lucky hadn't remembered strawberry shampoo ever smelling that good.

"It's probably best that you try to distance yourself from him," she said, her voice still soft. "Since you'll only be around him a couple more days, I don't want him to get too attached."

Lucky thought it might be too late for that. For both of them. But Marin was right. Noah wasn't his to claim, even though his feelings for Noah were the most real thing he'd felt since his sister's death. Noah was young and wouldn't remember him, but Lucky would certainly remember the little boy.

"The same applies to us," Marin added, scratching her eyebrow. She shifted her position and adjusted the sash on her robe. "That kiss in the closet shouldn't have happened."

He had to agree with that, even though saying it to himself didn't make the sensations go away.

"I want to kiss you again," he admitted.

Her shoulders snapped back. "But you won't," she insisted, sounding about as convinced as Lucky felt. "We need to keep our hands off each other."

"It's not my hands you should be worried about," he mumbled, causing her to laugh.

"Tell you what, if the kissing urge hits us again," she said, "let's make ourselves count to ten. That might give us just enough time to realize what a huge mistake we'd be making."

Right.

The side of her bathrobe slipped a little, easing off her shoulder. Her *bare* shoulder. And he got just a glimpse of the top of her right breast and her nipple.

"Oh, man. You're not wearing anything beneath that bathrobe?"

She jerked the sides together to close the gap. "I came out to check on Noah. Then, I was going to get dressed."

"So you're naked?"

Why couldn't he just let this subject drop? Because he was suddenly aroused beyond belief.

So, he did something totally stupid. He reached out, caught on to her shoulders.

And yeah, he kissed her again, all the while convincing himself that if he stopped, she'd give into the emotion caused by the danger and the adrenaline. She'd get worried and depressed again. He also tried to convince himself that he wasn't enjoying it, that it was therapeutic.

A bald-faced lie.

He was enjoying the heck out of it. The feel of her mouth against his. The way she fit in his arms. The hot-as-sin scent of hers stirring around him. Yes, he was enjoying it.

And he wasn't the only one.

Marin moaned in pure pleasure. That's when he knew he had to stop. With Noah only a couple of inches away, this couldn't continue.

He pulled away from her, ran his tongue over his bottom lip and wasn't surprised when he tasted her there. It was a taste that might be permanently etched into his brain.

"We shouldn't have done that, either," she grumbled. "With all the emotional baggage that each of us has, it wouldn't work between us. Every time you look at me, you'll see my brother, the man you blame for your sister's death."

"You're right," he said. Except it was partly a lie. Marin would always be Dexter's sister, but she was also her own woman.

And he was attracted to her.

Still, Marin was correct. They shouldn't be kissing. Maybe if he said it enough to himself, his body would start to listen. Heaven knows it hadn't listened to anything else he'd demanded it not do.

Lucky tried to get his mind back on business. "While you were in the shower, I got another call from my friend Cal Rico. He's a special agent in the Justice Department, and he's the one responsible for getting those surveillance disks to the sheriff who got them to me."

"Have you found anything?" she asked.

"Not yet. I'm still looking. But Cal let me know that he's using department resources to look into the e-mail Dexter sent your father."

"I think that e-mail was a hoax. It might be my father's way of trying to get you to leave."

Marin and he were obviously on the same page. "Either way, Cal will find out the origin of the e-mail."

Lucky didn't doubt his friend's ability, but verifying the e-mail was a long shot. If Dexter had indeed sent the e-mail, then he would have almost certainly covered his tracks.

Marin turned and tipped her head toward his laptop. "So, what have you seen on those surveillance disks?"

"A lot of people. Not Dexter though. But if he came onto the train, he was probably wearing a disguise." He paused. "Maybe you could take a look at them and see if you can spot him."

She frowned, then nodded. "All right. But for the record, I don't expect to see him. I think we should be looking for Grady Duran."

"Absolutely. But since you know what he looks like, as well, this might go faster with both of us going over the surveillance." But he rethought that when he glanced at the bandage on her head. "Then again, why don't you get some rest, and I'll finish reviewing the disks."

"I'll help," she insisted, going straight for the desk.

Lucky huffed, but he knew it wouldn't do any good

to try to talk her out of this. He was quickly learning that Marin was as stubborn as he was.

That only made him want her more.

"By the way," he whispered, just in case there was a bug in the room. "Are there any extra linens around?" He glanced at the bed as they walked past it. "I'm thinking it's not a good idea if we share the same mattress."

She understood completely. "The extra bedding's in the linen closet. Next to my parents' room. Probably not a good idea to advertise the fact we need two sleeping areas."

True. They already had enough issues with Howard and Lois. "No problem. I'll just take the floor."

"We could build a barrier with the pillows—"

He stopped and stared at her mouth. "I get your point," she conceded. "Pillows wouldn't be much of a barrier."

Heck, he wasn't sure being on the floor would be much of a barrier, either, but Lucky knew he wouldn't get a minute of sleep next to her. And he needed a clear head along with a little sleep to get through the next two days.

Lucky clicked the resume feature on the surveillance disk, and images immediately appeared on the screen. Marin dragged a chair next to his, and they sat, silently. Since Lucky figured a visual aid might help Marin, he took out the photo of Dexter, Grady Duran, his sister and Brenna Martel and positioned it next to his laptop.

"This is the station in Fort Worth, where we both got on," he explained. "The security cameras were on the entire time that passengers were boarding." He backtracked the disk to show her the recorded image of Noah and her.

Lucky was about ten yards behind them.

Several times during that brief walk from the terminal to the train, Marin glanced back, but each time Lucky tried to make sure he disappeared in the crowd.

"Well, if I didn't notice you," she remarked, "then I could have missed Grady Duran."

"Or your brother."

That earned him a scowl that he probably deserved, and they continued to watch the disk. "Okay, this is where I left off before I went to check on Noah. The train is about to leave. There are only a couple of people left at the terminal door. And none of them look anything like Grady Duran or Dexter."

"None of those people are carrying a large suitcase, either."

Without taking her attention from the screen, Marin got up, opened a bottle of pills that she'd placed on the dresser and took one of the tablets, washing it down with a glass of water she took from their dinner tray.

"Pain meds?" Lucky questioned.

"No. I took one of those earlier. This is for my seizures. I have to take them twice a day—a small price to pay for being as normal as I can be."

Yes. It was. But he wondered how all of this additional stress was affecting her health. "How old were you when you had your first seizure?"

"Twelve. I was riding a roller coaster at an amusement park. Scared the devil out of everyone, including myself. Before that, my parents were only overprotective. After that, they got obsessive."

He shrugged. "But you said you haven't had a seizure in years. That should cause them to back off."

"You'd think." She gave a heavy sigh and sank down next to him again. "They do love me in their own crazy way. I know that. But they just can't seem to give up control. They're scared I'll have another seizure, and they won't be around to help me."

Lucky understood that. He'd felt that way about his sister. And now Noah.

Hell, Marin was on that list, too.

Since it was starting to feel like one of those moments where he wanted to pull Marin in his arms and protect the hell out of her, Lucky just turned his focus back the surveillance images.

And then he saw it.

Just as the train was about to close the boarding doors, a passenger carrying a black suitcase hurried forward. Dressed in a bulky knee-length denim coat, the person wore jeans, gloves and a Texas Rangers baseball cap. With that cap sitting low on the forehead and with the bulky clothes, it was hard to tell who the person was.

Lucky backtracked the disk to the point just prior to boarding, froze the frame and zoomed in.

"Does that look like Dexter?" Lucky asked.

Marin moved even closer to the screen and studied it. "No. The body language is wrong. Dexter didn't slump like that."

"Maybe he would if he was trying to keep his face from being seen." Lucky advanced the disk one frame farther and got a better view of the face. Well, the lower part of it anyway. That cap created a strategic shadow.

Marin shook her head. "It's not Dexter. Maybe Grady Duran?"

That was the next possibility that Lucky had planned to consider. He rewound even more of the disk, looking for the best face shot possible. When he thought he'd found it, he zoomed in again. And this time, he didn't have to ask if that was Dexter or Grady Duran.

Because it wasn't either of the men. It wasn't a man at all.

He was looking at the face of a dead woman.

His sister, Kinley.

Chapter 9

From her chair in the sitting room, Marin finished her scrambled eggs and watched her grandmother feed Noah. Noah and her gran were doing great, but she couldn't say the same for Lucky.

He still hadn't moved.

He'd been at that desk in the adjoining bedroom for at least two hours, and it didn't appear he was going to move anytime soon. Right now, he was on hold, waiting for Agent Cal Rico to come back on the line. With his cell phone sandwiched between his shoulder and ear, his fingers worked frantically on the keyboard of his laptop. What he wasn't doing was eating his breakfast.

Marin stood, put her mug of tea aside and blew Noah and her grandmother a kiss. She went into the bedroom toward the desk. "Why don't you come with me for a walk?" she suggested to Lucky.

He didn't even glance up at her. He kept his attention superglued to the e-mail he was typing on the computer screen. "You should be resting."

"It's 9:00 a.m. I've already rested. You, on the other

hand, haven't. I know for a fact that you didn't get much sleep. You were in the bathroom talking on your cell phone most of the night."

"I'm sorry I kept you up," he grumbled.

She huffed. "I'm concerned about you, not me."

He huffed, too. "I'm not tired."

Oh, yes, he was. And he was frustrated and confused. Marin totally understood why. Before last night, all the evidence pointed to his dead sister having had no part in the wrongdoing at the research facility. But yet there she was in that surveillance video.

"I'm still here," Lucky quickly said into the phone. Agent Cal Rico had obviously come back on the line, hopefully with some answers.

Lucky paused. "I need your lab to keep trying to enhance that image from the disk." Another pause. "Yeah, I'm asking the impossible, but I have to know if that was Kinley getting onto the train."

Another pause, but she could see that Lucky was processing something. "Bits of money?" he questioned. "And you're sure that was in the suitcase, along with some clothes. Just how big was that explosive device anyway?"

Marin couldn't hear the agent's answer, but after several terse answers from Lucky, he jabbed the end-call button and cursed. He lowered his voice to mumble profanity, however, when his attention landed on Helen feeding Noah rice cereal for breakfast. Marin figured there was more cereal on her son and her grandmother than in Noah's tummy.

Noah grinned when he realized he had everyone's attention, and Lucky gave him a half-hearted smile in return before he groaned and rubbed his eyes.

That did it. Marin caught on to his arm, and in the same motion, she took his leather jacket from the back of the chair. "We're taking that walk," she insisted.

Lucky stood but didn't move. His stare was a challenge, and it let her know that he had no plans to budge.

"There are things we need to discuss," she whispered. "And I'd prefer not to do that in a room that's bugged. Plus, I could use some fresh air."

He glanced at his laptop, his silent cell phone and then at Noah.

"A *short* walk," Lucky finally conceded. "I don't want you out in that cold very long."

Marin didn't argue with the restriction. She turned toward the sitting room, but before she could even ask her grandmother if she'd watch Noah for a couple of minutes, the woman was already nodding. "Go ahead. Take as much time as you need."

She thanked her grandmother, grabbed her coat from the closet, put it on and led Lucky out the enclosed patio exit before he could change his mind.

Thankfully, it wasn't nearly as cold as it had been the day before. Still, it was in the low fifties, and Marin hugged her coat close to her so that she wouldn't get a chill.

"About an hour ago, I called a lawyer that I know in Fort Worth," Marin explained. "I asked him to contact the psychologist to see if he'd cancel the interview since I don't feel it's necessary."

"Don't count on that happening. The psychologist is probably in your parents' pockets, as well."

That might be true, but Marin had to try. Lucky wasn't in the right state of mind for that interview. Neither was she, and Marin hoped there was still some way to prevent it from happening.

She spotted her mother staring at them from the window, and Marin maneuvered him away from the yard and onto a trail that would take them to the edge of the one of the pastures. "Either way, I want you to leave this morning so you can find your sister."

He tossed her a puzzling glance. "Leave? If I don't do that interview, Marin, you could lose Noah."

Yes, and that terrified her. Still, she couldn't make Lucky stay, not when he had so much at stake. "But if you don't look for your sister before the trail goes cold, you might not find her."

"If that's really my sister."

So, he had doubts, as well. "You're thinking it's a look-alike?"

He shrugged. "I'm thinking if my sister had been alive for the past year, then she would have already contacted me."

"I seem to remember saying the same thing to you about Dexter."

"But my sister wasn't doing anything illegal." Then, he frowned. "At least, I don't think she was."

Neither was Marin. Anything was possible. "Let's assume then that it was a look-alike, maybe even someone in disguise. Brenna Martel, maybe?"

"No. I'd recognize Brenna." He said it so quickly that he'd obviously already considered it. "Plus, there's also the issue of the blood. Both Brenna's and my sister's blood was found all over the floor in Dexter's research lab. The CSI guys said there was little chance that the women could have survived after losing that much blood."

But survival was possible. And that led Marin to the next question. "Was the suitcase the woman was carrying the one that contained the explosives?"

"It appears to be. It also contained money and clothes. Agent Rico believes the explosives were hidden in a concealed compartment."

Since they'd already ruled out the logical explanations, Marin tried out one that was unlikely but still possible. "So, maybe your sister is alive. Maybe she has amnesia from her injuries at the research facility? That would explain why she hasn't contacted you."

"But it wouldn't explain why she got on that train."

Good point. Marin quickly tried to come up with something to counter that. "Maybe she didn't know she was carrying explosives?"

"I considered that at about 1:00 a.m. when I checked the records of everyone injured. There was no injured woman fitting my sister's description. If she hadn't known she was carrying explosives, then she would have been sitting near the suitcase."

"Perhaps not. She could have gone to the bathroom or something. She could have changed seats for a variety of reasons. Like maybe some guy was hitting on her."

The corner of his mouth lifted for a very short smile.

He stopped at a small rocky stream that cut through the pasture. The water created a miniature valley and was banked with chunks of white limestone and slate-gray clay. It was a peaceful spot where she'd spent a lot of time as a kid. A bare pasture was on one side and in the spring would be filled with Angus cattle that would graze there. On the other side was a barn that stored equipment, tractors and massive circular bales of hay.

Lucky could have easily stepped over the stream, but

instead he stared into the water. "I want to believe she's alive and that she's done nothing wrong. That'd be the best-case scenario. But even if Kinley has amnesia or whatever, she obviously needs help."

If Grady Duran was gutsy enough to press Marin for answers about Dexter, how hard would he press Kinley? Lucky's sister could be in danger.

"Let's go back to the house," Marin insisted. "I'll have someone drive you to the train station, the airport or wherever you need to go to find her."

He continued to look into the water. "That would make your parents very happy. They'd have you right where they want you. Here, alone and in fear of losing your son."

"I won't lose Noah," she promised. "I'll figure out a way to postpone or cancel that meeting." Though Marin didn't have a clue how she was going to do that. "Besides, the lawyer in Fort Worth is sending someone down to talk to the judge and the psychologist."

"If all that fails, you'd be giving up a lot," he said. "Just so I can leave."

He was thinking of her. Well, maybe more Noah than her. But whichever, he was putting himself and his needs after hers.

And Marin couldn't help but appreciate that.

There it was. That weird intimacy again. It was growing. They seemed to be racing toward some heated passionate encounter that neither of them seemed capable of stopping.

Worse, she wasn't sure she wanted to stop it.

He reached out and brushed his hand over her arm. Even through the wool coat, she could feel his touch.

Then, he trailed those clever fingers over her cheek. The moment was far warmer than it should have been.

But then, Lucky's hand froze.

"What's wrong?" Marin asked.

He didn't answer. He didn't have to. Marin heard the thick roar of the engine and looked in the direction of the sound. A large rust-scabbed tan-colored truck with heavily tinted windows bolted out from the barn.

Her first thought was a ranch hand had loaded the truck bed with hay to take out to one of the other pastures. But there was no hay. The driver, hidden behind all that dark glass, gunned the engine.

The truck came right at them.

Lucky's heart dropped. This couldn't be happening.

He drew his weapon and hooked his arm around Marin's waist. He didn't wait to see if that truck was the threat that he thought it was.

Waiting was too big of a risk.

Firing shots through that windshield might not be the best idea, either, because shooting would mean stopping to take aim. The driver could be low in the seat, or leaning far to the side, out of range. Lucky couldn't stand there and shoot when he might not even hit the guy. He had to get Marin out of the path of the oncoming vehicle and then figure out if he needed to stop the driver.

They jumped the shallow stream, and ran like hell. He hoped the soggy clay banks would be enough to slow down the truck.

It wasn't.

The four-wheel drive went right through it, sloshing rocks and water out from the mammoth-size tires.

So Lucky did the only thing he could do. He continued to run and pulled Marin right along with him.

Glancing back over his shoulder, Lucky tried to assess their situation. It damn sure wasn't good. That truck was closing in fast. And there was literally no place to hide in an open pasture. Their best bet was to try to double back and get to the barn.

Easier said that done.

The truck was in their path and coming straight for them. And it was quickly eating up the meager distance between them.

"Go right," Lucky yelled to Marin, hoping that she heard him over the roar of the engine.

Just in case she didn't, Lucky dragged her in the direction he wanted her to go.

The driver adjusted, and came at them again.

"Who's doing this?" Marin shouted.

But Lucky didn't have to time to speculate. Marin and he had to sprint to their right. The truck was so close that Lucky could feel the heat from the engine. And the front bumper missed them by less than a couple of inches.

Marin stumbled. Lucky's heart did, too. But he didn't let her fall. A fall could be fatal for both of them. Instead, he grabbed her and zigzagged to their left.

It wasn't enough.

The driver came right at them, and to avoid being hit, Lucky latched on to Marin even tighter and dove out of the way.

They landed hard on the packed winter soil.

Lucky came up, ready to fire. "Run!" he shouted to Marin.

Thankfully, she managed to do that and started sprinting toward the barn. The truck had to turn around and backtrack to come at him again. Those few precious seconds of time might be the only break they got.

So, Lucky took aim at the windshield and fired.

A thick blast tore through the pasture, drowning out even the sound of the roaring truck engine. The bullet slammed into the safety glass and shattered it, but it stayed in place, concealing the identity of the driver.

Maybe someone from the house would hear the shot and come running. But the house was a good quarter of a mile away, and it might take Marin's parents or the ranch hands a couple of minutes just to figure out what was going on.

By then, they could be dead.

Lucky dodged another attempt to run him down, repositioned himself and fired again. This bullet skipped off the truck's roof and sent sparks flying when it ripped through the metal. What it didn't do was stop the driver.

The truck came at him again.

Lucky dove out of the way. But not before the front bumper scraped against his right thigh.

He fired another shot into the windshield and prayed he could stop the SOB who was trying to kill them.

From the corner of his eye, Lucky spotted Marin running toward the barn. She looked over her shoulder at him, and he could see the terror on her face. Still, she was alive, and the driver didn't appear to be going after her.

Lucky dove for the ground again, but just like before, the driver adjusted and swung back around. He figured if he could keep this up until Marin got to the barn, then maybe she could call for help.

But on the next turn, the driver changed course. He

didn't come after Lucky. He did a doughnut in the pasture and slammed on the accelerator.

Hell. He was going after Marin.

She was still a good thirty feet from the barn, and even once inside, she might not be protected. This SOB might just drive the truck right in there after her. If that happened, she'd be trapped.

There was no way he could outrun the truck and get to Marin first, so Lucky took aim again and fired. This time, the back windshield blew apart, and he got just a glimpse of the driver.

Whoever it was wore a dark knit cap.

Lucky fired again. And again. Until he saw the truck's brake lights flash on. Maybe one of the shots had hit him. Lucky hoped so. But just in case this was some kind of ploy to make them think he was hurt, Lucky kept his gun aimed, and he raced forward.

Ahead of him, with the truck at a dead stop in between them, Marin ducked into the barn. Thank God. She might be safer there.

Lucky raced forward, keeping his eye on the driver and looking out for any weapon the guy might have.

Lucky slowed when he neared the truck and kept his gun ready. "Step out of the vehicle," Lucky warned.

He needed the guy out in the open because he could be just sitting there waiting for his best opportunity to kill Lucky so he could go after Marin.

Nothing.

No reaction. No sound.

Not even any movement.

Lucky inched forward. And with each step he prayed he wouldn't look inside that vehicle and see his sister. If she'd been the one on that train, if she'd set those explosives, then she might want him dead. Why, he didn't know. And he didn't want to have to find out.

He took another step, then another—aware that between the pulse hammering in his ears and the drone of the engine, he couldn't hear much. But he didn't need to hear well to realize that the driver was about to do something that Lucky was certain he wouldn't like.

The brake lights went off. In the same second, the driver jammed the accelerator again.

"No!" Lucky yelled.

He added another prayer that Marin had found some safe place in the barn.

To his right, he heard voices. Someone shouting their names. Two of the ranch hands were making their way across the pasture. Neither was armed, but because they were closer to the barn, Lucky figured they would stand a better chance of getting to Marin in time.

The driver must have thought so, as well. Because he didn't head for the barn.

Instead, he made a beeline for the back of the pasture, obviously trying get away.

"Take care of Marin," Lucky shouted to the ranch hands as he started sprinting after the truck.

Chapter 10

Marin glanced at the clock on the nightstand next to her bed. It was less than a minute since the last time she'd checked. It felt like an eternity, but it had only been a little over an hour that Sheriff Whitley and Lucky had been searching for the driver of that truck.

Maybe Lucky and the sheriff had already caught the man. Maybe he was already on his way to the jail, ready to tell the sheriff why he wanted her dead.

"Maybe," she mumbled.

She hugged Noah to her chest and rocked him. After nearly being killed in the pasture, she needed to hold her son and try to deal with the adrenaline shock and the aftermath.

"He's asleep," her grandmother whispered. "Want me to put him in his crib?"

Marin was about to decline, to say she wanted another minute or two to hold Noah, but then she heard footsteps. Because the overwhelming sense of danger was still with her, she bolted from the bed, ready to run so that she could protect her baby. But running wasn't necessary.

Lucky appeared in the doorway.

"The driver got away," he announced.

So much for her wish. "But the truck left tracks. The sheriff will be able to follow him."

Lucky shook his head. "The truck drove through a fence in the back of the pasture, and Sheriff Whitley thinks he escaped using an old ranch trail."

So, he was gone. Gone! And that meant Lucky, Noah and she weren't safe. There could be another attack.

Her grandmother came and took Noah, gently removing him from her arms, and carried him into the sitting room. Since Marin didn't want to wake him and they obviously had to talk, she grabbed on to his arm and led him into her walk-in closet.

"I'm sorry," Lucky mumbled. "I should have caught that SOB while he was still in the pasture."

His frustration and anger were so strong they were palatable. Marin knew how he felt. "He was in a truck. You were on foot. Catching him was a long shot at best."

She hoped her words comforted her as much as she was trying to comfort Lucky. This wasn't his fault. In fact, he'd done everything in his power to stop her from being hurt. He had literally put himself in harm's way to protect her.

"Are you okay?" he asked. He leaned away from her and checked her over from head to toe.

"I'm fine." Marin checked him, as well, and wasn't pleased to see grass and mud on his jacket and jeans. But then, he'd had to hit the ground several times to dodge the truck. "Were you hurt?"

"No." There was a thin veneer of bravado covering

all the emotion that lay just beneath the surface. Lucky held on to his composure for several seconds before he cursed. "First the explosion. Now, this. I brought all of this to your doorstep."

"I doubt it." She touched his arm and rubbed gently. "Since this particular doorstep at the ranch is also Dexter's, the danger might have happened whether you were here or not."

She saw the flash of realization in his eyes, and he glanced over his shoulder in the direction of the sitting room, where her son was sleeping. When Lucky's gaze came back to hers, there was a different emotion. One she understood because she was a parent.

Lucky cursed again and pulled her to him. His grip was too tight. His breath, hot and fast. She felt his heartbeat hammer against her chest.

He mumbled something she didn't understand. The words came out as mere breath brushing against her hair.

"I didn't get a good a look at the driver of that truck," he said. "Did you?"

"No. But I don't think it was Dexter." Marin immediately reexamined the images racing through her head. "Still, I can't be sure, especially since I didn't see the driver's face." She paused. "First there was that e-mail from Dexter. And then you see Kinley on the surveillance video. Two of the people we thought were dead might not be."

He nodded. "Now the question is, are they responsible for what's happening to us?" Lucky also paused. "But just like you can't believe Dexter would do this, I can't believe Kinley would, either."

Neither of them could be objective about the situation.

Marin knew that. But it didn't mean they were wrong. Maybe both of their siblings were alive.

And innocent.

There was a sharp knock at the bedroom door, and Lucky drew his gun from his shoulder holster. He headed out of the closet. Fast. He obviously wasn't taking any chances. But the vigilance was unnecessary because the person on the other side of the door was Sheriff Jack Whitley.

Marin had known Jack most of her life, and he hadn't changed much. A real cowboy cop. Tall and lanky with dark hair and gray eyes, Jack had on jeans and a white shirt with his badge clipped onto a leather belt.

Since Jack obviously wanted to talk to them, Marin thought of the bug, and her parents who were probably trying to hear every word. "We'll have some privacy out here," she told him, and Jack didn't say anything until they walked into the enclosed patio.

"My deputy wasn't able to find the truck or the driver," Jack announced, causing Lucky to groan. The sheriff volleyed glances at them and kept his voice low. "You're sure this guy tried to kill you?"

"Dead sure," Lucky insisted.

Jack nodded and seemed to accept that as gospel truth. "The ranch hands said the truck wasn't used very often and was put in the barn for the winter. Keys were almost certainly in the ignition, and the barn wasn't locked, either. They didn't see anyone around that part of the pasture."

"I guess that means no one saw the driver?" she asked.

"No one," Jack Whitley verified. "But there were footprints in the barn, and there's a Texas Ranger coming out from the crime lab. He'll take impressions and try to see if that'll tell us anything." His attention landed on Marin. "I spoke to your dad. He says this has nothing to do with Dexter."

It took Marin several long moments to figure out how to answer that. "I want to believe that."

Jack didn't answer right away, either. "Yeah. I understand. But since I have a job to do and since I'm sure you don't want to dodge any more trucks, I have to say that the circumstantial evidence is pointing to Dexter."

"Why do you say that?" Lucky wanted to know.

The sheriff took out the envelope he had tucked beneath his arm. "A visitor who just arrived and this." He extracted a photo from the envelope and handed it to Lucky.

Marin leaned in so she could see the photograph, as well. It was a grainy shot, taken from what appeared to be the surveillance camera outside the bank on Main Street. But even with the grainy shot, it wasn't hard to make out the woman's face.

"That's Brenna Martel," Lucky confirmed. "She's someone else I thought was dead."

Jack made a sound of agreement. "While I was looking around for that truck driver, I had the Justice Department give me a case update." Now, his attention turned to Lucky. "I know who you really are. And it seems your sister and now this woman might both be alive. Dexter, too."

Three people, all presumed dead. Now, all alive. Innocent people didn't usually let their friends and families believe they were dead unless something bad, very bad, was going on.

"You said something about a visitor?" Lucky prompted.

Marin held her breath. God, had one of those three come to the ranch?

"The visitor is the other player in the case," Jack explained. "Grady Duran."

"He's here?" And Lucky didn't sound any happier about it than Marin was.

"Duran's here," the sheriff verified. "And he's demanding to speak to both of you now."

Lucky would have preferred to delay this meeting.

After all, Marin was just coming down from a horrible ordeal. The last thing he wanted was to add any more tension to her already stress-filled day. But this chat with Duran might give them answers, and right now, answers were in very short supply.

"I'd rather you waited in the bedroom," Lucky repeated to Marin. But like the other two times he'd said it, she didn't budge. She walked side by side with him toward the front of the ranch house where the sheriff had said Grady Duran was waiting to see them. Sheriff Whitley was right behind them.

"If Duran's the one who just tried to kill us, then I want the chance to confront him," Marin insisted.

That's what Lucky was afraid of. That Duran had indeed been behind the wheel of the truck. And that Duran would try to kill them again.

But why?

Lucky kept going back to that critical question. If Duran was on the up and up and simply wanted answers as to Dexter's whereabouts, then he wouldn't want Marin and him dead. He'd follow them, demand to talk to them. But it would serve no purpose for Duran to kill them.

Well, at least no purpose that Lucky could think of.

Still, he couldn't take any more risks when it came to Marin. As they approached the great room of the ranch house, Lucky drew his weapon. He checked over his shoulder and saw that the sheriff had placed his hand over the butt on his own service revolver. Good. They were both ready in case something went wrong.

Duran was pacing in the great room. The man was just over six feet tall and solid. He wore a perfectly tailored suit. Cashmere, probably. He impatiently checked his watch at the exact moment his gaze connected with Lucky's.

Duran wasn't alone. On the other side of the massive room near the stone fireplace stood Lois and Howard Sheppard. They didn't look happy about their unexpected visitor.

"He said it was important, that it's about Dexter," Lois volunteered. "I was hoping he'd know where my son is. That's the only reason we let him in." She didn't go any closer to her daughter. Probably because both the sheriff and Lucky moved protectively in front of Marin.

However, Marin would have no part in that. She merely stepped to the side. "Were you the one who tried to kill us?" she demanded.

"No," Duran readily answered, though the denial hadn't come easily. The muscles in his jaw were so tight that Lucky was surprised the man could even speak. "I could ask you the same thing. Someone planted an explosive device in my rental car."

Lucky glanced at the sheriff who confirmed that with

a nod. "The device was on a timer, but failed to detonate. If it had, I would have been blown to smithereens."

"Well, neither Lucky nor I set an explosive," Marin grumbled. "But I'm sure you're not short of suspects. With your caustic personality, you've made your share of enemies."

Duran didn't react to her insult. He whipped his gaze toward Lois and Howard. "What about you two? Either of you into blowing things up to protect your son?"

Lois made a slight gasp and flattened her hand over her chest. Howard hardly reacted, other than a slight narrowing of his eyes. "I think you've already worn out your welcome."

Duran shook his head. "I'm not leaving yet. Not until you tell me where Dexter is."

"We thought you knew," Lois accused.

Lucky waited for someone to respond, but the room fell silent.

"All right. I'll get this conversation rolling," Duran continued a moment later, aiming his comment at Howard and Lois. "Here's my theory. You want me out of the picture because when I find Dexter, I'm going to haul his butt off to jail. Then, I'll figure out how to get back every penny he owes me. And by the way, that's a lot of pennies. Your son is in debt to me for the tune of nearly six million dollars."

Six million. Lucky had no idea it was that much. That was a big motive for murder. It also explained why Duran was desperate to find Dexter.

Howard took a menacing step forward, but Duran held out his hands. Then, he pulled an envelope from his pocket and slapped it onto the coffee table. "That's a copy of the letter my lawyer sent to the state attorney general and the Justice Department. I haven't had the best relationship with those two groups in the past, but I've decided to help them with their ongoing investigation."

"So?" Howard challenged.

But Lucky knew what this meant, and it had just upped the stakes.

So far, Duran had tried to find Dexter on his own. He'd not only refused to assist the Justice Department, he had likely withheld critical evidence. Now, Duran's cooperation could blow this case wide open, and it could lead them directly to Dexter or at least to the truth of what'd really happened in that research facility.

"So," Duran repeated, "I'd rather deal with Dexter on my own, but I'm willing to cut a deal with the Feds. I'm also willing to hang your son to get revenge for what he did to me. Understand?"

"We understand," Lois snapped.

The corner of Duran's mouth lifted. "I'm not going away. And I'm not backing down. I'm staying in Willow Ridge, and I plan to haunt you, your daughter and her fiancé until you lead me to Dexter."

"Just make sure your threats stay verbal," the sheriff warned Duran. "Because you'll be the one arrested if you cross the line."

Duran mumbled something and turned to leave. Lucky followed him. Marin would have no doubt done the same, but the phone rang, and several seconds later, one of the housekeepers announced that the call was for Marin.

Lucky went to the porch and caught Duran's arm before he could head down the steps. "Talk to me about Kinley Ford. What do you know about her?"

"She's dead." He paused, studied Lucky's expression and then shook off his grip with far more force than necessary. "At least the police think she is. You have any information to the contrary?"

"No," Lucky lied.

Duran kept staring. "Kinley Ford was at the research facility the night of the explosion. I know, because I was there, too."

"You saw her?" But Lucky already knew the answer. Or rather the answer that Duran had given the investigators when they had first interviewed him.

"I did see her. Dexter, Brenna and Kinley." Duran glanced around the grounds. The vigilant glance of a man who was wary of his surroundings. "Something was off, but I didn't know what. Dexter was acting even less normal than usual. I mean, he was forever pulling that prima donna genius crap where he'd say he couldn't be interrupted. But that night, he was wound up so tight that I could see he was about to snap."

Probably because Dexter was about to put his plan into action. "Did you ask why he was on edge?"

He lifted a shoulder, glanced around again "The prototype of the chemical project was due within forty-eight hours. Dexter kept saying it was ready, but that I couldn't see it until he'd given it one final test." Duran cursed. "I should have forced him to show it to me."

Lucky gave that some thought. "So, if the prototype wasn't ready, you think Dexter could have set the explosion, run with his research project and then faked his death?"

Duran met him eye to eye. "I think he faked not only his own death but maybe Kinley Ford's and Brenna Martel's."

Yes. After seeing his sister on that surveillance video, Lucky had toyed with that idea, too. Still, there was all that blood. "Why would Dexter have done that?"

"Simple. Because he needed their help to finish the project. Plus, he knew what a fortune that chemical weapon would make, and he didn't want to hand it over to the investors. Maybe he thought he could get away with it if everyone associated with the project was presumed dead. Then, he could wait a year or two and use an alias when he tried to sell it on the black market."

"There's a big problem with that theory. Kinley Ford wouldn't have cooperated with Dexter's illegal plan. She wasn't a criminal," Lucky insisted.

Duran shrugged. "Maybe she wasn't a willing participant."

Hell. That theory raced through and left him with more questions than when he'd started this investigation. "What could Dexter have used to force her to cooperate?"

"Right off the top of my head, I'd say maybe she was a fool for love. Brenna certainly was." Another glance around. "But I know that Dexter had already broken things off with Brenna."

Lucky hated to even put this out there, but it was something he had to know. "And you think that Dexter then started an affair with Kinley?"

Another shrug. "Something was going on between them. Hell for all I know, maybe Kinley Ford was the mastermind of that explosion. Or Brenna. *Women*," he added like profanity.

Lucky dismissed his sister's involvement. He had to. Because he couldn't deal with the alternative. "But if

Dexter and both women are alive, why haven't they surfaced?"

"Maybe they have." Duran extracted a set of car keys from his pocket. "My advice? Don't trust anyone around here."

"You think Dexter wants me dead, too?"

Duran blinked. "He has no reason to kill you. Does he?"

Oh, Lucky could think of a reason. If Dexter knew who he really was, then he might try to eliminate him. Dexter would figure out that Lucky wouldn't stop until he had justice for Kinley.

If Kinley needed justice, that is.

Lucky hated that he was beginning to doubt her.

"But I think Dexter's parents would do anything to keep you out of their daughter's life," Duran continued. "The stories Dexter used to tell me about them. They're manipulative enough to be very dangerous." He headed down the steps.

Like Duran, Lucky wasn't certain that Howard and Lois's parental concerns were all just threats.

He turned to go back inside, but as he reached for the door, it opened. Marin was there, and he instantly knew something was wrong. She'd probably gotten some bad news from that phone call.

"Is it your brother?" he asked.

She shook her head. "The psychologist, Dr. Ross Blevins. He called to let us know that the judge ordered that the interview be completed today."

"Impossible." Lucky didn't even have to think about it. "The driver of that truck might be sitting out there, waiting for round two." He glared at Lois and Howard.

They'd no doubt tried to orchestrate scheduling the interview when both Marin and he were not mentally ready.

"I know, and that's what I told the psychologist. But he said the judge insisted. He wants a preliminary report on his desk by close of business today."

Lucky cursed under his breath and intensified the glare at the Sheppards. Lois at least had the decency to look a little uncomfortable. Howard, however, couldn't quite contain his pleasure. To him, this was the next step in regaining control of his daughter.

But that wasn't going to happen.

"I'll call the psychologist," Lucky told her. He hooked his arm around her waist so he could lead her back to the bedroom. "I'll work out all of this."

But Marin didn't budge. "It's too late. Dr. Blevins is already on his way over here to conduct the interview. He should be here any minute."

Chapter 11

"Marin was nearly murdered today," she heard Lucky say to Dr. Blevins. Lucky had called the psychologist despite the fact the man was already en route. "The sheriff and his deputy are still here checking out the crime scene. Plus, she just got out of the hospital yesterday."

Marin continued to feed Noah his bottle, and she tried not to react to what was going on around her. Impossible to do. She still had dirt on the knees of her jeans. Dirt she'd gotten from trying to dodge that killer truck.

Lucky's appearance wasn't much better. He had triple the mud and dirt that she did, and unlike her, he was definitely reacting with anger. From what she could judge from the one side of the conversation she could hear, the psychologist wasn't going to postpone the interview.

Apparently aware that she had her attention elsewhere, Noah bucked a little and reached for her face. He pinched her chin, automatically causing Marin to smile. Looking down at him, seeing that precious little face, was all the reminder she needed that somehow she had to muster enough energy and resolve to get through this ordeal.

"This meeting needs to be rescheduled," Lucky continued. "Marin's attorney hasn't arrived." He paused again. "Yes, I know it's not necessary for her attorney to be there, but we'd like him to be."

Judging from his expression, that didn't go over well with the doctor.

"I couldn't change his mind," Lucky growled a moment later. He jabbed the end-call button and shoved his phone back into his pocket. "He's already here at the ranch and is waiting for us in your father's office."

That didn't surprise her. Her father would want to listen in on the interview, as well. "As soon as I'm finished feeding Noah, we'll go ahead and get this over with."

"Take your time. Let the guy wait." Lucky sat down on the bed beside her and brushed his fingers across Noah's hair. Her son responded with a smile and turned to face Lucky. Noah no longer seemed interested in the bottle and instead reached for Lucky. Marin let her son go into his arms.

"No barfing, okay, buddy?" Lucky teased. He put Noah against his chest and patted his back to burp him.

It was such a simple gesture, something she'd done dozens of times. Still, today it seemed, well, special. Maybe because of the near-death experience. But it also had to do with Lucky. With the way he held her son. The genuine pleasure in his eyes from doing something that many would consider mundane and even a little gross.

"Thank you," Marin heard herself say. Mercy, she was actually tearing up.

Lucky met her gaze over the top of Noah's head. "For what?"

"Everything."

But she immediately regretted that. It sounded gushy. As if she wanted this arrangement to be permanent. She didn't. They were on opposite sides of an important issue: Dexter. Plus, after her ordeal with Randall, she wasn't ready to risk her heart again.

Or Noah's.

Lucky had too much personal baggage of his own to be a real father to Noah.

"The kissing has screwed things up. It gave us this… connection. And it's complicating the heck out of this situation."

Since Marin couldn't deny that and since she had no idea what to say, she figured it was a good time to just sit there and listen.

"If this interview goes well…" Lucky continued a moment later. But he didn't finish it. He didn't have to.

"You'll be leaving the ranch right away," Marin finished for him. "I know. You need to find your sister."

He brushed a kiss on Noah's cheek. "I can't leave until I'm certain you're both safe."

It was tempting to try to keep him there, but she didn't have the right. Or the courage to make a commitment. Besides, he really did need to find his sister. She could be in serious danger. And if she was the person who'd tried to kill them, he might need to stop her from setting another explosive.

"Once the interview is done, I'll leave the ranch, as well," Marin assured him. "I have enough money to hire a bodyguard. Once I'm back in Fort Worth, I'll move again. I'll make sure no one finds Noah and me."

Lucky stared at her. "You can't be sure of that."

"True. But I can't be sure of it if you're with me, either." And then she played her trump card, the one thing that she knew would convince Lucky to leave. "Besides, if Dexter is behind this, Noah and I could be in even more danger just being around you."

It stung to say that, because she didn't believe it was true. She didn't honestly believe Dexter would come after her, even if he was trying to get to Lucky. Still, she needed some leverage to get Lucky to budge in the only direction he should go.

Lucky made an unhappy sound deep within his throat and gave a crisp nod. That was it. No more conversation. No rebuttal of what she'd just said. That nod was all she got before he stood and started for the door.

Marin followed, of course. "We can leave Noah with my grandmother."

He didn't comment on that, either. Lucky merely went down the hall and knocked on her grandmother's door. "Time for the interview," Helen commented, taking Noah from Lucky. "Don't let that head doctor bully you."

Marin assured her that they wouldn't and thanked her grandmother for watching Noah.

The walk down the hall had an ominous feel to it that only got worse when they passed the living room, and saw her parents.

"This is for your own good," her father insisted, again.

"Is it?" Marin fired back, but she didn't give them more than that. She didn't want them to get any satisfaction from seeing her upset. But underneath she was well past being upset.

Dr. Ross Blevins waited in the office. She'd seen him before around town, but had never been introduced. Too bad they had to meet under these circumstances.

Wearing a dark gray suit that was almost the same color as the winter sky and his precisely groomed hair, the doctor stood in front of the bay windows, the sprawling pasture a backdrop behind him. He looked like an inquisitor with his probing blue eyes and judgmental frown.

"Mr. Davidson," the doctor greeted Lucky. It made Marin cringe a little to hear Lucky labeled with the name of Noah's birth father. "Ms. Sheppard. Why don't you two sit so we can get started?"

But Lucky continued to stand, staring at the doctor. "I don't suppose it'd do any good to object to this on the basis that Marin has already been through enough for one day."

Dr. Blevins shook his head and remained perfectly calm. He sat at her father's desk. "This matter should be addressed immediately."

"Why?"

The doctor blinked. Hesitated. "Because the safety of a child is at stake."

"Noah's fine," Lucky insisted. "But this entire witch hunt of which you're obviously a major participant—or a pawn—isn't."

Marin took up the argument from there. "How much are my parents paying you?"

That caused a slight ruffle in his cool composure. A muscle tightened in his jaw. "The county is paying me for what will be an independent, objective assessment. But I have to tell you, you're not off to a good start."

"Neither are you," Lucky fired back.

Dr. Blevins got to his feet. "At least I am who I say I am, *Mr. Davidson*."

The room went silent, and Marin held her breath because that comment had a heavy punch to it. Coupled with the doctor's now almost smug glare, she knew this was about to take a very ugly turn.

"Sit down," the doctor insisted. He took his own advice and returned to her father's chair. "And then you can explain why you two lied about your relationship."

Marin lost her breath for a moment. Yes, this was an ugly turn. And it would no doubt get even uglier.

Lucky caught on to her hand and eased her into the chair across from where the doctor was seated. Then, he sat, as well, and they stared at the man who could ultimately take Noah away from her.

"You're not engaged," Dr. Blevins continued. "In fact, I suspect you're practically strangers."

"Why do you think that?" Lucky asked. Marin was glad he did. Her throat seemed to have snapped shut.

The doctor propped his elbows on the desk. "Because I know the truth."

"The truth?" Lucky repeated. "I doubt that. What you know is what Marin's parents have told you."

"Her parents didn't tell me. Someone else tipped me off, and then I did some investigating. I know you're not Randall Davidson. He's been dead for well over a year. I have a copy of his death certificate, though it wasn't easy to get since Randall was his middle name. The certificate was filed as Mitchell R. Davidson."

Since Marin couldn't deny any of this, she just sat there and wondered where this was leading. Would the doctor try to use this to challenge her custodial rights? And if so, how could she stop that from happening?

She glanced at Lucky, and in that brief exchange, she could tell he was as concerned as she was. But there was something else beneath the surface. Resolve. "It'll be okay," he promised in a whisper.

But Marin wasn't sure how anyone could make this okay.

Dr. Blevins stared at Lucky. "Since I know you're not Randall Davidson, would you like to tell me who you really are?"

"Quinn Bacelli." He paused a moment. Leaned forward. And returned the steely stare. "Marin's fiancé."

Marin hoped she didn't look too surprised. But the doctor certainly did. "You're lying."

Lucky shook his head and slid his hand over hers. "Why would I do that?"

"To help Marin keep her son."

"Marin doesn't need my help for that. She's a good mother who's been railroaded by parents who want to control her life." Lucky stabbed an accusing finger at Blevins. "And you're helping them do that."

The doctor shook his head. "I'm trying to get to the truth."

"You have the truth. No, I'm not Noah's biological father, but he's my son in every way that matters."

Lucky sounded sincere. Because he probably was. He did care deeply for her son. But would that be enough to get Dr. Blevins to back off?

"Why did you lie to everyone about who you were?" Blevins asked Lucky.

"Because I asked him to," Marin volunteered before Lucky could answer. "I came to the ranch to visit my grandmother. I wanted the trip to be short. And I didn't want to have to answer what I knew would be a litany of my parents' questions about my personal relationship. I figured it would keep things simple if they thought he was Randall."

The doctor obviously didn't like her quick response. His forehead bunched up, and he was no doubt trying to figure out a way to challenge what she was saying because that's what her parents had told him to do.

Marin pushed harder. "Lucky took care of my son while I was in the hospital. Do you think I'd trust a stranger to do that?" She didn't wait for him to respond. "Do you think I'd have a stranger sleep in my bed?"

"Well?" Lucky challenged when the doctor only stared at them.

"I'll have to tell the judge that you lied about your real identity," Blevins finally said.

"Go ahead. I'll have my attorney contact the judge, as well. And the state attorney general. Because, you see, you might think you're doing the right thing, but I don't believe your motives will hold up under scrutiny from someone who's not beholden to Howard and Lois Sheppard."

The doctor scrawled something on the paper in front of him. "Judge Carrick will get my report today. You should hear something as early as tomorrow."

Marin wasn't sure what that meant, but she had to hope that it would all turn out all right despite this horrible meeting.

She and Lucky stood, but the doctor spoke before they could even take a step.

"Judge Carrick tends to be conservative, even old-fashioned, when it comes to his cases," Blevins said. It sounded as if he were choosing his words carefully. "He wants me to tell you that you're to remain here at the ranch until you hear his decision."

"Lucky has to leave," Marin volunteered. "A family emergency."

The doctor made a sound to indicate he understood. But, of course, there was no way he could. "It could take weeks or even months for someone like the state attorney general to intercede. In the mean time, Judge Carrick could give temporary custody of your son to your parents."

Marin was glad that Lucky still had his arm around her. Still, she didn't want Blevins to see that she was on the verge of losing it. "You can stop that from happening," she told the doctor.

Blevins pulled in a long, weary breath and shook his head. "You were born and raised here, Marin. You know how things work."

That chilled her to the bone. She knew how much power and influence her wealthy parents had. This session had been nothing more than a square filler, the prelude to her parents getting what they wanted—her back under their control.

"I'll help if I can," Dr. Blevins finally conceded. But his tone and demeanor said that his help wouldn't do them any good.

Lucky led her out of the room. "I'll call my lawyer and get her out here."

Marin was so tired from the adrenaline crash and the stress that she nearly gave in. It would be so easy just to put all of this on Lucky's shoulders. But that's what had gotten her in trouble in the first place.

"I'll contact that attorney again in Fort Worth, and while I'm at it, I'll phone my friend Lizette, too. If she's back in town, I know she'll come right away."

Lucky nodded and caught on to her chin to force eye contact. "Are you okay?"

"No. But I will be, after I confront my parents."

"You think that'll help?"

"It'll help me," she insisted. She paused and moved closer so that her mouth was right against Lucky's ear. "I'm thinking about taking Noah and leaving tonight."

He didn't stiffen, nor did he seem surprised. Lucky simply slipped his arm around her and pulled her closer. He brushed a kiss on her cheek. That kiss went through her. Warm lips against cold cheek.

"Your parents won't give up. From the sound of it, neither will this judge. They'll look for you. No matter where you go, they'll keep looking."

"What other choice do I have? I can't let them have Noah. You heard what Dr. Blevins said about temporary custody. It could take me months to sort out everything and get Noah back. In the mean time, I'd be here, right where my parents want me to be."

"There is an alternative, something that might help you keep custody."

"What? I'll do anything." Marin was certain she sounded as desperate as she felt.

Lucky looked her straight in the eyes. "You can marry me."

Lucky watched his marriage proposal register in Marin's eyes. He'd dumbfounded her. She didn't utter a sound. Her mouth dropped open a little, and it stayed in that position while she stared at him.

"It makes sense," he insisted. "If we're married and I make it known that I intend to legally adopt Noah, then how could a judge object?"

But Lucky could think of a reason: Marin's parents were paying the judge so well that the man would find a way around the law. However, a maneuver like that would be temporary at best and highly illegal. Even this judge couldn't be out of reach from the state attorney general or Justice Department. Just like Duran, Lucky intended to use both if it came down to it.

"Marriage?" Marin finally mumbled. "That wasn't something I'd considered."

"I know. We've been in overload mode since we first met." Unfortunately, there were worse things to think about than temporarily losing custody of Noah.

Marin and Noah were in danger.

Marriage wouldn't keep them from a killer, but it would give Marin a little breathing room. He also hoped it wouldn't create a new set of problems. After all, Marin and he were attracted to each other. A marriage of convenience would muddy already murky waters.

She shook her head, but Lucky couldn't tell from her stunned expression exactly what she was thinking. She opened her mouth to answer, but she didn't get to utter a word before his cell phone rang.

"Blocked number," he mumbled, glancing down at the caller ID screen. And he immediately thought of his sister. Was she trying to contact him? "Bacelli," he answered.

But it wasn't his sister's voice he heard.

"Mr. Bacelli, this is Brenna Martel. Your sister and I worked together for Dexter Sheppard."

Well, that was certainly a voice he hadn't expected to hear. But it was welcome.

"I know who you are." He didn't want to put the call on speaker in case Marin's parents were still around, but he motioned for Marin to move closer so she could hear this. "I thought you were dead."

"A lot of people think that."

Of course, Lucky wondered why she was calling and if this call was related to the attempts to kill Marin and him. But right now, he had a more pressing question. "Is Kinley alive?"

Silence. Lucky held his breath. Beside him, Marin was doing the same.

"I'd rather not say anything about Kinley," Brenna finally answered.

"You don't have a choice. I want to know if my sister is alive, and you're going to tell me."

"Not over the phone," Brenna maintained, though her voice was shaky and hardly there. "It isn't safe. The less I say, the safer it will be for me. Someone wants me dead."

"Welcome to the club," Lucky snarled. "Your safety isn't my top priority, so start talking. I want to know if Kinley is alive and if so, where she is."

"No answers over the phone. I want to meet with you and Marin Sheppard."

Lucky didn't bother to suppress a groan. "I'll just bet you do. That way you can get another crack at trying to kill us."

"It isn't me who wants you dead." Despite that whispery, weak voice, Brenna sounded adamant. However, that didn't mean she was telling the truth. Killers were often very convincing liars.

"If not you, then who?" Lucky demanded.

"I don't know. Dexter, maybe. Or someone connected to him. Possibly even Grady Duran. God knows he's furious with everyone right now. I have information, or rather pieces of information, and I don't know how they all fit. That's why I need to see you. We have important things to discuss that involve both of you."

Lucky had to pause a moment to gather his composure. He wanted to know about Kinley, but this sounded a lot like suicide. "You must think Marin and I are fools. Meet with you so you can ambush us?"

"Fool or not, if you want to know about your siblings, you'll see me. Tomorrow morning, 6:00 a.m., at the abandoned drive-in theater. You must arrive together, without the sheriff or anyone else. And if you're carrying a weapon, hold it high so I can see it. Because I don't want to be ambushed, either."

With that, Brenna Martel hung up.

"The drive-in is on the edge of town," Marin immediately supplied, letting him know that she'd managed to hear the conversation. "It's surrounded by a flat field. Last time I saw it, the big screen and the concession stand were still there, but little else. In other words, there aren't many places a person could hide to ambush us."

Lucky was already shaking his head before Marin even finished. "I can't risk taking you out there. Heck, I can't risk taking you out of this house after what happened on our little walk this morning."

She caught on to his shoulders. "You can't miss this meeting, either. Lucky, this could be your best chance to find your sister and for me to know once and for all what happened to Dexter."

He made sure there was plenty of sarcasm in his voice. "You want to meet a potential felon who might have not only faked her own death and stole a chemical weapon, but also tried to kill us twice?"

Marin lifted her shoulder. "What's the alternative? Not ever knowing? Running? Hiding? Brenna Martel might have what we need to stop all of this. She could end the danger so that I can safely get out of here with Noah."

He couldn't argue with that. "Then, I'll go meet with her. I'll hear what she has to say and come back here to tell you."

She cocked her head to the side. "You heard what she said. This meeting will only happen if we're both there."

"Yeah, so it'll be easier for her to kill us."

"Not if we take precautions. I know that drive-in. We used to go there when I was a kid." Marin caught on to his arm when he started to move away. "We can arrive ahead of time, hours before Brenna will be expecting us, and stake out a safe place to wait for her."

Lucky couldn't believe what he was hearing. Or what he was thinking. God, was it even something he should consider?

How could he not?

Judging from the determined look in Marin's eyes, she felt the same. He cursed under his breath. "It's still too dangerous."

"Yes. But you can make it less dangerous. This is what you do. You know ways to minimize the risk."

"Yeah. And you staying here at the house is the best way to do that."

"No." Marin let that hang in the air. "Nowhere is safe until we learn who's trying to kill us. And if it's Brenna, then maybe it's time for a showdown."

"A showdown?" He threw his hands in the air. "With you in the frickin' middle?"

"With us in control of the situation." She pressed her fingers to his mouth to stop more of his protest. "We have to do this, so no more arguing. Instead, let's figure out how we can make this as safe as possible."

He saw it then. The sheer determination on her face. Marin wasn't going to back down from this. Worse? He couldn't let her back down. Because she was right—they had to know the truth.

"I'll set up a safety net. Some security," he said thinking out loud. "I'll get someone to provide backup so we're not out there alone."

"Does that mean we'll meet her?"

Lucky cursed again. There was really only one answer he could live with. "Yes."

He only hoped that he wasn't leading them straight to their deaths.

"I need to make lots of calls," he explained. "I have a PI friend who can get us some monitoring equipment so that no one can sneak up on us out there."

He would have added more if he hadn't heard footsteps. At first he thought the doctor was coming out of the office, but the footsteps came from the other direction.

Lucky pushed Marin behind him and drew his gun.

Just as Howard and Lois stepped into the hallway.

Lucky didn't put his gun away, and he hoped his glare conveyed his displeasure over what the two were trying to do to their daughter.

"Dr. Blevins just called me on my cell," Howard announced. He kept his attention nailed to Lucky. "He's writing his report now, but he wanted to give us a heads-up about the lie you told. Now, who the hell are you? I know for a fact you're not Randall Davidson."

"Guess there's no such thing as confidentiality when it comes to Blevins," Lucky grumbled. That was something else he could mention to the state attorney general. "My name is Lucky Bacelli."

"Marin, how could you do this?" her mother asked, snapping her attention to her daughter. "You hired this man, this imposter, so that we'd think Noah had a father?"

Lucky spoke before Marin could. "Noah does have a father. *Me*. My feelings for Noah aren't based on DNA. Good thing, too. Because after meeting you guys, I think that whole DNA connection thing is highly overrated."

Lois stiffened while her husband just stood there and stewed. "Judge Carrick will hear about your lies," she threatened. "You're obviously not thinking straight." She kept her eyes trained on Marin. "If you had been, you wouldn't have brought this imposter into our home. I don't care what he claims his feelings are for Noah. This is a sham of a relationship."

"A sham?" Marin stepped out from behind him and faced her parents. "For the record, Lucky asked me to marry him."

With Brenna's phone call, Lucky had nearly forgotten that. Though it was another critical cog in this complicated wheel they were building.

"You turned him down, of course," her father issued like a warning.

Marin's chin came up. "Actually, I hadn't given an answer yet. But now is as good a time as any." She turned, leaned in and kissed him. A real kiss like the one they'd shared in the closet.

"Yes, Lucky," Marin said. "I'll marry you."

Chapter 12

Marin waited, something she seemed to have been doing for hours.

Lucky was on the phone. She only hoped his efforts paid off and that this meeting with Brenna Martel ended with them alive and with crucial answers about Dexter and Kinley.

Lucky had certainly taken every conceivable precaution to assure their safety. It was midnight, a full six hours before the scheduled meeting. They weren't at the drive-in, but rather parked across the field, with their car nestled in some trees. Marin was armed with one of the handguns she'd taken from the ranch. Lucky had his own weapon and a backup that he'd slipped into an ankle holster.

To make sure they were safe and not sitting ducks in the field, Lucky had rigged the area around the car with a motion detector that he'd had delivered to the ranch. With the detector activated, no one would get close enough to ambush them without him finding out.

Lucky had called Dr. Blevins and the judge. There

was no word yet on the outcome of the so-called hearing. No decision about custody. It was a reprieve, but it wouldn't last. Marin needed to make some decisions before the judge made them for her and took her son.

But what were the right decisions?

Lucky was obviously on the same wavelength because in the middle of all this chaos, he'd made wedding plans. Right after announcing to her parents that she'd accepted Lucky's proposal, he'd taken her to town to see the justice of the peace and arranged for a marriage license. And he'd done that without so much as a flicker of emotion. If was as if he'd gone on autopilot.

Get safety equipment. Check.

Call the PI. Check.

Set up security for meeting. Check.

Marry Marin. Check.

It was stupid for that to sting. After all, Lucky was doing her a huge favor by marrying her. Or rather letting her parents *think* he was going to marry her. She wasn't sure he'd actually go through with it. After all, he wouldn't exactly jump at the chance to have a loveless marriage all because he cared for her son.

Marin wondered if there was more to his feelings.

Those kisses had confused her. And they'd made her burn. There was definitely physical attraction there between them. But that would only give her hope about having a real relationship with Lucky, which just wasn't a good idea. The timing was all wrong. She already had too many things to deal with. Lucky did, as well.

"You're positive there's no one around the drive-in?" Lucky asked.

Though Marin couldn't hear the answer, she knew that Lucky was talking to Burney Rickman, a San Antonio PI who had arrived earlier with a carload of security equipment. Lucky had told her that he trusted this man with his life. That was good because even though they had no choice about this meeting, they might need assistance to stay alive.

Thankfully, Noah was back at the ranch with her grandmother and a deputy that Sheriff Jack Whitley had sent over to guard them and the rest of the place. As a backup, her grandmother had an old Smith & Wesson that she definitely knew how to use. Still, Marin was eager to get this meeting over and done so she could get back to Noah, especially since her parents were also at home.

"Burney doesn't see anyone around the drive-in or in the concession stand, and he's searched the entire place," Lucky relayed to her when he finished the call. "He's also using equipment to make sure no one has set up surveillance cameras. If they have, he said it must be low-tech because his equipment's not picking up anything."

"Maybe the meeting is just that. A meeting. Maybe Brenna doesn't have anything up her sleeve." But Marin couldn't trust that. They had to stay vigilant when and if they ever went into that drive-in to talk to her.

It was entirely possible that Brenna wouldn't show.

And if so, they were back to square one.

Lucky's phone rang again, and he immediately glanced down at the caller ID screen. "It's Cal Rico from the Justice Department. I asked him to call if he found out anything about Brenna or Kinley."

Apparently, he had.

"I see," Lucky said to the Justice Department agent a moment later. Lucky sounded puzzled. "But it was my sister's blood on the floor of that research facility."

The comment had Marin moving across the front seat so she could hear what was being said. Unfortunately, the wind didn't cooperate. Winter had decided to return in full force, and the wind was howling right out of the north. Added to that was the sound of the overhead swishing tree limbs, so she didn't catch a word.

Lucky finally pressed the end-call button and slipped the phone back into his jacket pocket. "Cal Rico ran the surveillance disk from the train through some facial recognition software. It was a high percentage match for Kinley."

No wonder Lucky looked so shell-shocked. "You said something about the blood on the floor?"

Because of the full moon, she had no trouble seeing his expression. That call had not been good news. "Cal had the blood from the research lab retested. It belonged to Brenna and Kinley, all right, but there was a preservative present. They didn't find the preservatives in the earlier tests because they weren't looking for it."

Marin shook her head. "What does that mean?"

"Someone could have stockpiled their blood, possibly without their knowledge if they thought they were donating to a blood bank. Then the person could have used it to fake their deaths." Lucky paused. "Of course, they could have faked it themselves."

Oh, mercy. That put his sister not only alive, but in the thick of what could be the cover-up to a crime. "It doesn't mean she's behind the attempts to kill us," Marin pointed out. "She could be a pawn in all of this."

Anything was possible, including the prospect that her own brother was the one who was manipulating this situation. Though she didn't want to believe that, Marin had to at least consider the possibility. To do otherwise might be a fatal mistake.

"Just focus on what we can control," Lucky said. But it seemed as if he was trying to convince himself along with her. "Once we know the outcome of this meeting, we'll deal with the individual issues."

"Like the wedding."

Marin hadn't intended to say it aloud. It just sort of popped out of her mouth. And it earned her a puzzled stare from Lucky.

Since the subject was out there, seemingly coiled and ready to strike, and since they appeared to have several hours of free time on their hands, Marin continued. "You know a wedding might not do any good. I mean, my parents will probably just look for another way to challenge me for custody of Noah."

He made a sound that could have meant anything. "You're afraid of marrying me."

She thought about that a moment. "I'm afraid of us."

Lucky had apparently thought about that, too. "Yeah."

Marin thought it best to leave that comment alone. But she didn't. "I can't fall for you."

"Same here."

Surprised at his blatant honesty, she took a deep breath. "Good." They were in agreement.

Then, she made the mistake of looking at him. There he sat, looking hotter than any man had a right to look. He certainly had her number. He could take her mind off anything and move it straight to where it shouldn't be.

Specifically, on having down-and-dirty sex with him. She wasn't exactly the dirty-sex type, but he certainly put some bad ideas in her head. They must have crept into his mind, too, because he cursed. Something sexual and rough.

"I'm thinking about kissing you," he said.

"I'm thinking about it, too," Marin admitted. It was a stupid admission, but he could no doubt see and feel the need inside her.

He gripped the steering wheel. "How much are you thinking about it?"

She noted his white knuckles. His rapid breath. "As much as you are."

He squeezed his eyes shut. Groaned. And when he opened his eyes again, he reached for her.

It wasn't a slow, fluid motion. It was frantic and hungry and totally out of control. Exactly the way that Marin wanted it to be. Their arms tangled around each other, and lowering his head, he placed his mouth solidly on hers.

Lucky nudged her lips apart, though it didn't take much effort. She was ready to give him everything, even though she knew that wasn't possible here in the car. This car was her safety net. A way of counting to ten. Because Lucky wouldn't let things go too far.

Would he?

The whole forbidden fantasy thing spiked the heat. Lucky was the ultimate forbidden fantasy.

He pushed open her coat and slipped his hand inside to cover her breast. His touch was clever, wonderful, and he somehow managed to caress her nipple through her bra. Coupled with the fiery effects of his mouth, it sent her need soaring.

"We're in the car," she reminded him when he paused long enough for her to catch her breath.

"Yeah. I'm keeping watch."

She opened her eyes to see if he was truly managing to do that. He was. Damn him, he was. Here she was, body on fire, wishing she could strip him naked, and somehow he was kissing her, pinching her nipple *and* keeping watch.

For some reason, that riled her. Or maybe it just made her feel as if she weren't doing her part. "I'll watch," she insisted.

And because of her aroused, ornery mood, she slid her hand down his chest to his stomach. But her wrist brushed against the most aroused part of him.

Lucky sucked in his breath. "You can't do that."

"I'm keeping watch." Oh, it felt so good to say that and see the tormented pleasure on his hot face.

"We can't have sex in this car," he insisted.

"No. We shouldn't even be kissing."

She couldn't argue with that. So, they sat there. Staring at each other.

"Stupid, stupid, stupid," she mumbled. It seemed the threat of danger wasn't enough to cool them down. "Someone could come at us any minute," Marin reminded him.

"The PI would alert us." His mouth inched toward hers again. "And while I'd like nothing more than to be inside you right now, I don't want to have to multitask while we're having sex."

He continued to stare at her. His mouth moved a little closer. His hand slid up her jeans-covered thigh. Her breath stalled in her throat as his fingers touched her.

Marin could have sworn that her jeans dissolved off her. His touch felt that intimate, like breath against skin. She melted, her body preparing itself for more.

Which it wasn't going to get, of course. She repeated that to herself.

"Keep watch a second," Lucky instructed.

Before she could ask why, Lucky pushed her against the inside of the door, lowered his head and replaced his fingers with his mouth.

True, there was denim between his mouth and her sex, but he managed to make her feel ready to climax.

"Keep watch," Lucky repeated.

"I can't see," she warned.

He chuckled, and his warm breath and the vibration of his laughter creating some very interesting ripples in her body.

Lucky made his way back up. Kissed her mouth again. Then, her cheeks. All the while, he continued surveillance around them.

"This is driving me crazy," she said. "You know that?"

His phone rang, the sound slicing through the car and causing Marin to jump. Just like that, the lightness and the heat between them evaporated. Her heart immediately went into overdrive, and they pulled apart.

Lucky blew out several quick breaths to clear his head, and answered the call, clicking the speaker function. "It's Burney Rickman," the PI said. "A car's headed this way."

Thank God at least one of them was actually keeping an eye on things.

Marin fixed her clothes, tried to fix her brain and peered out into the darkness. "I don't see anything."

"The driver has the car headlights turned off," the PI provided.

In other words, the person didn't want anyone to

know she was approaching. Did that mean Brenna had arrived five hours early so she could set a trap for them? Or like them, was she getting a head start to ensure she didn't die tonight? After all, Brenna probably didn't trust them any more than they trusted her.

There was a slight clicking sound. "I have another call," Lucky told the PI. "Stay low. I don't want you spotted." He pressed the button to answer it.

"I know you're here," the caller said. It was a woman.

"Brenna Martel," Lucky supplied to Marin.

"I set up some small surveillance cameras in the surrounding area before I even phoned you for the meeting," Brenna explained. "So, I know what's going on. Who's the big guy with the gun trying to hide in the drive-in?"

Lucky hesitated and looked as if he wanted to curse. "A PI friend. He won't hurt you."

"I'm not willing to take that chance. Tell him to leave now."

"I will if you'll tell me what this meeting is all about."

Now, it was Brenna's turn to hesitate. A moment later, Marin heard another voice. Another woman.

Definitely not Brenna.

"Lucky?" the woman said, her voice little more than a raspy whisper. "It's me. Kinley."

Lucky's sister.

"I need you to do exactly as Brenna says," Kinley warned. "If not, I'm afraid she'll kill us all."

Chapter 13

"Kinley?" Lucky practically shouted into the phone. That was his sister's voice, all right—or else a very good imitation. "Is it really you?"

"Yes. You have to tell that man to leave. You have to come now."

He wanted to do just that. But he had to think of Marin and her safety. "How do I know it's really you?"

Lucky heard some whispered chatter between the women on the other end of the line. The woman next to him, however, sat silent and frozen. She was probably as stunned as he was.

"When I was six," the caller said, "you made me a dollhouse out of Popsicle sticks. You painted it lime-green."

Hell. It was Kinley.

Now, the question was, what was he going to do about it?

"We'll be there in a few minutes," Marin said, making the decision for him. His gaze snapped to hers, but she offered no apology. "We have to do this."

They did. But how?

"Sixty seconds," Brenna said, coming back on the line. "Tell your PI friend to get lost and come to the drive-in. Park just beneath the movie screen. Oh, and Bacelli, if you do anything stupid, your sister is the one who'll pay the price."

"Let's go," Marin said the moment that Brenna ended the call.

Lucky tried to push aside all his doubt, but he couldn't. He was taking Marin directly into the line of fire.

"Get in the backseat," he instructed Marin while he called Burney Rickman. "Burney, make it look as if you're leaving. But stay nearby, hidden, just in case I need you."

"Will do."

Lucky started the engine and drove toward the drive-in.

"There's no reason for me to stay in the backseat," Marin insisted. "I have a gun." She took the snub-nosed .38 from her purse. "And I'm not a bad shot."

"Doesn't matter. I don't intend for you to be doing any shooting."

She mumbled some protest, but thankfully did as he said. The backseat wasn't bulletproof, but if something went wrong, she wouldn't be an easy target.

Lucky didn't turn on the car headlights. Though Brenna had him under surveillance, he didn't want to announce his arrival to anyone else. This was a complicated game with a lot of potential players, and what mattered most was surviving this so that he could get Marin and his sister out of there.

He approached the drive-in slowly. Cautiously. On

one side was the concession building and projection room. The windows were all shattered. No doors. The concrete-block building was blistered with what was left of flamingo-pink paint.

On the other side of the drive-in was a thirty-foot-wide screen, that had essentially been a white wall, but it was now pocked with baseball-size holes. Moonlight spewed onto the ground, which was littered with metal poles that had once held speakers. Now, though, it looked more like some eerie haunted obstacle course.

Lucky checked his mirror to make sure Marin was staying down and came to a stop where the speaker rows began. He waited, the seconds ticking off in his head.

The phone rang again, and he snatched it up while keeping a vigilant watch on their surroundings. "Drive forward," Brenna instructed. "Stop directly in front of the center of the movie screen."

Of course. The center. The most vulnerable spot. Too vulnerable. And that meant it was time to set some ground rules of his own.

"I have a better idea. You drive forward, too, and meet me halfway. We both stop in the center." He made sure it wasn't a suggestion.

More seconds ticked by. He could hear the rapid jolts of Marin's breath. The wind. The pounding of his own heartbeat in his ears.

"All right," Brenna finally conceded. "But remember, I have your sister."

"And remember that I have something you want or you wouldn't have demanded this meeting."

Though Lucky didn't have a clue what it was that he had. Hopefully, it was something he could use to bargain so he could get his sister and Marin safely out of there.

Brenna ended the call again, and Lucky proceeded to drive forward.

"You think this is a trap?" Marin asked.

"I just don't know." He had a bad feeling, but then it would have been worse if he'd decided not to come.

He spotted the other car. A black two door. It crawled across the grounds toward him, and they stopped at the same time. About ten feet apart.

"Stay put for now," Lucky told Marin. He drew his gun and held it against his leg. After saying a quick prayer that firing wouldn't become necessary, he stepped out of the car, using the door for cover.

A moment later, the door to Brenna's car opened. There was a shuffle of movement, and two women emerged from the driver's side. A tall blond with a sturdy build who dragged the other woman from the vehicle. The other woman, a brunette, was practically frail in comparison, at least six inches shorter and twenty pounds lighter.

Because the brunette had her head hung low, it took him a moment to realize it was indeed Kinley. His sister was there, right in front of him.

And Brenna had a gun pointed at Kinley's head.

His sister had lost some weight, but other than that she looked the same. Short dark brown hair. The Bacelli eyes. One thing was for certain, unless this was some kind of hologram, she was very much alive.

He wanted to go to her. To hug her. To tell her how relieved he was that she was alive. All these months he'd grieved for her and blamed himself for not doing more to save her. But she'd already been saved.

Well, maybe.

After all, Brenna was holding the gun, and it was clear that Kinley was her hostage.

"I'm sorry, Lucky." Kinley was hoarse, and judging from the puffiness around her eyes, she'd been crying.

It took Lucky a moment to find his breath and another moment before he could speak. "What happened to you?"

But Brenna didn't let her answer. "I think Kinley's the one who's been trying to kill me."

Kinley shook her head, her hair swishing against the gun. "No. I didn't try to kill anyone. But someone tried to murder me. Many times."

Lucky wanted to know every detail about what'd happened the last year, but first things first. "Brenna, you need to put down the gun so we can all talk."

"Where's Marin Sheppard?" she asked, obviously ignoring Lucky's request.

He tipped his head to the backseat. "There's no reason to bring her into this. Marin just got out of the hospital, and she's not up to another confrontation."

Brenna jammed the gun harder against Kinley's head. "There are plenty of reasons to bring her into this. Get her out here now, or this meeting is over."

Lucky believed her. Apparently so did Marin because she stepped from the car and lifted her hands in a show of surrender. However, when she joined Lucky behind the door, he could see that she had her gun tucked in the back waist of her jeans. Maybe Marin wouldn't need to use it, but he hated that she was right back in the middle of danger.

"I want to know where Dexter is," Brenna demanded of Marin.

"Is he alive?" Marin demanded right back.

A sound of pure frustration left Brenna's mouth. "I figured you'd be the one person who could tell me that."

"I honestly don't know," Marin assured her. "In fact, I thought all three of you were dead. But now that you're here, I'd like to know if my brother is alive."

"So would we," Kinley agreed. "If he is, he hasn't shown his face. Not to me, anyway. Brenna thought you'd been in contact with him."

Kinley's comment earned her another jab from Brenna's gun, and it took every ounce of Lucky's willpower not to charge at the woman to stop her from further hurting his kid sister. But he couldn't do that. It would put them all at risk. Brenna was obviously on the edge.

"Why don't you put down that weapon," Lucky tried again. "We're all in the same boat here. Someone's tried to kill all of us, and we need to figure out who the enemy is."

Brenna continued to grip the weapon. "Well, it's not me."

"Nor me," Kinley insisted.

"I'm not a killer. I didn't try to run myself down with a truck," Lucky clarified.

Marin glanced at all of them. "I wouldn't have risked my son's life in a train explosion." Then, she stared at Kinley. "But maybe you did?"

"No!" And Kinley continued to repeat it.

"But you were on the train," Lucky reminded her. God, he hated to do this, to accuse her, especially under these circumstances while she was held at gunpoint. But it had to be done. And if she had endangered Noah and Marin, then heaven help her. Being his sister wouldn't give her immunity from his rage.

"I got on the train because of a note that threatened

to kill you. And someone else," she added in a whisper. "But I didn't set those explosives. Once I got on, I checked the suitcase, and it was empty."

"Someone sent you on the train with an empty suitcase?" Marin clarified, though it was more like an accusation.

"Yes," Kinley insisted.

Brenna shook her head. "There's too much missing information from her story. And it just doesn't make sense. A threatening note. An empty suitcase. An explosion, and she comes out of it without a scratch." Brenna spoke in raw anger, but Lucky thought she had a valid point.

"Who threatened to kill me, Kinley?" Lucky wanted to know. But his sister didn't answer. Apparently stunned by his demand and his rough tone, she just stared at him. "Dexter? Who?" Lucky pressed.

His phone rang again. He cursed. It was the worst timing possible. Still, he had to answer it in case something had gone wrong at the ranch.

"It's Rickman," the PI said. "We have a visitor. He arrived on foot and is coming up on the side of the concession stand. Judging from those pictures you e-mailed me, it's Grady Duran, one of your suspects."

Not just a suspect. The primary one.

"You want me to detain him?" Rickman asked.

Lucky snared Brenna's attention. "Grady Duran is here. You want him to join this meeting so we can get everything out in the open?"

"No," Brenna said at the same moment that Kinley said, "Yes."

"We need to know the truth," Kinley added.

Lucky agreed with her. "Escort him to where we are.

Disarm him first, and if he does anything stupid, pound him to dust."

"You can't trust Duran," Brenna said the moment he hung up.

"I can't trust you, either," Lucky reminded her. "Now, while we're waiting, how about an answer to my question. Kinley, who threatened to kill me?"

"I don't know. The threats came by anonymous e-mail."

"And you believed them?" Lucky asked.

Her eyes filled with tears. "I had to believe them. You weren't the only one they threatened. They threatened the child, too."

"Noah?" Marin immediately asked.

"No. *My* child."

Lucky damn sure hadn't expected her to say that.

"She had a baby four months ago," Brenna supplied. "Dexter's baby."

The tears began to spill down his sister's cheeks. "I left him with someone for safekeeping. Someone had been trying to kill me, and the person said he'd go after my son. I couldn't risk it."

Lucky waited a moment, hoping to process all of that. Here he'd just learned his sister was alive, and now there was another child involved in all of this mess?

"And this person threatened to hurt your child if you didn't carry that suitcase onto the train?" Marin asked.

"It's me, Rickman," the PI called out before Kinley could respond. "I've got Grady Duran with me."

Everyone's attention shifted in the direction of his voice. Lucky didn't have any trouble spotting the two men. The bulkier, meaner looking Rickman had a death grip on Duran, but Duran wasn't protesting. In fact, he seemed pleased to be present.

And that made Lucky very uneasy.

Lucky looked at Marin to see what her take was on all of this. Her too-fast breathing said it all. This had turned into a nightmare. But at least it had the potential to put an end to the danger.

"Keep a close watch on Duran," Lucky warned the PI.

"Finally, we're all together," Duran said, sparing each of them a glance before he settled on the gun Brenna was still holding on Kinley. "Either you two have learned how to return from the dead or else you've been hiding because you're guilty of stealing the plans for the chemical weapon. Which is it?"

"I didn't steal anything," Kinley insisted.

Brenna didn't deny it. "Are you the one who's trying to kill all of us?"

But any one of them could have asked the same question.

The corner of Duran's mouth hitched. "If Dexter's behind this, then he must be somewhere nearby laughing his butt off. He gets us all to turn against each other. Or better yet, kill each other. When the dust settles, he'll be the last man standing. And he'll have the plans for my chemical weapon."

"You don't own that weapon," Brenna pointed out.

"I'm the primary shareholder. Or maybe I should say, I'm the one who got stuck holding the proverbial bag when all of you decided to go into hiding." He rammed his thumb against his chest. "I'm the one who'd put up the most money, and I'm the one who had to answer the threatening lawsuits and letters from the silent partner that Dexter conned into investing in this project."

"Silent partner?" Lucky questioned. This was the first he was hearing of this.

As if she'd noticed something, Brenna suddenly jerked her head to the right, toward the old screen. Lucky looked in that direction, as well, though he'd heard nothing other than the wind and the normal sounds of the night.

Hell. Was Dexter about to join them? It didn't sound like footsteps. More like a click. Like the wind catching a piece of that tattered movie screen.

Brenna shook her head. Cursed. She curved her forearm around Kinley's neck and began to maneuver her back toward the car.

Lucky couldn't let them leave. For one thing, Brenna might truly kill his sister. And for another, he was going to get answers.

"Brenna," he said, trying to soothe her. He stepped away from the meager protection of the car door and inched his way toward the two women. Unfortunately, Marin was right behind him. "Don't leave."

She didn't listen. Brenna shoved Kinley into the car, pushing her into the passenger's seat.

"It's probably just the wind," Lucky let her know, going even closer. "But I'll check it out, just to make sure."

Lucky turned to do that, but before he could shout out the order, he heard another click. At first he thought it was Brenna putting the keys in the ignition because a split second later, her car engine roared on.

But that sound was soon drowned out by the deafening blast to his left.

He had just enough time for his brain to register that

it was an explosion. He turned, dove at Marin, trying to get her back into the car.

It was too late.

The explosion ripped through the massive movie screen, and it came tumbling right at them.

Marin dove across the front seat as a chunk of the screen slammed into the car and missed Lucky by what had to be less than an inch. He scrambled inside, and in the same motion, he started the car just as a massive slab crashed into the windshield.

The safety glass cracked and webbed, but it thankfully stayed in place.

With Duran still in his grip, the PI turned and began to race toward the concession stand.

Lucky shifted the car into reverse, turned to look over his shoulder and hit the accelerator. Even though Marin couldn't see Brenna's car, she heard the woman make her own getaway. But the screen was enormous, stretching across nearly the entire width of the drive-in. It would take a miracle for all six of them to escape without being crushed to death.

"Keep your gun ready," Lucky warned her.

That didn't help steady her heart. Of course, nothing would steady it at this point. It was a terrifying thought to realize that if they made it out of this situation, there might be someone waiting for them. After all, someone had set that explosive.

But who?

Marin took out her gun and waited.

Debris continued to rain down on them. The chunks pelted the car as Lucky maneuvered his way through the obstacle course of metal speaker poles. It seemed to take an eternity, and the seconds clicked by keeping time with the pulse pounding in her ears.

"Take my phone," Lucky instructed. "Call the sheriff. Tell him what happened and that I need him or one of his deputies to meet us at the ranch."

With all the horrible things that could happen zooming through her head, she made the 9-1-1 call and reported the explosion to the sheriff's dispatcher, who assured her that someone would be sent out immediately. Good. It was a crime scene and needed to be secured and examined. Maybe the person responsible had left something incriminating behind.

"Now, look through the recent calls to get the PI's number. Find out if Duran and he made it out," Lucky insisted.

Another lump of the screen smashed into the front windshield, dumping the sheet of broken safety glass onto their laps. With the glass obstruction now gone, she could see Brenna's vehicle on the other side of the drive-in. The roof of her car was bashed in on the passenger's side where Lucky's sister was sitting.

While she located the PI's number, Marin kept her attention pinned to the other car, but she also sheltered her face in case any debris came through what was left of the windshield. A moment later, she watched as Brenna's car disappeared into the darkness. Lucky noticed it, too, and cursed.

"You two okay?" Rickman immediately asked when he answered.

"We're alive." Marin put the call on speaker so that Lucky could hear.

"I want you to go after Brenna," Lucky ordered.

"I'm already on the way to my vehicle," was the PI's answer. "Should I take Duran with me?"

"No. He'll only slow you down, and you can't trust him." Lucky didn't hesitate, either. "By any chance, did you see who set that explosive?"

"I didn't see anyone near that movie screen. But once I catch up with Brenna, I'll check it out." With that, Rickman hung up.

Once they were clear of all the metal poles, Lucky did a doughnut to turn the car around. He slammed on the accelerator again and got them back onto the road. He slowed when he got to the connecting road, and his gaze darted all around, looking for Brenna's car.

"Are you going after her?" Marin asked. She wrapped her arms around herself to stave off the cold wind that was now gushing through the glassless windshield.

He shifted his posture slightly. "I can't. Too big of a risk." Lucky sped up again.

"Because of me?" But she knew the answer. He didn't want to put her at further risk. Even if that meant not trying to follow Brenna and his sister.

Lucky increased the speed even more, and even in the darkness she could see the troubled look on his face. "We need to get back to the ranch," he said.

That comment chilled her more than the brutal winter wind that was assaulting them. When Lucky had requested that the sheriff or the deputy go to the ranch, she'd thought it was so the person could take their statement. "You don't think this bomber would go to the ranch, do you?"

He glanced at her. Just a glance, but it said volumes. "If this person wants leverage against us, what better way to get it than to go after Noah."

Oh, God. He was right. If this person had no hesitation about blowing up four people, he wouldn't think twice about going after a child.

Marin grabbed the phone to call the ranch, and prayed they weren't too late.

Chapter 14

Lucky had his car door open before he even came to a full stop in front of the Sheppard ranch.

With his gun ready, he hit the ground running. But he didn't have to go far to find proof that everything was okay. Deputy Reyes Medina was right there on the front porch, standing guard.

"Like I told you on the phone," the deputy said, "there's no reason to panic. No one's tried to get anywhere near the house. There are two armed ranch hands out back. Three more are patrolling the grounds on horseback."

"You're sure Noah's okay?" Lucky pressed.

"He's fine," the deputy assured them. "I told Ms. Helen to call me if she heard anything suspicious. Plus, I reset the security system after your mom headed out a little while ago."

That temporarily stopped Marin, who'd already reached the front door. "Where did my mom go?"

"Wouldn't say. But she got a phone call and left not long after you two did."

Maybe that phone call had been from Dexter? Mercy. Was Lois meeting with her son right at this moment? Or was this late-night visit somehow connected to the explosion?

"Marin's father didn't go with his wife?" Lucky wanted to know.

The deputy shook his head. "No. He's not here, either. From what I gathered from Ms. Helen, he's been gone for hours."

"Hours?" Marin repeated.

That was troubling, but it didn't overshadow her need to check on her son. She hurried past the deputy, threw open the front door, disarmed the security system and began to run toward her grandmother's room.

Lucky was right behind her.

Her grandmother must have heard the footsteps in the hall because she answered the door after Marin knocked just once and called out her name.

"Noah's safe," Helen said immediately.

But Marin had to see for herself. She rushed across the room and checked the crib Lucky had moved there. He checked Noah, as well, and discovered the little guy was sound asleep. Not that surprising since it was a little after 1:00 a.m.

Marin mumbled a prayer of thanks, lowered the side of the crib, leaned down and lightly kissed Noah's cheek. Lucky couldn't help himself. He did the same, and he felt relief flood through him.

"Let him sleep out the night here," Helen whispered. "No need to wake him."

Lucky agreed, and he was a little surprised when Marin did, too. That probably had a lot to do with fatigue. She leaned against him, and he felt her practically collapse.

"She needs to rest," her grandmother insisted. "Stress can sometimes trigger a seizure."

Oh, man. Marin didn't need that tonight. He slipped his weapon back into his shoulder holster and scooped Marin into his arms.

"I can walk," Marin insisted.

But he ignored her and headed toward her bedroom. He only got a few steps into the hall when he saw Deputy Medina headed their way.

"Is Marin hurt?" Medina asked.

"No," she answered, trying to wiggle out of his arms, but Lucky held on tight.

"She's exhausted," Lucky explained. "The sheriff will want us to give a statement about what happened at the drive-in, but it's going to have to wait until morning." He didn't ask for permission. Besides, it'd take Sheriff Whitley hours just to process the massive crime scene. "I take it you'll be standing guard all night?"

Medina nodded. "I'll be here until the sheriff says otherwise. The ranch hands, too. I went ahead and reset the security system, and I'll be posted right by the monitor at the front door. That way I can see if anyone tries to open a window or anything."

Lucky thanked the man and carried Marin to her room. He eased her onto the bed, locked the door and took off her shoes.

"No need to treat me like glass," she said, sitting right back up. "I haven't had a seizure in years. But if you're squeamish about the possibility of it happening, I can go into the sitting room."

Now, that just made him mad. "Squeamish?" he challenged.

He pulled off his boots and practically threw them on the floor. He wasn't much gentler when he removed his slide holster and dropped it onto the nightstand.

She lifted a shoulder and pushed her hair from her face. "We've already been through enough without you having to be on seizure watch."

That also didn't help cool down his anger. "Marin, you might not have noticed, but I'm not here because someone forced me to be here. And hell's bells, I don't want you to have a seizure, but I imagine it'd be a cakewalk compared to what just happened to us."

"Then why exactly are you here?" she snapped. But she immediately waved it off. "What I'm trying to do—and failing at miserably—is giving you an out."

"An out?" There was still a lot of anger in his voice.

She groaned softly and stood. "I think after tonight we both know that Dexter is behind these attempts to kill us."

Lucky shook his head. "How do you figure that?"

Marin gave him a flat look. "He was the only key player not at the meeting. And he was the only one whose life wasn't in danger tonight."

He couldn't argue with the last part, but he sure as hell could argue with the rest of her theory. "So, why would I need an out? If your brother wants us dead, he won't stop just because we're no longer together. Our best bet is to catch the person responsible. And if it turns out to be Dexter, nothing changes. You need my help to keep Noah, remember?"

She looked exhausted, but ready to continue this ridiculous debate. Something Lucky instantly regretted.

He'd brought her in here to lessen her stress, not to cause more by arguing with her.

With that reminder, he ditched his own anger, and eased down on the bed next to her. "I'm not treating you like glass. I'm not leaving. I'm not blaming you because of Dexter. And if you have a seizure, I can deal with it. Okay?"

The emotion in her seemed to soften, too, and she sighed and leaned against him. The physical contact was a strong reminder that no matter what the devil was going on, his body always seemed to react to her.

"Now, what about you?" he asked. "How are we going to deal with your concerns?"

She looked up at him just as he looked down at her. "I'll calm down. I won't blame myself because of Dexter. Well, I'll try not to. And I'll continue to try to make you understand that you're not responsible for Noah's safety. Or mine."

The seriousness of the conversation was getting mixed up with all the physical stuff he was feeling for her. Or at least that was the explanation Lucky wanted to believe. He couldn't fall for her. Not with everything ready to crash down around them.

But he was.

"I *am* responsible for your safety," he concluded, causing her to frown.

"Why?"

Good question. He considered dodging the truth but decided against it when he looked into her eyes. He automatically leaned in. "Because I love Noah. And because I want you."

She blinked. "Want?"

He cringed. "Yeah. That shouldn't come as a surprise to you. Not after what happened in the car."

Another blink. "No. Not a surprise. I'm just trying to figure out why your desire..." She stopped. Shook her head. "How *our* desire for each other would make you feel that you need to protect me."

He brushed a kiss on her forehead and hoped he could change the subject with a little humor. "It's a guy thing. You wouldn't understand."

The corner of her mouth lifted. A weary, exhausted half smile. And a damn sexy one at that.

Before he could warn himself to back off from her, which he almost certainly wouldn't heed, his cell phone rang. He fished it from his pocket, glanced at the caller ID and answered it.

"Rickman," he said to the PI. Because he knew Marin would want to hear this, he put the call on speaker phone. "Please tell me you have Brenna and my sister."

"Sorry. I lost them. Or rather, I never found them. By the time I ditched Duran, got to my car and went in pursuit, Brenna and Kinley were gone."

Marin and he cursed at the same time.

"What do you want me to do?" Rickman asked.

Lucky scrubbed his hand over his face. "Go back to the drive-in. The sheriff should be there by now. Try to figure out what the heck happened. If either you or the sheriff find any answers, call me."

"Will do."

"If there's a lull, I also want you to check on what my sister's been doing for the past year," Lucky added. "See if you can confirm if she had a child."

"I'll see what I can do."

When Rickman hung up, Lucky turned his attention

back to Marin. No more hot, sexy smile. She looked alarmed again. And stressed. He caught on to her wrist to check her pulse.

"I'm fine," Marin insisted.

He took her pulse anyway and confirmed what he already suspected. "It's been a while since my EMS training at the police academy, but your pulse seems fast to me. Do you have something you can take to make yourself relax?"

"I'm not sure I want to relax."

Lucky understood that. He wouldn't be doing any relaxing, but Marin was a different matter. "Noah is safe, and it'll be hours before he wakes up. Security measures are in place. You're safe, Marin, and rest is the best thing for you."

She nodded, and got up from the bed. She took a prescription bottle of pills from her cosmetic bag on the dresser, popped one of the capsules into her mouth and went into the bathroom to get some water. A moment later, she reappeared. She stopped just short of the bed where he was still sitting and she stared at him.

"What are we going to do, Lucky?" she asked.

Since that sounded like the start of another stressful conversation, he caught on to her hand and pulled her onto the bed. But since he wasn't totally stupid, he draped the comforter over her so there'd be a barrier between them.

"Get some sleep," he insisted, turning off the light.

He started to move away from her, but she caught on to him and pulled him to her. And in doing so, she revved up his already interested body.

"One," he said, remembering the counting rule. "Two."

Marin pulled him even closer until their mouths were mere inches apart. His breath touched her mouth when he mumbled, "Three. Four."

"Does it help to count?" she asked, her voice like sin and silk.

"Yes," he lied.

Right before he lowered his head and kissed her.

Marin immediately felt a sweet tangle of heat in her stomach, and it spread like a wild blaze. Her nipples drew into peaks, the sensitive flesh contracting so that even a brush from Lucky's chest seemed like a thorough, eager caress from a lover's hand. And he kept right on kissing her.

Now, this was the ultimate way to relieve stress.

She didn't hesitate. Didn't give herself time to think. Because if she had, she would have stopped, opting for the more logical approach. But she didn't want logic tonight. She didn't want to think.

She wanted Lucky.

"Are you sure we should be doing this?" he asked with his mouth still against hers.

"I'm sure." She went after his shirt.

He went after hers.

It didn't take much for him to strip her stretchy pullover sweater off her. With his kisses now wild and frantic, he went after the zipper of her jeans while she still fumbled with the buttons on his shirt.

"What about a condom?" He groaned, stopped and stared at her.

"I'm on the pill."

She nearly cheered when she finally managed to open his shirt. And she wasn't disappointed. His body was perfect. All toned and naturally tanned. She gave herself the pleasure of touching him.

Lucky groaned and stripped off her jeans. He slid his hand down her breasts and then her stomach until he reached his goal, working his fingers into the wet entrance to her body. With the skill of an artist, he touched her so perfectly, so intimately that Marin thought she might unravel right in his hand.

Within moments he had her starving for him. What she had been unable to say in words, her body said for her. She wanted more. And she wanted it now. Marin pushed herself against his fingers, trying to relieve the desperate hunger that he had created.

She went after his zipper. Not a simple task. He was already huge and hard, which didn't make it easy for her to free him from his jeans and boxers.

Repositioning her, Lucky removed his hand and pushed himself into the slickly soft heat of her body.

Marin wrapped her legs around him and caught on to his shoulders to bring him even closer. Her body adjusted—no one else had felt this way inside her, no one else belonged inside her.

Marin realized that she had gone a year and a half without a man.

And a lifetime without a lover.

He drove into her. Treating her not like glass, but like a lover that he desperately had to have. Each new stroke, each assault of her mouth with his wildfire kisses became more urgent.

She heard herself moan. Felt herself go right to the edge. She considered trying to pull back, to wait for Lucky. But when she looked into his eyes, she realized, he truly was right there with her.

Marin gave in to the unbearable heat and pleasure. Lucky did the same.

He kissed her hard and deep as they went over that edge together.

Their breaths were the only sounds in the room, though Marin could feel her heartbeat. And his. It would have been wonderful just to lie there in his arms and let her sated body drift off to sleep. But she wanted to remain alert in case anything else went wrong.

Lucky didn't give into the moment, either. Breaking the intimate contact, he stared down at her. Their limbs were tangled together, their bodies slick with sweat. Marin felt so fragile that she thought she might shatter into a thousand pieces. Nothing could have prepared her for what had happened. Nothing could have been more beautiful, more perfect than what she had just experienced with Lucky.

She relaxed the harsh grip she still had on him, letting her fingers slide over the tightly corded muscles of his chest. She resisted the urge to ask how he felt about what they had just done. *Was it good for you?* She smiled. Anything she could ask would seem so clichéd, so ordinary.

But surely this couldn't be ordinary.

"Next time, I'll remember to count to ten," he said.

She laughed. A very short-lived moment. She knew he was right—they should have backed off. But she refused to regret this. Especially since this might be the only time they would be together like this.

Lucky moved off her, dropping on the mattress next to her and staring up at the ceiling. Silent. Thankfully, he didn't remind her that this probably hadn't been a good idea.

His phone rang, the sound slicing through the room. Lucky snapped up his jeans, dug his cell from the pocket and glanced at the screen. "The caller's ID is blocked."

The last time that'd happened, the call had been from his sister. Lucky hurriedly answered it and put it on speaker.

But it wasn't his sister this time.

"It's Grady Duran," the caller said. "There's been a murder."

Chapter 15

"Who's been murdered?" Lucky asked. And he held his breath and prayed it wasn't his sister.

"I don't know," Duran insisted. "The sheriff just found a body in the drive-in debris."

Lucky pressed harder for information he wasn't sure he wanted. "Is it Kinley?"

"They haven't identified the body, but it's definitely not Kinley. She's with me."

He felt the relief, followed by a slam of new concern. "How'd that happen?"

"I'd put a GPS device on Brenna's car this afternoon before I ever walked into that drive-in and encountered your PI. I knew Brenna would run if things didn't go her way in this meeting, and she did. When I caught up with them, she pushed Kinley out of the car. I nearly ran over her. And when I stopped to make sure she was okay, Brenna got away."

Oh, man. Lucky did not want to hear this. "Bring Kinley to the ranch," he demanded.

"She's already here. All you have to do is come out and get her."

Marin shook her head and mouthed, "No."

But as dangerous as Duran's offer sounded, Lucky couldn't just dismiss it. "Where are you?"

"In the hay barn on the east side of the pasture. I want you to come here and get your sister."

Lucky cursed. "You mean the same barn where someone nearly ran over Marin and me with a truck?"

"The very one." There was ton of cockiness and danger in his tone.

Before Lucky could even respond, there was another voice. One he recognized. "Duran says to tell you this isn't a trick," Kinley said. "All he wants in exchange for me is information." She hesitated. "Don't come, Lucky." Her voice was frantic, and it sounded as if she were crying. "I don't know if this is a trap—"

There was a shuffling sound. Definitely some frenzied movement. "It's not a trap," Duran said, coming back on the line. "And I'm not giving you a choice. Come now, or I'll make sure you don't see your sister again."

That punched Lucky hard, and he had to force himself not to panic. "What, are you going to kill her?" he calmly asked.

"No, but she'll make a good bargaining chip. You heard what she said. She had Dexter's kid. Dexter hasn't shown any interest in contacting her or the baby, but you never know. He might cave, especially if I remind him how his parents would feel about him casting off his own son. It might shame Dexter into cooperating and coughing up what he owes me."

That would put his sister right in the line of fire. "Kinley's not responsible for what Dexter did."

He hoped.

"Just come," Duran demanded. "We need to get to the bottom of all of this."

Lucky couldn't agree more. "Why should I trust you?"

"For the same reason I have to trust you. Because we have to learn the truth."

He couldn't disagree with that, either. "How will meeting with you accomplish that? According to you, you don't know the truth. Neither do I, and that means this little get-together wouldn't accomplish much."

"There has to be something, some bit of information that we're overlooking. And I'm tired of waiting for it," Duran snapped. "You've got ten minutes. If you're not here, I'm leaving. Oh, and Lucky? Don't alert the deputy or the ranch hands patrolling the place. Because if you do, this *little get-together* will be over before it even starts."

Before Lucky could bargain for more time so he could set up a plan, Duran hung up.

"You're not thinking about going," Marin said. She hurriedly put on her clothes.

While Lucky dressed, he went through his options and realized he didn't have any. Ten minutes wasn't enough time to get the sheriff out there. Of course, he could take the deputy with him, or the ranch hands, but that would leave the house itself vulnerable.

And that might be the real trap.

Duran could be using this meeting to lure Lucky out of the house so that he could get inside.

"If you leave, I'll go with you," Marin insisted. "I can be your backup."

Lucky shook his head, zipped up his jeans and put

on his shirt. "You can't. For one thing, it's too danger-ous. For another, you just took that sedative, and you're sleepy."

"Not so sleepy that I can't help you."

"You can help me by staying here." Then, he played dirty because the stakes were too high to take her with him. "Think of Noah. You need to be here in case Duran tries to get in the house."

Her breath froze. But there were no more head shakes. She knew he was right.

"I have to hurry," Lucky said, putting on his boots. "I don't think Duran will wait around past that ten-minute time limit he set."

"Then at least let me call the sheriff," Marin pleaded.

"He wouldn't be able to get here in time. Besides, I don't want him to do anything that might spook Duran. Okay?"

She nodded, eventually, though she didn't seem sure of any of this. Neither was Lucky. "I'll be careful," he promised. "I'll approach the barn from behind. I won't let Duran get the drop on me."

Another nod as tears watered her eyes.

"I'm going out the front door," he explained. "So the deputy can reset the security system."

Lucky wanted to give Marin more reassurance, but there wasn't time. The seconds were literally ticking away. So, he kissed her and hoped this wasn't the last time she'd ever see him alive.

Marin watched from the window of the sitting room.

With the curtain lifted just a fraction and with the lights off so that no one could see her, she waited and finally spotted Lucky. He glanced in the direction of the window and hurried toward the meeting with Duran.

She had a very bad feeling about this.

They couldn't trust Duran—this might all be a trap. Even Kinley had thought so. But Marin also understood Lucky's need to try to save his sister. If their positions had been reversed, she would have done the same. She just wished she could have gone with him.

Yawning, she leaned against the window frame and kept her gaze on Lucky until he disappeared into the night. Mercy, why had she taken that stupid sedative? It was clouding her mind at a time when she needed to think clearly about this meeting and the body that'd been found at the drive-in.

Should she call the sheriff?

Lucky had insisted that she not do that, but what if he was ambushed?

He'd need help.

She reached for the phone. Stopped. Rethought the whole argument. And while she was arguing with herself, she saw movement. It was a person walking along the fence, headed in the same direction that Lucky had just gone.

She froze. God, was someone trying to follow him?

Marin searched through the darkness, and when the silhouette stepped from the shadows of some mountain laurels, she saw who it was.

Her mother.

Marin blinked. At first she was certain she was seeing things. But it was indeed her mother. Lois was looking around as if she expected someone to jump out of those bushes.

What the heck was going on?

It was nearly two o'clock in the morning, and it was bitterly cold—hardly the time or the weather for her mother to take a stroll. That meant she was up to something.

But what?

Marin grabbed her coat and the gun she'd taken earlier to the drive-in, and she hurried out of her room toward the front door. "My mother's out there," she said to the deputy. "I need to see what she's doing."

Deputy Medina hesitated. "Lucky said I wasn't to let you leave."

Of course he had. Because he would have suspected that she might try to follow him.

Marin silently cursed. If she didn't get out there, her mother might already be gone, and Marin knew instinctively that something critical was going on. Her mother wouldn't be out there unless it involved her father or Dexter.

"I'll only be a minute, and I won't go far," Marin bargained with the deputy.

He frowned and mumbled his displeasure under his breath. "I'll go with you."

"No." To save further argument, she disarmed the security system. "Stay here. I don't want my son and grandmother left alone."

Marin hurried out before the deputy could stop her, and ran across the front lawn to get to the side of the house. Thankfully, the moonlight cooperated. She saw her mother on the trail just ahead.

Marin shook her head to fight off the dizziness from the sedative. Just in case, she kept her gun ready.

"Mother?" she called out, trying to keep her voice low. They were still far enough away from the barn that

Duran shouldn't be able to hear them, but Marin didn't want to take any chances.

Her mother stopped and turned. "No," she whispered. Her warm breath blended with the frigid air and created a wispy surreal haze around her. "You shouldn't be here."

"Neither should you. What are you doing out here anyway?" Marin asked.

"Taking a walk."

It wasn't a convincing lie, and coupled with the troubled look on her mother's face, Marin knew that something was terribly wrong.

"Why don't you come back inside," Marin suggested. "I'll make you a cup of tea. We can talk."

Lois frantically shook her head. "I'm too antsy for tea. I need to walk. But you look exhausted. Go back to your room, Marin. I meant what I said—you shouldn't be out here."

That sounded like a warning.

Marin didn't want to bring up Lucky and the meeting with Duran, so she took a different approach in the hope of learning what was going on. "Mother, is Dexter alive? Are you about to meet with him?"

She dodged Marin's stare. "I don't know if he's alive."

"You're lying again."

Lois looked around. Her breath was too fast. Her eyes, almost wild now. "You'll turn him in to the police."

Marin felt everything inside her go still. "Dexter's really alive?"

Her mother nodded and then groaned. "He didn't want you to know. He said you'd go to the police."

And she would have. Marin couldn't deny that. Her brother had put her son in danger, and Noah's safety came ahead of her brother's desire to go unpunished for the things he'd done wrong.

"He faked his death?" Marin asked.

Lois hesitated so long that Marin wasn't sure the woman would answer. But she finally did. "He faked his death, Brenna's and Kinley's."

"Kinley had his child."

Her mother's eyes widened. Her reaction was too genuine for it to be fake. "He didn't tell me that. He's been in Mexico. The people who invested in his project wanted to kill him."

That was not good to hear. Marin glanced back at the house to make sure it looked safe and secure. Thankfully, it did.

"But the investors are dead now," Lois continued. "Dexter took care of them."

Oh, mercy. "He killed them?"

"He had to. Don't you see? If he hadn't, they would have killed him. And he could have never come home."

That tightened the knot in her stomach. "But he's home now?"

Lois smiled and touched Marin's arm. "He's home," she said with all the joy of a mother who was about to see her son. Marin could understand that on some level—she had a son. But unlike her son, Dexter was a killer. "He called this afternoon to tell us that he was back. Soon, we'll all be a family again."

Not a chance. Dexter would know that she wouldn't want him anywhere near Noah.

Then, it hit her. "Lucky," Marin whispered under her breath.

God, was Dexter going after him? Did he plan to eliminate Lucky, too?

Blinking back another wave of dizziness, Marin considered running toward the barn. Maybe Dexter was there, waiting to ambush Lucky.

Her mother stiffened and whirled around to face the other direction. The direction of the barn. Her gaze flew to her watch and the lighted dial. "I have to go. It's time."

Marin caught on to her arm. "Time for what?"

"To meet Dexter. He should be waiting in the truck that I left for him at the hay barn. But you can't come. If he sees you, he'll leave." Lois began to run, staying on the trail.

Marin considered following her directly. But that would be a dangerous move, especially if Dexter wanted her dead. Instead, she waited several seconds until her mother had a head start, then went off the trail, using the mountain laurels for cover. She slapped aside the low hanging branches and began to run. She'd get to the barn taking the same path that Lucky had likely taken.

She prayed she wasn't too late to save him from her brother.

Chapter 16

Lucky eased his way through the darkness and the meager shrubs. There wasn't a lot of cover once he got close to the barn.

He was a sitting duck.

And there wasn't much he could do about it.

He kept telling himself that if Duran wanted to kill Kinley, he would have already done it. So, now the trick was to get to this meeting and come up with some kind of resolution that would set his sister free.

A twig snapped beneath his boot, spiking his heartbeat and causing his finger to tense on the trigger of his gun. Lucky paused, waiting to make sure the twig hadn't alerted anyone. It apparently hadn't. He continued forward one cautious step at a time.

There was no light on in the barn, but the entire structure was visible because of the watery white moonlight. The wind was still stirring and that made it next to impossible to know if he was about to be ambushed.

He saw a truck parked at the back of the barn. It

wasn't the same one that'd been used to try to kill him, but he was certain he'd seen the vehicle on the ranch.

Lucky walked toward it, keeping vigilant. He wanted to be sure he was mentally and physically ready for whatever was about to happen.

When he was within twenty feet of the barn, he picked up the pace. He practically ran until he got to the north side of the structure, and then to the passenger's side of the truck. He paused there and listened for any sound to indicate something was wrong.

Everything was quiet.

Too quiet.

He glanced inside the truck. It was empty. No keys in the ignition. There was no one in the back, either. Which meant the person who'd driven it, Grady Duran probably, was already inside the barn. If Duran had truly been the one who'd tried to run them down, then Lucky intended to make the man pay.

Trying not to make his presence known, he maneuvered his way to the back entrance, a double set of high wooden doors, one of which was slightly ajar. He peeked in, but it was too dark to see anything.

He stepped inside.

The toe of his left boot rammed into something soft and pliable that didn't budge when Lucky gave it a light shove with his foot.

He waited a moment, until his eyes could adjust to the darkness. Lucky saw the bales of hay stacked on both sides of the barn in staggered piles. They seemed to extend to the ceiling, and there was only a narrow path that cut through the middle of the barn.

And then he looked down.

What he'd walked into was no bale of hay.

It was a body.

"Hell," he cursed.

Without taking his attention off his surroundings, he stooped and fumbled around until he located the person's neck. He shoved his fingers against the carotid artery.

Nothing.

Not even the hint of a pulse.

Frantic now, he prayed this wasn't his sister. He turned over the body. Not Kinley.

Grady Duran.

There was blood. Lots of it. It spread out across the entire front of Duran's shirt.

Both the blood and the body were still warm.

That just had time to register in his head when he heard a muffled scream. But it wasn't so muffled that he couldn't figure out who'd made that blood-chilling sound. Kinley. He was certain of it.

With his gun ready and aimed, he stepped over Duran and began to make his way through the maze of hay bales. He had to find his sister. She was in trouble. The person who'd killed Duran might have already gotten to her.

There was another sound.

Lois Sheppard.

And Marin.

He couldn't understand exactly what Marin was saying, but she sounded close, probably just outside the barn. His first instinct was to shout for her to stay back. To tell her to run. To get away. But he didn't have time for that.

Then pain exploded in his head.

Lucky felt himself falling, but there was nothing he

could do to stop it. He hit the hay-strewn floor of the barn hard just as the world went blank.

His last coherent thought was that he wouldn't be able to save Marin.

"Dexter?" Lois called out again.

Marin caught up with her mother just outside the barn and tried to stop her from shouting Dexter's name.

"This could be dangerous," Marin warned. There were no signs of Lucky. Nor his sister or Grady Duran.

Not Dexter, either.

No signs of anyone. A meeting should be taking place, but where were all the parties? Where was Lucky?

"Dexter's in there," her mother said, and she bolted for the barn.

Since it was obvious her mother wasn't going to stop her quest to see Dexter, Marin got her gun ready and followed her through the front entrance. The place was pitch-black. She reached for the overhead light, only to realize that wasn't a good idea. She grabbed a flashlight from the tack shelf instead and turned it on.

She fanned the circle of light over the darkness, and the first thing she saw was Kinley.

Lucky's sister was tied to a post, gagged and blind-folded with rags. She was struggling to get free and mumbling something.

And that's when Marin noticed Lucky.

Lying on the floor.

"Lucky?" Even though it occurred to her head that it might be a trap, she couldn't stop herself from running to him. God, he couldn't be dead.

He wasn't moving.

Her panic soared when she saw blood on his head.

Not a gunshot wound. At least she didn't think it was. The wound was small, and he wasn't gushing blood. It looked as if someone had clubbed him across the back on the head.

"Lucky?" she repeated.

With the gun in her right hand and the flashlight in her left, she stooped down, rolled him onto his side and made sure he was breathing.

He was.

Thank God. But he still needed medical attention. She reached for her cell phone, only to realize she'd left it in her room.

"Mother, do you have your phone with you? I need you to call for help."

Her mother didn't answer. She looked behind her, turned the flashlight in that direction and saw nothing.

Her mother was gone.

Marin got up to run to Kinley, to see if the woman had a phone, but then she felt something.

Lucky gripped on to her arm. "You need to get out of here," he warned, forcing his eyes to open. He winced in pain and touched his fingers to his injured head.

Despite his weak voice, she felt relief. He could speak. However that didn't mean he didn't have serious injuries. "I need to get you to the hospital. You're hurt."

Lucky shook his head. "You have to leave. *Now.* Duran's dead."

An icy chill went through her. "Dead, how?"

"Shot."

Mercy. Was Dexter responsible? Probably. But she didn't have time to point fingers now. "Can you stand up? I have to get you to the hospital. Kinley, too."

"Where's Kinley?" He sat up and wobbled, so Marin

helped him to his feet. Somehow. She cursed her own dizziness and weak legs.

"She's here in the barn. Alive." Marin hadn't seen any obvious injuries, but that didn't mean there weren't some.

And where the heck was her mother?

With Lucky leaning against her and with her gun clutched in a death grip, they made it through the hay bales to the front of the barn.

The moment Lucky saw his sister, he reached for her, and though he was clumsy from his injury, he pulled the gag from her mouth.

"Watch out!" Kinley immediately shouted.

From the corner of her eye, Marin saw the movement. And the gun. It was aimed right at Lucky.

"No!" she yelled and automatically turned the flashlight and her gun in the direction of the shooter.

White light slashed across the barn like a razor, blinding the shooter. That didn't stop him from shooting.

Kinley screamed.

But it took Marin a second to realize the bullet had missed her and that it had smacked into a hay bale on the other side of the barn. Bits of dried grass burst into the air.

Praying that the dizziness from the sedative would go away, Marin readjusted her aim and braced herself to return fire. And then she saw the shooter.

Her father.

He re-aimed and pointed his gun right at Lucky.

Marin didn't think about the situation or anything else. She just reacted. She dove in front of Lucky, just as he tried to pull her behind him. They collided, both ending up right in the line of fire.

"Get out of the way, Marin!" her father ordered.

There was no chance of that. In fact, she moved back in front of Lucky. Well, as much as Lucky would allow her to do.

"Dad, what are you doing?" she shouted.

"Saving you. You need to get out of here." His gaze was frozen on Lucky. And Marin knew in that moment what her father was doing.

He intended to kill Lucky.

"Did you murder Duran?" Lucky asked her father.

Howard moved to the side, obviously trying to position himself for a better shot. He had a set of keys hooked to his belt that jangled when he moved.

Marin didn't believe her father would kill her to get to Lucky. But she couldn't be sure. She couldn't be sure of anything right now. Her world had just tipped upside down.

"I had to get rid of him. He got in the way."

Oh, God.

Her father was a killer.

"You've gotten in the way, too," Howard continued, aiming his comments and his gun at Lucky. "And like Duran, you're getting too close to finding out the truth about Dexter."

Blinking back tears and trying to deal with the horrific image of her father as a cold-blooded murderer, Marin moved, intending to use herself as a shield.

"And what truth would that be?" she asked.

"That Dexter's alive," Kinley provided. That hung in the air for several seconds. "Howard helped him fake our deaths that night in the research lab because Dexter took money from the wrong people. Not just from Duran, but from other investors. Dexter promised both he'd deliver a weapon I learned that we couldn't deliver. We only had the technology for components of the weapon, not the entire package."

"So, Duran and the other investor were going to get their money back any way they could," Howard supplied. "One of them put a contract on Dexter's life. That's when I knew I had to help my son."

"You helped him by blackmailing me into staying quiet," Kinley fired back. She looked at Lucky. "I'm so sorry."

Lucky glanced at her, but like Marin, he kept his attention on Howard.

And on his trigger finger.

"Now that Duran's dead and I've discovered the identity of the other investor who's after Dexter," Howard continued, "the only thing I need to clear up is this mess." He tipped his head first to Kinley and then to Lucky.

"You aren't going to try to kill them," Marin insisted.

"I won't try. I'll *succeed*. I have to, for Dexter's sake." Turning to the side so he could still keep an eye on them, her father pulled the barn door shut and, with his left hand, used the key on his belt to lock them in. Of course, the back entrance was still open. If possible, they could use that way to escape.

Because she had no choice, Marin tried again. She had to make her father see that what he was doing was crazy. "You'll be arrested. You'll go to jail for murder."

"No. Brenna will take the blame for this. She has to be eliminated, too. After I'm done here, I'll find her and plant this gun on her."

Lucky inched closer to her father. "The deputy's at the house. You plan to kill him, too?"

"No. He won't hear a thing," he said, waving the silencer at Lucky. "Neither will the ranch hands that I asked to patrol the place. I told them to stick to the front of the ranch. They won't come back here."

Mercy. He had planned all of this. She had to do something to stop him. It would have been easier if he were ranting and out of control. Then, maybe she wouldn't have seen the small part of her father that still remained.

"Why would you risk killing your own daughter?" Marin asked.

He looked genuinely insulted. "I don't want to hurt you. I'm only doing what I have to do to save your brother."

"But you nearly killed Marin and Noah on the train and then again at the drive-in," Lucky pointed out. He took another step closer.

"I didn't set those explosives. Dexter did. And even though I was furious when I learned what he did, I forgave him because he was desperate. *I'm desperate.*"

Marin didn't doubt that. She could see the pain etched in his face. That meant she might be able to talk him out of this insanity.

"And what about Mother? Is she in on this with you, too?" Marin asked, wondering if her entire family had gone stark raving mad. She also wanted to keep her father occupied so that maybe he wouldn't notice that Lucky was maneuvering himself closer.

"Not a chance. Your mother has no idea. That's why I sent her back to the house. I told her that Dexter would meet her there. That's the plan, anyway."

With his gun still aimed right at Lucky, her father

walked closer and latched on to her arm. "I don't want you to see this. It might trigger a seizure."

She wanted to laugh at the irony. Her father didn't want to trigger a seizure, but he was willing to kill the man she loved.

In that moment, Marin realized that she loved Lucky. Talk about lousy timing.

"I can't let you do this," Marin said.

But before the last word left her mouth, her father reached out, lightning fast. With a fierce grip, he knocked the gun from her hand. Lucky bolted forward, but her father turned his gun in Kinley's direction.

"Back off," Howard warned.

Lucky froze and stared at Marin. She could see him process their situation. He couldn't risk killing his sister, or getting himself killed. Because every minute he stayed alive was another minute he had to get them all out of there.

Only then her father latched on to her and started dragging her toward the back exit of the barn, away from Lucky.

Chapter 17

For Lucky, this was a nightmare.

Marin's father was ready to kill him and Kinley, and now Howard was literally dragging Marin away from the crime scene. God knows what the man would do to her when she didn't cooperate with his plan to protect Dexter.

And Marin wouldn't cooperate.

Lucky was certain that it was that lack of cooperation that would get her killed. Because despite Howard's assurance that he wouldn't hurt her, the man would obviously do anything to protect his precious son. Lucky understood that on some level. He loved Noah and would protect him. But not like this.

"Stop," Lucky warned Howard, and he stepped toward the man cautiously. Lucky didn't want Marin's father accidentally firing that gun and hitting her.

But Howard didn't stop.

Marin didn't stop struggling, either.

"Don't come any closer," Howard threatened Lucky.

"You and your sister better stay put, or Marin will pay the price. I'll kill her if you try to escape."

Marin dug in her heels and punched at him, trying to knock the gun from his hand. Cursing, Howard finally gave up and pushed her at Lucky. The impact sent them both crashing into a wooden post.

Howard aimed his gun again, this time at Marin.

"Put down your weapon," Howard warned him, "or I'll shoot her."

Lucky wanted to believe it was a bluff, but he could tell from the stony look in Howard's eyes that it wasn't. Howard had chosen which child to protect.

It wasn't Marin.

"You're doing this for nothing," Lucky insisted.

"Put down the gun," Howard repeated. He took a step closer to them. At this distance, he wouldn't miss, and the shot would be fatal.

Lucky dropped his gun onto the floor and inched himself in front of Marin and Kinley. "Dexter is dead." It was a bluff. A calculated one.

Howard shook his head and stepped even closer. "You're lying."

"No. I'm not. A little while ago Sheriff Whitley found a body at the drive-in. It's Dexter. He died when he set the explosions to kill us."

Marin's father froze.

"Think about it," Lucky continued, hoping that if this was a bluff, it'd stand up to scrutiny. "You haven't heard from Dexter since the explosion, have you?"

"That doesn't mean he's dead."

No, it didn't. But Lucky had put enough doubts in Howard's head. With his hand shaking, Howard unclipped his cell phone from his belt and pressed a button.

The seconds crawled by.

Because the barn had gone deadly silent, Lucky could hear the rings to Dexter's number. No one answered.

Howard's concern kicked up considerably, and while volleying nervous glances between them, he pressed in another set of numbers, looking for someone who could verify Dexter's whereabouts.

Just in case Dexter happened to be alive, Lucky got ready to launch himself at Howard. It would be a risk, of course, but doing nothing would be even a bigger risk. Even if Howard changed his mind about killing Marin, there was no chance he'd let him and Kinley go.

Lucky kept a close watch on Howard's body language while he waited for an opportunity to strike. He glanced at Marin and hopefully conveyed that when the time came, he wanted her to get down.

Marin shook her head, just a little, but enough to let him know that she wasn't going to let him do this alone.

Hell.

"Think of Noah," he mouthed. "He needs you."

It was the second time tonight he'd used the little boy to get her to cooperate, but if this was the only way to save her life, then Lucky didn't feel the least bit guilty. He wanted Noah's mom alive so she could raise him.

"Sheriff Whitley," Howard said when the person on the other end of the line answered the call. "Tell me about the body you found at the drive-in."

Lucky shut out everything else but Howard Sheppard. He watched his face, and Lucky knew the exact moment that the sheriff confirmed exactly whose body had been found.

A hoarse sob tore from Howard's throat. A wounded, helpless sound. But Lucky didn't let it distract him. Nor did he let it allow him any sympathy for the man who'd been about to kill them all.

He launched himself at Howard, plowing into him with full force and knocking him to the ground. Howard's phone went flying.

His gun didn't.

Howard somehow managed to keep a firm grip on it. He could fire at any second, and the bullet could hit Marin or Kinley.

"Get out here now, Sheriff!" Lucky shouted so that Whitley would hear him.

Lucky heard Marin move, first to recover her gun, and then to join the battle. Not good. He wanted her far away from this, but Marin obviously wouldn't have that. She pushed at her father, trying to force them apart.

Howard threw out his hand, and the gun. Lucky was certain he lost ten years of his life when he saw the barrel aimed at Marin.

"Get down," Lucky yelled.

The imminent threat gave him the extra jolt of adrenaline he needed. Despite being bashed in the head, Lucky gathered every ounce of strength he had, grabbed on to Howard's right wrist and slammed his hand against the barn floor. It took three hard jolts.

Then, the gun skittered across the floor.

Lucky didn't waste any time. He drew back his fist and landed a punch to Howard's jaw. Howard stopped moving, stopped fighting.

He surrendered.

"Make sure the sheriff is on his way out here," Lucky instructed Marin. He grabbed Howard by his shoulders and flipped the man onto his stomach. "And then untie Kinley so I can use those ropes."

He didn't want to risk Howard having second thoughts and trying to come at them again. Lucky didn't want to have to shoot the man, especially not in front of Marin.

With the cell phone sandwiched between her shoulder and her ear, Marin worked frantically to set Kinley free. Once Marin had her unbound, she tossed him the rope. Lucky reached up to catch it when he heard something.

He whirled around toward the sound. It'd come from the back of the barn, from the path he'd taken between the stacks of hay.

Someone was there in the darkness, directly behind Marin. Because she was still working to free his sister's feet, she probably hadn't heard the sound or noticed the other person.

Lucky aimed his gun at the newcomer and tried to make sure Howard didn't get free. He was obviously having second thoughts about his surrender because he began to struggle.

"Marin," Lucky warned. "Watch out."

She, too, spun around, just as their visitor stepped from the shadows. The illumination from the flashlight was more than enough for him to recognize the person.

Brenna Martel.

She had a gun clutched in her right hand, which she held just beneath a bulky blanket.

Lucky's heart dropped to his knees when he saw what Brenna had in that blanket.

Noah.

Marin felt the scream rise in her throat.

Her son wasn't moving.

Noah was just lying there bundled in the blanket in Brenna's arms. It took Marin several terrifying seconds to realize that he was asleep, that Brenna hadn't hurt him.

Both Lucky and Marin bolted toward Brenna, but Brenna merely raised her gun. "I wouldn't do that," she warned, her voice hardly louder than a whisper. It didn't need to be any louder for them to understand that Brenna meant business.

And that she had the ultimate bargaining tool.

"Give me Noah," Lucky insisted.

Marin tried to demand the same, but her mouth was suddenly so dry that she couldn't speak.

Her father, however, had no trouble responding to the situation. Without Lucky bearing down on him, he got up from the floor.

Brenna shifted the gun in Howard's direction. "You're not going anywhere. Back on the floor. While you're at it, I want the key to the front door."

Her father actually looked ready to argue, and that infuriated Marin. And terrified her.

"Do as she says," Lucky warned Howard, giving him a chilling glare that seemed much more threatening than Brenna's gun.

Mumbling something under his breath, her father tossed the keys in Brenna's direction. They landed, clanging, just at her feet.

Howard sat back on the floor. He'd be able to strike easily from this position. If he'd been on their side, Marin wouldn't have minded that, but she had no idea what her father would do if cornered.

"Did you hurt my grandmother?" Marin asked Brenna.

"No." Brenna picked up the key, slipped it into her pocket and checked her watch. "I didn't hurt anyone, not even the police officer guarding the place. I covered my face with a stocking cap so he wouldn't see who I was and then sneaked up on him and held him at gunpoint. I tied him up after I forced him to disengage the security system. I found your grandmother, tied her up and took Noah."

Marin wasn't sure she could believe her, but she held onto the possibility that her grandmother was safe. She had to be alive and well.

"Please," Marin said to Brenna, "give me my son."

"I won't harm him," Brenna promised though she didn't seem convincing. Actually, she seemed disoriented. Her eyes were red and puffy. "I just wanted him here to make sure you would cooperate."

Oh, she'd cooperate, all right. First chance she got, she would get Noah away from this woman.

"Dexter's dead," Brenna whispered a moment later.

"Yes," Marin confirmed. "I think he died while trying to kill us." This wasn't a conversation she wanted to have right now. All she wanted to do was run to her son and get him out of Brenna's arms.

Brenna shook head. Then, the tears welled up in her eyes. "Dexter didn't mean to hurt me." Just as quickly though, she blinked those tears away and shot Howard a look that could kill. "But you wanted to hurt me. You were going to murder Kinley, Marin and Lucky and set me up to take the fall. Thanks a lot, you miserable piece of slime."

Howard didn't deny it. In fact, he seemed defiant.

"I can't let any of you live," Brenna continued. She glanced at Howard. "Especially you." And then another glance at Kinley. "And you."

"Kinley has nothing to do with this," Lucky insisted.

"She has everything to do with it. Dexter slept with her. He cheated on me—"

"He broke things off with you," Kinley volunteered. "I would have never gotten involved with him while he was still with you."

The pain and tears in Brenna's eyes instantly went away, and in their place was raw anger. Marin had already been terrified for her son, but that look took her beyond that. It took every ounce of her willpower not to launch herself at Brenna.

"Don't," she heard Lucky say. Obviously, he knew what she was thinking. He had the same need to protect Noah.

"So, what are you going to do?" Howard snarled.

"I'm leaving."

"Leaving?" he questioned. "And what makes you think I won't come after you?"

"Noah," Brenna answered without a shred of doubt in her voice. "He lives if all of you stay put. It's as simple as that."

Mercy. Brenna would use Noah to save herself.

"You mean if we stay put and die?" Howard countered.

"I mean if you're willing to sacrifice yourself for the life of a baby. For your grandson," Brenna added. She looked at Kinley. "Your death will be quick. Painless. Because in five minutes or so, this place will be a fireball. That'll happen with or without Noah here inside. Your decision."

"Oh, God." Marin pressed her fingers to her mouth and tried to figure out how to get away from this. "Please don't hurt Noah."

"Don't worry," Brenna said almost calmly. "I'll make sure he's raised by a good family."

And with that, she started to back out of the barn.

"You don't have to do this," Lucky said.

He took a step toward her, but Brenna lifted her gun. She didn't quite aim it at Noah, but she sure as heck implied that's what she would do.

"I do," Brenna said, spearing Howard's gaze. "Don't I?"

"What does she mean?" Marin demanded when her father didn't say anything.

"I'm a wanted woman, thanks to your dear ol' dad. The man I love is dead. I'm flat broke. I don't even have the components to the chemical weapon that I helped create. Why? Because Dexter sold them on the black market to make some money, and when he did that, he leaked my identity to Howard."

"Brenna Martel is the other investor that the Feds are looking for," Howard supplied. "She used every penny of a trust fund her grandmother set up for her." That helped put the puzzle pieces together.

Brenna continued, "I'll be wanted for murder of the security guard who was killed in the explosion at the research facility once the authorities find out I'm the one who actually set the explosives. I'll be looking at the death penalty."

So Brenna had nothing to lose.

"Without money, where will you go?" Marin hoped it would make Brenna rethink this lethal plan.

"Somewhere I can start fresh." Brenna took another step back. It wouldn't be long before she was out that door. With Noah as a hostage, there was no way Lucky could stop her with his gun.

Plus, seconds were ticking away. It wouldn't be long before the explosives went off. And as much as Marin wanted to live, she didn't want her son anywhere near the place if it blew up.

"Wait," Lucky said to Marin. "Let everyone leave. Give Noah to Marin. I'll go with you. I'll be your hostage. And everyone here will be sworn to secrecy. No one will know you're the investor. I'll use my contacts in the Justice Department to help you clear your name."

But that didn't stop Brenna. She continued to move back. Faster now. While volleying her attention between them and her watch.

How much time did they have? A minute, maybe two? Was that enough time to get Noah from Brenna and save themselves?

Marin didn't think so.

Knowing she had to do something, fast, Marin glanced at Lucky. He looked at her at the same moment. A dozen things passed between them, and with that look, he promised her that he would save her son.

Even if it cost them their lives.

Marin nodded. And braced herself to do whatever it took to get Noah to safety.

A deep growl came from Lucky's throat. It was the only warning she got before he charged at Brenna. The woman had just glanced at her watch again. It took her several seconds to re-aim her gun. She managed to do that, just as Lucky got to her and wrenched Noah from her arms.

Marin was right there, behind him, ready to take her son.

"Run!" Lucky yelled.

Noah yelled, too. The sudden movement and the shout

woke him up, and he began to cry. His screams blended with the sound of the struggle.

Somehow, Marin made it past Lucky and Brenna, though their arms and legs seemed to be blocking every inch of the narrow path between the stacked hay bales.

Marin wanted to help Lucky. She wanted to help him get that gun from Brenna. But it was too huge of a risk to take. She had to get Noah out of there.

So, she ran. Just as she reached the back door of the barn, a shot rang out.

Chapter 18

Lucky ignored the deafening blast from the shot that Brenna fired. He wasn't sure, but he thought it'd landed in the barn loft. He had Brenna's right hand in a death grip and had purposely turned the weapon upward in case she fired.

Which she did.

Lucky ignored the shot so he could keep up the fight to gain control of the weapon. But Marin, Noah and his sister still weren't safe. Worse, Howard might use this particular battle to subdue Kinley so he could use her as a bargaining chip. But there'd be nothing to bargain for if those explosives went off.

"Get out," Lucky shouted to his sister.

From the corner of his eye, he saw Kinley try to do exactly that. Howard, too. Marin's father charged at them while he was still trying to free himself from the ropes that Lucky hadn't had time to secure tightly enough.

Lucky bashed Brenna's hand against one of the posts, and the impact dislodged the gun from her grip. He pinned her against the hay long enough for Kinley to get by. His sister went running to the back exit.

With Brenna in tow, Lucky grabbed her gun and followed his sister.

Behind him, he heard Howard, and Lucky tried to keep watch to make sure the man didn't ambush him. But thankfully, Howard must have realized they were in dire straits because he was as eager to get out of the barn as Lucky was.

Brenna, however, was a different matter. She continued to fight, scratching at him, while he maneuvered her through the hay. Once he reached the exit, he latched on to her and started to run into the cold night air.

"Marin?" Lucky called out.

"Here," she answered.

She sounded a lot closer to the barn than he wanted her to be, and he spotted her running toward the pasture. She had Noah clutched to her chest, and the little guy was still crying.

Kinley followed Marin, and since Lucky needed to put some distance between the barn and him, he wasn't too far behind. He glanced over his shoulder though and saw something he didn't like.

Howard wasn't anywhere in sight.

Lucky didn't have time to react to that because behind them, the barn exploded into a fireball.

Brenna finally quit struggling, thanks to a chunk of the roof that nearly landed right on them. Lucky latched on to her even harder and raced them across the pasture to safety.

Ahead of him, Marin stopped and looked back. She was far enough away, he hoped, to avoid being hit with any of the fiery debris. He caught up with Kinley, and the three of them raced to join Marin. Out of breath now and unnerved with adrenaline, they stopped and looked at the blaze that had nearly claimed their lives.

"How dare you endanger my child!" Marin warned Brenna. Her eyes were narrowed, and her breath was coming out in rough jolts.

Lucky checked Noah to make sure he was okay. He appeared to be, despite the crying. They'd been fortunate. A lot could have gone wrong in that barn.

He pulled Marin and Noah into his arms for a short but much needed hug before he turned back around to face Brenna. He was about to add to Marin's warning when he heard the sound of an engine.

Slowly, he looked behind them, fearing what he would see. His fears were confirmed.

A truck was coming right at them.

"It's my father," Marin announced.

The interior truck cab light was on, and the driver's door was partly open, clearly revealing the driver.

"Run," he instructed the others.

However, Lucky didn't move. The man was obviously hell-bent on killing them. Lucky was hell bent on making sure that didn't happen. Noah, Marin and his sister had already been through enough, and this had to end now.

Kinley latched on to Brenna's arm and got her moving.

"Run!" Lucky repeated when Marin stayed put.

He looked at her, to make sure she understood that he wasn't going to let her and Noah die. She said a lot with that one look. A look that made him realize he would do anything to protect her. That look also made him realize that this could be goodbye.

With the truck closing in on them, she nodded. "I love you," she said. And she turned to run.

I love you.

Powerful words. Words that would have normally shaken him to the core. But he'd have to deal with Marin's admission later. Because right now, he had to do something to stop Howard Sheppard.

Lucky lifted his hand. Took aim at the truck. And waited. Behind him, he could hear Marin running with Noah. His sister and Brenna weren't too far ahead of them. Yet something else to concern him—he didn't want Brenna doing anything stupid.

But for now, he speared all of his attention on Howard.

He watched the truck barrel over the pasture. Howard no doubt had his foot jammed on the accelerator. Pedal to the metal.

Everything inside Lucky stilled. Focused. He adjusted his arm. And when the truck was within range, Lucky double tapped the trigger. The windshield shattered, and Lucky dove to the side so he wouldn't be run over.

He immediately got up and raced into position for round two, so that Howard couldn't get anywhere near Marin and Noah.

But it wasn't necessary.

The truck careened to the left, going right into the rocky stream. Just yards on the other side, it came to a stop. No brake lights. No signs that the driver had tried to bring the truck under control.

Lucky soon learned why.

With his gun ready, he approached the vehicle. But his vigilance and caution weren't necessary.

Howard was slumped in the seat.

Dead.

"Hell," Lucky cursed.

Now, he was going to have to tell Marin that he'd killed her father.

Chapter 19

The morning sun was too bright, and it glared directly into Marin's eyes.

She didn't move from the glass-encased patio off her bedroom. She couldn't. There seemed to be no energy left in her body so she stayed put on the wicker love seat.

This was the aftermath of a nightmare.

And in some ways, the continuation of one.

Seemingly oblivious to the fact that he'd recently been kidnapped and endangered by Brenna Martel, Noah was playing on a quilt at her feet. He batted at her leg with a small stuffed dog and laughed as if he'd accomplished something phenomenal. Marin couldn't even manage a weak smile in response, though with every fiber of her being, she was thankful that her child hadn't been harmed.

In the bedroom, she could hear the conversations that were going on. Lucky and the sheriff were discussing what had happened. Her grandmother was talking to her mother.

Consoling her.

After all, her mother had only hours ago learned that her husband was a killer and that both her son and husband were dead. That was a lot for anyone to absorb.

Marin, included.

It'd been years since she'd felt real love for her father, and she had already grieved her brother's death a year earlier when she thought he'd been killed. Still, it hurt. It hurt even more that Dexter and her father had been willing to risk her life, Noah's and Lucky's just so they could cover their tracks. It would take a very long time for Marin to get over what had happened. If ever.

"Lucky wanted me to check on you," she heard her grandmother say. She was now in the doorway, examining Marin. "He'll be finished up with the sheriff soon."

"Good." Because she didn't know what else to say, she repeated it.

Her grandmother walked closer and dropped down into the chair next to her. "Your mother says to tell you that she's sorry."

Marin peered into the bedroom. Her mother was no longer there. "Why didn't she tell me herself?"

"The wound's too fresh. Give her time."

Maybe it was her mood or the fact that she didn't trust her mother, but Marin didn't like the sound of that. "I hope that doesn't mean she'll try to get custody of Noah."

"Not a chance. She'll be lucky if she doesn't get jail time for aiding and abetting Dexter. Your brother was a fugitive, and the federal agents aren't happy that she kept his whereabouts a secret from them."

Neither was Marin.

But then, she wasn't pleased about a lot of things.

"What about Lucky?" Marin asked, almost afraid

to hear the answer. "Has he said anything about when he'll be leaving?"

"Not to me." Her gran hesitated. "I'm guessing from your tone that you expect him to go?"

Marin didn't trust her voice and settled for a nod. Lucky would have to tend to his sister and tie up the loose ends of this investigation. Without a custody hearing, there was no reason for him to hang around.

Or was there?

So what if she and Lucky had slept together? That didn't obligate him to be part of her life. But God help her, that's what she wanted. Still, she couldn't cling. She'd spent a lifetime being coddled, and if this brush with death had taught her anything, it was that she was strong enough to stand on her own two feet.

She heard the footsteps, glanced in the direction of the sound and saw Lucky making his way toward them. Marin straightened her shoulders and lifted her chin. She doubted that she could completely erase her gloom-and-doom expression, but she tried. She didn't want this conversation to turn into a pity party.

"How's your sister?" Marin asked when Lucky joined them.

"She's fine. She's at the Justice Department office in San Antonio. There won't be any charges filed against her, but she needs to give her statement about what happened the night of the explosion and assist them with the case against Brenna. Once she's done with that, she can leave and get her baby. My nephew," he added, causing a brief smile to bend his mouth.

"Good." Marin winced. It sounded like a token well-wishing. It wasn't.

Looking totally uncomfortable, Lucky stared at her a

moment, moved closer and sank down on the floor next to Noah. He immediately got a bop on the forearm from Noah's stuffed dog, and her son giggled.

"Are you playing with your da-da?" her gran asked Noah. She goosed his tummy, causing Noah to laugh even more.

Marin frowned at the question. Her grandmother knew the truth. Lucky and she had lied about, well, pretty much everything—he wasn't Noah's father or her fiancé.

Helen stood. "I think I need a nap. Let me know if you need me to babysit." And with that, she kissed all three of their cheeks and left the room—but not before she winked at Marin.

With her exit came plenty of silence.

Noah volleyed glances between them, trying to figure out what was going on with the sudden silence. Marin wanted to know the same.

"Brenna was arrested, of course," Lucky informed her. He sounded as grim as his expression.

Marin choked back a laugh. "Between your sister and her, maybe we'll learn the truth about what happened at that research facility."

He grunted. "From what Brenna said before they took her away, Dexter couldn't deliver the chemical weapon so he forced her and Kinley to fake their deaths, and then spent the last year trying to eliminate them so there'd be no witnesses as to what he'd done."

Now, it was her turn to make that sound. "And Dexter used your sister as a decoy for the train explosion."

Lucky nodded. "The Justice Department thinks Dexter used a disguise when he got on the train. They'll take a harder look at those surveillance disks."

They'd no doubt take a harder look at all the evidence. But in the end, it would lead them back to Dexter and her father. "I figure that's why Dexter was trying to kill you. Because he knew that between you and Grady Duran, you were close to figuring out the truth."

She paused because she had to and then added, "I'm sorry."

"I'm sorry," Lucky said at the exact moment.

Marin stared at him and blinked. "Why are you sorry? My brother terrorized your sister, forced her to put her child in hiding, and then my father and Dexter tried to murder you."

Lucky held the stare for several moments and then looked away. "I killed your father."

She heard it then. The pain in his voice. It cut her to the bone. Because Lucky was obviously agonizing over something he couldn't have prevented.

"My father didn't give you a choice. And I don't blame you for his death. In fact, if you hadn't killed him, he would have done the same to us. You saved my life, again."

Tears threatened, but Marin blinked them back. She needed to stay strong.

So she could tell Lucky goodbye.

He already had enough guilt without her adding more. The trick was to make this quick. She couldn't make it painless. But she could do Lucky this one last favor.

"As soon as the sheriff gives me the all clear, I'll call a taxi to take me to the airport." She reached for Noah, but he batted her hands away and climbed into Lucky's lap.

Her son grinned up at Lucky. "Da-Da," he said with perfect clarity.

Marin groaned and buried her face in her hands. It

was Noah's first word. And it couldn't have come at a worse time.

"I think my grandmother taught him that," Marin said as an apology. She risked looking at Lucky then.

He was glaring at her. "You'll call a taxi to take you to the airport."

It wasn't a question. It was more like a snarl.

"Your rental car is wrecked from the drive-in explosion," she reminded him.

Just then, Noah said, "Da-Da" again. In fact, he began to rattle it off, stringing the syllables together while he snuggled against Lucky.

"You'll call a taxi?"

Both Lucky and Noah gave her accusing stares as if they were waiting. But waiting for what? Marin couldn't give Noah the nod of approval for his Da-Da mantra. Nor could she back down on calling that taxi. She couldn't be clingy. She had to be strong.

Even though her heart was breaking.

Lucky kissed Noah on the forehead and mimicked what her son was saying nonstop. "Da-Da is right." And then Lucky turned those sizzling gray eyes back on Marin. "I might have started out as a replacement father, but as far as Noah and I are concerned, I'm the real deal. Any objections?"

She glanced at her son's happy face and then at Lucky. Not happy, exactly. Hot and riled.

"No objections," she managed to say.

The silence came again.

Marin just sat there. What was she supposed to say or do? The right thing was to give Lucky that out.

Wasn't it?

He had a life, one that hadn't included her before

he started investigating Dexter. But then, she'd had a life, too. A life she no longer wanted—it didn't include Lucky.

"You about got it figured out?" Lucky asked.

Marin frowned at his question, which seemed not only eerily insightful, but also like a challenge. Yes, she'd figured out what she wanted. Marin wanted the life in front of her. Lucky as Noah's father. And Lucky as her lover.

No, wait.

She wanted more than that.

The corner of Lucky's mouth lifted. "Count to ten and tell me what you want."

"One," she mumbled. Marin slid down out of the love seat and sat on the floor next to him. She was about to move on to two, but it seemed rather pointless.

"I'm in love with you, Lucky," she confessed. "I don't want a taxi, and I don't want to go to the airport unless you're with Noah and me."

The other corner of his mouth lifted for a full-fledged smile. "And?"

She leaned in and kissed him. "And I want to be your lover and your wife. I want to marry you."

A chuckle rumbled deep within his chest. "And?"

Marin wasn't sure what he wanted her to say. She'd already poured out her heart. But what she hadn't done was take the ultimate risk. "And I want you to be in love in with me, too."

She held her breath.

Waited.

Heck, she even prayed.

"Then, you have everything you want, Marin. I'm crazy in love with you."

Lucky slid his arm around her neck, pulled her to him and kissed her, hard.

The kiss might have gone on for hours had it not been for Noah. He bopped them with the stuffed dog and laughed when they pulled away from each other.

"Da-Da," Noah announced.

Noah certainly knew a good thing when he saw it. And so did Marin. She pulled her family into her arms and held on tight.

* * * * *

We hope you enjoyed reading

That Forever Feeling

by *New York Times* bestselling author

LINDA LAEL MILLER

and

Security Blanket

by *USA TODAY* bestselling author

DELORES FOSSEN.

Both were originally Harlequin® series stories!

From passionate, suspenseful and dramatic
love stories to inspirational or historical,
Harlequin offers different lines to
satisfy every romance reader.

New books in each line are available every month.

His hands cupped her face. She blinked up at him.

"They buried me," she said, fighting the emotion
trying to take over at the thought of never seeing him
again.

Anger flashed in his blue eyes, and his jaw muscles
clenched. "They better never touch you again. We can
make an excuse to get you out of here. Say one of your
family members is sick and you had to go."

"They'll see it as weakness," she reminded him. "It'll
hurt the case."

He thumbed a loose tendril of hair off her face.

"I don't care, Ree," he said with an overwhelming
intensity that became its own physical presence. "I can't
lose you."

Those words hit her with the force of a tsunami.

HIEXP0622

Neither of them could predict what would happen next. Neither could guarantee this case wouldn't go south. Neither could guarantee they would both walk away in one piece.

"Let's take ourselves off the case together," she said, knowing full well he wouldn't take her up on the offer but suggesting it anyway.

Quint didn't respond. When she pulled back and looked into his eyes, she understood why. A storm brewed behind those sapphire-blues, crystalizing them, sending fiery streaks to contrast against the whites. Those babies were the equivalent of a raging wildfire that would be impossible to put out or contain. People said eyes were the window to the soul. In Quint's case, they seemed the window to his heart.

He pressed his forehead against hers and took in an audible breath. When he exhaled, it was like he was releasing all his pent-up frustration and fear. In that moment, she understood the gravity of what he'd been going through while she'd been gone. Kidnapped. For all he knew, left for dead.

So she didn't speak, either. Instead, she leaned into their connection, a connection that tethered them as an electrical current ran through her to him and back. For a split second, it was impossible to determine where he ended and she began.

Don't miss
Mission Honeymoon *by Barb Han,*
available August 2022 wherever
Harlequin Intrigue books and ebooks are sold.

Harlequin.com